Cinnamon and Salt

By C.j. Ethington

Cinnamon and Salt (Sentinels, Book 1)

ISBN 978-0-99070-260-3

Library of Congress Cataloging-in-Publication Data is available.

Printed in the United States of America
First Printing, 2015

Cover design and layout by Tron Johnson

For Jecca, who loves every single one of the voices in my head despite how annoying, sarcastic, and mean they can be at times. It takes a true friend to accept all of them.

Also, for my husband, Tron, who encourages me when I need encouragement, pesters me when I need to be pestered, and for the most part, knows the right time to shut up. I love you for all that you are.

Cinnamon & Salt

Sentinel Series

– Book One –

Chapter 1

NEW YEAR'S EVE:

A night for celebrations, new beginnings and more alcohol than one can imagine.

I stand on the frozen lawn outside of a large, white house. The sounds of muffled music, voices and laughter waft past me. I try to convince myself that the reason I haven't gone in yet is because I'm just not a people person, but I'm lying and I know it.

It's too cold to be standing out here. I pull my corduroy jacket tighter around my chest. The last two fingers on my right hand have already gone numb. Frostbite is on its way.

Tonight will be the night. I will finally do this, I tell myself in the worst mental pep talk ever. Not even I believe me. Not after the last forty times I've chickened out.

The door swings open as I quietly mount the steps. Spencer Adams stumbles out the door and folds over the railing in a regurgitating heap. I've never been a member of the Spencer Adams Fan Club; however, I have been a little more sympathetic to the inebriated ever since I had a similar experience at the pool last year.

"Are you alright?" I ask, only mildly concerned.

He crumples to his knees before passing out on the porch floor. An inaudible groan writhes out of his throat before his eyes flutter shut.

Hunkering down on my heels, I hoist him up using the infamous forearms-under-the-armpits maneuver I've had to learn over the years. I was bound to learn something from hanging out with drunken people who are drawn like magnets to the kitchen floor whenever they feel like puking or passing out. Being that I am usually the sober one, I'm also the one who usually has to move them.

So why do I still do it, you ask?

Got me.

1

Using my elbow, I pound on the door and count how many seconds it takes before someone comes to let us in. Spencer has at least fifty pounds on me and with each one, his weight seems to double. My arms ache like my bones are bending backwards.

Finally someone opens the door.

Not anyone helpful, but someone nonetheless.

"Can you... um, move out of the way, or help, or something?" I grunt at Melinda Carter, or as I like to think of her, Melin-Duh. Her expression is two shades less interesting than her normal blank expression as she slowly moves out of the doorway. If she were to move any slower, I might throw him at her. It's not like I really expected her to help, but it would have been nice if she did something other than stand by and watch.

Spencer makes *oomph* and *umph* sounds as I jostle his body back and forth, aiming him through the house. Halfway down the hall, I turn and push the door to Brady McGowan's father's study open. I don't bother to see how many couples are tucked into the corners of the room. Why should I be considerate? These are his friends, not mine. As far as I'm concerned, they should be the ones to deal with him.

Since the couch is occupied, I lower him to the middle of the floor. Before I leave, I turn his head to the side in case he pukes or something. If he were to asphyxiate, I would probably feel guilty as hell for leaving him there, which is exactly what I intend to do.

A man I've never seen before sits on the couch watching me, his forefinger tapping against his knee. I wonder what he is doing in the designated make-out room all by himself, but decide I don't want to know. The answer would probably just make me dry-heave. Just looking at him with his stone grey eyes and his pale blond hair makes my skin itch, and the way he stares back at me doesn't make matters any better.

"Can you keep an eye on him?" I ask. "He'll probably pass out, but just in case."

He nods slowly, his gaze fastened to my face. It feels like he's trying to connect me to some fuzzy memory, but can't quite do it.

2

Feeling awkward, I thank him and leave the room. I've done my part and in a latent gesture to be nice, I even shut the door behind me.

I've been coming to this house for years now and still love it. It's large, clean and best of all, parentless. Brady's parents vacation a lot because they can afford it and when Brady turned thirteen, he suddenly became too much of a hassle to drag along, so he was allowed to stay home. Some people might think it a psychological cry for help that he started testing the waters of rebellion around the same time, but I call it opportunity. So far, he's been able to get away with everything.

I pass by the stairs and down the hallway that leads to the kitchen and entertainment room. I trail my finger along the wall just below Brady's school pictures. I almost don't recognize him as a kindergartner. He's pudgy with freckles everywhere and soft auburn hair parted down the middle. I've seen the picture before, but it startles a laugh out of me anyway.

I walk toward the sound of girls laughing and the relieved sigh of beer cans being plucked open. If I were to make a soundtrack of Brady's life, this would be the introduction.

"Nicky! Good to see ya," Brady says. He waves a martini glass at me; gold flecks swirl in a thick, clear liquid. There's a beer in his other hand. "Want a drink?"

"Yes, please," I nearly beg, stripping off my jacket and tossing it onto the back of a chair. "What you got?"

"Anything and everything. Name your poison."

Liquor store boxes line the counters and walls. In each one is a cardboard sectional that makes it possible to fit twelve bottles into one box without any breaking. Doing the math in my head, I realize that he probably has at least seventy-two bottles of liquor in the kitchen alone. Give or take whichever ones have been drained.

"I see you're cutting back on the alcohol, Brady," I say wryly, motioning around the kitchen. "How much did you spend on this thing anyway and who did you get to buy it?"

"Don't you worry about that, Kitten," he replies. "Besides, the champagne is from dear Daddy's personal stash. It's an amazing batch and I doubt he'll even know it's gone."

Michael McGowan is as big a lush as they come.

The kitchen is so crowded that I have to pull my arms close to avoid touching anyone by accident. Otherwise, I may get accused of trying to feel someone up. It happened once to Greg Tandy and turned into a huge debacle. Better to be safe than sorry.

"I'll take whatever," I say. Brady's been a good buddy since junior high. I'm pretty sure I can trust him with whatever I might ingest.

Brady winks at the girl beside him. Her bra is green with pink martini glasses patterned across the cups. I know this because her shirt is already missing. That is, if she ever had one. She giggles and fingers the collar of his shirt.

Brady turns back to me. "Harder or softer than beer?" he asks.

"Harder. But don't knock me out. I'll have to go home eventually."

"Or you could stay here. There's a spare bedroom, you know," Brady says, his grin so wide I can make out the sparkle of his toothpaste.

"Nah, I'll pass, but thanks."

Martini Girl shoots me a sharp look. I lean forward and flip her hair behind her shoulder for her. "Do you know what a wasted effort is, darlin'?"

She sticks her tongue out at me and stomps off.

Her absence doesn't even faze Brady, who is mixing cocktails like they are potions and he is a wizard.

Moments later, I have a drink in my hand made by The Amazing Martini Master. I raise it in a toast to him and take a swig. It tastes of vodka, champagne, sprite and some sort of fruit juice. It actually isn't that bad, just kind of tart.

"Good, right?"

I make a face and he laughs.

"It gets better, I promise you. Just keep drinking."

4

I thank him and move toward the entertainment room with drink in hand. It's stifling in here from all the natural heat being passed around. It's not long before I realize that half the crowd doesn't even know me. I know most of them. We've only attended the same schools for most of our lives, but they have no idea who I am.

Except one person: Alex Berkley.

He pushes his way through the crowd, patting someone on the back here, tossing out a knuckle bump there, and finally pointing in my direction to indicate that he's seen me. I get a little thrill seeing that the drink in his hand is identical to mine. Stupid, I know.

Alex is the king of this crowd. Guys follow him like he is a snake charmer and girls beg to talk to him. It's disgusting really.

Oh, and he's also my best friend.

Alex bumps me with his elbow and says, "You're late."

Heat floods my cheeks. I fidget with my hair to hide it. "Fashionably," I reply.

He laughs. "Sure. I was starting to worry that I'd have to hide the alcohol just so you could have some if you ever showed up."

I look toward the kitchen. It looks like a liquor store threw up in there, save for Brady dancing with another shirtless girl. "Sure you did."

Something to his right catches his eye. That's why I hate these things. There's so much going on. It's like you can't have an uninterrupted conversation with anyone.

"So whatcha think?" he asks, gesturing to the party with his glass.

There are so many people here I can hardly breathe. If this were any other night, the cops would have already come and sent everyone home, but it isn't. This is New Year's Eve. As long as the drunks stay indoors and don't bother the sober people, they can usually fly under the radar. Even the underage.

I don't fit in with this crowd. I never have. Like oil to water, I have floated among these people. While they were out drinking on weekends, I was home reading, or studying, or doing anything else I could come up with to avoid repeat embarrassments like the one last year. But here I am. I'd like to think I put up one hell of a fight when I was invited tonight, but in reality, I gave in to Alex like I always do.

"It's just...great," I manage to say.

"Don't lie," Alex says with a laugh. "I know you. You'd rather be home with Cynthia. Am I right?"

Cynthia is my DV-R. Not many people know that I call her that.

Unfortunately, he's right. The whole walk over, I imagined what it would be like to sit in a dark room and watch episode after episode of *Supernatural*. It was a beautiful fantasy, albeit short-lived.

Rather than admit how lame I am, I change the subject. "So what'd I miss?"

"Same shit as always."

I take a breath then down my drink in one gulp. I have to do this now and it requires a large reserve of alcohol-infused courage, and by god, I am going to do this. No matter how much it hurts.

"Hey, Alex?" I say quietly, half hoping he won't hear me.

"What's up, Nic?"

It doesn't bother me that he calls me Nic instead of a more feminine version of my name. If anything, it's kind of comforting.

That's what he and Brady have called me since I was little.

"Can we talk?"

Alex glances at me sideways. When a girl says she wants to talk, it triggers a natural fight or flight response. Well, more flight than fight, but still. So I'm not surprised when he looks around with unabated panic clear in his eyes. "Good or bad?"

I wish I could tell him it's good – not bad at all – but I can't.

I slap him playfully on the arm. "You tell me."

"Hang on. I'll get drinks first. The countdown is about to start." He doesn't wait for an answer before he turns and melts into the crowd.

A fissure opens up in my chest. The warmth of the alcohol breathes out of it.

"He'll be back. Just went to get champagne," I say quietly to myself.

The gigantic television is on and tuned in to one of the fifteen stations that are airing the New Year's celebration recorded live in New York City. Millions of people mill around, dance to music, and toast each other in Time Square. The ball sits at the ready. Big shiny numbers cling to the sphere in declaration of the next year. I contemplate all the new beginnings I will face in the year to come. Above all of them, senior year of high school scares me the most. They say it's supposed to be one of the greatest years of my life, but I have a feeling it will just bring more change. I'm allergic to change. It gives me hives.

The ball is in motion. Soon, a chorus of drunken voices will intone the countdown like the numbers still make sense. With how drunk everyone is, it's possible that a few of them will count out of sequence.

My eyes dart around, trying to pick Alex out of the crowd. Stretching up on the balls of my feet, I find that almost everyone is taller than me. I can't see him.

An elbow bumps into my side. At first, I ignore it, thinking some inconsiderate person decided to walk through me instead of going around, which happens a lot at these shindigs, but then it happens again.

"Got a problem?" I snap, wheeling on a stricken-looking Brady. I don't look at him when I apologize. Where did Alex go?

"You know, Kitten, maybe your one resolution this year should be to chill out. You're so wound up these days," Brady says. He never was one to waste his time on tact. "And drink more. Everyone should definitely drink more."

"Sorry," I say. "Have you seen Alex?"

"Yeah. He told me to bring this to you," Brady says, offering me a flute glass with pink champagne bubbling up the sides.

I take it and breathe in the scent. It smells a little more girly than regular champagne, which is exactly why it's my favorite: it's different, unexpected. "Where did he go?"

"Um. Jen grabbed him. I think they went that way." He uses his head to gesture toward the front of the house where the bedrooms are.

An ache forms in my stomach, slowly churning the alcohol into a dangerous mixture. I clutch the glass a little tighter and hope it doesn't fall from my numb fingers.

And the countdown begins.

"Ten."

Brady wraps an arm around my shoulder. "This is it, Kitten. This is our year."

"Nine."

The alcohol is taking effect. The room spins. I rest my head against his shoulder.

"Eight."

All I want to do is get the hell out of here. I want to go home, curl up in my flannel sheets, pull the blankets over my head…

"Seven."

… and scream like I've never screamed before.

"Six."

Then cry myself to sleep and stay in bed until someone makes me move. Likely my parents.

"Five."

On Wednesday for school.

"Four."

Where he'll be.

"Three."

"You're a good friend, Brady," I say through the hot lump constricting my throat. My eyes water.

"Two."

"And don't you forget it," he says.

"One."

"Happy New Year!" a hundred drunken voices yell. Guys high five each other and girls fall into inebriated kisses with their dates that would make a blind man blush.

8

And I stand there, my head resting heavily against Brady's shoulder, already feeling like a failure. He turns his head and kisses my hair. "Happy New Year, Nicky."

The champagne flute is all but forgotten in my hand. If I were to drink it right now, I would probably puke all over the girl in front of me, declaring my first embarrassing moment of the year.

"I'm gonna head out," I say quietly.

He eyes me knowingly and gently tucks an errant lock of hair behind my ear. "Okay. Text me when you get home?"

I nod, hand him the glass and slowly push my way toward the front of the house. The door to the McGowan's study is open and all of the lights are on. Everyone is up and has congregated in the center of the room. At first, I shrug it off. Maybe the countdown was just that exciting.

But then, between the feet of two people, I see something that makes my stomach turn. Lying motionless on the floor is a person.

I claw at my throat, suddenly unable to breathe.

Because the body lying so still, so lifeless, is Spencer.

And I'm the one who left him there.

Chapter 2

"What's going on?" I ask.

No one hears me. They are too busy arguing about who is going to take responsibility for the drunkard on the floor.

Louder than before, I say, "What the hell is going on?"

That gets someone's attention. Melin-duh eyes me accusingly. "He passed out. We can't wake him up."

"Did someone call an ambulance?" I ask, numbly. Spencer isn't moving. If he's breathing, I can't tell. And I certainly can't hear it over the ringing in my ears.

"We can't," she responds.

Well, they could, but no one wants to risk exposure as an underage drinker, even if it means Spencer's life. I glare at each of them in turn. "You guys are his friends. Call a damn ambulance."

Now everyone is looking at me. These are the faces of my classmates, no more than acquaintances.

"Can't someone just drive him to the hospital?" Tori Cavers asks.

I never did like her. Stepping toward her, my glare turns to a burning glower. "And who here is sober enough for that?"

"You just got here," Melinda suggests.

"Someone with a car," I snap back.

A loud roar tears out of Spencer's throat. The sound reminds me of every exorcism performed in every television show. It sounds like he's trying to eject a demon from his body. A chill runs down my spine.

"You." I point to a boy whose name I never bothered to remember. "Go get Alex or Brady. I need their keys." I might have been feeling tipsy before, but now I am stone cold sober.

The boy shifts his weight from foot to foot. He pauses for a second to look at Spencer then takes off running out of the room.

I elbow my way through the crowd and kneel next to Spencer. After a mental evaluation, I know three things: his hands are cold and clammy, his eyes are unfocused and dilated, and he is breathing. Barely, but that's better than nothing.

Sliding a hand under his neck, I tilt his head back. His pulse slows in his throat. I curse myself for skipping school on CPR day in health class. Does CPR even help when someone is still breathing?

The boy comes back, jingling a set of keys in his hand. He's alone.

So irritated I could spit, I turn on him. "Where's Alex?"

He shrugs. "I don't know. Brady says to take his."

"Awesome," I respond dryly. "What the hell am I supposed to do? Carry him by myself?"

"I can help," a voice says from the doorway. It's deep and smooth: the kind of voice that can send me into shivers or throw me into a tornado of annoyance. Right now, his voice is having the latter effect. I don't glance over my shoulder to see who the speaker is. All I care about is that he sounds sober.

"Fine," I sigh. "Let's get him to a car."

In two swift movements he has Spencer up and dangling at his side. He smiles at me cockily. "Lead the way."

I open the door for him and realize that Brady's car, having been the first one here, is blocked in. In a fit, I almost throw his keys into the street.

"Hang here. Be right back," I tell Mr. Helpful. Then I dash through the house, bumping people out of my way with my shoulder like a linebacker.

Maliciously, I hope it leaves bruises. I call out for Brady, who appears around the wall.

"What's up?" he asks. He may have been outside this realm of sober before, but his expression is grave. That's why I love Brady. He knows when things need to be taken seriously.

"Gotta take Spencer to the emergency room. Your car is blocked in. You know where Alex is?"

"Upstairs somewhere."

"Somewhere" means one of the bedrooms, probably Brady's since that's where he usually takes girls. I dart up the stairs, almost

11

trip over my own feet, and pound on the first door to my left. Someone inside makes a strange noise. I pound again.

"Alex," I say, unable to contain the bitter edge to my voice. "Get your pants on. I need your keys."

The door opens just an inch. Alex's hair is in disarray. Lipstick smears his cheek. "What's going on?"

I imagine drawing a blade down my arm would hurt less than seeing him like this. "I have to take Spencer to the hospital," I say, though would rather scream obscenities in his face and kick him in the shins. "I need your car."

He stares at me for three seconds too long.

"Now," I add, waving my hands for emphasis.

"Okay." He ducks behind the door.

I close my eyes against the image of Jen Bowers in Brady's bed. I've seen it before with other girls and "awkward" is not a strong enough word to describe it.

Keys jingle in front of my face. I open my eyes. Alex has pushed his hair back and wiped the lipstick from his cheek, but it's too late. I can smell him. He smells of sweat and slutty girls.
I grab the keys out of his hand without even so much as a "thank you."

My heart feels too big for my chest as I dash down the stairs. I don't expect Alex to come after me, but wish with all my might that he would.

He doesn't.

I hold my breath and don't fully release it until I arrive at the hospital two miles away. By the time I pull into a parking space, I'm lightheaded. But it's better than suffering through the stabbing sensation in my chest whenever I inhale.

Mr. Silent carries all of Spencer's weight as he walks through the sliding doors into the Emergency Room waiting area. There are very few seats unoccupied. After a quick survey of all other patients, I think Spencer might qualify for a line jump. Unconscious is to broken bone as I am to I don't give a shit.

A lady with silver and red hair sits behind the counter. She has a warm smile and a pink swoosh of blush on her cheeks.

"What are we seeing you for today, dear?" she asks.

"My friend. He passed out and he's not breathing," I explain. I don't like how my voice shakes.

The lady pulls out a form and passes it to me on a metal clipboard. A pen is chained to the right hand corner. "Fill these out and we'll get you back just as soon as we can."

I glance at the form, surveying the questions. "Ma'am," I say, trying to get the woman's attention again. She's already turned back to her computer screen. "He's my friend not my brother. I don't know any of his history or his insurance information."

She gives me an uneasy look before smiling. "That's alright, dear. Just fill out what you know. We can get the rest later when we call his parents."

His parents? Oh no. If Spencer's parents find out he was at Brady's then Brady could get into some serious trouble. Like court-time trouble. In the back of my mind, I formulate a cover story as I neatly scrawl out the information. I don't even bother to sit down – that's how little I know about Spencer's history. Any of what I do know comes from the driver's license I fished out of his wallet. I hand the clipboard back to the lady. She takes it and asks me to bring Spencer into the next room.

"Hey," I call over my shoulder. "Can you bring him around here?"

The guy smiles at me as if we are standing in the middle of the school hallway and not in the middle of the hospital emergency room. Then he nods, his thick dark hair brushing across his cheeks. With a fluid movement, he has Spencer up and balanced as he walks around the side.

The thermometer says he has a fever, though I don't ask how high. The nurse doesn't seem like the type to waste her time explaining medical results to teenage kids. She nods when she sees the blood pressure results. I don't know if that's good or not. The pulse oximeter, however, I can read. His oxygen is in the low seventies and I know that's not good.

What does he win? Access to a room immediately. I hesitate before going with him. I'm not family after all. I don't even constitute as being a friend. In fact, my overall opinion of Spencer Adams is that he's a ginormous asshole.

Once Spencer is settled onto the hospital bed, I pull a stool over and perch on it, sliding back and forth on its wheels.

A male nurse with muscles straining against his shirt comes in with an IV pole, a computer monitor, and an oxygen mask. Before he regards either of us, he starts the oxygen and plugs the nasal cannula into Spencer's nostrils. For a moment, I have a guilty thought about how much more I like Spencer when he isn't talking.

"How are you two doing tonight?" the nurse asks.

Neither of us replies. The question was probably rhetorical anyway.

"The doctor will be in shortly. Has he ingested any drugs or alcohol this evening?"

"He drank a little bit," I offer. "I don't know how much, though."

He nods and marks something down on the chart. "No illegal drugs, though?"

"I'm not sure." I think for a moment. "Probably not. He's not really the illegal drug type." I raise my voice so Spencer can hear me, unconscious or not. "A stupid drunk, but no drugs."

He raises his eyebrows. "You are his friends, right?" he clarifies.

Against my better judgment, I nod. But my companion jumps in, saying, "Not really. He's kind of an ass."

I look at him in shock. Respect for him builds like Legos, one on top of another, somewhere deep inside me.

The nurse looks taken aback. I suppose he doesn't hear such blatant honesty here. "Have you two been drinking?" he asks. Apparently he only hears honesty from teenagers who are inebriated.

"A sip of champagne," I answer, omitting the other drink. Like I knew what it was anyway.

Mr. Honest waves his hand in the air and says, "Yeah, a few of those. I didn't drive, though."

The look on the nurse's face says, "Stupid high school kids," but his mouth says, "Okay, let me tell you what we're going to do. The doctor will be in soon to check your, um, him out." He nods toward the lifeless form of Spencer. "But first, we're going to call his parents. I recommend the two of you wait here until you are completely sober before you leave. More often than not the people who die in a drunken driving accident are not the drunk driver. Got me?"

I nod slowly. I've never felt so sober in my life.

"I mean it," he says, crossing his arms over his chest. "Don't make me pump your stomach." He fidgets with the wires hooked up to Spencer. "I'll be back to check on him soon." Then he leaves.

I don't even have time to roll my eyes before a woman walks in with a no-nonsense swagger. She looks irritable all the way to the ends of her auburn hair. Glancing down, I see she's wearing heels. I consider telling her to wear something easier to walk in, but bite my tongue. No wonder she's irritable.

She doesn't talk at all while she works over Spencer. Either because she heard the drinking comments or thinks we're too young to handle it. Her silence grates on my nerves.

"Will he be okay?" I ask.

Mr. Silent glances at me from across the room with a look of relief. He sits in the chair next to the bed, which puts him right in the way.

"He hasn't woken up yet?" the doctor asks curtly without lifting her head.

"Nope," I respond.

Her head moves slowly back and forth. "There's not much we can do without a full medical history. We'll have to keep him here until he wakes up. I called his parents. They're on their way."

My stomach tightens with unnecessary anxiety. His parents know me – they know my parents – and word travels fast. I twitch with the need to get out of here. Why did I ever decide to go out tonight? I wonder if Cynthia misses me as much as I miss her.

In panic, I look at the boy across the room. Our eyes lock.

While I may feel like fleeing the scene, his grey eyes regard mine with no emotion whatsoever. None pertaining to the situation anyway. He looks confused, how someone would look at a painting they have only seen once before in their lives. He's trying to place me, find some familiarity.

Every noise outside the room startles me. It would probably be impolite to book it out of here now before anyone else shows up. I did bring Spencer here. Shouldn't I care about his well-being, too?

Every set of footsteps sounds like they are coming toward us. I squirm in my seat and breathe a sigh of relief when I see they belong to the nurse.

"His parents are here, should I send them back?" he says.

The doctor nods.

"That's our cue to go," I say, nodding to the door. "We don't want to be in the way."

"I suppose you can call his parents for updates," she says without looking up.

"Sure." I grab my companion by the hand and pull him out the door.

At the end of the hall, I see Mr. and Mrs. Adams. They look like they just got out of bed and threw coats on. My heart pounds in my chest. Without thinking, I shove him into the empty room to our left.

He reaches out and grabs onto me, pulling back and turning to the side. Somehow during our impromptu game of tug-o-war, we end up with his body pinning me to the wall.

"What—" he starts to say.

I clamp a hand over his mouth in the universal sign for "shut the hell up." For a moment, I barely breathe.

When I hear Mrs. Adams' sobs echoing through the hall I drop my hand to let him speak.

He doesn't move for what feels like forever.

This was not how today was supposed to go. It began with a steely resolve. I was going to finally tell Alex how I felt about him. In my head, I saw him jumping for joy and professing his undying love to me, too. But now, I know that never would have happened.

Instead, I find myself in a dark vacated room at St. Mark's hospital with a strange man pressed up against me.

How do I get myself into these situations?

For the first time tonight, I actually meet the eyes of the man pinned up against me. And that's when I recognize him. Not from anywhere special, just school. I may not have known him at all if he wasn't on Alex's basketball team.

His name is Asher Rowan and the only way to describe him is from his lips outward. That's the first thing you notice about him: his lips. They are perfect and pale pink. The rest of him seems to emphasize that. His smoky grey eyes even direct your stare back to his mouth like each lash is an arrow pointing downward. If he were to have a caricature done of him, his mouth would be stretched and wide while the rest of his face would be painted smaller with lighter colors.

His black hair brushes his chin in straight jagged strands. Asher has one of those faces: one that seems familiar only because you see something of him in everyone else's features.

"What was that?" Asher breathes into my face, without even the slightest effort to move away from me. His chest brushes against mine with each breath.

"Spencer's parents," I say by way of explanation.

"So? You're a hero. Who else was going to get him here?"

I sigh. "Yeah, I'm a hero who was at the same party, drinking the same alcohol. Right." The sarcasm burns through my ears.

He smiles. "But you left."

"So did you," I respond. "So why don't you go talk to them? You can take all the credit for this one." With my hands against his chest, I add, "And could you move, please?"

"If I remember correctly, this was your fault."

"Fine, but I can't move until you do."

Reluctantly, he puts his hands against the wall on either side of my head and pushes off. He gives me a long look then sighs and strides over to the door where he sticks his head out, looking this way and that. "I think the coast is clear," he says. "Crisis averted."

"Great." I push past him out of the room. Turning left, I walk straight and true down the hall and toward the freedom of the exit doors. He scrambles to keep up.

"Nicoletta, right?" he asks.

"Huh?" I say, not even sparing a glance over my shoulder at him.

"Your name is Nicoletta, right?"

I nod, still walking. The sooner I'm out of here, the better. Especially since I still have to drop Asher off at home and return Alex's car. My legs feel heavy suddenly and each step more difficult. It's just what Asher needs to catch up to me.

"I'm Asher," he says, by way of greeting. "I, um, play basketball with Alex."

"I know who you are." I sound annoyed, but then again, I always do after a couple hours spent in the emergency room with an unconscious Spencer Adams. Not that this has ever happened before, but I imagine if it did, this would be my normal response.

"Have we met before?"

"Nope," I say. "I make it a point to know every member of Alex's fan club."

His steps falter; he jogs to catch up. "What makes you think I'm a member of Alex's 'fan club'?" You can almost hear the air quotes.

I shrug. "Isn't everyone?"

He doesn't respond.

The lady at the counter wishes us luck and gives us a threatening look. Nothing is sacred in the Emergency room. I smile and nod at her in reassurance. Yes ma'am, I will drive safely. No ma'am, I am not drunk.

In fact, that one drink I had earlier feels like a distant memory.

The doors slide open letting in a gust of chilly air. I pull my jacket tighter around me and button the middle button. Not much of an improvement, but what can you do? Asher doesn't have a coat, I notice, just a long sleeved shirt.

"Don't you have a coat?" I ask.

"I left it at the party. It didn't seem very important at the time."

I don't look at him. My gaze is fixed on Alex's Mustang. I have a destination in mind: my bed with my three pillows and my fluffy blue quilt just three blocks away. "We don't need to go back, do we?"

"Nah. I'll get it later."

I unlock the doors, using the key fob hooked to the keys. "So where am I taking you then?"

He stops walking. I know this only because his footsteps no longer echo mine. I turn to see him standing a few feet away from the car. He looks confused.

"What?" I ask impatiently.

"No offense or anything," he says slowly. This can only mean one thing: he's about to offend me. No one ever declares that they don't intend to offend you, unless they plan to. "I've heard rumors about you being, um, stuck up."

I roll my eyes. "Gee thanks."

"No. What I mean is that you don't really give the time of day to anyone who isn't Alex or Brady. Why are you willing to take me home?"

I take a second to think about that. "The golden rule or some shit," I explain. "You helped me out so I offer to help you out. Do unto others, blah, blah, blah. Do you want the ride or not?"

He looks from me to the empty road. "I would love a ride," he says after a moment's hesitation.

I turn and close the distance left to the car. I jump inside. He climbs in after I shut my door. I look at him. His face is half hidden in shadow, but I can still see the uneasy set of his jaw. "So... where to?"

Asher's house ends up being a block away from Alex's, which is only two blocks away from mine. Finally, I get a break. Thank God for small miracles.

The silence in the car is unfaltering, but welcome. I'm not in the mood to talk after the night I've had. The only mood I'm in is for sleep, days and days of sleep.

Given that Asher's greatest opinion of me is that I'm stuck up, I half expect him to jump out of the car before I have the opportunity to stop. So imagine my surprise when he doesn't tuck and roll to the curb, but rather sits very still for a long, agonizing moment.

When he finally looks at me, it's with an odd expression. Before I can ask why he's glaring at me, he says, "I'll see you around, I guess."

"Sure," I say without any enthusiasm.

He scrutinizes my face a moment more before shaking his head, climbing out of the car and stalking off without even a glance over his shoulder.

He is so weird.

After five long seconds of careful deliberation about the importance of moral imperative versus exhaustion, I decide that Alex can live without his car for the night. Since the thought of seeing him before eight blissful hours of sleep fills me a homicidal desire, I'm sure any judge and jury would prefer I keep his car an extra twelve hours to avoid any risk of hitting him with it.

Besides, I have an appointment with exhaustion and this car is the only way I'll make it there on time.

I'm surprised to see the television light flickering in the front window of my one story house when I pull up. After locking the car, I let myself into the house with fingers crossed that my parents fell asleep on the couch. No such luck. My parents are still up, sitting on the couch, watching an old movie. My mother asks how the party was. I grunt in response. If there was ever a time I didn't want to talk, this was it.

"I'm going to bed. 'Night," I say before waving my hand at them and bee-lining it for my room.

I wonder what my parents will think when they wake in the morning to notice Alex's car in the driveway, but that's the last thought before I fall into bed and cry myself to sleep.

I had such big plans for this year and so far it feels like everything's crumbling. Four hours in and I already feel like a failure.

Chapter 3

Wednesday morning. Olympus High School. Home of the Titans. Ugh. I may not have felt hung over yesterday, but today is a whole different story. Then again, maybe I'm just getting sick. I could hope. A good sick day might be just what I need.

I dropped Alex's car off to his mom yesterday morning. So once again, I am a lowly pedestrian. The school is only a block and a half away, but on days like today it feels like miles. I make a mental note to get a job so I can invest in my own car.

The school hasn't had a chance to warm up after winter break. My breaths exhale into billowing clouds of smoke. The cold air presses in on my already pounding head. I really hope I still have some pain killers in my locker.

Last year, my locker was in an inconspicuous corner of the hall. No one bothered me and I liked it that way. This year, it's in the middle of one of the busiest hallways at school. On a normal day, I get bumped five times during one stop and no one ever apologizes. Today, though, the hall seems abnormally quiet. I grab my books, shove them into my backpack, and slam the door. Alex is there. I glare at him unintentionally before turning to walk away.

"Wait," he says, reaching out to grab my wrist.

Yanking my hand away, I turn and pin him with my best glower. "What?"

"Just wondering how Monday night went."

"Oh just great," I say sarcastically. "I totally got some and left my best friend high and dry. Oh wait, that was you."

He shoves his hands into the pockets of his coat, his shoulders slumping forward. "I'm sorry, Nic. It just... happened. I didn't mean to leave you alone with Spencer. Is... is he okay?"

I try to push the thought of his messy hair and the lustful look in his eyes and fail miserably, which only makes me more irritated. "He's wonderful. You should probably go see him sometime since he's your friend and all," I snap out. "So you have your car back and everything is peachy. Can I go now?"

I don't wait for an answer before turning on my heel and stomping my way down the hall.

Alex bounces beside me, trying to catch up. "So, there's this rumor going around that you went home with Asher the other night," he says. Seeing the shocked look on my face, he adds, "I told everyone it was a lie."

I consider telling him that I did in fact go home with Asher just to see how he would respond. But since it probably wouldn't faze him either way, I tell him the truth. "Remember Spencer? Your friend who had to go to the hospital with a wicked case of alcohol poisoning? No? Then maybe I should remind you that someone had to take him to the hospital." I narrow my eyes at him. "*Asher* was the only person willing to help me. So, yes, I took him home afterward."

"Oh," he responds.

I shake my head in disgust. There was a time when Alex would have been playing EMT with me, but apparently booty calls are too important to pass up these days.

"You're mad at me," he muses. It seems to hurt his feelings.

The way his eyes seem to frown at the corners tugs at my heart strings. This is exactly the reason why I can't stay angry at him for very long. I hate it, but it's the truth.

I sigh. "Why Jen? I thought you had better taste than that." It's true. Not why I am angry, but true. Asking that, though, is much better than asking why he isn't affected by me like I am by him.

Affected? More like afflicted.

"There's nothing wrong with Jen," he says. He doesn't sound defiant like I would expect. He sounds almost worried.

We turn the corner that leads to my English class: first period of the day. I hesitate outside the door. Alex won't meet my eyes.

"We'll talk later," I say, urging him to remember his own class. He has History, clear on the other side of the building. If he's late again, his coach might kick him off the team. Of course, he'd only be off the team until next semester. Next semester is like a "Get out of

Jail Free" card for all athletes. Not so much for the rest of us.

"Yeah. See you." He turns to leave.

I watch silently as Alex drifts off into the din of the hallway then shake it all off and step into class.

Sitting next to my normal desk is Asher Rowan. I wonder to myself why Asher would choose to sit next to the snotty stuck up kid in the front of class instead of in back with the rest of the slacker basketball team. Maybe his seat was taken.

When his head lifts, his eyes meet mine. I nod in response.

Without him, I would have been on my own the other night. The least I can do is be nice, or at the very least, polite.

Mr. Warren, our English teacher strides in just as the bell rings. He holds a steaming mug with the words printed in bold white across the front that say: *If you can't say anything nice at least make it funny.*

He's my favorite teacher.

"*Persuasion,*" he says without preamble. "By now you should have read the book in its entirety. So, what did you think?"

No one responds. Not even me. The question is too ambiguous for my taste. A simple "I liked it" or "I hated it" is one of Mr. Warren's pet peeves.

"Mr. Rowan," he continues with a nod. "Nice to see you up front for a change."

Asher returns the gesture before turning back to the paper he's doodling on. It's already half filled with circles. Probably some sort of playbook. Most of the basketball players keep them. Alex has three. He's tried to explain the necessity multiple times. I still don't get it.

"Anyway, does anyone have insight on this book?" he asks.

Melinda Carter raises her hand.

"Yes, Miss Carter?" Mr. Warren asks. He looks positively pleased.

"Can I have a bathroom pass?"

The smile fades from his face. He waves his hand in a gesture toward the stuffed raven sitting on the chalkboard. Around its neck are dog tags that say who it belongs to. He even has a name: Sheldon.

"How about something relative?" Mr. Warren says to the rest of us.

I raise my hand.

"Finally. Miss Dubois. Yes?"

"I've noticed a pattern in Jane Austen's writing," I respond, my heart racing. I'm not a shy person by any means. That doesn't mean I like to be put on the spot, though, either.

He smiles. "Yes, please continue."

"Men only want one thing."

A girl in the back snickers, but he urges me on with a gesture of his hand.

I glance around, taking in all of the bored expressions on my classmates faces.

"Money. Power. Position. Possession."

Jane Masters raises her hand. "I thought it was romantic," she offers before being called on.

"Well, that's a given," I say rather than the "dur, dur, dur" hanging off my tongue. "But that's just one plotline. *Persuasion* isn't just about the romance between the hero and heroine. It's about financial difficulty, pain and betrayal."

"I don't see how," Jane argues.

"Every story," Mr. Warren cuts in, "has an antagonist, Miss Masters. Without opposition, the story would be quite boring. Without opposition, you and Miss Dubois here would agree completely. There wouldn't be a class and I would be out of a job." He smiles ruefully as if that's the most pleasant thought he's had all day. "But Miss Dubois has a point. While you may have been interested by the romantic plot, she was more concerned with lies and betrayal."

Someone behind me burst into laughter.

"It's all about preferred interest," he concludes.

Asher glances at me sideways sympathetically. I ignore him and don't talk for the rest of the class even when Jane Masters declares her preference for Louisa and Frederick Wentworth's union over any union he could have with Anne. She pretty much handed that right to me. Still I stay quiet, letting the insults form in my head where only I can hear them.

The bell rings. I'm halfway out the door when I hear Asher say, "Hey, Nic, wait up. I'll walk you to your next class."

"That's alright," I respond dismissively. I think about ducking into the girl's bathroom in an attempt to ditch him. I wouldn't want to be late to P.E. again, though. Oh no, I love being all sweaty for the rest of the day.

Great, now I'm sarcastic and stuck up. I slow down and wait for Asher to catch up.

"Have you been back to the hospital?" he asks.

I shake my head. "You?"

"Yeah right," he says with a snort. He gives me a sideways glance and smiles. "You coming to the game after school?"

Are we really having small talk? Was that why he wanted to walk me to my next class— to have an awkward conversation?

I smile blandly. "I don't think so."

"Oh. Well, I guess I'll see you in Psych then," he says, slowing in front of the girl's locker room. At least it was a short walk.

"Yep." I push open the door and head into the locker room. It smells like deodorant, shampoo, sweat, and my own hatred for this class.

English and Psychology? I swear I don't remember having so many classes with him. I shrug it off. Asher wasn't the first thing I hadn't noticed this year and I doubt he would be the last.

"It's a travesty that we have to change for P.E. in this frigid air," Ashley Marinello says loud enough for everyone to hear.

A few shouts of "Amen!" echo off the tile floor.

"I mean, come on," she says louder, "Pneumonia is a real thing. What if we all catch it? Is that what they want? All of us in the hospital?"

I roll my eyes.

Changing next to me is a girl whose name I can't remember. "What the hell is she rambling on about?" I ask her.

Her cornflower blue eyes shift toward me then back to her locker, barely giving me the time of day. "Ashley? Oh, she's protesting gym class. Some chick last period – I think her name was Lisa something-or-other – passed out and was taken to the hospital. They said she had a 104 fever. That's, like, fatal or something. They think she had pneumonia. She's still unconscious." She slams the locker door and turns her back on me with finality.

Cold fingers tickle my spine and I shiver. "Is she going to be okay?"

"She's got pneumonia not the plague," she says over her shoulder.

Miss Hess, the P.E. teacher, steps into the locker room and glances around at all the girls who have yet to change into their running sweats. She looks exhausted. "Alright, class. Knock it off. Today is officially lecture day. No need to dress down."

She exits on the sound wave of cheers. Even I cheer a little. Silently, of course, and on the inside. This day may have just gotten a little more bearable.

Chapter 4

"Come on, let's go," Brady says, grabbing me by the elbow.

"Where we going?" I ask, confused.

"To lunch. Where else? I'm not eating here," he says with a mischievous smile.

The air is cold in here, but it's frigid outside. I shiver just thinking about it. He grips my arm and steers me toward my locker. We pass by a blur that almost looks like Alex. He's talking to another blur that definitely looks like Jen. I divert my eyes back to Brady.

"So where exactly are we going?" I ask loudly.

Brady's face twists into a thoughtful look. "Hmm, I didn't think that far ahead. To somewhere where the air is fresh and the food is edible."

I'm suddenly on board. "Perfect."

I open my locker to stuff my bag inside. Brady leans against the locker next to mine. He's wearing a black hooded sweatshirt and jeans. Not the best attire to brave the weather in. If he needed a coat, though, he would have taken me to his locker.

"So... let's talk about the other night?" he asks.

"Not much to tell. Went to a party, took a detour to the hospital, went home, and went to bed. I didn't even get to watch *Supernatural*," I respond.

"I know that." He eyes me suspiciously. "What happened with Alex?"

"Shut up Brady," I warn.

"Fine. We have all lunch to talk about it."

I groan loudly and slam my locker door with a lot more force than necessary. Brady offers me a smile and his hand.

After we order food at the local Arby's, we sit down at a table in the far corner. I like corners, though I've never understood why. I imagine it's because no one can sneak up on you when your back is to the wall. A little paranoid perhaps, but I like to see what's coming for me.

"So?" Brady says impatiently. "Want to tell me what's going on?"

I take a bite of my sandwich and gesture to my mouth as if to say, "I can't talk with my mouth full."

"Fine. I'll get it out of you eventually."

Of all the restaurants in all of town, Alex just happens to walk into the same one I am in. Okay, so it's not that crazy of a coincidence. This is the closest restaurant to school. But why today? The one day I swore the most solemn oath to ignore him.

He steps away from the counter, pausing for a second. Once he sees us, he calls out our names and lopes toward us, leaving someone else to pay the bill. Two girls step out of the crowd and fight over the honor. It appears half the student body decided to join him for lunch.

"Did I miss a memo? Is the pep rally meeting here today?" I whisper to Brady.

He gives me a look warning me to be nice and turns halfway around in his chair.

"What's up, man?" Alex asks, pulling a chair from an empty table and plopping down backwards onto it.

I take another bite of my sandwich so I can pretend my mouth is too full to talk and wave my hand at them like I'm apologizing.

"Not much," Brady says, cocking an eyebrow. "Pre-game meeting?"

"Nah. Just craving some roast beef," Alex replies with a grin.

My chest tightens up. I tell myself to be brave even though part of me is already running for the door. When did things get so complicated between Alex and me? I'll tell you: when I started to like him as more than a friend. That's when.

Six out of eight of the cheerleaders, their hair dyed an array of colors, are included in Alex's entourage today. The sight of their green and white uniforms makes me cringe. This is just one more way for High School to be hypocritical. While the rest of us have to meet certain dress code standards, the cheerleaders are allowed to wear their uniforms – sleeveless shirts and short, short skirts – to school as long as it is on the day of a game. If I were to wear a mini skirt to class, I'd get the "lecture" about how my skirt makes me a slut. But if you're a cheerleader, showing your ass means you have school spirit.

Jen Bowers is a cheerleader. Go figure.

It feels good to know how much they have to suffer in the cold with their bare legs and boobs hanging out just waiting to freeze off. I smile a little at the though.

A few more of the basketball players, wearing their green and white jerseys, are quickly taking up more tables than they need.

I'm suddenly craving a burrito from the Mexican food joint next door. Then a boy with dark hair turns from the counter and catches my eye. Asher.

He walks over and comes to a deliberate stop between Alex and me. "Nicoletta," he says, like he is appreciating the sound of my name in his mouth. To be honest, I like it, too. His tongue sounds like it clicks against his teeth with each consonant. In other words, he pronounces it the way it was meant to be said. I wonder if I could spell it different so everyone would pronounce it like that.

"Asher," I say, refusing to let anyone see how his voice saying my name could affect me.

Alex shoots an upwards glare at him. He looks angry – pissed off even.

I get a sick sort of enjoyment from seeing his reaction. Who knew that instant gratification was on the menu? I sure didn't.

Asher ignores the heat barreling out of Alex's eyes, nods a greeting to Brady, then turns back to me. "Not much. I looked for you after class, but you were already gone."

I feel like I'm sitting precariously on a boulder between two different viper pits. I could either turn the conversation back to Alex, which he would love, or I could pretend to pay sole attention to Asher, which he would hate. There is nothing Alex likes more than being the center of attention.

I choose Asher. Now, if only I knew how to flirt. That would be perfect.

"Yeah. Sorry," I say, propping my chin up on my hand, and feigning apology. "Brady grabbed me after class."

Brady clears his throat to hide a laugh. "We only get so much time for lunch. I, myself, want to take as much advantage of it as possible."

"Good on ya," Asher says with a smile only for me.

I can feel Alex's eyes getting hotter and hotter. With the right concentration, he could probably shoot lasers. When his number is called, he jumps up to get his food and doesn't come back.

"I hope I didn't interrupt anything," Asher says.

"Nope," I say nonchalantly while staring daggers at Alex's back with my eyes. "Care to join us?"

Brady kicks me lightly under the table. I turn a glittering smile at him. He shakes his head. Not in warning, but more of an I-don't-know-what-I'm-going-to-do-with-you type of look.

Asher doesn't respond. Something outside the window in the parking lot has caught his attention. His demeanor may have been warm and comforting before, but it's ice cold now. Every muscle in his body is clenched. Unable to resist, I look over my shoulder. A man with pale blond hair and a long gray coat retreats slowly. By the time I turn back around, Asher is already focused on me instead of the window like nothing even happened.

"Nah, I better get back to the group. We're talking strategy about the game. But I'll catch you later?" Asher says.

"Sure," I shrug. "Later."

When he is out of earshot, Brady turns slowly toward me, leans across the table, and says, "You play with fire and you're gonna get burned."

"What's that mean?"

"You know what it means," he says, jerking his head to the side to indicate Asher.

"He's harmless, but," I trail off as I pick at my sandwich without any intention of eating it. "Am I stuck up?"

He laughs. "You? Right. Where the hell did that come from?"

I shrug. "I don't know. I guess it's a rumor going around about me."

"Huh," he says like he isn't at all surprised. "People don't know what they're talking about. You ready?"

I nod.

There was a time when I would have been sitting right next to Alex, hanging on his every word. But now, seeing Jen staring at him with her pretty brown eyes, I can't imagine ever sitting there again. Actually, staying home from the game is the biggest middle finger at Alex I can come up with.

I've been to every game since Alex started playing and I don't even like basketball. I don't play it, I don't follow it, and I sure don't care to watch someone else play it.

I groan under my breath. Maybe after tonight I can start talking to Alex again. I don't think I've been this mad at him since the third grade when he stole my cupcake out of my lunchbox without telling me. It feels strange like I gave up my favorite CD or something. Not detrimental, just wrong.

Brady elbows me on my way out the door. "You know you're going to forgive him. You always do," he says.

I let out a loud sigh. "You're probably right."

"I usually am, Kitten."

***

I realize just after Math that I forgot to grab my Psychology book and make a mad dash toward my locker to retrieve it. Alex is leaning against it when I get there. It isn't like I've never given him the combination because I have.

It wouldn't have surprised me to catch Alex ditching his backpack in my locker or borrowing my English notes or something. What does shock me, though, is that he's just sitting there waiting for something.

Since I don't usually come back to my locker between Math and Psych, I ask him none-too-friendly, "You lost?"

His expression is priceless: unease mixed with horror. "God, what did I do?" he says, pushing his weight off of the locker with his elbows.

I open my mouth to release numerous unprintable words, but recoil at the last second. "Nothing," I say, shaking my head in disgust with myself. "You didn't do anything."

"Was I supposed to?" His eyebrows draw together like it will help him remember the last forty-eight hours.

He looks so cute I can't help but laugh. Though, it may be a touch on the nervous side. "No. You weren't supposed to do anything either."

I turn the dial on the combination lock a few spins. My locker always sticks so I have to wiggle the handle a few times before I can yank it open. On the inside of the door is a picture of Jensen Ackles posing at a promotion shoot for *Supernatural*. I can't help it, I smile. That's what Dean always does to me.

"What is it then?" he asks over my left shoulder.

I shake my head, suddenly very interested in the items in my locker. When I pictured us having this conversation, the setting was not the hall at school in the middle of the day. "I don't know, okay? I'm probably just PMS-ing."

Now is his turn to laugh. "Girls." He sighs as if that answers every question he ever had.

"Yeah." I shut the door with a bit more force than necessary. The sound vibrates the locker next to mine. I wheel around and start heading toward the direction of my next class. Despite the fact that his class is this way, too, I really hope he doesn't follow.

"You know, you've been my friend for so long I forget you're a girl." He smiles and adds, "Sometimes," to spare my feelings.

"Well, that's a comforting thought," I say, wryly.

"You're my best friend. You're one of us," he continues.

"One of you?"

"Well, yeah." He glances at me sideways and almost runs into a fellow Junior. He places his hand on the kid's shoulder so he doesn't topple over him. One of Alex's known traits is his civility among the rest of the student class. It's part of his charm, part of what got him nominated for class president all three years of Junior High. "One of the guys."

I stop walking. A sophomore veers to the left at the last second to avoid bumping into me. Aren't we a hallway hazard today? "Is that supposed to be a compliment?" I clarify.

He nods. "Of course, why wouldn't it be?"

At that exact moment, we come up on my Psychology class. Thank God. I don't turn to look at him as I wave goodbye and duck into the room. A year ago, I may have been able to consider his words as praise, but now, with these feelings and emotions rampaging on inside of me, I just want him to see me as something else. Like, I don't know, a girl maybe? I take a long look down at myself. I'm not at all flat-chested. In fact, my mother's side of the family was pretty blessed in that department and I am no exception. I'm wearing a black t-shirt, which doesn't exactly accentuate my greatest asset, but doesn't hide it either. My jeans aren't tight, but aren't loose. They fit just like I like them. I don't like bending over and showing the whole world what color my underwear is and what style.

The least feminine thing I wear is my boots. They're Doc Martens. Black. I like them and they've lasted forever. Maybe if they were pink...

Yeah, me in pink. Ha. The only pink I wear is on the inside of my glasses, which incidentally, I refuse to wear in school because of that fact.

A maelstrom of thoughts and suggestions suddenly smack me between the eyes. What if I curled my hair? Dyed my hair? Changed my makeup? Hell, if I even did my makeup? What if I wore a dress? Heels? Jewelry? What if I started dancing around like a Barbie doll, wearing half the clothes I do now and talking like every girl out of every cheesy teenage drama sitcom?

What am I thinking? Am I really thinking about changing my looks for a guy – for Alex? That's against everything I believe in. I might as well make an appointment to get "Poser" tattooed across my forehead.

"Miss Dubois?" Mrs. Jarvis, Psychology teacher extraordinaire, says, "Whenever you're ready."

Blood burns my cheeks. I didn't even hear the bell. Looking around, I notice the desks have all been rearranged into groups of four. Lab day. I like Lab days. What I don't like, however, is that in the course of my musings, all of the seats have been taken. All except one.

Mrs. Jarvis is wearing the same dress she always wears on the third of the month. I wonder if she does this to test our analytical minds. That seems like something she'd do. Her dress is black with a swirly silver pattern across the stomach. Very elegant. The neck connects in a V and shows a little more of her breasts than any high school teacher should. Her red hair is in its usual style. Half up, held with a pen, and curly down her shoulders. She's a very pretty woman. When I was little, I probably would have wanted to grow up to be her.

With a sigh, I walk over to join the group with the one empty chair. The same group with Jen, Asher and April Goody, head cheerleader. Dropping my backpack to the floor, I fall unceremoniously into the chair. Immediately, I prop my elbows on the desk and let my head flop into my hands. Jen sits across from me, Asher to my right, and April is across from him. I never understood why people name their kids after months. It makes almost as much sense as naming a dog Bob. Then again, who am I to talk? I'm not named after just one dead woman, but six of them.

"Great," Mrs. Jarvis says once I'm all settled. "Now taped to the underside of each of your chairs is a psychological disorder. It is important that you don't show anyone what's written on your paper. The purpose of this assignment is to display what you have learned so far in my class. For the next week, I want you to spend the time exhibiting key symptoms for this disorder. Then you will psychoanalyze the members of your team."

At least she gave us fake illnesses to analyze. I wouldn't be in anyone's good graces if we were to do it in reality.

You know how you read symptoms and think of people you know? Well, that's how I remember them.

Jen is a delusional sociopath. I suspect she also suffers from Bulimia Nervosa, as well, but have never been able to prove it. She could be a nymphomaniac, though. Or would she just be a slut? If I were to combine my Health class lessons, I would say she has a ninety-seven percent chance of contracting an STD and a seventy-two percent chance that it will be fatal.

April suffers from a form of narcissism. I sub-categorize it as Look-At-My-Ass syndrome. Because she and Jen are so close, I have to commit her to the bulimic and slu… nymphomaniac categories as well. Guilty by association and all that.

And that brings us to Asher. Well, I'm not exactly sure about him yet. He's new this year, just moved here from some city in the Northeast. Probably New York or somewhere extravagant like that. I make a mental note to analyze him later.

"You can look now," Mrs. Jarvis instructs. "Make me proud."

I reach under my chair and feel around for whatever role I am assigned to play. A couple of snickers roll through the room. I try not to imagine what disorder would cause someone to giggle. The bottom of my chair feels empty. I climb off the seat, hunkering down on the balls of my feet to see underneath it. There, wedged underneath one of the metal bracings, a small piece of scotch tape flapping off the corner, is my assignment. I rip it free with my nails. Before climbing back into the chair, I open the paper.

Depression with suicidal tendencies.

I bite my tongue so I don't laugh out loud. After the week I've had, playing depressed should be a piece of cake.

When I get back into my chair, I see Asher looking at me with a mischievous smile.

"What?" I ask, hoping he didn't see what was on my paper, too.

His look lingers across my eyes. "Nothing," he says before turning back to the group.

I watch him for a minute before joining the discussion myself. When I say that I "joined" the discussion, what I really mean is that I pulled on my role as if it were a new sweatshirt. I flip open my notebook, grab my pen, and doodle anything dark I can think of: black voids, teddy bears crying, knives, and bleeding hearts.

Sometimes, my acting skills astonish even me.

Chapter 5

There's a note stuck to our chrome-plated fridge when I get home. It's written on a piece of white lined paper with hearts bordering the edges. I pull it free and read it.

Nicky.

You probably went to the game. Dad and I will be out late. Hope you went out to eat with the guys, but if not, there is left over Chinese in the fridge. Love you.

Mom

Of course she would think I was at the game. I probably should have gone, but I just couldn't bring myself to do it. Even when Brady begged me to go with him.

I think I'm allowed a girly fit every now and again.

The left over Chinese food containers are at eye level and wrapped in cellophane. It may be my imagination, but I swear a choir of angels sings as scoop three different entrees on to my plate. When it goes into the microwave, it has to be separated carefully. If the juices mix, it doesn't taste as good. After it's re-heated, though, I always mix the Cashew chicken and the rice together. Don't ask me why it tastes different after instead of before, but it does. I'm just glad I don't have to eat left over chicken. Nothing tastes as good the second time like Chinese food.

While I wait, I search out the number to the hospital on my cell phone. They may not be able to tell me anything, but at least I can tell the guilty feeling in my stomach that I tried. So, while my food turns mechanically in the microwave, I dial the number I've found to St. Mark's Hospital.

After a few transfers and one disconnection, I finally get through to Spencer's room. This must be how they weed out the undesirable calls: frustrate them to death.

The last thing I expect is for Mrs. Adams to answer the phone.

"Hello?" she says, her voice rough from very little sleep.

I panic for a second, but after reminding myself that I did nothing wrong and am completely anonymous, I am able to reply.

"Hi, Mrs. Adams. This is Nicoletta Dubois," I say, though I'm not sure why I'm being so formal. Debra Adams has gone to church with my mother for as long as I can remember. She's a nice lady. Too bad Spencer didn't get any of those genes.

"Oh, Nicoletta," she says, sounding surprised.

Frankly, I'm surprised, too. "I heard that Spencer was in the hospital," I lie. "I just wanted to see how he was doing."

Her voice is tinged with raw emotion now. She's crying. God help me. "It is so good of you to call, dear. Spencer's hanging in there. I'm surprised that more of his friends haven't called, though."

"Yeah. Me, too." I have to fight the urge to correct her that I am an acquaintance, not a friend. "So, will he be alright?"

There's a long pause. I check my phone to make sure it didn't disconnect. Still connected.

"We don't know, honey. We just don't know."

I'm taken aback. That's not how these things work. Alcohol poisoning is common, right? Plenty of people from school have gone to the hospital with it before. They get their stomach pumped and go home. Cut and dried. So why would it be life and death now?

Mrs. Adams clears her throat to hide the sobs. "I don't know why Spencer would be so irresponsible. With his condition, he never should have been drinking. I'd be hopping mad if I wasn't so worried."

"Condition?" I repeat. The microwave dings. I shush it with a fluttering hand without knowing why. It can't understand me.

"Oh, honey. Spencer was born with a very weak heart. We haven't told anyone because he didn't want to be treated differently, but he is on the list for a heart transplant. Unfortunately, it is a very long list and not a very easy one to get through, I imagine. Your mother hasn't told you this?"

"No," I say regretfully.

She pauses again before saying, "Oh. Nicoletta, dear. Please don't tell anyone. Spencer would be so upset with me."

Guilt rises up in my throat like bile. I still don't like him, but fatal illnesses make a little asshole behavior acceptable. "I won't."

"Thank you."

"Do you guys need anything?" Aside from a new heart.

She chokes out a laugh. "That is so thoughtful of you. Spencer still hasn't woken up and I don't want to leave him, but I think we're okay."

"Okay. Just let us know. Anything at all." I pull the nuked food from the microwave and dump it into the trash can under the sink. I'm suddenly not hungry anymore. I repeat my cell phone number for her three times and assure her that she can call me any time, day or night. A nurse must have walked into the room, because she agrees quickly and hangs up without saying goodbye.

I lean back against the counter and stare at the phone. Nothing like a little brush with mortality to put your priorities back in order.

I pick up my keys and head out the door, locking it behind me. It may seem awful to go cheer at a Basketball game after learning that one of their players is on his death bed, but I would feel awful if I didn't.

I'm half frozen by the time I walk into the school. The smell of heat, sweat and people stings my nose. The first thing I do is strip off my jacket and shudder as the cold air is nearly ripped from my pores.

The door to the gym doesn't enter into the stands like so many other high schools. Once you walk in, you have to skirt the court and hope you don't get hit, which is exactly what I do. I sidestep a few people who are leaving and make my way up the steps.

Brady calls out to me from the middle of a row to my left. The seat next to him is open and he's waving like a maniac to get my attention. I have to step around people's knees to get there. Some are considerate and stand up. Most aren't.

"What did I miss?" I ask, sitting on the metal bench and setting my jacket beside onto the seat next to me.

"I don't know," he scoffs. "I don't come here to watch the game."

I flash him a knowing smile. "Right."

You may think Brady's ability to understand me is a paranormal ability, but it's not. Brady and I understand each other because we have the same interests. For instance, Brady comes to the games for the same reasons I do: to support Alex and to watch sweaty guys running back and forth on the court. Oh yeah, Brady's gay. Did I forget to mention that? Maybe it's because Brady being gay is just a part of his genetic makeup like his unruly auburn hair or his green eyes. We don't tell Alex, though, or anyone else for that matter. Brady thinks people will look at him differently. I don't push him. If I were to announce I was a lesbian then the whole male population of the student body would be enthralled with my very existence. But if a guy announces he is gay, he magically turns into a pariah. Talk about your double standard.

"Asher is playing awesome today," Brady says, a little under his breath. He glances around to see if anyone can hear him and adds, "Not that I was noticing."

I force a lopsided smile in his direction. But it feels wrong somehow. More like a grimace.

"What? He's cute," Brady says in defense.

I make a theatrical display of rolling my eyes before turning my focus back to the game. Alex dashes up and down the court blocking and bouncing, all without getting the ball. That doesn't seem right. He usually gets the most one-on-one time with the ball. The player he blocks, a thin wiry boy with blond hair that sticks to his forehead in an annoying way, ducks to the right where he juts out an elbow and catches Alex in the kidney. Alex drops to the floor in a heap of limbs.

I'm out of my seat before my heart has a chance to beat. A few groans ruffle the audience, drowning out my gasps. Blood pulses in my ears. I don't hear Brady stand up next to me.

"Shit. That looks like it hurt," he says, sounding very far away.

But Alex pulls himself up off the floor with Mikey Masters' help. He jumps up and down a few times like he can shake off the pain, but his face shows the pink stain of embarrassment. His hands cover his face, rubbing it as if he can wipe it clean.

When he steps up to the line, setting up to take his first shot, I take my first full deep breath. My chest burns when the air hits my lungs. Brady and I sit back down.

"I hate basketball," I mumble.

Brady laughs. "Why do you come to every game then? Aside from the cute boys, I mean. Not even I come to every game."

"Because we don't have a hockey team?" I suggest with a shrug. "I have to show my school spirit somehow."

Brady slaps my knee. "Good one. School spirit. Ha!"

We both laugh. It's easier than admitting the real reason I come to every game: to watch Alex Berkley from afar. Sure, to support him, too, but from the stands, you can stare without question. Everybody stares.

"Hey. I'm having another party this weekend. You coming?" Brady says, still chuckling.

I stare at him with a confused look, no humor, not anymore.

"You're going to throw another party after what happened with Spencer?"

He shrugs, not looking at me. "Why not? Out of all the parties I've thrown, Spencer has been the only mishap."

Mishap? I want to shriek.

"What better way to get back on track than to throw another party? Aside from the situation," He makes quotation marks in the air with his fingers. "That party was epic."

"I wouldn't know," I say glumly. My mind replays the conversation I had with Mrs. Adams before I left the house. Her masked sobs still make me cold.

"So you'll come, right?" He nudges me with his elbow. "I bet Asher will be there."

"I'll think about it."

I agonize over whether or not to tell Brady about Spencer's heart condition for a moment. How would Brady respond if I told him that if Spencer hadn't been drinking the alcohol Brady provided then he wouldn't be in a coma? He would probably launch into a speech about free will, and he would be right. No one made Spencer Adams drink except Spencer Adams.

The final buzzer vibrates through the seats. Game over. We won. Happy dance and all that jazz.

**

Brady and I are the only ones left in the hall. We always wait after to see if Alex wants to get something to eat. A big game makes him hungry. Since I didn't eat dinner, I'm a little bit hungry myself.

The door to the guy's locker room shoves open and steam escapes into the hall. It sounds like a party is going on in there.

Brady wags his eyebrows at me. I look away, embarrassed.

Out comes Asher. His dark hair hangs in wet cords across his cheeks. He's changed into loose fitting jeans, heavy combat boots, and a Rangers shirt. He looks absolutely delectable.

Brady smiles and bobs his head toward Asher, directing my attention to his shirt. He knows how big of a Rangers fan I am.

I nod to let him know that I noticed.

"Nicoletta," Asher exclaims. "I thought you weren't coming."

I try really hard not to smile when he says my name. Seriously, how could I spell it to get that pronunciation every time someone says it – add a *k* after the *c* or change the *i* to an *e*?

"Well, I was afraid you'd lose if I didn't come," I joke. *Stuck up people don't joke*, I think to myself with satisfaction. Two points for me.

"Good thing you came then." The corners of his lips creep up in a lopsided grin just for me. Then he turns his focus on Brady, "What's up, man?"

Brady looks like a cat basking in the glow of the sun. "I was just telling Nicky about my party this Saturday."

43

"No you weren't," I interrupt.

He nods emphatically. "Yes. I was. But I'm afraid she's nervous after the last one. So, I'm looking for incentive."

Just then, incentive… err, I mean Alex, walks through the door of the steaming locker room. He nods at Brady and sweeps me up into a rib-crushing hug. Over his shoulder, I see Asher's expression turn hard and disconcerted. Then within seconds, it's gone and he's back to nonchalant and careless.

"Nic," Alex says excitedly. "Did you see that last shot? I was amazing."

I nod tightly. "Yeah. I did."

He sets me onto my feet and says to Brady and me, purposefully ignoring Asher at his back, "So where we going to eat? I'm starving."

I'm too stunned to speak. It isn't like Alex never hugs me. It's just usually when I am upset or something of the like, but never with that much emphasis.

"Fat Cats," Brady exclaims. "I gots me a date with *Dance Dance Revolution*."

I snicker. Not because of Brady's butchered English, which I'm pretty used to, but because of the images that come to mind. Even though Brady is awesome at the game, it's still hilarious to watch.

"Sounds good," Alex agrees.

I look around his shoulder to Asher, who is inconspicuously trying to walk away. It feels weird to let him just go without inviting him since he has been standing right there listening to us. Besides, I kind of want him to go.

Then again, it might be a good time for Alex and me to have that talk.

Alex shorts out my train of thought by saying, "Hey, I invited Jen. That's cool, right?" It's not lost on me that he stares at me when he says it.

"Um, sure," Brady responds, his eyes shifting between Alex, me, and the floor.

I hold up a finger to tell them to hang on and duck around Alex. Asher is already to the side doors a good twenty yard dash down the hall. I'm not proud of what I do next. Breaking into a run, I reach him just before he gets outside.

"Ash...," I gasp. I may walk every day, but running has never been my strong suit. That's what happens when you have asthma.

He turns with a confused look on his face as if the last thing he expected to see was me barreling toward him. Though, in all fairness, it probably was. "Not many people call me that," he says with a chuckle.

"Sorry," I pant. Very attractive, I know.

"Don't be." He smiles and puts a hand on my shoulder. "You alright there?"

"Fine." I clutch my chest where it burns like I've been impaled with a hot poker. "Asthma."

He shifts back and forth impatiently like he isn't sure whether to have me sit down or administer CPR.

With one hand still pushing into the burning hole in my chest, I use my free one to locate the inhaler deep in my pocket. Three puffs of gritty air later, I exhale, feeling the burn ebb.

"Really. I'm fine. God, that isn't embarrassing." I roll my eyes to emphasize how embarrassing it actually is.

He breathes out a nervous laugh. Then he glances over my head to where Alex stands, glaring at us. "So did you run all the way over here just to give me a heart attack?"

"No," I respond without turning. I don't have to see Alex's expression. I can feel it heavy on my neck. "I came to invite you to dinner with us."

He doesn't look at me, just stares past me. "Um, I probably shouldn't. I have a sneaking suspicion that Alex doesn't like me much these days."

"So?" *He has Jen*, I add silently. "You aren't going to hang out with Alex. You're going to hang out with Brady and me. I'll tell you what: if it gets awkward, I'll treat you to a game of pool." I wrap my hand around his forearm and pull lightly. As if a string were attached from his arm to his head, he looks down at me. "Please?" I say with an innocent smile. "I will be forever indebted to you."

Asher makes an adorable face that says he is weighing all the options in his mind. It's a look that makes ugly guys look creepy and sexy guys look sexier. Asher evidently belongs to the latter of the two.

I take his hesitation as agreement and pull him by the hand back down the hall. He doesn't fight me.

Asher's hand is warm. The touch of our palms together makes me feel different somehow. Like there's a part of me I've never realized before moving forward through the shadows. Where our skin meets is a tingling sensation like you get after touching a live wire or something, but better.

Alex looks like he could combust any moment by the time we catch up to them. His eyes rake over our interlaced fingers and the muscles in his jaw jump.

"Alright. Ready to go," I say with a devious smile.

Chapter 6

Fat Cats is a combination arcade, bowling alley, pool hall, and restaurant. The restaurant, otherwise known as The Pizza Factory, has a separate entrance from the gaming hall. According to the parking lot, Wednesday nights are not very busy.

Brady walks right up to the hostess and splays his fingers to indicate that we have five in our party. She grabs the menus with a fake smile and ushers us around the salad bar to a booth.

I put a hand to Brady's chest to hold him back while Asher climbs in first. He gives me a look of astonishment. I never give up the corner. Then I climb in with Brady to my left. That puts Alex, Jen, and all of their fake gooiness across from us, where I have to watch every disgusting glance. I curse quietly.

"What was that? I didn't hear you," Brady says with a grin worthy of the Cheshire cat.

I glare at him. "I said the breadsticks here are amazing."

"Yeah they are," he says with a wink.

Before the waitress goes away to do whatever it is she does on quiet nights like tonight, we give her our drink orders.

Alex turns halfway in the booth to talk to Jen. Her fingers are wrapped around and strangling his. It hurts my throat to watch, but I can't seem to make myself look away either.

Brady hands a menu over to me. I pass it on to Asher without looking at it. He glances at me curiously.

"I'm not hungry," I tell him. Actually, I feel nauseous, but that's better left unsaid.

He follows my eyes across the table to Alex, who is playing up his injury from the game. Jen gushes about how she'll take care of him. He frowns slightly and nods.

Everyone else is hungry, though. Brady orders a full pizza for himself. Alex gets the Chicken Alfredo, as I suspected he would. Jen gets a salad with lemons and no dressing – also not a shocker,

47

and Asher gets a concoction that includes bowtie pasta with Alfredo sauce, chicken, broccoli and extra pine nuts.

I look at him with a smile.

"What?" he says in defense. "I like pine nuts."

Asher's order is really close to what I normally get, extra pine nuts included. Brady elbows me hard enough in the side to leave a bruise in an effort to point that out. That jab says, "You're perfect for each other" when Brady can't.

"I like them, too," I say quietly, elbowing Brady back hard enough to warrant a grunt.

In the end, I order a single breadstick. Really it's like two breadsticks braided together up a chop stick, but they are amazing. Add Alfredo sauce and they are sweet perfection.

We don't say much during dinner. I refuse to play *20 Questions* with Asher because I don't want to exclude Brady. Alex sure as hell isn't going to keep him involved in conversation. I've been the third or fifth wheel enough times to know what it feels like and frankly, it sucks. Unfortunately, that means dinner is awkward and quiet. So with the least amount of food to consume, I make an effort to spark conversation.

"What did you guys think about the assignment in Psych?" I ask Brady and Asher. Alex isn't taking Psychology until next semester so he can't weigh in. I purposely want to exclude him. I want to hurt him for making me hurt. Not that he can hear anything we say anyway with Jen's boobs distracting him.

Brady laughs. "I got Schizophrenia. I love it. I get to sit there and have conversations with myself all day. Best conversation I've had in a long time. What did you guys get?"

My mouth opens in automatic response. Asher speaks over me. "Nicoletta and I are in the same group. So we can't say," he says, shooting a pointed look in my direction.

"Right," I say, embarrassed. "I'll tell you later."

"I got a good one," Jen says, jumping in. "Oh Alex, I wish you were in this class. Our teacher always does the most interesting assignments."

Damn it. I forgot Jen was in our group.

Alex shrugs and takes a bite of his food. "Maybe next year."

Jen makes doe eyes at him and says in a seductive voice, "Maybe I'll just have to fail it this semester so I can take it next semester with you."

He glances at me in silent communication. His look says, "Really, she's not that bad." I look down, concentrating on my breadstick. So much for conversation.

Asher pushes his half-eaten food toward the middle of the table and rubs his hands together. "Hey Brady, can you let us out? Nicoletta promised me a game of pool."

Brady climbs out, grabbing the check on his way. "Sure. I've got a date with DDR anyway."

Alex nods. But neither he nor Jen say anything as we walk away.

The girl at the cash register slips a piece of paper to Asher without any subtlety. I focus on the check to make a show of how little it bothers me despite the burning in my chest.

I've gotten really good at pretending not to care when girls are interested. Alex taught me well years ago and I've had a lot of practice since. I fish a ten dollar bill out of my pocket and try to hand it to Brady in order to give her more time.

"Don't worry about it." Brady says, waving me away. "You shouldn't have to pay for awkward situations."

When the waitress finally employs herself with ringing us up, I take the opportunity to look her over. Alex usually asks what I think of a girl after this type situation happens so it's best to be prepared. Of course, I usually judge with prejudice. I won't come straight out and say that I hate her, but it doesn't hurt to point out any flaws I notice: Knobby knees, high-pitched voice, or fat wrists. Yes, I said fat wrists.

I don't see any of those things on our waitress, though. I mean she's really pretty. She has dark hair that curls around her neck as if attracted there and big brown eyes with thick eyelashes that could make every girl at school scream in jealousy. Her face is proportioned like a portrait. In art class, we learned how to draw the face in dimensions. This seemed weird to me at the time because my features don't match those dimensions: My eyes are set just a little more than an eye-width apart, my mouth is not as wide as the outside corners of my eyes, and I can't imagine anyone's eye line marks the center of the head.

Now I can.

This girl's features are perfect in proportion and it's even likely she's our age. I hate to admit it, but I can't find anything wrong with her, and believe me, I can usually spot something wrong with anyone.

Asher grabs Brady's shoulder and tries to hand him a twenty dollar bill.

Brady glares at it as if he's offended. "I'll tell you what. I pay for dinner and you get Nicky to my party."

"Take his money then," I suggest quietly.

But Asher is already tucking the bill back in his wallet. "I'll see what I can do."

The restaurant has a dimly lit hallway to the left of the cashier counter that connects to the bowling alley. I run my finger along the wallpaper as we walk so I don't bump into the wall like an idiot.

"Nicoletta," someone whispers from behind me.

I look over my shoulder, but the only person there is Brady, and I know it wasn't his voice. I shrug it off. Must have been Asher.

Brady pushes me along. "I'm so glad we brought separate cars. Let me know when you guys want to leave." He pulls open the big glass door

Along with the sounds of pins crashing together and video games beeping, the music of Social Offense welcomes us. Their latest single, *I Almost Miss Hating You*, pounds through the speakers.

Asher leans in close to my ear and says, "I love this song."

The thick drum beats pulses out into the air adding energy to the room. I nod in agreement. I love this song, too.

"Did you know they went to our school?" I ask him, though it feels like I'm yelling.

"They're from Utah?" he replies, sounding genuinely interested.

"Yep." I cock my head to the side. "Well, originally."

"And I thought nothing good could ever come from that school."

Yeah, I did, too. Until now.

***

The room is dark. Not so dark you can't see, but dark enough that you could bump into someone without realizing it. The only illumination comes from the rectangular lights hanging over the pool tables. There are three. The restaurant is just on the other side of the billiards area. I think about Jen and Alex, wondering if they are still in there.

Asher bumps my shoulder with his bicep. "You're up."

I line my stick up to the cue ball. It stopped in an awkward position so I have to lean half over the table. I'm losing, horribly.

I call out, "Six. Corner pocket," and let the stick fly. When I say "fly," I mean literally. I lose my balance on the follow through and the stick launches from my grasp. It jumps over the cue ball without touching it and bounces against the six, ironically, knocking it into, you guessed it, the corner pocket.

Asher doubles over with laughter.

"I'm not usually this bad," I say, defending my hurt pride.

He holds his hands up in surrender. "Hey. It went in. Works for me."

"Still doesn't count," I argue. The table is one of those pay tables so you can't fish out a scratched ball, only the cue ball, so it has to stay.

"Suit yourself." He shrugs, still chuckling. "I would have given it to you, though."

"Don't do me any favors," I mumble.

He walks around the table, calls his shot and hits the cue ball with such force that he sinks two balls.

I shake my head in awe. "How do you do that?"

"Practice," he says, tapping the table with the tip of his stick to call his next shot. The sound of bowling balls racing down the lane to tackle pins makes it hard to hear so both of us are talking really loud. I'll probably be hearing crashing noises for days to come.

I glance around the room, trying to look anywhere but where Asher is bent over the table in front of me. His shirt clings to his skin, showing the muscles constrict in his back, each line so defined I could press my fingers into them and feel how solid he actually is. My breath catches at the thought and I thank God for the extra noise.

Asher pauses and turns around without making his shot. He motions me over.

Warily, I walk toward him.

"I'm not going to hurt you. I just want to help you practice."

A wry smile crosses my lips. "God, this is so cliché."

"What?"

"The guy teaching the girl how to play pool. That happens on all dates, doesn't it?"

After I say the words, I immediately regret them. A girl wouldn't complain about a guy wanting to help her better her skills at pool. She would walk right over and let him lean over, around, and into her without hesitation. I cover my face with my palm to hide my mortification.

"Date," he repeats. "Wow, if I had known that, I would have taken you somewhere nicer. Somewhere less… prone to awkward situations." He looks himself up and down. "And I probably would have dressed nicer. Probably."

"Sorry. Not a date," I amend, waving my hand in the air to erase the last few minutes. "Thanks for your help in there, by the way."

He smiles. "You're already forever indebted to me." He gestures to the pool table and says close to my ear. "So humor me."

I roll my eyes. "Fine, one cliché coming right up."

I shrug my jacket off and throw it over the drink table next to us. If I'm supposed to be serious about this, maybe I shouldn't be wearing a tight jacket. There's a thought I wish I had earlier.

Asher's hand slides up my back sending warm tremors through the knuckles of my spine. Then, with barely any pressure, he pushes me down over the table until I am eye level with the cue ball. His hand is like a weight on the back of the cue stick. He bends down, his body bonding with the curve of mine. His face is so close that his breath stirs my hair. His left hand cradles mine on the tip of the stick, his thumb rubbing gently along my palm.

"Easy," he breathes into my ear.

No wonder this situation is so overdone. With his chest rising and falling against my shoulder blades and his callused fingers stroking mine, I finally understand the excitement. Goosebumps march up my neck.

Asher's head droops and he inhales as if smelling my hair. Every inch of me goes warm. "Now," he says. The cue stick launches out and smacks into the cue ball with a crack! I don't see any balls go in, but I hear two of them sink home and bang down the return tracks under the table.

"Wow Nic. Nice shot," says a familiar voice from the doorway. It's Alex.

I launch up so quickly that the back of my head collides with Asher's.

He groans and pushes one hand into his forehead.

White lines lance my vision. I turn to see Alex leaning against the doorframe with an amused smile on his face. At least I think it's amused. Between the horrible lighting and my disintegrating vision, I can't be sure.

"You alright?" I ask Asher.

He's collapses into a chair, holding his head. "I think I'll live," he moans.

I drop to my knees in front of him and pull his hands away. No blood so far as I can tell. Good. I'd feel bad if I broke his nose.

"I'm so sorry," I say quietly.

He waves one hand dismissively. "Just give me a minute."

I get to my feet with a little bit more effort than usual, fighting the dizziness that threatens to take me back down.

"We're out," Alex says, still smiling. And that's when I notice the black figure next to him that must be Jen.

I grip the table for support. What does he want, a bon voyage party? "Alright. See ya."

My heart feels full and heavy in my chest. He's going home with Jen, my mind screams. Early!

"See ya," he says. Then he disappears.

When I look back at Asher, he stares at me with a confused look in his eyes.

"You sure you're alright?" I ask again.

He bobs his head up and down once. "Yeah. I'm really tired, though. Rain check on the game?"

My eyes take in the table with four billiard balls still waiting to be played. "Sure," I say with a mark of disappointment.

Brady runs us back to the school parking lot to get Asher's car. When we pull up to the red shiny jeep, I have to force myself not to ask him a million questions all at once.

I turn so I can see him over my shoulder. "Wait, you have a car?"

He nods from the back seat of Brady's Camry. "Yeah, why?"

Because you could have driven Spencer to the hospital that night, I think to myself.

He can probably tell what I'm thinking because he says, "My sister borrowed it the other night. She doesn't have one yet. So I let her take mine." He lays a hand on Brady's shoulder. "Well, thanks man." Clutched in his fingers is the twenty dollar bill. He drops it, letting it float to Brady's lap.

Brady picks it up with his thumb and forefinger as if it were contaminated. Then he flings it back at him. "No way. We have a deal."

They both look at me. I shrug. Twenty dollars just doesn't seem like enough money to get me to another party. Besides, they aren't offering me the money.

Asher shoves the bill back in his pocket. "Alright," he mumbles. "See ya around."

On impulse, I tell Brady to wait for a minute and climb out of the car. I don't know why I do it. It's not like I'm going to hug him goodbye or anything. I don't know him well enough for that.

Asher strides over to stand in front of me. For a long awkward moment, I stare at him in the harsh light of the parking lot. Again, he doesn't have a jacket on. I'm cold with one so he must be freezing without. Pink powders his cheeks and nose.

He must be crazy being out here in below-twenty weather without a jacket. People who are mentally stable are already donning ski gear, but here he is in just a Rangers t-shirt and jeans.

I consider scolding him for it, but decide it would just make me sound like my mother. Besides, he doesn't look that uncomfortable. So I don't say a word about it.

"Thanks for coming," I say. Out here, the world seems quiet and empty. I'm surprised when my voice doesn't echo back.

"No worries," He runs a hand through his hair. It dried in waves. I notice for the fiftieth time tonight how good looking he is.

"Oh," he says suddenly. "I have something for you." He holds up a hand to tell me to wait while he rummages around in his pocket with the other one. Out comes a thin piece of paper. He shoves it into the pocket of my jacket.

"What's that?" I ask, confused. The knock to my head still smarts. I wonder if his does, too.

He shrugs. "Something I don't need. Give me your cell phone."

I hand it over without question.

He punches a total of three keys – not enough to equal a phone number – and hands it back with a smile. I take it back and shove it into my pocket. I want to check what he did, but not in front of him.

He gives me a sexy, mischievous smile. "Well, see ya tomorrow."

"Sure," I say slowly. Then, shaking my head, I turn to climb back into the heated car.

That has to be the most ambiguous conversation I've ever had.

I find myself staring at Asher as he climbs into his jeep. The way his jeans tug around his thighs as steps up, the bulge of his bicep as he wraps his hand around the door to haul himself in, and the ease in which he does it. It feels like the world just stops for a solid moment and the only thing still moving in it is him.

Brady laughs, bringing my attention back to the here and now. "This is going to be a great year," he says. "Don't you think?"

I shake my head and then raise one eyebrow in his general direction. "Take me home, Jeeves."

He wags his eyebrows, chuckling, and puts the car into gear.

My house looks utterly abandoned when we get there. I must have forgotten to turn on the outside light and during the time we were gone, it got dark enough outside to need it. I'm not saying I'm afraid of being alone in the house at night, but I am saying that after you watch enough scary movies it isn't your favorite thing.

After checking the clock on my phone twice, I study the bushes in front of my house. I swear something moves behind them.

When I don't move right away, Brady asks, "Want me to wait with you?"

I shake my head mechanically. Look at me, sixteen years old and still afraid of the boogeyman. I swallow hard, trying to silence the raging drumbeat of my heart. "No, I'll be fine."

"You sure?"

"Yeah," I lie. I'm not sure at all.

Brady lets out a long breath, but doesn't move. Only when his eyes roam over me do I realize that I'm scratching my right arm straight through the jacket. I force my hands into my pocket and pretend like nothing ever happened.

"Alright. Call me if anything goes bump in the night," he jokes, but there's a hint of seriousness to his expression. Aw, Brady worries about me.

"See you tomorrow," I say with a whole new fondness for my best friend. Then I exit the car.

"See ya," he calls out as I am shutting the door.

He sits in the car, watching me until I am safe inside with the door locks. If anything, that's the only reason why I don't bolt inside like this is Pompeii and his car is the volcano. You know, I think to myself, it's too bad Brady isn't interested in girls. The female race really is missing out on a good guy.

The house feels too big and too quiet. It reminds me of the beginning of every slasher flick right before the phone rings or someone walks behind the unsuspecting girl in the hall. If this were *Supernatural*, the lights would be flickering and I would be standing on the verge of getting my heart ripped out by a demon.

Shut up… shut up… shut up!

In an effort to direct my thoughts elsewhere, I flip open my cell phone and scroll through the numbers. There's no Asher in there. Weird. Going through my texts yields the same results. I turn on the hallway light, push the phone into my jacket pocket, and retrieve the piece of paper Asher not-so-subtly left there.

Call me, it says in bubbly letters that could only be written by a girl. There are even two hearts strategically placed in the corners. How cute. And there's a number.

I stare at it for a minute, thinking about the look the waitress gave Asher when she slipped the paper to him. Could this be that paper? It has to be. Though, I can't imagine why he would give it to me. The waitress was pretty without a doubt. Why wouldn't he keep it and call her?

Instead of an answer, a dull pain slithers up the back of my neck and settles into the base of my skull. I cringe and rub at forehead, thinking only beautiful thoughts of my migraine medication. I shrug my jacket off, hang it on the hook by the door, and head to the medicine cabinet.

"Oh how I love you," I say to the bottle as I pop it open and toss back three white tablets, swallowing them dry.

I'm asleep in almost no time at all. I don't even hear my parents come home, if they ever do.

Chapter 7

I wake feeling like I haven't slept at all. The only offerings from my unconscious mind were nightmares. I can't even remember them, but I can feel the remnants of my racing heart, the burning in my chest, and sore muscles like I was running. Like vapor left after the water has boiled away. Was I running? I could be having an asthma attack. I reach over to grab my inhaler, put it to my mouth, and take one long drag of gritty air. Then I realize the pain isn't in my lungs, but in my heart.

Oh god, I must have fallen asleep thinking about Spencer. My alarm clock tells me that it's four forty-five in the morning. Damn it. I'm not even tired anymore. If I were to go back to sleep now it would be next to impossible to wake up in time for school in an hour and a half. I turn my head and groan loudly into my pillow. School. Not something I'm prepared to deal with yet.

Since I've already decided I'm not going back to sleep, I grab the remote. The television clicks to life in the form of a blue glow. Grey sky is visible through the edges of my curtains reminding me of early morning showers and hot chocolate. Winter. I shake my head thoughtfully.

This early in the morning all of the local channels are off air and the cable channels are stuck on infomercial repeat. When I finally reach a channel that isn't trying to sell me something, I put the remote down and close my eyes, falling into the steady beat thrumming in my head.

"Who believes I can hear the dead?" the man from the T.V. says to his audience. "I need myself a believer."

I focus on the rhythmic pulse in hopes that I might hypnotize myself into a state comparable with sleep.

"I do, Rev!" an old woman says. "I be-lieve!"

"Good," he replies. I don't have to see him to know that he's robbing her blind with every word. "Now what can I do you for, ma'am? Where you from?"

"Well, Rev, I'm from a little town in Utah and I believe I am afflicted!"

The crowd gasps in unison.

"What, my dear, do you believe you are afflicted with?"

"I believe a demon is feeding off my life force," she says, sounding a little embarrassed.

It's enough to make me open my eyes and watch.

What must a woman look like who believes she is demon buffet?

What I expect to see is a woman who looks like she just walked out of her trailer in her muumuu to talk about the tornado that just missed their trailer park by "this much," but what I get is a woman who is not much older than me with blond hair and blue eyes. She certainly doesn't look crazy.

"Well, ma'am, that's not usually my thing. But take my hand and let's see what I can do," he says, reaching out the hand that isn't holding the microphone.

She takes his hand and suddenly there's a bright light in my vision.

Then I'm driving down the freeway in my car. My eyes shift to the engagement ring on my left hand. In this light, it actually glitters. I think about how excited I am to get home and tell Brett the good news: that I'm cured. I knew if I had enough faith that God and the nice psychic man would see me through. I pass a freeway sign. Not too far from home. My blood feels like it's alive in my veins.

I'm not sure the guy in front of me could go any slower. Even though the speedometer says he's going 60, it feels like he's going 25. I check my blind spot and begin my transfer into the next lane over.

"Sarah," someone says from my back seat. I know that voice. It's like glass and gravel scraping away at each other. It's awful, like claws raking down my back. "Sarah," he says again. "You didn't actually think you'd get rid of me so easily, did you?"

He breathes in. With each deep inhalation, I feel myself get weaker. I know this isn't right. I'm only twenty-one, and at the prime of my life. I rarely even get sick, but now, I think I'm dying.

My arms go numb as the first stage of panic sets in. I pull on the steering wheel with all my might, but my muscles don't respond.

I have to get off the road.

"Sarah," the voice says again, this time much closer to my ear.

I have to see who is calling me by that name, but I can't turn my head. I'm frozen in the driver's seat, barreling down the freeway at ten over the speed limit. If anyone pulls into my lane... if anything gets into my way... if I can't stop...

"What are you doing here?" the voice asks accusingly, no longer lilting. "You don't belong here."

An ice cold hand brushes the hair off my neck. I'm not sure what he sees there, but there's a sound like a sharp intake of breath.

Almost instantly I'm able to move, but it's too late. There's a car in front of me and there's nothing I can do to avoid impact. So rather than fight with physics, I yank open the door and take my chances with the road.

A horn honks. I look up just in time to see my vehicle – Sarah's white sedan – slam into the sound barrier with a crunch! The car bounces back into the lane, does a half turn, then slams into the barrier again, this time from the driver's side.

Smoke billows out from under the hood. In the distance, I hear three, maybe four, sirens already headed this way.

It doesn't matter. They won't make it in time. She's already dead.

I open my eyes to six-thirty. The past hour has disappeared and I don't feel refreshed at all. In fact, I've never felt more on edge in my life. And now I'm late. Awesome.

I probably spend more time deciding on whether or not to take a sick day than it would take for me to get ready. My mother wouldn't be pleased, but at least I wouldn't have to watch Jen and Alex all day.

We have block days at school. It was explained to us as a great and wonderful idea that would create the option of earning more credits in less time. The catch is, we take eight classes instead of seven. I suspect they had ulterior motives. Though, I have yet to figure them out. So today I have Anatomy, History, Spanish and Art in that order. Alex and Jen are both in my Anatomy and Spanish classes. I wonder how awkward that will be. I think I'd rather take my chances with P.E. and math.

After a nice hot shower, I take my sweet time drying my hair. I'm already late so why bother rushing?

My cell phone rings. My top callers have their own assigned ringtones. When my parents call, it plays an old Jimmy Buffet song they used to play all the time. Nostalgia at its worst. Alex's is a song by Social Offense called *How I Breathe*. It's only available on the Japanese import CD. I made the ringtone myself. The people who only call me on occasion get the generic song: 3Oh!3's *Don't Trust Me*. I like it. It makes me laugh.

Not as much as the song playing now, though. Brady got to choose his own ringtone: the theme song from *The Smurfs*. I giggle for the first time in what feels like forever.

"Seriously, Brady, you have got to call me more often," I say into the receiver.

"Miss me that much, did you?" He doesn't ask why I'm laughing; he already knows.

"Well, of course."

"Aw, that's sweet. So, Kitten, you on your way to school?"

I look at the jeans and t-shirt sitting on my bed. "Something like that."

"Why Nicky," he says in mock horror, "you aren't planning on ditching are you?"

"I might have thought about it. But no."

He gasps. "Well, why the hell not? It's, like, forty degrees outside. We should take a day off to enjoy this warm weather."

I laugh. "Tempting."

"Good. Get ready. I'll be there in five."

I pin the phone between my ear and shoulder. It's hard to pull on jeans while balancing a cell phone, but I manage. "What are you thinking?"

He scoffs. "I don't care. Whatever. Bring Sam and Dean if you want to."

I remember the last time I watched *Supernatural* with Brady. His eyes widened to the size of saucers and there were days of drool to clean up thereafter.

"You better hurry," he warns. "I'm almost there."

"Fine. Bye."

Suddenly, with school out of my mind, it doesn't bother me to hurry. It's hard to believe, isn't it?

On the way out the door, I notice the kitchen light on. Nice to know my parents made it home safely last night. I duck my head in and blow them each a kiss goodbye.

"Have a good day at school, honey," My dad calls over his newspaper.

I feel a little guilty. My parents have always understood the need to occasionally ditch school and they probably wouldn't care. But just in case this is the one time they would, I shrug it off and say, "See ya tonight. Love you."

Brady taps his watch as I get into his Toyota Camry. "That was seven minutes," he scolds.

"Just drive before my parents come outside," I tell him.

Down the street, out of view of my house, I turn and ask, "So what inspired ditch day?"

He laughs. "Just wasn't feeling school today. I got there and started sneezing. I think I might be allergic."

"You should see a doctor for that," I suggest sarcastically.

"What about you? I thought I was going to have to pull a covert op to get you out of the building. What were you doing still at home, my dear?" He glances at me sidelong before nodding knowingly. "Bad dreams again?"

I shiver in response. There are some people in this life who just get you. Brady is my person.

He smiles empathetically. "Looks like ditch day was just in time." Then he turns left when we should be turning right. If we were going to his house, that is.

"Um. Where we going?"

"One more stop," he informs me without meeting my eyes.

That "one more stop" turns out to be a gas station because apparently Brady's tank is only half full. Curiosity burns in my empty stomach.

Brady climbs out of the car then leans back in. "Want coffee or anything? It's a long drive," he says.

"What's a long drive?"

He grins and shuts the door. I jump out and race after him.

"Where are we going?" I demand.

He shrugs and walks over to the coffee carafes, calling over his shoulder, "Be a dear and grab some doughnuts. I'm starving."

"Tell me where we're going."

"It's a surprise. Chocolate, please."

I head down the doughnut aisle in frustration. Brady fills two monster sized coffee cups with the fake French Vanilla Cappuccino stuff in the tall standing machines. I grab a box of six chocolate doughnuts and lick my lips. I hope we aren't going too far. With that much coffee in me, I'm going to have to pee right quick.

As Brady pays for the doughnuts and gas, my attention is drawn to the daily newspaper in the bin next to the counter.

On the front are class pictures of three girls side by side. They all look slightly familiar, but if you live here long enough then eventually you'll run into just about everyone in the city and I've lived here my whole life.

I touch the newspaper and read the headline:

Three local girls found dead from possible epidemic.

I snatch my hand back like the paper bit me.

The soft material of my shirt now feels like steel wool scraping into my skin. I itch at my wrists where it seems like the biggest problem.

I swear I saw the front of the newspaper – this same newspaper – as my dad read it from the kitchen table and that was not the headline. I shake my head like I can clear my vision and look back at the paper. The head story has transformed into some awfully tedious political article.

My blood turns to ice. What the hell is going on with me?

Once we are in the car, Brady says, "I hope you don't mind, but I invited someone else to come along."

Dread clenches my heart in its fist. "Who?"

Please don't say Alex. Please. The greatest aspect of today is that I didn't have to see him. There is only so much awkwardness one can take before you internally combust.

He smiles without answering. I hate it when he acts all coy. "So tell me what's going on with you and Alex. Things have been… tense… lately," he says, changing the subject.

"Is that why you invited me along?" I accuse. "You wanted a story out of me?"

"Nah. That was a bonus."

I roll my window down. Not for the air, for the noise.

"You like him, don't you?" Brady asks, pitching his voice louder to be heard over the whistling wind.

"No," I respond too quickly, but then I hesitate. This is Brady. I've never hidden anything from him. He knows everything from when I got my first crush in Elementary school to when I got my first period. If I'm just one of the guys, he's one of the girls. "Yes," I finally admit. "I don't know when it happened. Not that it matters. He doesn't see me like that. I'm not even a girl to him."

"Sucks, don't it?" he says ruefully.

"Yeah, it does."

He pulls onto a side road by the school. From where we are, I can see the side windows where the cafeteria is. If anyone were to look outside then they could totally see us. Seems this is Brady's idea of hiding in plain sight.

The heater breathes out into the silence, a soft whooshing noise fighting to be heard over the air rushing in through my window. For some reason, I'm reminded of last night. The look on Alex's face when he walked in on Asher and me playing pool has been bugging me. And if anyone would have insight on it, that person would be Brady.

"But then…," I begin, but trail off to organize my thoughts. How do I want to say this?

Brady concludes the thought for me. "There's Asher."

"Exactly."

"No," he says, reaching out and directing my chin toward the window with his hand. He chuckles. "There's Asher. Surprise."

He's right. Asher lopes toward us from across the street, not even bothering to be stealthy. I would have at least ducked. I glance back and Brady who looks smug and satisfied.

If it weren't for the little extra kick in my heart, I would be furious. "You didn't," I say, closing my eyes as if it would make him disappear.

"Oh yes I did. You can sit in the back with him if you want." He wags his eyebrows emphatically. "I won't mind."

A noise like a growl resonates in my throat.

"You're welcome."

Asher climbs into the back bringing a gust of cold air with him. I roll up my window as if that will help keep in the warmth.

"I'm so glad I don't have to deal with that shit today. I owe you man," Asher says, setting his backpack down by his feet. I notice he isn't wearing a jacket again.

"Do you even own a jacket?" I ask before realizing I've opened my mouth.

Asher cocks an eyebrow at me. "Yes, I do, but I save it for cold days."

"This," I gesture outside the car at the freezing temperatures, "does not constitute cold?"

He passes a hand over his face to hide his smile. "Have you ever lived back East during a freezing rain storm?"

I shake my head.

"That is cold. This is light hoodie weather."

Brady cuts us off and says, "These are the rules. This is a mission. We do not talk about anything we do today. Ever. With anyone. The chosen few in this car are the only exception. If either of you have issues with this, school is that way."

He doesn't have to point. We know where school is.

I don't meet his eyes. Even though he included both of us, I'm pretty sure he's not talking to me. I've earned Brady's trust, but Asher hasn't yet.

"Ya got me?" he says with more authority than I've ever heard from him.

Asher's expression is unwavering. "I got ya, man."

The tension seems to flow out of Brady to be carried away by the heater. "Great." His hard expression melts into a lop-sided smile. "Because I want Nicky to meet someone."

They both laugh at my terrified expression.

Funny that I've already had a nightmare and a hallucination, I feel like I'm going crazy, and that one sentence is the most ominous thing I've heard today. In response, I pull up my sleeves and itch at my forearms.

"Oh relax, Kitten," Brady says, consoling me. "It's a good thing."

Chapter 8

The car comes to a spine-jolting stop. I must have passed out before we even got out of the city limits. I don't remember much after we climbed on the freeway heading South.

"Where are we?" I ask. My breath is bitter with the taste of coffee drunk long ago.

The driver's side is already empty. In the back seat, Asher sits up and strokes his hair back behind his ears. He must have fallen asleep, too. Good thing I didn't sit back there with him. With his long legs and broad shoulders, we never would have fit.

"Um," he mumbles. "I don't know. Looks like the middle of nowhere."

I flip out my phone to check the time. We've been on the road for an hour. "Well, at least he didn't take us to Vegas."

Asher laughs once then turns serious. "Would he do that?"

I rub my face, hoping to smooth out any lines imprinted on it from the seatbelt. "There are no limits to what Brady is willing to do."

"So where are we then?"

I look around. We are in a Walmart parking lot. I don't tell him that because it should be obvious to anyone who lives on this planet.

"My guess? Provo," I say. "I think anyway. Unless Brady hit impossible speeds, which is possible knowing him."

"If he did?" Asher prods with a sleepy smile.

"Then we could be across state lines by now."

Both of us laugh at the thought and impossibility.

When we quiet down, Asher asks, "So where'd he go?"

Just then, two people climb out of a car parked a row in front of us. One of them is Brady. The other, I'm not entirely sure, but he seems really familiar.

"There." I point then wish I hadn't. The man Brady's with isn't much taller than he is, which means he's about five-nine. His hair is too white and pale to be called blond and his eyes are ice blue, almost iridescent. It's like someone tried to erase him, but only managed to eradicate the color. On the right side of his face is a scar in the shape of a lightning bolt. They walk toward us. He clutches Brady's hand as if it were a life preserver.

"Oh," Asher says, his eyes widening.

I am just about to read Asher the riot act, making him swear to never tell another soul when he follows up with, "I get the rules now."

"Do you?"

He looks at me for a moment before averting his eyes as if he sees something he doesn't like. "Yeah, I do. Cause people are assholes."

A knock on the window makes me jump. Brady stands just outside, laughing as if my nerves are the funniest thing he has seen all year. I take a few breaths before opening the door.

"Nicky," he says. "I want you to meet Jac."

I climb out of the car. Shaking someone's hand while sitting down is not only uncomfortable, it's rude. My grandfather taught me that.

"Nice to meet you, Jac." I extend my hand by way of greeting.

His hand meets mine firmly. Where my skin touches his, it feels rough like sandpaper. The way he looks at me is so intense. It feels like I'm backed into a corner. He seems to sense my discomfort and releases my hand. "You look awfully familiar."

"Funny. I thought the same thing about you." I may believe in coincidences occasionally, but not often.

Brady glances back and forth between us. "You guys probably met at my New Year's Eve party," he suggests.

And suddenly I remember him.

I asked him to watch Spencer.

And Spencer almost died.

The light dawns across Jac's face as he realizes where we've met. I make myself a promise that I won't say anything if he doesn't.

It's all enough to make me grateful when Asher climbs out of the back seat and introduces himself, too. The handshake seems to affect him a little differently than it did me. He steps back, coming to my side and stares at his hand, pumping it as if to get blood flowing again. With Asher's body heat radiating against me, I'm able to shake the uneasy sensation.

"Let's go somewhere," Brady says, bouncing up and down like a toddler with a new toy at Christmas.

I turn back to the car before Brady grabs my arm, stopping me. He catches my eye and winks. "Sorry, Kitten. You've been demoted. To the back seat with you."

I'm not surprised. I was about to offer up the seat anyway, but that doesn't stop me from rolling my eyes theatrically. "So we share beautiful moments like that and you just toss me to the back seat?" I ask, feigning the defensive.

"Hey," Brady jokes back. "If I wanted your opinion, I'd give it to you."

While climbing into the back seat, I begin to understand why Brady invited Asher along. He didn't want me to feel left out. Being the third wheel feels like being left out in the cold while watching others drink hot soup in a warm living room. I feel guilty when I realize how Brady must have felt the night before. But we couldn't just go without him. Brady and I are a package deal. I guess I could have left Asher out of it, but the thought of not having his presence as a buffer makes me shudder.

All four doors shut and we are on our way.

"How's your head?" Asher asks, reaching out and pushing a strand of hair behind my ear.

"Better. How's yours?"

He rubs his forehead as if remembering. "I think you broke something."

"I doubt that. You have an extremely hard head."

He raises one dark eyebrow at me. He looks so cocky when he does that. Not that I'm complaining. "The correct answer would be, 'I'm so sorry. What can I do?'"

"Aw. I'm so sorry. What can I do?" I repeat, faking sympathy.

He smiles, wryly. "Thank you. You almost had to take me back to the hospital you know."

I shrug against the seatbelt. "Sorry, but I've hit my quota for hospital visits this month."

"What if I was dying? Would you just drop me off and make me go all by myself?" He sounds a little whiney. And it's cute. Damn it.

I turn toward him, my back to the door so that Brady and Jac don't feel like they have an audience. He mimics the motion, turning toward me.

"Nah," I tell him. "You would just have to wait until the month end to receive medical attention."

"Next month?"

"Um, preferably never." My chest tightens at the thought of taking another friend to the hospital. I need to change the subject quick. "I called to check on Spencer yesterday," I blurt out without meaning to.

"Oh?"

"Yeah. His mom is in hysterics."

"Well, that was nice of you," he says, brushing the topic aside.

I look away. The roads aren't really busy here. I recognize one of them from a movie I watched with my parents years ago. "Hey." I say excitedly. "We are in Provo. I'm so good."

Brady and Jac laugh. Brady's is warm and soft like a teddy bear. Jac's is kind of pointed like the touch of a cold blade.

"Where did you think we were?" Brady asks.

"Hell if I know. I slept on the way here."

Jac shoots me a speculative look over his shoulder, but just like that, his attention is back to Brady.

I don't like how he looks at me. It's like he's looking into me instead of at me. It feels oddly intimate and highly unsettling. I remember the handshake. It was so cold. Like the hand from my dream.

Something doesn't feel right.

"You alright?" Asher asks quietly.

From the look on his face and the tension in his shoulders, he has the same creepy feeling about Jac as I do.

I shake my head to clear my thoughts. "Yeah, fine."

I shift back into my seat, but closer to Asher this time. His warming presence seems to chase away the cold feeling deep inside me. He slips an arm around my shoulder and draws me against him. If I shrug him off then I fear that aching cold would freeze and splinter inside of me. So I do what anyone would do: I slip off my seatbelt, scoot over to the next seat, and slide into the heat of him.

We make the mistake of letting the newcomer pick lunch and since Jac was the only one of us not at the restaurant last night, he was craving spaghetti. So we end up at Fazoli's for lunch. I haven't had Italian twice in a row in ages. However, as long as you eat inside, they offer you as many buttered-down-to-the-crisp breadsticks you can eat. Breadsticks are always good by me. I just hope that awkwardness isn't on the menu here.

"So where did you guys meet?" Asher asks Brady after the silence has gotten too thick to swallow. There's something in his voice, a sort of suspicion no one else seems to pick up on.

Brady and Jac appear so enthralled with each other that they've forgotten all about us.

"We met at the party on New Year's," Brady says, glancing at Jac like he is asking permission to tell the story. Jac nods his okay so Brady continues, "Jac came with a couple of friends. He goes to UVU. But his friends ditched. So he ended up having to stay the night."

I watch Asher's face as he listens. He doesn't look disgusted or anything, just interested. Smart boy. I've never had to kick anyone's ass for Brady before, but that doesn't mean I wouldn't make an exception.

However, I can't help but feel a little irritated. While Asher and I were taking Spencer to the hospital, Brady was working his mojo with a college boy? In that aspect, he is no better than Alex.

"That's cool. You from around here, Jac?" Asher asks, a little coldly. I wonder if my tension is contagious. Though, perhaps he's just showing the same distaste he has been all along.

71

Jac regards Asher with his pale eyes. Pretty wouldn't be the word to describe that color. I guess they would be unique. Something you might see on an animal, but not on a human.

"No," he drawls. "I'm originally from Louisiana."

"You don't sound like you're from Louisiana," I blurt out. Everyone I know from the Eastern side of here has an accent. Or at least not a Utah accent, depending on how you look at it. This guy sounds like he's always lived here.

Brady glares at me. Right. We aren't supposed to be drilling him, I remind myself. We're supposed to meet him. Nothing else.

"I should hope not," Jac says with a chuckle.

I force myself not to respond, for Brady.

"I moved away from there a long time ago. We moved a lot," he explains.

Asher nods like he understands.

When Brady starts waxing nostalgia about the party, I zone out completely. A boy with red scraggly hair and black rimmed glasses comes by to offer us more breadsticks. I take two and busy myself with chasing marinara sauce around my plate before eating them. I wish Brady had just wanted to stay home and watch movies.

To my dismay, Jac offers for us all to hang out at his apartment for the duration of the day. He lives off-campus by himself so we wouldn't have to worry about any roommates coming home upset about visitors.

Just because Jac has an apartment doesn't mean I want to go hang out there, though. But I can't just tell Brady that. He looks so happy.

We clean up the table and head out into the parking lot. I step in front of Brady while Jac and Asher climb into the car. He eyes me suspiciously.

"What's up, Kitten?"

"Is it cool if I take your car? I have a friend who lives here. Haven't seen her in a while. I'll come back and get you when we have to leave," I say, hoping I sound convincing.

Excitement flickers across his face. The thought of having alone time with Jac is enticing, which is what I'd hoped for. But then it's gone replaced by a look of scrutiny. "Yeah? What's her name?"

Shit. I spout out the first name I can think of. "Samantha."

"Samantha, what?"

"Samantha… Smith."

Brady smiles like he's having fun playing this game. "How do you know her? I know all your friends."

"Girl's camp," I reply automatically. The only place I ever went where Brady couldn't go, too. Though, in hindsight, it probably would have been better for him than Boy Scouts. What a disaster that was.

He laughs. "Which year?"

"All of them. God, Brady, do you want to be alone or not?" I say, throwing my hands up in the air.

"Of course, but you don't have to lie."

I don't think Brady understands that I do, indeed, have to lie. What am I supposed to tell him? The truth? How would he take it if he found out his new boy toy gives me the creepy crawlies?

"Can I take your car or not?" I repeat slowly enough for him to understand this time.

He thinks about it for a second before saying, "If you take Asher with you."

No hesitation. "Deal."

He puts his hand on the door handle. "I knew you liked him," he says before climbing into the driver's seat.

I let out one long frustrated sigh before doing the same.

I mentally count the money in my wallet. How much would it cost me to take a cab back home? Probably more than I have.

Damn.

Chapter 9

"They really don't have coffee shops here?" Asher asks, his brows forming an unhappy dip between his eyes. He is turned sideways in his seat, eyes wide as they scan the stores in hopes of caffeine.

"Not that I've heard of." I gesture a hand at the scene outside. "Welcome to Provo. Now, would you please put your seat belt on?"

"They have to have something." Asher's face is the picture of unabated panic.

"Oh, they do. Just nothing as morally deprave as caffeine."

He laughs. "Since when is caffeine 'morally deprave?'"

"You really haven't lived in Utah long, have you?" I say, rolling my eyes theatrically.

"A few months," he admits. "Alright, then. Since caffeine, drugs, alcohol and premarital sex are all outlawed here, what are we going to do?"

I shrug at the implications, silently hoping that was a joke. "I guess we make up our own fun and debauchery."

His right eyebrow arches up. "And we do that, how?"

"How long we got?"

Asher slides his sleeve back to look at his watch, which surprises me. Not many people wear watches anymore. I wear one, too, but that's because cell phones die despite their excellent time keeping. And I don't like being late.

"I have to work at five. So we have approximately three hours before we have to head back," he says.

"Approximately?" I tease.

He smiles. A dimple creases his left cheek. "Approximately. Now, bring on the fun and debauchery."

Without warning, I maneuver a life threatening U-turn. A few cars honk loudly as we cut in front of them.

Asher has one hand on the roof of the car and the other gripping the handle. "Jesus, Dubois," he says with a start.

"What? I was going the wrong way."

He mutters something about how you should always slow down before a U-turn and how it's best to do them at a green light or something like that. I'm not really paying attention.

The Walmart we visited earlier is up ahead and on the right. I slam on my brakes and pull into the lot. We score a space close to the front doors. That's pretty good for any Walmart at any time.

"Did I slow down enough for you?" I ask, grinning maniacally.

It's like he tries to shake his head, but the movement is restricted. It reminds me of my dad when I ask him a question after his favorite hockey team loses in the playoffs. It's a look that says "You're killing me," without ever having to actually say it.

"Shopping is your idea of deprave?" he asks instead of responding. "I don't get it."

"You will."

I motion him out of the car. The automatic doors whoosh open for us as if they've been waiting to invite us in all along. I take a deep, cleansing breath. The place smells of paint and white trash. It must be a new store. They haven't febreezed all the previous smells out of it yet.

"Can you keep a straight face?" I ask.

A look of curiosity passes over his face. "I'll try."

"That's all I can ask."

I take his hand and pull him along past a display of cupcakes on sale for a dollar. I pause for a moment, wondering how the item might fit into the plan. It won't so we move on.

"What the hell are we doing?" Asher says, following me down the pharmaceutical aisle.

Ever-so-subtly I reach out and snatch up the biggest box of condoms I can find. Asher stares at me with a quizzical expression. Somehow I've baffled him. Amazing.

"What is the most embarrassing item in here you can think to buy?" I ask, showcasing the shelves with my arm like I'm Vanna White.

"Seriously?"

I nod, plucking a bottle of KY Warming Lubricant off of the next shelf and tossing it in the air.

"Come on, Asher," I prod. "Is it toilet paper? Rogaine? I know. It's Tampons, isn't it? You seem like the type of guy who would get embarrassed by having to buy feminine products."

"Nope," he says proudly, crossing his arms across his chest. It's hard not to notice the bulge of muscle straining against his shirt. "I have a sister, remember?"

"What then?" I weigh the decision of grabbing yeast infection cream or Maxi pads next, the huge bulky kind. Ooh, maybe adult diapers instead. That's an idea.

"I don't know," he responds finally, his arms falling to the side. "A pregnancy test, maybe?"

I glance at him sideways before turning my head and staring at him with the most surprised look I can muster: wide eyes, unhinged jaw, the works. "Oh my god, you're serious, aren't you?"

He nods shyly.

"How many times... you know what? I'm not going to ask." I flick a pregnancy test off the shelf and into my hand.

"Now will you tell me what the hell we're doing?" he asks, sounding a bit nervous.

"Sure." I steer us down the next aisle, which is lined with body soaps, loofahs and – Aha! – body massagers. I reach for one shaped like a frog, but he grabs my hand, spinning me to face him. Our eyes meet inches apart. My breathing hitches up a notch.

Who knew a simple gesture could be so sexy?

"What. Are. We. Doing?" Asher says slowly, gripping my palm with such ferocity my hand cramps up. "You want to embarrass me for fun, is that it?"

"Not you," I say, staring into his eyes. I swear they smolder back. My hand waffles back and forth in his grip. "Can you let me go, please?"

He loosens the hold, but doesn't release me. His hand is warm and soft with rough edges. I wonder what it would feel like if he ran his hands up my arm or down my neck. Blood rushes into my face just thinking about it and I shiver.

"Who then?" he says. He sounds tired.

"You'll see. It's kind of a personal psychology experiment."

Just then, a guy with short spiky hair wearing an AC/DC shirt and pushing a full shopping cart turns down the aisle. Asher releases me instantly as if he's afraid this guy is going to accuse him of abusing me. Short and Spiky barely notices. He abandons his cart and ducks around to peruse the end cap. My brain takes inventory of which items I managed to hold onto with my free arm: condoms, a pregnancy test and lubricant is all I've retrieved so far. With great care, I lower the pregnancy test into his cart without considering which item I'm surprising him with. Then I grab Asher's hand and drag him further down the aisle where we can see him, but he won't see us.

"This is what we're doing?" he says. "Wow. He's not going to buy it."

"Probably not," I agree. "But that's not the point. I just want to see what he'll do."

Asher scoffs. "That's easy. He'll put it back."

When Short and Spiky lopes back to his cart, he's on his cell phone. There's a lot of "mmhmm's" and "okay's" before his eyes light on the pregnancy test. He stops dead, all color draining from his face. "What's this?" I imagine him saying. Then he thoroughly cases the aisle before shoving the test underneath the bread in his cart.

As he strolls past, I hear him say into the phone, "Apparently I already have the test... No, really... It's right here in the cart... Weird, right?"

"What...?" Asher mutters over my shoulder.

I shake my head in disbelief. It appears today is a day of coincidences.

"Is that how the game works? We see if we can guess what they are trying to buy?"

"Not usually. If that was the game we were playing, I probably would have given him Xbox points or the cupcakes."

Asher looks like he's trying to figure me out. "So what do we do with the rest of the items?" he asks, gesturing to the condoms and lubricating jelly still tucked into the crook of my arm.

"New game," I announce, clapping my hands and bouncing on the balls of my feet. "We're going to find items that have nothing and everything to do with these."

"Like?" His voice is still distant. For a boy from the big city, he sure gets shaken easily.

"Duct tape. Finger paints. Come on, Rowan, be creative. I know you have it in you."

"Then?"

"Then we buy them. We don't have to keep them. Maybe we can give them to Brady for a Valentine's day gift or something."

He shudders.

After browsing the store for a half hour, we end up with rope, duct tape, peanut butter, whipped cream, a single apple and a negligee for emphasis. If I did my math right, it will come to somewhere around forty-five dollars. Good thing I brought my emergency credit card. Depravity doesn't come cheap. Unless you steal it, which I won't do.

We don't go to the express lane because no one else is in line there. The point of this experiment is to see people's reactions. I consider asking Mrs. Jarvis for extra credit. This would make a killer essay.

Without being told, Asher seeks out an older lady at check stand five. Four people are in line. "That one, right?"

"You're learning well, grasshopper," I say, pulling him down the lane. My eyes catch on the shelves of odds and ends standing by the aisle. While Asher flops the items onto the conveyer belt, I look over each item carefully just in case we forgot something. Doesn't seem like it.

I turn and survey the items. It's satisfying to see how quickly Asher caught on. I smile up at him.

An uncomfortable laugh barely makes it out of his mouth. "I can't believe I'm doing this."

I offer him a pseudo seductive smile and a wink.

"You must really love Psych," he says, chuckling under his breath.

I smile in spite of myself. "It's my favorite class. What's yours?"

He taps his chin. "Last week I probably would have said I didn't have one, but now… I think Psych and English are my favorites."

I mimic him, tapping my chin with my credit card. "Oh? Why would you like those classes? And be honest. Remember, I'm in them with you."

His lips curve into a blinding smile. "Exactly."

For a moment, I am lost in the depths of his dark eyes. People don't usually call dark eyes beautiful, but his remind me of wood smoke on a wintry day. As I argue with myself about whether the flecks in his eyes are gold or amber, the scanner beeps rhythmically.

"We're up," Asher says, bobbing his head toward the register.

To the common shopper, we probably look like we are counting the moments until we can be alone. Good. That's all I could hope for.

The cashier is three shades of pink when I step up next to the card reader.

On impulse, I rub Asher's arm and say, "I can't wait for tonight. I can't believe it's been three weeks already."

He forces a shaky smile. The apple, the peanut butter and whipped cream go in one sack. Now comes the fun part. She scans the duct tape.

"You're sure your wife isn't coming home tonight, right? Because this," I wave a hand at the items, "could be really embarrassing."

Asher's face cracks a little. I'm afraid he's either going to laugh or run screaming from the store. The cashier does everything in her power not to look at us. She's probably afraid of going to hell as an accomplice.

"I told you, honey, she's gone until Friday," Asher says. He's finally playing along. I couldn't be more surprised.

I don't have to fake the mischievous smile spreading across my face. The only item left is the lingerie. "You sure that'll fit?"

He glances at me as if he's trying to picture me in it. He's a better actor than I thought. He licks his lips. "Oh, I'm sure."

"Good," I say with a fake sigh of relief. "Because that is going to look so hot on you."

While Asher scowls and the cashier fights off a heart attack, I swipe my credit card through the reader. Probably the best forty-three dollars and thirty-seven cents I've ever spent.

"That was fun," I say once we are back in the car.

Asher doesn't speak. He just stares at me.

I burst into a fit of giggles. Somehow, he manages to keep a straight face.

"Fine," I say, slapping him playfully on the arm. "You can pick the next activity. I'm sorry you didn't enjoy it like I did. What was it you didn't enjoy? Was it too childish? Too much fun? Tell me, what was it?"

He blinks. "It was, um, interesting," he says like "interesting" is synonymous for "horrible."

I start the car. All the while, mumbling, "Well, I had fun."

We pull out of the parking lot and head right. I roll down my window and let the smell of crisp winter air inside. There are days in the valley where you can barely see the mountains because of the pollution, but here on the other side of the mountain is clear. I feel like I can finally breathe.

"Let me know when you figure out what you want to do," I tell him.

"You owe me for the lingerie comment," he retorts.

Canting my head toward him, I say, "Is that what's bothering you?"

"It was a little over the top."

I nod. "I'm sorry. I thought it was the top. You'll laugh about it someday. Trust me." When he doesn't respond, I add, "Fine. I owe you."

His eyes light up. "I was hoping you'd say that."

Evidently my little game was so immature that Asher wants to do something more old lady-ish. However, in the process, we learn that while there is no caffeine in Provo, there is plenty available in the adjacent city of Orem. I wonder what makes the difference. Either way, it feels like an invisible line between mine and my parent's version of paradise.

"Pull in here," Asher instructs as we approach the parking lot to Barnes and Noble.

"A book store?" I ask, incredulously. "Don't get me wrong. I, myself, love a good bookstore trip, but we're ditching school, Asher. Shouldn't we take advantage of our wrongful acts by compiling them instead of redeeming them?"

I aim for a parking spot near the doors, but almost slam into the car parked in front of me when he says, "Well, if you'd rather, we could take advantage of that Walmart bag back there."

A blush creeps up my neck and colors my face hot. I turn into the nearest parking space, slam the car into park and yank the keys from the ignition. "Now that you mention it, there is a book I wanted to look at."

He laughs and jumps out of the car. "I thought so. I'm getting coffee. I'll come find you. Do you want anything?"

"Sure. Whatever. I'm not picky," I lie. I'm totally picky when it comes to my coffee, though, I could probably choke down anything right now.

We part ways just inside the door.

Isn't it funny how a chain store can be set up so differently in every location? The Barnes and Noble I usually go to has two levels. Downstairs are the Non-fiction sections like Science, Computer Programming, Reference, and Magazines. Upstairs you can find Fiction, Art, Photography, New Age and a music section. This store seems smaller because it's one level. Fiction is in the back.

When Asher finds me, the air around him feels completely different. The irritated boy from the car has dissipated into the steam rising off of his coffee. He smiles at me as he hands me a cup. It's the smile not the coffee that warms me all the way through. I can't help, but smile back.

"I should've figured I'd find you in the Mystery section," he says.

"Why's that?" I look up him from where I'm crouched on the floor devouring the new Jeff Lindsay novel.

"You just seem like the Mystery type. Actually, I have to admit, I checked out Science Fiction first."

I don't tell him that I've already been through that section because I don't want to seem predictable. Instead, I take a sip of my own cup. It's a White Mocha Latte. Maybe I am predictable.

I close the book and sit back on the floor. "And what section are you? Wait, let me guess." I make a show of tapping my fingers on the cover of the book like I'm thinking. "Sports, right?"

He laughs, dropping down to sit on the floor next to me. "Wrong. Reading about sports is as pointless as watching people play golf."

"I hate golf," I muse, nodding my head.

"Me, too."

"I guess I'm a little of everything," he says. "Though, history bores me."

I could sense that about him. He seems the type of guy who would rather live the present, plan for the future, and forget all about his past.

He doesn't seem to notice me watching him as he nurses his coffee. With each sip, he seems more and more relaxed. I suddenly feel guilty that we didn't get him a cup this morning. He seems as addicted as I am.

Nonchalantly, he leans back against the bookcase behind him. "Better?"

He nods. "Much."

I slide the book back into its place, careful not to disrupt the flow of titles, and turn around so I am facing him. I lean back against the shelf and stretch my legs out in front of me. If a manager were to walk by right now, we would probably get yelled at for being a fire hazard. Who says you can't cause mischief in a bookstore?

"So, what's your story, Asher?"

He lifts his head, his dark eyes meet mine. The dark tendrils of his hair brush along his cheekbones. "My story?"

"Yeah. I would have bet money you were just another jock," I reply, shifting a little on the floor.

"What makes you think I'm not?" he asks. His smile gives him away, though. He looks amused.

"Well, jocks don't hang out with stuck up kids like me," I mock whisper, turning my head this way and that as if I'm afraid someone might hear my secret. "It's bad for the reputation."

He flinches at his own words. His smile fades. "Alex hangs out with you."

"Yeah, except Alex and I grew up together. His mom and my mom are best friends. We didn't have much of a choice."

"Oh," he says. The thought that there might be some underlying reason behind our strange friendship must not have occurred to him. "I doubt that's the only reason. Anyway, you're not stuck up. Quiet, maybe. A little crazy, but not stuck up."

I look away. "Gee, thanks. Just what every girl wants to hear – that she's crazy."

"A little crazy," he corrects me. "And without the right amount of crazy, things would be really boring."

I pretend to look at him. What I'm really doing, though, is studying the titles over his shoulder. Agatha Christie. Dan Brown. Nora Roberts. Great authors all eavesdropping on our conversation.

"Nicoletta," he says, claiming my attention with the way he says my name.

I chew my pinky nail nervously. "Yeah?"

"I don't think you're stuck up," he repeats. "I have this problem. I tell things how they are. Someone told me you were stuck up and I told you I heard it. I'm sorry if that hurt you, but it's just a rumor. I'm sure there are plenty of those floating around about me."

I shake my head. "Not that I've heard. Well, aside from the one about you being an amazing basketball player."

"And that's not a rumor," he says, puffing out his chest. "That's true."

"What else have you heard about me?" I want to know. Actually, I need to know so badly that I'm willing to let this torturous conversation drag out.

An uneasy expression crosses Asher's face. "You sure you want to know?"

Oh god. Judging by his reaction, there are more rumors. I'm willing to bet that none of them are good. Why can't gossip be about how great someone is at Science? Or what awards someone has won? Why does it all have to be crippling to your character?

I nod reluctantly, setting my coffee aside and wiping my sweaty palms on my jeans.

"Well," he pauses, taking a long pull off of his coffee as if it will fill him with strength. "First thing I heard about you was that you are a foreign exchange student, which is obviously not true."

I roll my eyes. "Obviously."

"I've also heard you like *Supernatural*."

I nod. Anyone who has walked past my open locker can tell that much.

"You hang out with Brady, Alex – the boy wonder – and… that's pretty much it until now."

That startles a chuckle out of me. "Boy wonder?"

He ignores me. "And I've heard you have a thing for Alex," he concludes.

My smile fades. Only one person knows about my feelings for Alex and he just found out. But if I find out Brady was anywhere near that one, I'll kill him.

When I see Asher scrutinizing my expression, I force a shaky smile. "Stupid rumors."

"Yeah well." He puts the cup to his lips, never taking his eyes off me. Halfway there, he pauses to say, "Oh and I heard that you've never been to a school dance."

I look up from picking at a stray thread on my jeans. "You did not," I argue. "That's not even a good rumor."

"So it's not true?" he asks, intrigued.

I shake my head. "No. It's true. It's just a really stupid rumor. I guess I expected something more defaming."

Asher smiles. "Sorry to disappoint." Then he smiles wider.

"What?"

"Remember how you owe me?" he asks.

I hesitate before nodding. "Where are you going with this?"

His eyes light with mischief. "I think I just figured out payment."

"Oh god," I mumble.

"Yep." He nods emphatically. "The Sweetheart Dance."

"You want help sabotaging it?" I ask, hopefully. "I have some great ideas."

He shakes his head.

"You want me to help find you a date? Sometimes I help Alex do that," I offer. Once the words are out, though, I wish I could take them back. The last thing I want to do is help Asher find a date to some stupid dance.

He laughs. "No. I'm asking you to go. You know? With me?"

My eyes fix on my boots. Thoughts of what it would be like to dress up, do my hair, and go to a dance fill me with an alien feeling. It's almost like anticipation and terror mixed into a fatal concoction. If I went to this dance then there's no way anyone could confuse me with one of the guys, but the dance is still a month away. What if Alex asks me to go?

"I'll think about it," I say finally.

Asher looks almost shocked, but only for a second before relaxing into his cool composure. "Alright, but don't think too long. I might come up with something worse for you to do." He gets to his feet and holds a hand out to help me up.

I stare at it as if it might bite me. "What are you doing?"

His eyes shut slowly, regretfully, as if he doesn't want to say the words that are already sitting in his mouth. "We need to go so I can get to work. I need to pay for this book first, though."

I take his hand and all but jump to my feet. "What book? You didn't have a book."

He reaches over to the shelf next to him. He must have stashed it when he walked up. Now, he retrieves it and holds it out for me to see. The silver letters embossed on the front are in a language I don't speak, let alone read.

"And that is?" I ask.

"It's a gift for, um, my dad," he says. "He collects French editions of old books."

I touch the leather bound cover. It's a plain book with just a title. No author, no border, and no pictures. "And this one is?"

He scratches his chin with his thumb and nudges me with his elbow. "I don't know. It's not like I take French. I just thought it looked pretty."

His words feel wrong to my ears somehow. I could have sworn Asher said my name the way only someone with a French accent could. It's not like any American accent I've ever heard.

"You alright?" he asks.

I shake myself out of it. "Yeah, sure. Let's go."

The cashier who checks us out is an older man who is all ears and nose with less hair on his head than coming out of the collar of his shirt.

Asher places the book on the counter.

The man, whose nametag introduces him as Truman, looks at the title and immediately launches into a French monologue.

Asher doesn't look fazed. He patiently waits for the man to finish before saying gently, "I'm sorry. This is a gift. I don't understand."

His eyes narrow in confusion. "But you...," he begins.

Asher cuts him off with a sharp shake of his head. "No, sorry."

After paying for the book, he takes my hand and guides me away from the counter, tossing his empty coffee cup in the garbage can as we go.

"You alright?" he asks, leading me to the driver's side door.

There's a strange feeling coalescing inside my chest like something's not right. If I'm not mistaken, that man acted like he knew Asher. He sure spoke to him like he did even if I didn't understand what he was trying to say. Damn it! Why didn't I take French instead of Spanish?

"Yeah," I say, shrugging off that strange feeling. "It's weird. Normally people mistake me for being French."

Asher laughs all the way around to the other side of the car. "People believe what they want to believe, Nicky. Once they make up their mind, there's no telling them otherwise. Not even if the evidence is right in front of them." He opens the door and ducks inside.

"What the hell does that mean?" I ask no one in particular. No one answers.

Chapter 10

On the third call, Brady finally picks up. I roll my eyes in annoyance. School has been out for an hour; he should have been expecting us.

"Yeah?" Brady snaps into the phone.

"Good morning to you, too," I quip back. "We're outside and Asher has to work at five."

"Shit," he says. Then, "Shit, shit, shit. I fell asleep. What time is it?"

"Three-thirty."

"I'll be right out."

"Right out" for Brady usually means at least twenty minutes so I'm shocked when he comes bolting out the door two minutes after the phone disconnects.

I climb out of the driver's seat and drop the keys in Brady's hand. He looks like hell. His eyes are bloodshot, his hair even more disheveled than usual and...

"Are those hickeys?" I ask, pointing to the five dark circles mottling his skin. I can't help but smile. Hiding those is going to suck.

He grins. "Sure are, Kitten. Now get in the car."

When we pulled up, Asher was in the passenger seat so I climb into the back without even thinking twice. Once inside, though, I realize he is now sitting in the back with the grocery bag on his lap. He grins as I eye them suspiciously.

The Camry squeals out of the parking space and barrels down the road going too fast.

"Did you have fun?" I ask him.

He makes an illegal left hand turn. "Of course I did, but you know me, I never kiss and tell. How about you guys?"

"Let me guess," Asher mumbles, patting the seat of the car as if expecting a floatation device to be hidden in the seat cushion. "You guys learned how to drive from the same teacher."

I flash Asher a smile before trying to catch Brady's eye in the rear-view mirror. If he weren't in such a hurry, he might catch the warning written on my face. If he doesn't slow down, he's going to get pulled over. Or worse. I don't want to spend the night in Provo if we get into a wreck. Besides, how would I explain that to the parents?

"So much fun," I say coolly. "Hey, do you want me to drive?"

Finally, he catches the hint and slows down to only ten over the speed limit. To my right, Asher grips the door handle. I wonder if he thinks throwing himself out of the car would be safer. I rest an assuring hand on his arm. Brady's driving is terrifying when he drives the speed limit. He's much safer at racecar speeds.

Slowly, Asher releases the handle and covers my hand with his.

Brady reaches into the middle console and produces his iPod. He nearly changes lanes while fiddling with the auxiliary cord. I lean forward and snatch it out of his hand.

"I'll do it," I say, reaching into my pocket and switching my iPod with his.

Asher gives me a questioning glance. I shrug and offer Brady's iPod over in explanation. He turns it on, scrolls through the artists, and covers his mouth to keep from laughing out loud.

"Seriously?" he whispers, pointing to the screen. "There isn't one song from this century in here."

I nod. "Keep scrolling. It gets better."

"Wow." He sounds more amused than appalled. "Let me see yours."

I hand it over.

His head bobs up and down a few times before he hands it back. I raise my eyebrows, daring him to comment. "Good taste," he whispers.

The exchange reminds me of just how vague he often is. I frown at him then pull my legs up onto the seat, folding them under me.

"Question," I say quietly.

"Yes?"

"What did you do to my phone the other night? I checked all the numbers and texts…," I trail off.

He smiles. "I stole your number."

He stole my number? I didn't even know you could do that. I guess if you were to look at an incoming text message then it might say the number it was sent to, but still. That's it. I'm locking my phone with a passcode the first chance I get. "You could have just asked for it," I say.

"I could have," he says. "But this was more fun."

The drive back to into the city is a funny one. For some reason, the trip out feels like it takes hours, but the return trip seems to take no time at all. Maybe it's because of traffic or just the excitement of being back in the city. Who knows? It feels like we just jumped on the freeway and already we are halfway home.

"God, I'm exhausted," Brady complains as he takes the interchange heading east.

I close my eyes and shake my head. He should have gotten plenty of sleep while he was making Asher late for work.

Asher checks his watch then pipes up with, "I still have a little time. You can drop us off at my place and I'll give Nicoletta a ride home."

"Aren't you helpful?" I say wryly.

They ignore me.

"Not a bad idea," Brady replies. "You only have two days to talk her into going to my party anyway. Tick, tock."

I turn away from them to stare out the window, but to my dismay, I can still hear them talking. On the side of the road is a familiar looking sedan pushed up tight against the barrier, half of it missing. I sit up a little straighter. The vehicle turned on impact, smashing the driver's side in and stripping the passenger side clean away.

"Jesus," Brady says, slowing the car to a crawl.

Three cop cars block off the far right lane with an ambulance in front of them. Two EMT's rush a stretcher toward the little white sedan. Lights spin and flash in a hypnotizing pattern.

The car, if you can even call it that anymore, is overwhelmed with policemen yanking at doors in search of other passengers. They won't find any, though. I know because I've already seen this crime scene. There was no one else in the car except the driver and she, Sarah, was dead on impact.

A man with white blond hair and pale eyes looks up from where he's been leaning back against the trunk of the car. He turns his head as if one of us called his name and I swear he looks right at me.

I gasp. "Jac."

"What's that, Nic?" Brady asks, checking his mirror while he maneuvers through the gathered onlookers.

"Nothing."

All the warmth in my body leeches out of me. The EMT: he looks so much like Jac. I can even see a small mark on his face like a tiny lightning bolt shaped ink stain. I argue to myself that it would be impossible for him to beat us here. No one drives faster than Brady on the freeway. When Brady's behind the wheel, we do the passing, not the other way around. Besides, Brady would have recognized him. Right?

A woman's body is pulled from the vehicle. She is utterly limp. For a second, I'm surprised that she's is wearing a red shirt. Her shirt wasn't red when I saw her in my dream. Then it hits me: It's her blood.

Something glitters in the sunlight and blinds me. I blink rapidly, trying to clear the spots from my vision. When my sight comes back, we are past the wreck and almost to our exit. A headache builds from the pressure behind my eyes. I press my fingertips into my temples.

A hand rubs my back. Asher. "You alright there?"

I shake my head but say, "Yeah I think so. Her diamond ring. It blinded me for a second."

I don't open my eyes, but I can hear the concern in his voice now. "Her what? There's no way you could have seen a ring."

I look over at him. He's right, of course. With as far away as our car was, there's no way something that small would be visible, and definitely no way it could have blinded me. "I guess I just assumed," I tell him.

"You need some Excedrin?" he asks, still rubbing small circles into my back. "I have some at my house."

"That would be great."

Silence yawns between us the rest of the way to Asher's house where Brady drops us off. After tolerating a long speech from me on driving safely, he leaves.

I pause for a few minutes, staring at Asher's house. It's not exactly what I expected. The only other time I've been here was at night when the only thing visible was the outside light. Now I can see that it's a split-level with a built-in garage. The exterior walls are made of alternating beige and sandy colored stones. It reminds me a lot of the beach. Except for the door, which is painted red. It looks odd, but a lot of people in this area paint their doors to match the season. Maybe theirs was painted for Christmas.

"You coming?" Asher says from the top step. The grocery bag swings from his right hand and bumps against his leg. Relief washes over me. I sure wouldn't have remembered to grab it. I could just imagine how much fun that would have been to explain when Brady found it in the back seat.

Blinking against the light of day, I nod. Why does it always seem brighter when the sun shines in the winter? It's not like it's a different sun or anything. Its thermostat just breaks down for a few months. So why would that make it brighter?

"You sure you're alright?" he clarifies.

I shrug. "Yeah. It's just really bright out here."

"Well, let's get you inside then."

We walk past the Jeep in the driveway. I gesture at it as if it appeared out of nowhere. "Did you walk to school?"

He shakes his head. "My sister brought it home."

"She goes to school with us?"

In lieu of a lock, they have an electronic box. All it takes is a code and it unlocks. I've seen them before and while I like the idea of them, I don't think I'd ever feel safe enough. Not unless I was sleeping with a baseball bat by my bed.

"Yeah, you wouldn't know her, though. She's a sophomore."

I wonder if that's supposed to be a reference to my being "stuck up."

"I know sophomores," I grumble as we step inside.

He laughs. "No you don't."

"I'm only a junior. It's not like it's a different world."

The house is like a sauna compared to the frigid air outside. You'd think Utah would be all snow, right? Sometimes it is. Like during the months of February through April. Otherwise, the snow comes and goes as it pleases, but the cold perpetually lingers, even when the sun up. There could be no snow on the ground and you still run the risk of slipping on black ice.

My face burns from the change in temperature.

"I'm sorry. You're right," he says sarcastically. "In fact, I'm sure you know her. Her name is Acacia." He pauses, waiting for me to jump in.

I stare at him.

He laughs again. "I didn't think so." He gestures in front of him. "This way."

Asher drops his backpack in the entry way and motions for me to follow him down the hall. One set of stairs leading up to a second level are just a few steps in from the front door. Around them and to the right is the living room, dining room and the kitchen. The rooms are so large I almost expect to hear an echo. Just off the kitchen is a door. When opened, there's a second set of stairs that take you down to the basement, which his evidently where we are headed.

When I think about basements, I picture wooden steps, concrete walls and maybe a small unfinished room with a washer and dryer. That's every basement I've ever seen anyway. The basement in my head, however, is not the one we walk down into. The stairs may be concrete, but they are padded and carpeted with blue shag. The walls are insulated and boarded with a mahogany colored wood. And its space is as large as the house it sits under.

"You could fit my room in here like four times," I say to myself.

A large TV is mounted on the wall to the right with a small couch in front of it. His bed is to the left next to a desk in the corner. A Mac computer sits on top of the desk, the screen dark. On the other side of his bed is a door standing slightly ajar, a sliver of light shining through. Must be a bathroom. Wait, he has his own bathroom?

"Where's your kitchen?" I ask, faking boredom. "Seems like it's the only thing missing."

He smiles, unloading his jacket and the grocery bag onto his bed, but doesn't respond.

Pasted up on the walls are posters of all shapes and sizes. I recognize the Social Offense promos pinned all around the room. He has all six albums. Tampering down my jealousy, I walk over to scope out the bookshelves of CD's and DVD's behind his TV.

"While you do that," he says with a chuckle. "I'm going to shower. If you still need some Excedrin, there's some in the cupboard above the microwave in the kitchen. I'll be right back."

I wave a hand dismissively. I'm too awe-struck by his collection of TV series to care. He has *Roswell*, *CSI* and – yep, there it is – *Supernatural*. My fingers caress the spines of the collection reverently.

Next, I venture into his bed area to be nosy in there. His bed is twice the size of mine (mine is a full so his must be a king). His blankets are red and blue, his sheets patterned with the logo for the New York Rangers. My breath catches in my throat. He may be a dork, but he could very well be my soul mate. If I believed in that.

When the water shuts off, I jump. What is he going to think if he comes out of the bathroom to find me snooping around his bed? I've always felt like beds are too intimate for strangers to hang around.

Just as I turn to go, something shiny catches my eye. I turn and stare at it in disbelief.

That's when the door to the bathroom opens, snatching my attention. Asher walks out wearing a pair of jeans riding low on his hips and he doesn't have a shirt on. While towel-drying his hair, his muscles jump and writhe under his skin. Who knew drying your hair could use so many muscles?

It's a good thing I have a lot of practice with staring at half-naked guys. Otherwise, I might need help retrieving my jaw from the floor.

"So you're one of those guys," I say, hoping he can't hear me silently thanking God for placing him shirtless in front me.

He tosses his towel back into the bathroom and runs his fingers through his wet hair. While it might be straight when it's dry, it curls ever so gently when it's wet. I consider starting a petition to keep his hair wet always.

"What guys?"

Waving my hand toward the sword hanging above his bed, I say, "One of those guys."

He laughs. "I guess I am."

"Doesn't it freak you out having it there? I'd be worried it'd fall and decapitate me in my sleep or something." Though, I guess that does make a little bit of sense as to why he's fine having a door that locks by code. Anyone who tries to break in wouldn't see that coming.

He shrugs. "It makes me feel better to have it there. Besides, it's mounted really well."

I scrutinize the wooden mounting. There are four nails holding up the wooden cross backing, but there are only two metal pegs below the hilt to secure it in place. "Not well enough for me," I say, shaking my head emphatically.

Asher shrugs a shirt on.

A silent "No" forms in my mouth and I purse my lips to keep it in. I have to keep talking, though. It's the only way to keep my hormones in check. "Do you know how to use it?"

"Sure. Poke 'em with the pointy end, right?"

His shirt is a flat black with five buttons and a collar. His hair falls against his neck, blending with the material. He catches me staring with my jaw unhinged and misinterprets my expression as a look of shock. "Just kidding," he continues, as if I even heard him. "I took fencing lessons at my last school, but obviously that one is a little heavier than a fencing sword," he explains.

It takes a certain level of brute force to peel my eyes away from him and focus back on the blade. The "pointy end," as he put it, is at least as long as my arm. The hilt looks like it's made of really old iron, half of the handle wrapped in something that resembles duct tape, but shinier, almost reflective, and green. Parallel to each side of the blade protrudes a shiny metal spike that curves like an hourglass before jutting out backwards at the end in a sharp point. A thought blindsides me. If someone were to plunge that sword into someone else and turn, the metal prongs would cut a hole right out of the person. I can even see it in my mind. I shudder involuntarily.

"Where did you get it?" I hear myself asking from very far away. As dangerous as it looks, it's still quite beautiful.

I take a step forward and reach out to touch the silver symbol that spans the length and width of the hilt. I'm sure to anyone else it would look like a mass of swirls, but I feel like there's something else there… something more. It almost looks like a tree split at the branches and roots while a massive snake wraps itself around the trunk in an attempt to hold the splintering wood together against a raging storm.

Something niggles at the edge of my mind.

I've seen that symbol somewhere before, but I have no idea where.

Asher looks up and around the room like he can't remember what we were talking about. "What? Oh. The sword. It was my grandfather's grandfather's grandfather's or something like that. It's been in the family for centuries. My father gave it to me when my grandfather died."

I turn my head from side to side watching the light glint off of it. "It's spectacular. Shouldn't it be in a museum or something?"

He walks over to his desk and starts shoving things into his pockets: money, keys, and cell phone. Then he sits in the chair and pulls on his boots.

"Nah. My great-great grandfather – or whatever – was a nobody. No one would want it."

I'm taken aback. "But it's old and it looks really unique. Museums love stuff like that."

"Oh it's old." He finishes lacing up his boots and walks over to the side of the bed where he can gesture at the sword like a game show host. "Most blades were sculpted out of iron and steel at that time, but this is iron and silver. Even the handle is wrapped in some sort of silver grip tape, and you see this?" He gestures at the symbol swirling around the hilt.

I nod.

"Those are onyx and jade. I don't know how they did it, but they did. It's wicked heavy, hard to hold."

"So how come you ended up with it? Why not some other great-great-great grandson?" I ask, still staring.

He shrugs. "Because I'm special." The words may be arrogant, but his tone is wistful. He pauses a second, staring at his birthright, then shakes his head as if denying some voice only he can hear. "We better go. I'm already late."

Chapter 11

"So are you going to get Brady off of my back or what?" Asher asks as he turns the corner to my house.

I don't reply.

"Come on, Nicky, help me out."

That gets my attention. "You never call me Nicky.'"

"Sure, I do. Besides, I thought you liked 'Nicky.' That's what everyone else calls you."

"I do. It's just... weird to hear you say it."

I'm not sure how to tell him that I love the way he pronounces my name without sounding like a total moron. When he says it, it sounds exactly how it should be said, with the original French pronunciation, even though he claims he doesn't speak French.

"You're changing the subject," Asher reminds me.

"I don't know."

The Wal-Mart bag between my feet gives me a good excuse not to look at him. We decided it was best if I kept it since it was my idea and all. Although, I suspect Asher was worried his father might get the wrong idea if he found a nightgown in his son's room.

"It just feels wrong, you know?" I continue, speaking to the floor. "I mean, Spencer's still in the hospital and last I heard no one has even bothered to visit him. Not even his friends. I really don't care to hang out with people like that."

Asher braves a glance at me when we pause at the stop sign two houses down from mine.

"You don't have to hang out with them. Just me." His smile makes me feel like I'm missing an inside joke.

"What makes you think I want to hang out with you?" I say, flashing him with a comparable grin.

"Just come. Please? You owe me."

"Does that mean you're rescinding your invitation to the dance?" I ask, nudging him with my elbow.

We pass through intersection and ease to a stop in front of my house, which is when I notice the strange car parked in my driveway. It's hard to divide my attention equally between Asher and the Mustang and it shames me to admit that Asher gets a lesser amount.

"No. You owe me a lot."

Alex is still sitting in the driver's seat of the car. I can see his head shaking at me through the tinted windows. Is that disappointment I smell coming off that car? What right does Alex have to be disappointed in me? What the hell is he doing here anyway?

"Alright fine," I say in an effort to appease him.

"Really?"

"Yes, fine. As in: Fine, I'll think about it. Now get to work. I'll see you later."

The smile fades from his face like the sun dropping behind the mountains. I wonder if he knows why I'm in such a hurry to get out of his car. So without thinking, I throw in, "Call me later," and jump out on to the sidewalk.

The Jeep pulls away just after Alex climbs out of the Mustang. He looks almost concerned. His voice, however, is unabated anger.

"Where were you?" he demands.

Suddenly, I would rather punch him in the kidney than talk to him. I change direction and veer past him toward the house. It's amazing how my reaction to Alex has been electricity in my veins and butterflies in my stomach for months, but now, all the butterflies are dead and the electricity feels more like electrocution.

Alex reaches out a hand and catches the sleeve of my coat. He tries to spin me around. Damn corduroy. It's so easy to grip.

Remember the unexpected black ice I was telling you about? Yeah, well, I hit that and go down with an ungraceful thwack. My palm skids across the pavement and sharp pain shoot up my wrist. My vision goes checkerboard and the back of my throat burns.

Alex pulls me to my feet before I'm ready, apologizing profusely.

I push him back with a shoulder and stumble toward the Mustang where I lean down on my elbows and try not to vomit. Though, that would serve him right. I look down at my hands and my stomach clenches hard. The left one appears to be fine, but the right one looks like it fought a cheese grater and lost. Blood wells up from the abraded skin. I force myself to breathe in and out slowly. I'm a big girl and we don't cry. Or so I'm told.

"Let me see." Alex says, reaching out for my hand.

I don't give it to him. It hurts too much to move. The fall replays in my head. Did I land on my wrist while trying to catch myself? It all happened so fast. Could it be broken?

Once Alex realizes I'm not relenting, he stuffs his hands in his pockets. "We should probably get that cleaned up."

"Ya think?" I say, still stunned. The cold air turns my hand numb. Unfortunately, that makes it hurt worse. Somehow I manage to move toward my house without puking on the sidewalk.

Alex heads back to his car while I walk inside and straight to the kitchen. He knows his way through a door and honestly, I could care less if he decides to stay or leave at this point.

I stand at the sink running my hand under luke warm water. The anti-bacterial beads in the soap feel like tiny needles in my flesh. I flinch and try to hold in the high-pitched squeal resonating in my throat. My dad used to tell me that if I focus on something else then I can make it through any pain. Right now, though, I can't even imagine imagining.

Even after the abrasion is all rinsed out, I still don't feel any sort of relief. I leave the water running and go to retrieve the first aid kit from the hall.

When I return, the water is off and Alex is sitting at the table. In front of him is a white plastic sack. Seeing it reminds me of the grocery bag I accidentally left in Asher's car. Oops.

"What's that?" I ask, sitting down opposite him. With my good hand, I open the first aid kit and rummage through the different creams and bandages. Good thing I didn't land on both hands because I'd be screwed.

"Chinese. You weren't in school so I figured I would bring your homework and dinner," he says sheepishly. Then he reaches for my hand again. "Let me do that."

I slide the kit over before surrendering anything to him. He pulls out a tube of Neosporin and some sterile strips then he slowly takes my hand into his palms. The contact of my flesh on his sets my nerves on edge. A blush climbs up my neck. It should be a crime to have hands that soft and warm.

He sucks a breath in through his teeth. "God Nic, I'm so sorry."

"It'll heal," I say, but why I'm reassuring him, I haven't the slightest idea. Maybe it's the intoxicating aroma of Chinese food in my kitchen. What girl wouldn't love that?

He turns my wrist back and forth in the light. I wince as a new line of pain darts up my arm.

"Is it broken?" he asks.

"I don't know. I hope not."

"Want to go to the hospital?"

"No," I answer a little too quickly.

"Urgent Care?"

I consider it for a moment. If my wrist is broken and I don't get treatment then I might lose the use of my dominant hand. While I hesitate, Alex makes the decision for me. The chair squeaks across the linoleum floor as he gets up from the table, places the delicious smelling bag in the fridge and says, "Come on."

"Why? The food will get cold." And even to me it sounds whiney.

"Because I'm going to fix you."

"I wouldn't need fixing if you hadn't broken me."

He sighs. "I always fix things I break."

"That's not true," I argue. "Don't you remember the porcelain clown my parents bought me for my fourth birthday? You broke that and never fixed it."

Alex lifts me to a standing position by my elbows. "Okay, so I fix all the things I don't mean to break."

I glare at him as he ushers me out of the kitchen and to his car. "You meant to break my clown?" I accuse.

"Hell yeah, I did. That thing was seriously creepy. You should be thanking me right now."

Funny, I think I should return the favor by breaking his face. In fact, I consider all the different ways I would do it as we arrive at the Urgent Care building and get checked in.

By the time a nurse ushers us back to the room, I'm ready to go back home and punch someone on my way out.

There's no way that sitting in an examination room with bloody gauze taped to my hand could've had any effect on my irritation meter, could it? Alex is trying to be nice, but I haven't listened to a word he's said since we got in the car. As soon as he mentioned school, I zoned out.

Until he says, "So, you and Asher ditched school together, huh?"

I can't say I didn't expect him to ask eventually. Luckily, the X-Rays have already been taken. We are just waiting for doctor to come in with the results, bandage my hand, and send me home.

"Actually, I ditched with Asher and Brady," I say, turning my wrist back and forth. The sting keeps me in the present where I can think clearly.

"I didn't see Brady." Alex pulls latex gloves out of a box and stretches them on to his hands. It must be easier to ask questions when you look like you don't really care.

I shrug. "He was tired so he went home. Asher offered to drop me off."

"Oh," he says.

Is it just my imagination or do I sense a hint of jealousy in that one word? Is it even possible for Alex Berkley to get jealous?

"So what's going on between you two?" He slides the latex together. A satisfied grin slips across his face when it snaps and pops.

"We're friends," I say dismissively. I've spent so much time downplaying other guys to Alex that it just comes naturally. But why do I do it? To seem readily available? If anything, it probably makes me look pathetic. I don't want to seem pathetic so I add, "He asked me to the Sweetheart Dance."

Alex's hands pause in mid-motion and fall to his lap. He looks at me in horror. "What did you say?"

C.j. Ethington

I open my mouth to respond just as the doctor walks in. So I press my lips shut.

"Good news, Miss Dubois. You did not break your wrist. It is a pretty nasty sprain, though. That must have been a nasty fall," the doctor, a middle aged man with prematurely grey hair, says. He looks nice enough, but when he gets too close, the hair on the back of my neck stands on end.

I inch to the side, hoping to put some distance between us. Something doesn't feel right about him.

He glances over his shoulder at Alex. I know I'm not imagining the accusatory look he gives him, but I ignore it anyway. I'm tired of explaining what happened. I've already had to tell three different people that (1) Alex is not my boyfriend; (2) we were not fighting; and (3) my "boyfriend" does not beat me. Besides, Alex is a big boy. He can handle a few glares.

The doctor stops at the door and says, "We'll fit you into a splint, wrap your hand and you can go. I'll be right back with some bandages."

The thought of him touching me sends shivers down my spine. I don't even know the man, but he still gives me the creeps. I wonder what the hell that's about.

"I won't mind a nurse doing it. You seem awfully busy," I suggest with a sweet smile. The waiting room really only had five people in it, but I hope it's enough.

The man nods with a predatory smile like he either wonders what you look like naked or can't wait to get back to his office to finish looking up porn. I go rigid to hide a shudder.

"We are pretty busy. If that would be alright with you then I'll arrange it," he responds.

I assure him that it will be perfectly fine.

He closes the door, leaving Alex and me in an awkward silence.

Alex looks me over with his blue green eyes. When he sees me, it's like he sees through me to the core. Now that the creepy feeling has passed, I notice my chest has gotten really warm. It feels like my lungs are filled with sunlight, which reminds me of my New Year's Resolution.

After a short internal pep talk, I resolve myself to tell him about my feelings.

"I wanted to talk you," I say at the exact same time he says, "I wanted to ask you something."

We both laugh.

Curiosity gets the best of me. "Go ahead."

"You sure?"

I nod.

Using the heels of his boots and the wheels of the chair, he scoots his stool over to me where I sit on the examination table. His chest bumps my knees and my stomach does a little flip from the impact. Resting his arms across my thighs, he leans in.

I stop breathing. Is it possible his eyes could be any brighter than they are at this exact moment?

"Nic, you are my best friend," he says, looking up at me through his eyelashes.

"And you're mine," I respond automatically. The warmth from his forearms seeps through my jeans, making the rest of me cold.

"You know I'd do anything for you."

My mind is a blank slate. I nod shakily. Excitement fills me so fast I think I may have to jump out of my skin to make room for it all.

"And you are the only person I really trust."

I close my eyes slowly, willing him to get on with it. Alex is usually a foot taller than I am, but since he's sitting down and I'm on the table, his face is lower than mine by a few inches. An image flies through my mind. If I just leaned down, I could kiss him. I could taste his cinnamon breath whispering against my lips.

"I wanted to ask you," he says again, his eyes searching my face.

And as if some superior force knows how close I am to euphoria, the nurse walks in.

Alex shoots back across the room, the wheels of the stool screeching across the floor. The cushion hits the cupboard behind him with a loud *thunk*! There is no way we could be farther apart and still be in the same room.

The nurse pulls a metal wheelie cart in behind her. On it is a generic wrist splint I'm pretty sure you could get at any pharmacy, a roll of gauze, antiseptic cream, and scissors. I give Alex a look that says "I told you so." We could have saved the money and done all of this at home.

The nurse is pretty enough, I notice, but Alex isn't looking. His eyes are glued to his phone. I assume he's playing a game (Alex is addicted to his games) and focus on the nurse to avoid feeling anything. She has curly blond hair riding down her shoulders, a tongue ring that clicks against her teeth when she talks, blue eyes and an ugly pair of coral-colored scrubs on. Then again, I guess black would be too morbid for her to wear to work.

As she cleans my wound, I try to focus on something else entirely, like what Alex might have been trying to say. I've dreamt – hell, fantasized – about him coming to his senses about me. I've pictured what it would be like to date him, kiss him, or play boyfriend/girlfriend out in public. We've known each other forever. You don't stay friends with someone that long without some sort of feelings forming on either side. You just don't. Not when you're the opposite sex. Or sex preference in Brady's case.

Back when we were little, our mothers used to joke about us getting married someday, making them in-laws. At least I think they were joking.

The nurse clicks her tongue ring against her teeth to the rhythm of some song. I stare at her working over my hand with the gauze. I imagine what kind of person she is. I mean, she seems nice enough. Does she even know she works with Dr. Douchebag?

"Now try to keep this on as much as possible," she tells me. "You can remove it to shower, but it's best to keep the wrist immobile."

"How long do I have to wear it?"

She doesn't look at me. "The doctor says six weeks, but it's really hard to tell with sprains. Six weeks would be adequate if it were broken." She looks up finally and smiles. "I'm gonna say two weeks. But wear it as much as you can bear to after that to avoid further strain." Her voice drops down to a whisper. "But I'm not the doctor. I could get him if you would like a second opinion."

"No, I like your opinion just fine. Thank you." I'll take two weeks in a brace over six any day.

She squeezes the brace around my wrist then rubs her hands together. This must be her moment of magic. I laugh at the idea of her saying something absurd like, "Presto fix-o."

"Alright. You're good to go. Be careful." Then she tacks on quietly, "That ice can be a bitch."

I laugh, startled at her choice of words. They don't really fit the atmosphere. But maybe her bedside manner isn't really a bedside manner at all. I appreciate a nurse who tells it like it is.

I try to maneuver myself off of the table, but realize how much harder things like that are going to be. Alex comes to my aid. He reaches out his right hand and helps me slide down.

The nurse watches us leave with an expression on her face that says, "How cute."

I wave back to her over my shoulder, but the image I see chills me. She's no longer standing in the hall wearing her coral pink scrubs, but frozen in ice, her face the mask of death.

The breath in my lungs turns thick. I cough hard and pull back on Alex. He turns us around so we are facing back down the hall from which we just came.

"What?" he demands and is awarded with nasty looks from every nurse there. "Good god. You almost pulled me over."

My eyes search the whole room for my nurse. She's nowhere to be found. Just as I'm about to force Alex into taking me all the way back to the room, the nurse steps through the doorway, pulling the metal cart.

"Did you forget something, hon?" she calls out.

It takes me a long time before I can speak, move, or breathe.

"Nic, you okay?" Alex asks.

Finally I can shake my head. "I'm good. Just wanted to thank you," I call back.

She looks at me as if I've just grown two extra arms, which still wouldn't be the most confusing experience I've endured today. "You're welcome."

Alex pivots, turning us back around, but I'm not ready to go yet. There's something I have to tell this woman, though I'm not sure what it means.

"Annie," I say.

She turns, clearly startled. "Yes?"

"Don't take it," I continue ominously. "It's safer to just wait until your boyfriend shows up. Trust me."

Her face pales. She takes a step back and knocks the scissors off the cart. While she crouches down to gather the items, I pat Alex on the chest. "Now I'm ready to go."

Alex's feet shuffle down the hallway. Once we are through the exit doors to the waiting room, he says, "Nic, how did you know her name?"

"Um, nametag?" I say, though I don't really mean it to sound like a question.

He nods slowly, but doesn't say anything until he loads me into the car. Once we are all buckled in, he replies, "Um, Nic, her nametag said her name was Cassandra. There's really no way you could have known she went by Annie."

I think on that. He's right. There's no way I could have known she went by Annie. So how did I?

Furthermore, how could I possibly know that while waiting for her boyfriend to pick her up after work she will be approached by a strange black Volkswagen Jetta with an 8-Ball hanging from the rearview mirror? It's not so strange that someone might pull over and offer a pretty girl a ride home when it's cold out. It's not even strange that the pretty girl might accept it. So how could I know that if this pretty girl – Annie – accepts the ride, she'll end up dead?

The car still hasn't moved. Alex has turned almost completely toward me in his seat waiting for a response.

"I must have heard someone call her name while we were being checked in," I say. "And since when is it a crime to remind nice people of stranger danger? It's not like I could give her a tip."

Alex shakes his head dubiously. "Whatever," he says. Then without another word, he takes me home.

Chapter 12

Alex never really got my homework. Well, in a way, I guess he did since we have two classes together, but that's it. He does offers to re-heat my food while I sit on the couch, though. He must be feeling guilty.

The TV mounted on the wall beeps to life. I access the DV-R screen for my choices. I still haven't watched the last episode of *The Office* and I think I deserve some humor. After we left the doctor's office, my body started to ache in places I hadn't noticed. Bloody hand obviously trumped the deep tissue bruise on my thigh and butt.

Alex walks in balancing two cartons of Chinese food in his hand. We don't like the same dishes so there's no need to use plates. He always gets the Moo Shoo Pork and I'm a Cashew Chicken kind of girl. He hands me the container, hot from the microwave, and a fork. Then he sits next to me on the couch. Immediately and without thinking, I lift my legs into his lap.

He doesn't protest, just shifts to make himself more comfortable. I push play on the episode and we eat in silence, except for the laughs.

We're both finished by the time it's over. His is gone. Mine is ready to go back into the fridge.

The question burns in my mouth. I want to ask – no, beg – him to finish the topic from earlier, but I've been patient this long. I guess I could wait a little longer.

"You're fortune," he says, offering it to me with a flourish. Then he presses his own fortune cookie between his palms. "On the count of three."

One. Two. Crack!

I pull the paper out of my crumbled cookie and start eating the shell. My mother used to tell me that your fortune wouldn't come true if you didn't eat the cookie first. I guess it was like an offering to some god or something. Alex doesn't like the cookie so he drops it into his empty container and spreads the fortune out.

"What's it say?" I ask around a mouthful of orange-flavored cookie.

He raises his sandy eyebrows and smiles. "'The journey of many lands awaits you.' I think I'm supposed to go on a trip. What about yours?"

I gesture to my mouth, still chewing.

"Right. Not until the cookie is gone," he observes with a roll of his eyes.

I nod.

It takes me a little while longer than normal to finish the cookie because it's just too much fun making him suffer.

"Oh god," he says impatiently. "Just give it to me." He reaches out for the paper resting uncomfortably between the fingers of my bandaged hand.

I hold it back and away from him. Then I swallow. "Okay, I'm ready."

"Finally."

Clearing my throat, I read, "'Investigate new possibilities with friends. Now is the time.'" My stomach lurches. I really wish I'd read that once over quietly.

"Interesting," Alex says with a grin. He rubs his chin as if thinking it over. "Brady?"

I punch him weakly in the arm with my left hand. He laughs at me. "You, my dear friend, are a weakling."

"That's what happens when your best friend breaks you," I argue.

Staring at the fortune, I wonder if it's a sign. I've only chickened out like five times already. Maybe it's time to just spit it out. How hard can it be to tell someone you like them?

"Alex?" I begin.

He looks at me sidelong. "Oh yeah. What we were talking about earlier."

"I wasn't reminding you," I reply.

"I know, but I remembered and I don't want to forget. It's too important."

I move my feet from his lap and tuck them under me. "Go ahead then."

He twists on the couch so he can gauge my reaction. The excitement builds again. This is it. All out on the table.

"I have something to ask you."

I nod a little too excitedly and have to remind myself to be calm, collected.

"I was just wondering..." He drags his fingers through his hair. "Would you be willing to go out with—"

"Yes," I blurt out, cutting him off.

He smiles. "Really? You'll do it? I told Jen. She didn't think you would."

"Why wouldn't I?" Then his words sink into me like acid. I hold my hands up in front of me in the universal sign for "Stop!"

I backpedal. "Wait, what?"

Alex catches sight of the brace and frowns. He must not notice that not only are we not on the same page, but we appear to be reading from two totally different books.

"Well, Jen's ex-boyfriend – his name is Taylor, by the way – has been giving her a lot of grief about dating me. It's kind of irritating. They've been trying to stay friends so we thought that if we could hook him up with someone else, he might leave us alone."

"And you thought of me?" I realize I'm only a breath away from yelling. I bite my lip in order to force my anger back down.

"Well, yeah. You don't get out enough and Jen thought –"

"She could pimp me out?" I snap out.

He holds up his hands like he's afraid I might lunge at him. His face has gone pink. "No, not at all. It's just dinner and Taylor's a great guy, I promise. What would it hurt? It's not like you're seeing anyone. Unless you and Asher..."

"Nothing is going on between Asher and me," I say deliberately. I want to scream at him, tell him that I'd hoped something could happen between us. Every part of me throbs from the tension.

"Well, then what's the problem?" He drops his hands and moves closer to me. I don't want him closer so I inch up the arm of the couch like he's a creepy bug who wants a piece of me.

He gets up and looks at me with a fevered glare. I must have offended him by moving away. Why don't I feel bad about that?

"Is there something you aren't telling me, Nic?"

I didn't picture any of this going the way it has. To tell him about my feelings now would put me on a journey down a path of destruction. I can't foresee it going well at all. Another time would be better.

Make that six times I've officially chickened out.

"No. Nothing. Never mind," I grind out.

"Please, just think about it then? I would really appreciate it, and Jen says he's a really good guy," he bargains.

Suddenly, I'm very tired. I just want to go to bed. "But he's not you," I whisper.

Either he doesn't hear me or he ignores my words. His eyes plead with me. He only unleashes the full power of his eyes when he really needs me to do something. "What did you say?"

"If he's such a great guy, Alex, then why isn't Jen still dating him?"

He looks surprised. "Well, because Jen and I are together."

"Jen cheated, you mean," I say. He doesn't have to answer. The look on his face says it all. "Fine. I'll think about it," I tell him.

His face splits into a grin. It's like I just handed him a whole bag of candy rather than promising him that I'll think about sharing. "You're the best, Nicky."

If I'm the best, then why do I feel like a tiny little shadow of myself?

Alex leans over and kisses my cheek. "Thank you. Thank you. Thank you. I'm going to go tell Jen."

"I said I'd think about it," I remind him.

"I know," he says, still beaming. "Will you be alright?"

I nod reluctantly. My cheek tingles from the touch of his lips. Talk about adding insult to injury. At least if it burned or stung, it wouldn't hurt so much when the sensation drifts away.

"I'll see you later." He touches my shoulder briefly before bouncing excitedly toward the door.

It opens before he gets to it. My parents walk in. My father is still in the suit he wore to work, but my mother has traded her dress slacks for an ankle length jean skirt. Must have been a church function.

"Alex," My mom says, giving him a hug. "Good to see you."

"Mrs. Dubois. Mr. Dubois," he says by way of greeting. "I'm on my way out, but it's good to see you, too. Bye, Nic." And he's gone. Too excited to sell me off to the highest bidder, I gather.

My parents laugh.

"Such a good kid," my father muses.

"Hi honey," my mom says, coming to stand behind the couch. Her face turns pale when she sees the splint on my wrist. "Oh dear, what happened?"

That gets my father's attention. He walks around the couch and kneels on the floor next to me. "Are you okay? Do we need to go to the doctor?"

"No need. Alex and I already went. It's just a sprain. I slipped on some ice in the driveway," I explain.

"Oh my," my mother gasps. "I told you to put some salt out there, Jeffrey."

"It wasn't snowing. I didn't think there would be ice," he argues.

I remain utterly silent. Anything I say at this point will only fuel the fire and I would rather be in bed before the real fighting starts.

My parents are pretty stable people separately, but their relationship is a touch bipolar. When they're happy, the birds sing, the heavens open up, and the angels smile, but when they're unhappy, a chasm splits open the earth and the flames of hell lick at your heels. There really is no in-between.

"Well, what do you think happens when the snow melts off the roof? In this cold, it's bound to freeze to the pavement," my mother says, her fists planted firmly on her hips.

"There wasn't any snow on the roof, Pauline," my father snaps back, clipping his words. He's originally from Boston and when he gets angry his accent comes out big time.

I can't take much more. An ache works its way up behind my right eye. "I didn't slip in our driveway," I lie. "It was someone else's."

They both look at me. The tension is thick enough to choke on.

"Whose driveway, dear?" my mother asks.

I hate lying to her, but if it will avoid an argument, I'll tell them anything. "Brady's. His parents are out of town and they were out of salt. He felt really bad."

"What were you doing at Brady's?" Dad asks. He doesn't sound angry. If anything, the way he says Brady's name is almost piteous. He knows how seldom Brady's parents are home.

"I let him borrow my English notes. They were at his house."

The tension thins out to a bearable pressure. I take in a deep breath. Crisis averted.

"Look, I'm really tired. I was studying late last night. I'll see you in the morning." It's a good thing that I'm too tired to feel guilty for all the lies spilling out of my mouth. Guilt never tastes very good.

I climb off the couch awkwardly and retrieve the food container with my left hand. That's going to take some getting used to. Tucking it into the crook of my right arm, I grab for Alex's empty container. Then I kiss them both on the cheek and head to the kitchen.

As I'm brushing my teeth, a feat in and of itself, I hear my parents bickering again. This time it's about bills. There was this one time when I marked all of their fights down on a calendar to see if I could prophesy when the next storm would hit. Nothing came of it. Their highs and lows are like the weather in this state: too scattered to predict.

I roll my eyes. None of my lying had even helped. I guess the Argument Fairy had us on her list tonight.

I turn off the light and crawl into bed. My phone beeps as I'm putting my glasses up. I grab it and squint at the screen. It's a text message from Alex saying: *Talked to Jen. Taylor is really hoping to meet you. Please, please, please think about it.*

I sigh, put the phone back on my nightstand, and roll my face into the pillow. The tears come hard and fast, intensified by the screaming downstairs. I shake and cry until I am burning up and just can't do it anymore.

Next thing I know, my phone rings. I must have fallen asleep at some point because my eyes are crusted with the salt of my tears. I pry them open and answer the call. If it's a telemarketer, they're going to get an ass-reaming they'll never forget, and if it's Alex, he'll get worse than that.

"Yeah?" I croak into the phone.

"Oh god, did I wake you?"

My brain sparks to life, but I still don't recognize the husky voice on the other end of the line and the ringtone was generic. "Who is this?"

"Asher. Were you asleep? It's only ten-thirty."

"It's been a shitty night."

"Tell me about it," he agrees. "I had three brain wraps. I wish this place would just go digital already."

"Huh?" My eyelids slip closed. Whatever a "brain wrap" is, I feel like I'm having one now. The sound of his voice, like smoke, is enough to put me back under.

"Sorry. It's a movie theater term. In patron terms, the film was being a gigantic pain in my ass."

"You work at the movie theater?" Had I never thought to ask where he worked?

He laughs. "Yeah. Projectionist. The job sucks, but I can do my homework when I'm not threading. Of course, if they would just go digital then I wouldn't have to thread."

"Whatever the hell that means."

"Yeah. We didn't sell to the last set so they let me go early," he explains. "So I get in my car to head home and guess what I find."

"Shit," I mumble.

"I can bring the bag to you, but if you're asleep, it's cool. I'll just hide it somewhere in my car. Hopefully my sister won't find it." The lightheartedness in his voice makes me smile.

"Are you trying to give me a guilt trip?"

As I listen for his answer, I notice for the first time that the house has gone still, quiet. I wonder if my parents are in bed or just recharging for the next battle.

"Yeah." He laughs again. "That was sort of the point."

"To drag me out of bed?"

"It's ten-thirty. You shouldn't be going to sleep this early. It's bad for you."

"I must have missed that lesson in Health class."

"It was a good one. It was the same day we learned about the dangers of missing sarcasm. Good times."

I laugh quietly. "It's awfully cold out there and my bed is really warm. I might need another incentive."

"Besides returning this bag, along with all its beautiful memories, to you?"

"Besides that."

He sighs. "What if I said I wanted to see you?"

"You just saw me."

"It's a reason, isn't it?"

"Fine. Give me five minutes."

"Okay. I'm outside." Then the line goes dead.

I don't bother getting dressed. If Asher wants to wake me up, he can deal with seeing me in my black sweat pants and Rangers hoody. I pull on my boots and shrug a black leather jacket on over my sweatshirt. I don't tie my shoelaces because I can't with the brace, but I do take out the braid I wore to bed. The curtain of hair might add a little extra warmth. After putting on my glasses, I'm good to go.

The hallway bends at the edges because of the thickness of my lenses. It always looks like that when I go a long time just wearing contacts. It almost feels like I'm walking through one of those funhouses they always seem to have at carnivals.

The house is too dark to see. If my room wasn't a direct shot from the front door I would for sure run into something and wake my parents. At least this way I have the porch light guiding me.

I duck out the front door and shut it quietly behind me. Since I'm not going far, I leave it unlocked. That way I can't be accused of sneaking out just in case my parents wake up and bother to come looking for me.

Salt crunches beneath my boots. The driveway is covered with it. I shake my head. Mom – one; dad – zero.

The Jeep sits at the curb with its lights off. I walk around to climb into the passenger side. After fumbling with the door handle for a minute, I finally get it open. Heat washes over me, reminding me of my warm bed.

"Looking good, Dubois," Asher says, motioning for me to shut the door.

"I try," I say wryly.

His eyes roam over me, stopping at my chest. "Excuse me," I snap, pulling the jacket tighter around me. I'm not used to having guys stare at me.

He smiles. "Sorry. It's just – I didn't know you were a Rangers fan."

"Oh." I breathe a sigh of relief. "Yeah. My dad roots for the Bruins, though. I think my mom got me the sweatshirt to torment him."

He laughs and the sound reverberates through the Jeep. "That's funny."

I shrug. "He didn't think so."

"I'll bet. So what happened to your hand?" he asks, gesturing to the brace and gauze protruding from my jacket sleeve.

"Alex," I tell him. I'm not going to lie. I reserve that function for my parents.

He cocks an eyebrow. It's not a happy eyebrow. There's an edge to his voice when he says, "Berkley did that?"

"Inadvertently. He wanted to talk. I didn't want to. I tried to walk away and when he grabbed my arm, my ass somehow ended up on the ice."

"Sounds like an adventure," he says through gritted teeth.

"Oh yeah. Going to the doctor's office is almost as good as Italy or Paris." I look at the brace. The gauze is starting to itch. Funny how it was all but forgotten before we started talking about it.

"Is that why your night sucked?"

I nod. "More or less."

"What's the more?" He stares at me like I'm the most interesting thing he's seen all night. Hell, maybe I am. I don't know what working at a movie theater is like.

I laugh cynically. "Why am I telling you this?"

His face scrunches up for a second, contemplating. "Because I'm easy to talk to. So why was Berkley here?"

"Because," I say, sounding exasperated. "He wants to set me up on a blind date with his girlfriend's ex."

"Awkward."

"Seriously."

"What did he say when you said no?" He smiles like the thought intrigues him.

I stare at my hand some more.

Asher says, "Oh god, you agreed?"

"I told him I'd think about it."

"Why?"

"I don't know." I glance up at him. The darkness of his hair contrasts against the neighbor's porch light, leaving his face in shadow. "Because he asked as a favor. Besides, it's just one date."

"With Jen's ex-boyfriend."

"Yep." The pain from being asked out by Alex only to find out it's for someone else flows into me. My heart falls like a rock.

"Do you know him?"

I shake my head. "Alex says he's a good guy, though."

Asher surprises me by laughing. "Forgive me. I don't exactly trust Berkley's taste in friends."

A muscle in my jaw tightens. "And why is that?" I challenge.

"Don't get me wrong," he argues, knowing he offended me. "You and Brady are the coolest people I've met here, but Berkley is a social whore."

I glare at him some more.

So he continues, "He tries to be friends with everyone. It's what makes him popular. He doesn't have to care. He just has to pretend to. He gives everyone the face he thinks they want to see." He shrugs. "I thought you could see that."

Torn between my newfound love and even newer found hatred for Alex, I feel compelled to stick up for him anyway. "Who died and made you Dr. Phil?"

His eyebrows rise as he turns his head away. "Look, I'm sorry. I don't like the guy. He's fake, but I didn't mean to offend you."

"Well, you did." I reach toward the door handle with my left hand. Asher watches as I struggle for a good three minutes before he holds up a finger and climbs out of the car. A few seconds later, he opens my door.

I swing my legs out, still sitting on the passenger seat. I feel around on the floor for the grocery bag. Asher leans down and across me to help. His hair brushes my nose. It smells like Tea Tree Shampoo and campfire: natural and musky. As I lose myself in the scent of him, he seizes the bag and holds it down by my thighs. This is the point where he should move out of the way and let me go back inside, but instead of pulling back, he leans into me, his face inches from mine. My heart beats wildly against my ribs.

"I'm really sorry," he whispers. His breath forms white clouds in the air between our lips. "I warned you. I say what I think. Always."

"Always?"

He nods. His eyes, the shade of burnt almond, glued to mine. The light from behind me dances in them, bringing out flecks of gold. The depth is astounding.

"Yes, always. Or when the opportunity arises. I'm trying to work on it."

I shift a little in the seat. My balance is off and I have to fight the reflex to brace myself with my right hand. It's an awkward position. If I move too far this way, I'll fall off the seat and if I scoot forward, I'll bump right into Asher.

"And what are you thinking now?" I ask, a little out of breath.

He leans in closer, tilting his head like he might kiss me. With his lips a mere centimeter away, he says, "I think you should come to the party with me on Saturday."

My senses stabilize. Pressing my knees into either side of his hips, I push him away. "Ugh. You are relentless."

He laughs, rubbing his sides through his shirt. Seriously, doesn't he ever wear a jacket? "Come on. You'll consider going out with a complete stranger, but you won't come to a party with me?"

I wiggle off of the seat, using my legs to propel me forward. When I get to the edge, Asher reaches out a hand to help me, which I accept so I don't end up breaking something more vital than my wrist. I hit the ground and stumble a little. Asher catches me before I fall. His arms are warm despite the cold.

"I refuse to agree to anything tonight," I inform him. "Try me tomorrow."

He doesn't release me right away. His hands linger on my waist as he looks down at me. "You haven't agreed to anything with me. Not once."

"I'm sure you'll get over it," I respond, nonchalantly.

He shakes his head while a smile flirts with his lips. "No, I'm not sure I will."

"You will," I snatch the bag out of his hands and turn to go inside.

"Nicoletta," he says, but in the still winter night, he might as well be yelling.

I turn back to look at him.

He shuts the passenger door. It echoes in the night like a gunshot. I expect to hear the sound of my father getting his shotgun.

Asher lopes over to me. With his right hand, he pushes a lock of hair behind my ear. His eyes scrutinize mine.

"What?" I ask, suddenly feeling self-conscious.

"Your eyes haven't always been two different colors, have they? I could have sworn they were blue. Not green and blue."

"I wear colored contacts," I tell him.

"Why?"

I can't help but look away. People have been commenting on my eyes for as long as I can remember. The majority of those comments are not always pleasant. The last thing I need tonight is to hear how I'm a freak because of a genetic trait I had no control over. "Are we gonna do this tonight? It's cold."

He leans in to whisper into my ear. His breath is hot against my skin. "Another time then. But remember, just because I'm thinking about getting you to the party doesn't mean that's all I'm thinking. All you have to do is ask."

Then his hand falls away from my face, leaving me cold. I turn toward the house as he drives away.

My skin vibrates from the electricity of his touch.

I may never get back to sleep now. At least not without a cold shower first.

Chapter 13

The halls at school are thrumming. The air smells of the weekend. As soon as I'm through the doors, I head straight toward the office with a forged note excusing my absence yesterday. I've done this so many times that if my mother were to ever write me an excuse, they would probably think that one the fake. This time I had to write it three times to get it right. After all, I'm the one with the wrist splint, not my mother. It made for a good excuse, though.

Mrs. Adams is the school secretary. She hasn't come back yet, so I wait for the vice principal, Mr. Jackson, to help me. It doesn't shock me anymore to see him. I used to panic. Something about him makes my throat tight, my skin itch, and my hair curl. After the first year, I learned to breathe through it. It usually works as long as he doesn't try to pat me on the back or something.

"Miss Dubois," he says with a nod. He looks likes any vice principal in my mind: short and stocky with a belly hanging over his belt. His hair is thinning around the middle and his eyes and nose are too big for his face. Mid-life crisis hit him last year. That's when he started driving a Miata to work.

"Mr. Jackson," I reply, aiming for cool and collected. "I have a note from my mother." Then, before he has a chance to graze my fingers with his, I drop the note onto the counter and take a step back.

"Good. Thank you. Now get to class. We don't want a smart girl like you falling behind," he says with an elbow nudge and a wink. I try not to read into his actions. He's just trying to get along with the student body, I tell myself. Yeah, body being the key word.

My morning coffee starts a long climb back up my throat. I nod and duck out of the office, nearly running into Ashley, our very own protester.

"Sorry," I say, side-stepping her so she can move past me.

She doesn't seem to notice or care. Her usually perfectly styled hair looks like something straight out of a Tim Burton flick. She has no make-up on and is clutching her chest like it hurts to breathe.

"Are you okay?" I ask.

She stumbles a little to the side. I catch her elbow and guide her to the nearest chair. I thank God that I remembered to wear my wrist splint when she presses her weight into it.

"Miss Marinello," Mr. Jackson says. "Are you feeling alright?"

"I...," she coughs and tries again, "I... can't breathe." Her voice reminds me of mine when the asthma attacks.

"She might be having an asthma attack," I suggest.

Mr. Jackson's gaze swings toward me. He reaches out a hand to touch my shoulder, but I bounce back out of his reach. "Thank you, Miss Dubois. I think we can take care of Miss Marinello just fine without you. Now head to class, would you?"

It only takes a second for me to weigh my options. I can either wait for Ashley's mom to show up and take her to the hospital, which puts me at risk of Mr. Jackson's constant pats on the back and/or head, or I could get as far away from our vice principal as possible. In a moment of selfishness, I take the latter option.

But not before I make sure she'll be okay. Too many of my peers are taking up residence in a hospital bed for me to feel comfortable abandoning her.

"Ashley," I say quietly. "Take deep breaths. It'll all be okay. Do you have an inhaler?"

She shakes her head.

I reach into the backpack I haven't stuffed into my locker yet and pull out mine. Clicking the mouthpiece into place over the canister, I put it to her lips.

"Breathe in on the count of two, okay?" I say.
She nods.

I count silently then press down. The inhaler makes a sound like someone breathing. Ashley coughs once, twice, three times.

When she looks at me, the color is bleeding back into her cheeks. "Thanks," she says. "Wait, I know you. Aren't you the foreign exchange student?"

And that's all it takes to make me forget why I helped her. Being mistaken for an exchange student comes with the territory when you have a name like mine. Actually, it's not my name. It's my grandmother's. Her name has been passed down from generation to generation for centuries until it became hers and then eventually landed on me.

I force a smile at her. "Yep, that's me. Well, good luck to you," I say, giving her a thumbs-up.

I shake my head as her words ricochet around in my head. Foreign exchange student? Nice. It's not like Ashley and I have gone to school together since she moved here when we were seven. Oh, wait – we have.

When I get to English class, Asher is sitting in the seat next to mine again. He's slouched down in his seat, his long legs folded under the desk with his knees peeking out on either side. He's wearing boots, jeans, and a grey sweater, which is dotted with spots from his wet hair. I've never seen anyone look so relaxed in school before. Though, I imagine he could look comfortable anywhere.

He sees me and smiles.

I take my seat, turned in my chair so I'm facing the room. If body language is honest, it would probably seem like I was opening myself up to him. As soon as I realize this, I shift back toward the front.

The bell rings and Mr. Warren walks in right on cue. Somehow that man manages to always be exactly two seconds late. He probably sits in the hall waiting for the bell to ring.

"Ah," he says with a smirk, "The weekend. What a great time for a new book."

Half the class groans.

"Oh don't be like that." He takes a sip of his ever-present coffee. "To read is to be enlightened. To be enlightened is to... yes, Miss Carter?" he says, pointing to Melinda Carter in the back. "No, you may not be excused if that's what you are asking."

She looks down at the desk sheepishly and lowers her hand.

"Very good. Now, your assignment is to read something of your choice. The catch is that it must be one of the books located at the back of the room. You will go by rows to choose your selection. Choose wisely for you will be working with this book until the end of the year," he explains. He walks forward and taps the desk in front of me. "Front row, go."

I look at Asher. I like assignments that are creative and personal, but they also make me nervous. I don't like being vulnerable to my peers. Especially since I now know that most of them think I'm stuck up. Or they don't know me at all.

He returns my look with a lazy one of his own. It doesn't surprise me. I think I'm getting used to his "let things fall where they may" attitude.

The first row sits back down.

Mr. Warren takes a long draw off his coffee and instructs, "Second row. Go."

I slide out of my seat and make my way to the back of the room. Using my left hand, I sift through the books stacked on the back counter.

Asher already has his book. So do the rest of them, I notice. Everyone's waiting on me.

"Let me help," he says, moving books to the side.

Chaucer. Austen. Shakespeare. Wilde. Steinbeck. Flaubert.

"That one," I say, pointing to John Milton's *Paradise Lost*.

"You sure?" he asks, but hands me the book anyway.

I nod. "The never ending battle between good and evil? Who doesn't like a story like that?"

He chuckles as if I've said something funny.

We make our way back to our seats. When the third row is called, I point at his book in silent question. In response, he tilts it up so I can see: John Milton's *Paradise Lost*.

"Seriously?" I whisper.

He nods and says, "The never ending battle between good and evil? How could I resist?"

Mr. Warren walks past desks, checking out our selections and jotting them down onto a clipboard. "*Wuthering Heights*. Good selection, Miss Ivey," he says. "*Dracula*. Interesting, Mr. Brown. I hope you aren't planning on renting the movie. It's nothing like the book."

I haven't read the book or seen the movie, but I imagine he says that to discourage it. Personally, I passed on that one because vampires bore me. As far as mythological creatures go, I would rather read about something more believable than a blood-sucking romantic.

Steven Brown's face falls. I have to force myself not to smile. He'll have to read the book just to find out if Mr. Warren is right.

The last row is still shuffling around the back of the room retrieving their books when Mr. Warren walks down the aisle between Asher and me. "Was this planned?" he asks.

"No, sir." Asher responds. "It was kismet."

Mr. Warren smiles, his eyes crinkling at the edges. It makes him seem warmer, friendlier, like you could tell him anything. "Then if you'd like, the two of you can be partners. I expect great things from both of you. I am, however, surprised at your choice, Miss Dubois."

"Why? What did you expect me to choose?" I ask.

"I don't know. Maybe something that would pay homage to your background. *Madame Bovary* would have been an excellent choice for that."

I feel a warm crimson creep up my face. "I've read *Madame Bovary*," I tell him. "It was awful."

He doesn't notice my embarrassment, but accepts the answer. "Have either of you ever read Milton?"

I shake my head. Asher hesitates then says, "No."

"Well you are both in for a treat." And then he moves on.

I look down at the book, willing the blood out of my face. Why couldn't my parents have named me something different? The last name was bad enough, but not only did they name me Nicoletta, but they also gave me the middle name Cheri. That's three foreign names. Ridiculous! No wonder people mistake me for a foreign exchange student. I mean, come on. They could have named me Lilly or Rachel. Even Charlotte would have been better. Apparently no one was thinking in that hospital room.

When I look up, Asher is staring at me with a confused look.

"I hate my name," I whisper to him.

"That's too bad," he whispers back, his eyes softening. "Because I kinda like it."

I roll my eyes emphatically. "I just had someone ask me if I was a foreign exchange student,"

"What's so bad about that? I thought girls liked being called exotic."

The rest of the class is returning to their seats. I lean forward so no one can hear me except him. "I've gone to school with her for ten years and she had no idea who I am."

He nods as if he understands, though I'm not sure how. Looking like he does, I doubt anyone could forget him.

"Sometimes," he whispers, leaning across the aisle until his breath stirs my hair, "it's not a bad thing to be invisible."

"Okay, Crazy. As if you know what it's like to be invisible." The corner of his mouth quirks up. "Oh, you'd be surprised."

Chapter 14

Ms. Kelley, the Phys Ed. teacher is obviously unimpressed with my inability to play dodge ball. She shoots daggered glares at me every chance she gets.

Honestly, even if I wasn't hurt, I probably would have faked an injury to get out of it. I mean, come on, dodge ball is fine for third graders, but high school? That's just asking for broken bones and bloody noses. So I sit on the side lines in my jeans and hooded sweatshirt while everyone else has to wear their green gym shorts and white school t-shirts. Hey, protests only last as long as the instigator is there. Without her, the sheep wandered away from the flock.

I flip the pages of my book back and forth between my fingers. I always like to get a jump start on my assignments. I'm not very good with deadlines.

Brady and Asher wait outside the gym doors when I get out of class. I shove the book in my bag and try to zip it up with my left hand.

"Why can't I be ambidextrous?" I complain.

Brady laughs. Asher takes my bag and zips it up for me.

I take the bag back and shrug it over my shoulder. "Thanks, but I'll never figure out how to do it on my own if you keep helping me."

"I think that's the idea, Kitten," says Brady, wrapping an arm around my shoulders. "Now come on. I need me some nourishment."

"Nourishment, my ass," I mumble under my breath. I'm going to gain twenty pounds if I allow him to talk me into eating off campus much more, especially since I can't exercise it off thanks to Alex.

Asher must have heard me. He covers his mouth to hide his snickers as we follow Brady through the crowd. I wonder what he did for lunch before coming with us. Surely he had a huge group of friends he went with or something. I mean, we did see him out with the basketball team and cheerleaders a few times, but that was usually just before a big game. Maybe he went with his sister, whom I still haven't met. How is it possible that we could go to the same school and never meet? Maybe sophomores and juniors really do live in different worlds.

Rather than load up into Brady's car, we pile into the Jeep. I get the front seat because "Gimpy always gets the front," according to Brady.

"What sounds good?" Asher asks, reaching over to flip on the heater.

I stare at him with a lecture on my lips. Why the hell wasn't the heater on before? It's like thirty degrees outside. All heaters should be on all the time.

"What sounds good? Or what's close?" I say through chattering teeth.

We finally agree on bagel sandwiches. It's better than what we've been eating the last few days. I'm going to get sick if I eat one more plate of pasta, I swear.

I order a bowl of soup in an attempt to feel warm and healthy then head to the table with my spoon. Once I sit down, I realize I hadn't considered how I would eat anything that required the use of my right hand.

"So, have you decided to come to the party yet?" Brady asks me, but wags his eyebrows at Asher.

Asher clears his throat and answers for me, "She's still thinking about it. But trust me, I've been trying."

"Well," Brady continues. "I feel it imperative to inform you that the party has been changed to a *Supernatural* affair."

"Oh? Like that one time we were going to watch it instead of going to school, but ended up in Provo instead?" I splash my spoon back into the bowl, frustrated. "Unh uh. I'm not buying. You've used Sam and Dean against me for the last time, Brady McGowan."

Brady and Asher laugh. Brady says, "Well, that's a bit melodramatic, but no. Not like that at all. This is different."

"How?" I ask indignantly.

"Because this time I'm serious. I even bought the seasons."

Asher nods. "It's true. He ditched last period. They're in his locker. And I could bring mine for insurance."

"What are you?" I snarl at him. "His wingman?"

They laugh again.

"Fine. I'll go. But you better not be kidding."

"I swear on my dog's life," Brady says, holding his hand over his heart.

"You don't have a dog."

"But if I did, I would swear on its life."

I retrieve my spoon just to point it at Asher. "I am holding you personally responsible for all of this."

He smiles. "Of course."

I scoop a spoonful of soup with my left hand, which is a lot harder than it looks, and also makes it really hard to take me seriously. "I hope you two assholes are happy," I mumble around the mouthful of hot liquid.

"Ecstatic," says Asher.

Brady agrees. "Amazingly so."

***

I hate Math. Enough said. The square root of Pi multiplied by the cosign of "A" makes my head hurt.

"When are we ever going to use this?" I ask Jessica Wayland on the way out of class. She's a cute girl and one of the few I like. She turns to look at me. Her curly brown hair is straight today, which makes it look really long.

"I don't know. You could be in a radio contest or something."

I laugh cynically. "Right. Like the winning question is going to be: Name the variable in the equation when Pi equals A, B is the square root of C and C is the fifth decimal point in D," I rattle off.

"Did you make that up?"

"Yes, and it doesn't make sense because it wasn't supposed to."

She giggles. "I think that question was actually on the test. Besides, it could happen."

"And I could be Miss America," I joke. I always have so much fun with Jessica. She's the only reason I even go to math, which gives me an idea. "Hey, you know Brady McGowan, right?"

"Yeah, I went to his New Year's party."

I shudder involuntarily. "Well, he's having a *Supernatural* party at his house on Saturday. You should come."

She hesitates, thinking it over.

"He swears it's low-key," I say, cutting off her line of thinking. "Nothing like New Years. In fact, it's just snacks and the best episodes. Not really a party at all."

She smiles. "Yeah, okay. Sounds fun."

I grin back at her. There's no way Brady can get out of it now. Asher can bring his DVD's as insurance for all I care because I'm bringing Jessica as mine.

"Awesome. See you then," I say, waving at her over my shoulder.

By the time I make it to Psych, I've already channeled my inner depression. I even wore black jeans and a black sweatshirt. I would have thrown on some heavy black eyeliner, but my hair already seems really dark and my skin really pale, which is perfect.

Look at me. I'm a team player. Who says I don't have school spirit?

Asher sits at his desk, chatting up Jen and April as if they might actually have something interesting to say. I don't interrupt him because I suspect he's really asking the interview questions Mrs. Jarvis suggested.

I've already figured out what April's disorder is. It wasn't hard. Trust me, her acting abilities could use some work. She "suffers" from delusional paranoia. All through class, she prattles on about the leprechauns coming to steal her lucky charms, and I'm not kidding, either.

I take out my notebook and open to a new page. My pencil squeaks as it lays down doodle after doodle in the margins. My pencil is a piece of me, undirected and free. I let it roam as I eavesdrop on the interview playing out before me. One of the lines becomes a design of thorny vines. They reach up and snake around a sword that bears a remarkable likeness to Asher's. I flip the page before he can see. Then I draw a ghost with pale blond hair and grey eyes. On his face is a lightning-shaped mark. I look at the sketch in awe. Even with the wrist brace, the lines are clear and hardly blurred. It looks so real.

"Jac, right?" Asher says, startling me.

"Um. It wasn't supposed to be," I admit. Maybe my voice sounds shaky, but I don't care.

"Well it looks just like him. You're really good at that. Of course," he adds in a mocking tone, "I could show you a few things. My sketches are sublime, I must say."

I nod, thinking. Asher "suffers" from Narcissism. It's blatantly obvious. I file that away for later use. Of course, that could just be how Asher is. Outside of class, it might be called confidence. No wonder I didn't figure it out before.

I still haven't placed Jen, which means I have to pay more attention to her than usual. Exactly what I don't want to do. Just being in close proximity of her makes my blood boil. I'm not normally a jealous person, but I've also never had a reason to be jealous before.

Aside from her flirty ways, I'm totally stumped, and since Mrs. Jarvis doesn't seem the type to assign someone with a "slut" disorder, I'm doubly so. Maybe the hints lie in her words. I close my eyes and focus on the little girl voice she uses around guys. Do they really find that endearing? To me it sounds like someone's letting the air out of a balloon excruciatingly slow.

"Asher," she says. "Did you get the notes from History? I could really use some help."

"Of course I did. Don't I always?" The fabric of his shirt whispers against itself as he stretches his arms above his head. "I'm meticulous like that."

"Great. You're sure they're right, aren't you?"

He scoffs. "I'm always right. It's one of my most admirable qualities. One of many."

"Well, as long as they are accurate, I would love to borrow them."

I shake my head, trying to think past the flirtation. Everyone else's disorders are extremely obvious. So why am I having such a hard time with hers? I'll tell you why: it's because I've grown used to blocking her out.

"I feel," Asher continues, "that only my notes would be accurate enough to help my lesser peers."

A laugh explodes out of me, shattering my angsty façade. Asher looks over and grins haughtily.

"You're sure I can borrow them?" Jen clarifies.

"Yes."

"You're positive?"

"I'm always positive." He doesn't look at her. He stares at me like he's trying to convey some message.

I try not to smile.

"So, Nicoletta," he says only to me. "What are your plans this weekend? Would you be enjoying the honor of my company?"

Time for aggressive acting. I have to make up for breaking character. It's only fair.

I clear my throat and say in a small voice, "I don't know. I don't plan that far ahead."

He stretches his arm across the back of my chair. Jen glares at him.

"Pity that." He traces circles on his desk dismissively. "I plan every day in advance. I wake up every morning knowing how blessed I am to live another day being me."

"I wish I could be someone else. I hate being me," I mumble, careful not to make eye contact.

"You should be more like me." He chuckles. "Life is great from where I stand. Of course, everyone loves me."

Not breaking into a laughing fit is one of the hardest things I've ever had to do. His acting is just so thick.

"Oh Nicky," Jen chimes in. It doesn't bother me when my friends call me that; however, Jen is not my friend. Actually, she is the bane of my existence. She should call me Miss Dubois. "I wanted to thank you for going out with Taylor."

Asher's head swivels back and forth from her to me. Slowly, he removes his arm from behind me. He's broken character. That's not good. I reach under his desk and tap his knee in reminder.

"Alex and I really appreciate it and you'll love Taylor. He's such a great guy. A true friend."

It feels like someone just dumped ice water down my back.

She rambles on. "We do appreciate it. So thank you. I really think you'll hit it off. I just wanted to make sure to say... you know, thank you."

I stare at her. Asher's attention is on anything except for the conversation playing out right now. April mumbles something about her pen disappearing. She's sure someone took it.

"Who's Taylor? He probably took my pen," she mutters to herself.

"Actually," I say, my voice dripping with venom, "I haven't agreed to anything yet."

She smiles, her eyes flitting from Asher to me and back. He stares off somewhere toward the window with a look of unabated rage. "Well, I'm sure you will."

What the hell is that supposed to mean? I'm tempted to ask, but that means I would have to keep up this awful conversation with Satan's child. Deliberately, I turn in my chair and focus all my attention on Asher to bring him back to the game. "So what are you doing this weekend?"

He doesn't look up. "Any weekend is perfect as long as I can be with myself," he says, but his heart is no longer in it.

I know Asher doesn't like the idea of Jen and Alex pimping me out any more than I do, but his reaction has me baffled, especially since I haven't even agreed. I turn back to my notebook, flip the page, and write at the bottom: What's wrong? Then I tap my pen against the page repeatedly like I'm thinking.

He glances over before looking down. His mouth forms the word, *Later*.

The bell rings. End of a school day. On to the weekend. Two glorious short days before Monday.

"See you guys at Brady's on Saturday," Jen says, beaming.

I look to Asher in horror. But did I really think that Brady would have a party – any type of party – without inviting everyone he knows? Well, no. But I hoped.

"You know there's a theme now, right?" Asher asks her.

"No. What is it? I love themes." She smiles, showing her perfect white teeth through bubblegum pink lipstick. I remember the Playboy Bunny costume she wore for Halloween. It wasn't really a costume, more like a bra and panties with a cotton tail and big fluffy ears. My stomach rolls at the thought.

Asher picks up his books and then automatically loads my notebook into my bag like it's a normal, everyday occurrence. "It's a *Supernatural* party so everyone is dressing up like a supernatural creature to watch the seasons," he says.

Jen's smile fades. She's not happy about that. "Oh. Really?"

"Yeah." He nods. "If you guys can't make it, though, I'm sure Brady will understand."

A fake smile replaces the faded one. "No, we'll be there." Her eyes zero in on me. "But I doubt Alex and I will be watching the show if you know what I mean."

It takes all my strength not to hit her. I want to scream and go crazy ninja on her ass, but somehow I manage no reaction. My expression is empty.

"See you there," she says. She turns and walks out of the room, swaying her hips all the while. Whether for Asher's or my benefit, it's hard to tell.

"What a bitch. Come on," he says, wrapping an arm around my shoulder to lend comfort. "I'll drive you home."

I move mechanically with him. I'm afraid to bend. My heart might shatter. I have to get it together before we get to the car. Otherwise, I may have to explain and I don't want to talk about it. Definitely not with Asher anyway.

Chapter 15

"Costumes?" I ask in terror. "No one told me we had to dress up."

"We don't," he says, smiling mischievously.

I laugh. "You're a dick."

"Am I?"

We've been sitting in front of my house for close to an hour. Thirty minutes ago, he turned off the car. Both cars are in the driveway. My parents must have gotten home early. They must have entered the realm of happy sometime after the storm blew over. The thought alone makes me want to hurl.

"Nah," I respond, still laughing.

Asher says, "Maybe they won't come."

I need to change the subject before we start having the heartfelt talk I've been avoiding since we left school. The clock on the dash reads three forty-five. I wonder if I should get out of the car and let him go.

"Don't you have to work?" I ask, gesturing at the time.

He shakes his head. "No. I don't work again until Monday."

"You get that much time off at a movie theater? Aren't the weekends supposed to be, like, super busy?"

"They are. We have three projectionists. The other ones don't like to work weekdays," he shrugs. "So I get weekends off. I'm fine with it."

"Oh." I pick at the gauze on my hand. Peeling off the bandage sounds really appealing. "Do you need to go?"

He leans his head back against the seat. The muscles in his neck look like they might jump through his skin. The knob in his throat bobs up and down in a steady rhythm. "Not really. Do you?"

Something like a scoff comes out of my mouth. "I'm not going in there. Actually," I pause, trying to organize my words, "I thought about going to the hospital. When I talked to Spencer's mom, she said he hadn't had any visitors. That's just doesn't seem right, you know?"

He looks at me sideways, his eyes reading something in my face.

I add quickly, "If I were in the hospital, I would want someone to visit me. He may be an asshole, but he's a person, too."

Asher's voice softens to almost a whisper. "I'd visit you."

The tone in his voice sends a warm rush down my spine. I shift uncomfortably against the seat. "Thank you, but I'm sure a lot of Spencer's friends would have said the same thing."

He hesitates then nods. "You make a good point."

"Trust me, I really wish I didn't. But it seems like the right thing to do."

"Then I'll take you. Save Brady the trip."

"You sure?"

He nods and turns the key in the ignition. "He's got a party to plan." Glancing over his shoulder once, he pulls away from the curb. I notice that when he shifts, the Jeep responds like a cat would to a good petting. If I could drive a manual like that, I'd feel like a badass. He just seems tense.

"If you want to drop me off, you can," I tell him. "I can find a way back."

He smiles tightly, a thin curve to his lips. "And make you miss out on my company? Never."

"Wow." I shake my head in mock incredulity. "Psych's over. You can drop the act."

"Was I that transparent?"

"I don't know," I say. "I haven't figured you out yet."

"What's there to figure out?"

I try not to look at him. "Where to start? First, you play basketball, but aren't enthralled by any sport other than Hockey, and you spend all your time at school with Brady and me – so not a jock thing to do. So why play a sport you care nothing about?"

While maneuvering a perfect U-turn, he says, "That's easy. I'm looking for a scholarship."

"To?" I prod.

He shrugs. "Don't know yet. Waiting to see if I get any offers."

"So I was right. You don't care about basketball."

"Not particularly, no."

"Then why don't you quit?"

He lets out a long breath. "I'm good at it. I didn't expect to go to college. I just always figured I'd go into the family business. My...," he pauses as if he's trying to come up with a word, "dad decided to switch jobs. So if I'm going to college, it's on my own dime."

"But you're good at school, too. Couldn't you just get a scholarship because of your grades?" I pause then ask, "Is this too personal?"

"No." He slams on the brakes to avoid hitting a cat sitting in the middle of the road. His arm reaches out and braces me to the seat, which would be fine if I was a guy, but I have boobs and his forearm is pressed up against them. He snatches his arm back with an apology.

I don't mind, honestly, but I'm not about to tell him that. His ego is big enough. I don't need to feed it anymore.

"Anyway." He turns the Jeep left on to the main road using only one his left hand on the steering wheel. "In theory, I could get a scholarship based on my grades if I were a four-point-oh student. Regrettably, I am not."

"What are you then?"

"Three-point-eight-nine."

A breath whistles out through my teeth. "That sucks."

"Seriously."

"You know," I say, feigning authority. "If you didn't sluff school with us hoodlums, you might have a four-point-oh."

He laughs.

A tangent forms in my head. I grab onto the tail end and let it pull me along. "Seriously, though. You shouldn't spend so much time doing something you don't like to do. There are always grants and student loans – that type of thing."

He glances at me out of the corner of his eye. "And what about you? Don't tell me you actually want to go out with Jen's ex-boyfriend. Why would you waste time on something you don't want to do?"

He has a point. Just the thought of going out on a blind date gives me dry heaves, and every time I hear Jen or Alex say his name, my skin itches like a million fire ants have been using me as a snack bar. "First of all," I say, lifting a finger defiantly, "I haven't agreed to go out with anyone yet."

"But you haven't said no."

"That's true," I concede.

"So why even consider it?"

I take a long breath. The answer is as true as it is embarrassing. "Because Alex asked me to."

He sighs unhappily. "Do you always do everything Berkley asks you to?"

"No," I say in defense, but I know I'm lying. If Alex asked me to jump off the diving board at a public pool naked, I'd do it. Hell, I did do it. Two summers ago, a game of Truth or Dare got out of hand. There was a lot of alcohol involved, too. Yep, it was that summer that I threw up at the pool. All because Alex kept passing me shots. Quietly, I amend, "Fine. Yes."

Asher bursts out with a harsh laugh.

"What?"

He shakes his head, still laughing. "And I can't even get you to go to a dance with me despite the fact that you are forever indebted to me."

"I'm not forever indebted," I say, rubbing my face to hide the color staining my cheeks.

"Not yet, but you will be."

The road opens up to two-lanes. The hospital is two lights away. Not much time to finish Q and A with Asher.

"Why do you even want me to go? And don't give me some bullshit about making sure I taste everything high school has to offer either."

"That's not it," he admits with a half shrug. "I want to go, but I don't like anyone else in our class. It's either you or my sister."

"Oh Asher," I say, holding a hand to my chest theatrically and feigning a swoon. "I'm so flattered." The thumping of my heart actually hurts.

He looks at me with an unreadable expression before he turns back to the road just in time to take the middle lane. His blinker clicks in the silence as we wait for our turn to enter the parking lot.

"That sounded wrong," he hedges. "What I meant to say is that I like you. I'd like to think of you as a friend."

"We are friends," I agree. My heart begs him to shut up with each painful beat.

"You're so easy to be around. You don't expect anything from me. You're just…," he trails off, looking for the right words.

I've heard this speech so many times I could give it to myself. Ruefully, I say, "I know. I'm just one of the guys." And my heart opens up and bleeds out.

That seems to confuse him. He pulls into a parking spot and gets out without another word. I fumble with my door handle uselessly.

A second later, he opens the door and offers me his hand. When I'm on the ground, he leans in and whispers, "Not what I was going to say."

I have this strange urge to run my fingers along the bone of his jaw. What is going on with me?

"What, then?" I ask, breathlessly. His face is so close to mine I can feel the warmth of his cheek. My knees wobble a little.

He shakes his head. His lips brush across my ear. He rests his temple against my hair. "Another time. Let's get this shit over with."

We walk in silence all the way to the information booth. Blood rushes loudly in my ears.

"Spencer Adams," I tell the little old lady at the desk. She's a total grandma type. Just being near her makes me think of warm chocolate chip cookies and smell peppermints.

"Hang on a second, dear." She turns to her computer and expertly types in a few keys. "Oh yes. He's in room two-fourteen. The elevators are that way." She points one wrinkled finger down the hall.

"Impressive," Asher tells her. "My grandmother is still learning how to use a typewriter that well."

I shoot him a warning look. Most women wouldn't consider that a compliment. No woman likes to be reminded of their age after twenty-five.

But she smiles sweetly and says, "Thank you." And she's sincere. Weird.

"Excuse me," I cut in. "Could you also give me an update about two of the girls from my school? They both came in this week."

"Sure, honey, what school do you go to?"

"Olympus."

"Oh yes," she says. "We have had three students picked up from there this week alone. What is going on over there?"

My stomach feels hard as a rock. "Three?" I ask.

"Yep, one came in just an hour ago, in fact. Unfortunately, they are still in admitting so I cannot discuss anything until after they sign a release."

I give Asher a startled look. Three students from our school, not including Spencer, all end up in the same hospital. That doesn't seem like a coincidence. That seems more like an epidemic.

Asher's eyes fixate on something over my shoulder. I turn my head, but can't figure out what it is he's staring at. Unless he has a sudden fascination with water fountains that I know nothing about.

The woman's fingers tap over the keys. "Names?" she says. I nearly jump. "I'm sorry, what?"

"You asked for an update on the girls from your school. What are their names?"

I rack my brain, trying to remember their last names, but all I can come up with is, "Lisa? And Ashley Marinello."

The woman chuckles. "Do you have a last name for Lisa?"

I'm about to tell her that I haven't the foggiest idea what Lisa's last name is when I get a strange urge. I open my mouth and the name "Tannis" falls out.

Her manicured nails tap against the keyboard again.

"Maybe I was wrong," Asher says quietly. "Maybe you do know everyone at the school."

I smack him playfully in the arm as if to say, "You're such a kidder." It's all an act for Miss Information Lady, but in all reality, I have no idea how I knew Lisa's last name. I've never met her before in my life.

"Now, It seems Miss Marinello has been diagnosed with a rare lung infection while Miss Tannis is being treated for seizures, pneumonia, and possible liver failure," she reports.

I stare at her as if she is speaking gibberish. Liver failure? Really? I mean, I may have only seen this girl in P.E., but she's not really the partier type. If anything, she should have the heart condition while Spencer Adams suffers from liver failure.

While I'm busy swapping diagnoses in my head, Asher thanks the woman and pulls me by the left hand down the hall.

After we step onto the elevator, I turn on him. "Does any of this seem weird to you?"

"What? That there might be sick people at our school during flu season?" he jests. There's an under-tone to his voice, though, that tells me he thinks this whole situation is as weird as I do.

I'm still trying to think of an adequate response when the doors ding open. At a straight shot down the hall stands a man dressed in scrubs. He's not moving, just standing there like he's waiting for something. A chill pierces through me.

I gasp and smack Asher in the chest with my brace. "Asher," I say, pointing down the hall at the man.

"Damn it, Nicky, that brace is half metal, you know," he replies, rubbing at the center of his chest. He looks up, but just before he does, the man turns his pale blond head and disappears into a room.

"What?" He leans this way and that trying to make out what I'm pointing to. But no one's there. Not anymore. "What am I looking at?" he asks.

I wave my hand like I could wipe the image away. "Never mind."

"Who was it? You sounded panicked." He rests a hand on my shoulder and turns me toward him.

A long jagged breath. "Jac. I thought I saw Jac. He was coming out of Spencer's room."

Chapter 16

Mrs. Adams is happy to see us. So happy, in fact, that she offers us one of the ten cups of pudding she brought back from the cafeteria.

I tell her it isn't necessary, but when that woman puts her mind to something, she doesn't let go. So off she goes to retrieve us two extra spoons.

Asher and I are left alone with the sleeping body of Spencer Adams. His face has gotten plump since I last saw him. Actually, all of him has. I wonder if it's the heart medication. I hear that stuff can produce some wicked side effects.

The room is overflowing with Mrs. Adams' luggage, bottles of water, toiletries, blankets and cards. I glance at one. From the basketball team. Spencer is second-string.

Handing it to Asher, I ask, "Did you know about this?"

He reads it, his eyes going wide. "Nope. No one mentioned it. But apparently I signed it. Wasn't that so nice of me?"

As I fiddle with more cards, I realize just how irritated I am. Sure, Spencer shouldn't have been drinking, but I couldn't possibly be the only one who knows of his condition, can I? If nothing else, the coach has to know what his limitations are. I've had to provide a note to each and every one of my P.E. teachers to notify them of my asthma so surely Spencer has to tell them that he could die of a heart condition at any time.

I look at the monitor standing like some sort of guardian next to the bed. The heartbeat sounds too slow and deliberate. My own heartbeat is running at racecar speeds in comparison. Placing my finger over my pulse, I count two of my heartbeats to each of his.

What am I doing? I'm probably just being paranoid. If the nurses aren't worried then why should I be?

"So you really think you saw Jac?" Asher says conversationally.

"I don't know. I saw something, or rather, someone. They were wearing scrubs, though." I slide a bag off of one of the chairs and plop down in the seat. The room smells of alcohol and other medical supplies. Where is Mrs. Adams? Suddenly, I want to go.

"Maybe it was a doctor," he suggests.

I run a hand through my still cold hair. Using my fingers, I bounce it up and down on my back to separate it so it can warm up. "Maybe."

I wonder if Spencer can hear us. Some doctors say that comatose patients can still make sense of the outside world. So you should always offer words of encouragement. But I have nothing encouraging to say. It's like he's lifeless, just waiting to move on.

Asher folds a strewn blanket over the chair next to me. Then he sits down. "So what's wrong with him?"

"I don't know what you mean," I lie.

"This is not alcohol poisoning. I know you know. So what is it?"

Can I tell him? It's not really my secret to tell. But if Brady can trust Asher with the secret of his sexual preference, then maybe, just maybe, I can trust him, too.

"He has a heart condition," I tell him. "His mom says he's on the transplant list. So, basically, the dumbass shouldn't have been drinking."

"Oh god." He wraps an arm around my shoulder. I bury my face into his shirt. When I pull back, it's wet. "Are you crying?"

I sniff. "No."

He doesn't say anything witty like I would expect him to, just pulls me back into the warmth of his chest. His hand wraps around my neck, cradling me. "I'm sorry. I didn't know."

With the sleeve of my sweatshirt, I wipe my eyes. "It's like, we're not even friends, you know? I mean, not really. But no one else can spare the time and for some reason, I feel awful about that. What is wrong with people?"

He rocks me a little, back and forth. "Where do you want me to start?"

The sound of heels on the linoleum floor shakes me out of it. I sit up straight and wipe my eyes one last time.

Asher still has one hand on my back, but he's looking at Spencer's monitors now. His eyebrows tighten into a concentrated line and something like worry crosses his face.

The door opens and Mrs. Adams walks in holding a handful of spoons. It's nice to see that staying in a hospital hasn't broken her spirit. She's dressed in her regular work clothes. More power to her. I'd be wearing pajamas.

"So I have chocolate and tapioca. I hope that's alright," she says with a motherly smile.

"Either one is perfect," I say, but I'm actually wondering how Spencer can be such an asshole with Mrs. Adams for a mom. I'll bet his parents almost never fight, and if they do, I bet it's about something cute like who loves who more.

Asher eats his pudding in silence. My throat is still thick from tears. Each bite is saltier than the last so I nibble at it slowly.

"It's so good of you kids to come. Spencer would love to see that his friends care enough to visit."

I'm quick to respond before Asher can correct her. I can't imagine she would respond so well to Asher's "We're not really friends" speech. "Seriously," I say, "it was our pleasure. How is he doing, by the way?"

She sits down on the edge of the hospital bed. The room looks enormous around her; she just looks so small and frail. "Well, the new medication is stabilizing him, but I'm afraid he still has a long way to go. We pray." She chokes on a sob. "But sometimes, just sometimes, I wonder if God is listening."

"I'm sure He is." I say to comfort her. My parents are Mormon just like the majority of this state, but I adopted the belief that God has more important things to do than listen to me a long time ago, and really, it would be selfish of me to expect Him to care about my problems while wars rage on and children are dying of cancer.

She smiles so I know I said the right thing. "I just wish He wasn't so mysterious all the time."

I try to laugh. It comes out sounding like a derisive snort. "Don't we all?"

For this being the first time Asher has ever met the woman outside of school, he is doing remarkably well. He finishes his pudding and tosses it like a basketball into the garbage can. It goes in. Nothing but net.

"I'm sorry, but we should probably get going," I say, standing up. I don't toss my pudding cup toward the garbage can. I walk it over. Knowing my luck, I'd miss and leave an unsightly pudding splatter down the wall.

"Of course," Mrs. Adams replies, her tone oozing sadness. "You kids probably have a date or something planned."

I blush. "Actually…" I don't know what to say, so I leave the word hanging in the air like a forgotten thought.

"Asher, it was so nice to see you outside of school," she tells him.

He nods. "It was nice to see you, too. I just wish it was under better circumstances."

I stare at him. Does he have a book that tells him what to say around women older than him? I didn't see How to be Prince Charming sitting on his nightstand. Could be shoved under the pillow, I guess.

"If you need anything," I repeat for what feels like the millionth time to regain my ground, "anything at all, don't hesitate to call, okay?"

She steps forward and envelops me in an awkward hug. Her arms are tight. "Oh Nicoletta. You are such a dear."

Spencer's heart monitor goes silent for a second. Collectively, we hold our breaths. Mrs. Adams' arms tremble around me. I picture nurses and doctors rushing in like on all those medical dramas my mother used to watch. In my mind, they push us out the door as Spencer flat lines. My heart races. Oh god. Could this be it?

But just then, the beeping continues at a non-rhythmic pace.

With a trembling hand, Mrs. Adams wipes a tear from the corner of her eye.

I squeeze her shoulders one last time then release her. Her arms cross over her chest a second before she turns to face her son. Once her back is to me, I reach for Asher's hand and guide him out the door.

In the hallway, Asher dips his head close to my ear. "Are you okay?"

I shake my head. "Not really. It's weird to me that a woman so sweet could have a son who puts her through so much shit. I doubt my parents would even notice if something was wrong with me and they definitely wouldn't be camping out at the hospital."

Asher shrugs and wraps an arm around my shoulders, guiding me down the hall toward the elevators. "You never know until it happens. I'm sure you're wrong, though."

I roll my eyes. "Yeah, sure."

We pass by a long counter with nurses bustling around behind it. There's no rest here at the hospital on a Friday night. Asher steers me forward just as the elevator doors are getting ready to close.

"Hold the elevator, please," I say, reaching out as if I could stop it with my sheer force of will.

The doors ding once then yawn open.

Standing inside the box is Seth Baldwin, a guy I recognize as a senior from our school. He's wearing a heavy black hooded sweatshirt with a giant green "O" imprinted on it and a pair of baggy jeans. His hair pokes out the bottom of his green beanie and he stares at his shoes. When he looks up, his mouth twitches into a half smirk. Of course it would. He was at the pool that one time.

"Nicoletta," he says by way of greeting.

The light on the first floor button is already lit up. Asher presses it again anyway.

"Fancy seeing you here," I reply. "Wait, what are you doing here?"

He points to the visitor badge adhered to the right side of his shirt. "Visiting my sister. She was just admitted."

"Oh my god. What happened?" I ask, racking my brain for his sister's name. Seth and I were never really friends. Not for any real reason other than the fact that our groups seemed to orbit around each other rather than mingle.

"She passed out in the middle of school. By the time the nurse got there, she had a hundred-and-four fever. They aren't sure what happened yet. I'm sure she's fine. Steph has a tendency to overdo it at times," he explains.

"I'm so sorry to hear that. I hope she gets better quickly."

The elevator door dings open. Asher extends an arm through the gap and gestures outside the box with a bob of his head. He has a strange expression on his face: like he might have swallowed something really bitter.

"Thanks," Seth says, stepping off the elevator and pointing down the opposite hall. "I'm this way. See ya around."

I stand there for far too long, watching as yet another acquaintance disappears down a hospital hallway, until long after he is gone.

Asher touches the small of my back with his hand and I jump.

"Whoa there, Tiger," he says.

I don't look at him. "So what do you think are the odds that four people from the same school, all relatively close to the same group, come down sick?" I ask him. "And no, I'm not talking about the common cold or normal winter sicknesses. I'm talking debilitating diseases."

I feel silly for asking. If I were speaking to Alex, he would tell me to get real and laugh at my naivety. If he were Brady, he would shrug it off as a conspiracy theory. Not positive responses and they are two of my best friends. There's no telling how Asher will respond.

So I'm nearly blown away when Asher cants his head to the side and regards me with smoldering eyes. "Pretty limited," he admits. "But the real question is: what you think the chances are?"

He may be right. That may be the real question.

And hell if I know the answer.

Chapter 17

My parents are at it again. Too much time spent together, I guess. You know how they say couples should go on vacation at least once a year to keep the spark alive? Well, I agree. But in this case, I think separate vacations would be appropriate.

In a few days, it will cool down, I hope. All of the bills are due before the fifteenth of the month. Their happy period should follow close behind. Go figure. Nothing, not even the pillow over my head will drown them out. I need a thicker door.

A loud shriek comes from the front room. Then a door slams. I wonder which of them left this time. I am not, however, curious enough to go check. In the past when I have emerged from my room to comfort whoever was still home, I've been treated like a traitor by the other parent for days – like I picked sides or something.

Tentatively, I go to the window. My father's car is the only car left in the driveway. So it was my mother who left this time. She'll do what she always does and go to the store. Shopping is therapy. Good thing, too. We are getting dangerously low on caffeine. They may not drink coffee, but I do, and they usually keep me pretty well stocked. I wonder if it would be bad taste to call her and ask her to pick up some good creamer. Something named after an ice cream flavor perhaps. Probably shouldn't. I wouldn't want to risk getting caught in the crossfire.

I turn on the bedside table lamp since the light isn't bright enough to cast a glow under my bedroom door. I sit on my bed with my legs crossed under me and drop my face into my hands. Usually after one of their episodes, I would call Alex. He would listen to me ramble about mundane things, knowing all the while that something bigger was brewing underneath the surface. Then he would wish me a good night, and as if he performed some great miracle, I would then be able to sleep. I realize that it's been about a week since we last talked on the phone. Something seems wrong about the fact. He's my best friend. We should talk.

I grab my phone off the nightstand and call him. No answer. Frustrated, I throw the phone into my blanket and flop down onto my pillow. After a good muffled scream, I notice my phone has been ringing with a familiar song.

Scrambling to get to the screen, I finally manage to answer. "Alex?" I croak. Screaming always does that to my voice.

Background music thrums so loud, I almost can't hear him. "Yeah, what's up? You alright?"

My fingers find the end of the blanket and absently tug at a loose strand. "Yeah, just wondering what you are up to."

"What?" he yells.

"What are you up to?" I ask loud enough that my dad can probably hear me in the next room.

"Hey, Nic," he says as if he can't hear me. "I'm at a show right now. I'll call you later, okay?" Then the line goes dead.

I stare at the phone like it committed some terminal offense. My chest burns. I didn't even know there was a concert in town. Why wouldn't he invite me? The answer is obvious, even if I don't want to believe it. He didn't invite me because he's with Jen. I find myself wishing I hadn't turned down Asher's offer to go out.

***

I was quiet the whole way back from the hospital. Asher didn't ask why. He just let me stew. It felt horrible knowing that my silence wasn't out of respect for Spencer, Ashley, Lisa, or Steph. No, I was too busy agonizing over Jac's presence at the hospital. Why does he always seem to appear when something bad is happening? And furthermore, why do I feel like there are insects crawling through my skin whenever he is around?

"Everything okay?" Asher said when I didn't jump out of his car. I nodded, but didn't offer more.

"You want to go do something else? We could go out. I happen to know someone who works at the movie theater and could probably get us in for free," he said with a wink.

I thought about it, but all I wanted to do was be alone. My bed was the only comfort I thought I could handle. I shook my head. "No thanks."

"Alright," he said. He sounded worried as if he was afraid I might go inside and hurt myself or something. "Let me know if you change your mind."

"Thanks. You really don't have to make me your charity case, though. I'll be fine."

His eyes shifted toward me then to the steering wheel. I took that as my hint to let him go. The only way he could have been less subtle is if he was staring at the clock and counting down the seconds.

"Thanks for the ride and for going with me. I really appreciate it," I said, forcing the door open. Then I climbed out and walked inside without another glance back. I still don't know why my chest hurt so much when he didn't respond. Maybe because I knew I was right.

For a fleeting moment, I think about calling Asher, but right now, it might kill me to get brushed off again. Once in a night is more than enough for me. I know of one person who won't turn down a call from me, though, and he should be home getting ready for the party. Nothing I can't interrupt. My fingers find the number and make the call before I even finish the thought.

"There is no way you are cancelling on me, Kitten," Brady answers. He doesn't ever say "Hello." This is as close as he gets. It's like he makes it a point to answer his phone in such a way that it feels like we are in the middle of a conversation. He'll say something like, "The most awkward thing ever…," or "And why do I even bother…" or anything really, but never just a good old-fashioned greeting.

I would never admit this to him, but I love him for it. There's no better way to feel like you are always in contact with someone then to have a string of conversations on pause, waiting to be resumed.

"I'm not calling to cancel," I respond. Thank God for Brady, the perpetual leaning post. "What's up?"

"Just—" He's interrupted when something falls and clatters to the floor on his end of the line. "Shit. Sorry. Just getting the place ready for tomorrow night. I want it to be Dean-worthy," he emphasizes.

"The only way it will be Dean-worthy," I counter, "is if I'm there. Are you alone?"

He lets out a loud, sardonic laugh. "Yeah, I'm alone and mostly decent, too. Why?"

"Sorry. No reason," I apologize.

"Eh. It's alright. By the way, I looked for you after school. I heard Asher took you home."

I fiddle with the tie from my sweatshirt. The long lace is tied into a knot that resembles something very close to a noose on either side of my hood. "Actually, we went to the hospital," I admit.

"The hospital? Did you get hurt again or were you just looking for an empty bed?" he asks, with a chuckle.

I'm not surprised he would think that. Though, I probably should be. "Oh shut up."

Now that I'm more relaxed, I lie back down and roll to my side. Tacked to my wall is a *Supernatural* throw blanket I found on the internet a few months ago. Sam and Dean lean up against Dean's muscle car and stare at me with serious expressions.

"You have to admit," says Brady. "Asher Rowan is delicious."

"I don't have to admit anything."

"Okay. Then you can't deny it." The sound of tape tearing away from the roll catches my ear.

"What are you doing for this thing anyway?" I ask, not really sure I want to know the answer.

"Oh, no. You are not spoiling the surprise, and besides, you're changing the subject. Why did you go to the hospital?"
I kind of wish I hadn't called him now, but I guess it's too late to take it back. I sigh loudly. "We went to see how Spencer was doing." Brady chokes on whatever he's drinking in the silence. "You mean Speenis?"

"Yeah," I respond quietly. We came up with that nickname last year. When I said I didn't like him, I wasn't joking.

"Can I ask why?"

153

I take a deep breath. "If you can tell me why Jac might have been at the hospital."

"Jac?" he repeats. "My Jac?"

"The one and the same."

There's a long pause before Brady says, "Impossible. He had to work tonight."

"I swear I saw him," I argue.

"Nic. I talked to him after school. He was in Provo. How could he have gotten down here and back in time for work? It's like a forty-five minute drive."

"He works in Provo?" I ask. I know deep down to my bones that I saw him. It had to be him. Birthmarks are identifiable traits, aren't they? However, for Brady's sake, I'm willing to hope for reasonable doubt.

"Well, yeah. Why wouldn't he? He lives there so I would assume."

"Assume?" I cut in. "So you don't know for sure?"

"Well, no," he says defensively. "Look, Nicky, if you don't like him, just tell me." He sounds so hurt. Like me hating his boyfriend would be the worst thing to ever happen. If that's the case then I can pretend Jac doesn't give me a case of the shudders. First and foremost, I want Brady to be happy.

"It's not that. Forget it. It's just been a long night. I'm projecting," I lie.

As far as I'm concerned, lying is only acceptable in three situations: (1) when your parents are about to tear each other's throats out in front of you, making you the only witness; (2) when you're about to break someone's heart – and only if that someone's heart is good and fragile; and (3) when your life is on the line. Oh, make that four. It is absolutely okay to lie when you are trying to conceal your identity during a fight against evil to save all of mankind. That's the number one demon hunter rule on *Supernatural*. Can't forget that one.

"You know if you're that curious, you can ask him tomorrow night. He'll be here," Brady tells me.

"Yeah," I scoff. "I hear everyone will be there." Including Jen and Alex, but I don't pick them out specifically.

"A party isn't a party without a hundred of your closest friends."

"And how are you going to keep your secret if your boyfriend is around those friends?"

Brady makes a tsk-tsk noise. "Oh ye of little faith."

I turn off the bedside lamp, having found my exhaustion again. I roll into the covers and turn the television on. I know I won't be able to sleep until my mother gets home, but the second her car is in the driveway, I'm out.

"I'm going to bed," I announce. "It's been a long day."

Brady laughs. "Alright. Goodnight, Kitten. See you tomorrow."

Since there's no school tomorrow, I don't bother setting an alarm. To be honest, I don't really bother seeing where my phone lands among the covers either. I doubt anyone will call me anyway. Not that I would want to talk to them if they did.

The television projects an eerie blue glow into my room. I flip through the channels in hopes to find a cartoon that might lull me to sleep or something.

Instead, I find the news. Enlarged on my screen is a picture of a girl I recognize. I recognize her because I dreamt of her last night.

"Police have identified the victim as one Sarah Crocker," the reporter says into the screen. "At three o'clock today, Sarah was returning home from a trip to Nevada where she was featured on the popular television show, *Beyond the Curtain with Reverend Jimmy*. Her boyfriend, Brent Wilkes, said that the last he heard from Sarah was at eleven o'clock this morning when she called to check in. In his statement, he confirms that there was no reason to suspect foul play on either Sarah's part or an outside party. Though, he did state that Sarah's trip to Nevada was what she considered a pilgrimage."

A new face fills my screen. Brent Wilkes is a skinny man with a day and a half of stubble growing on his chin. He wears a red baseball cap turned backwards and speaks around a wad of chewing tobacco tucked inside his right cheek. He's not even crying.

155

"It never would have worked out between the two of you," I say, shaking my head at the screen. "She deserved so much better."

"Sarah was a good girl. We was set to be married come June," he says. He turns his head to the right and spits. "Sadly, her mental illness was just too strong. That's what took her, you know. Her brain fog."

I cringe. It's hard to reconcile Sarah's thoughts about Brent with the man – if you can even call him that – on my television screen.

The sound of my mother's car beeps in the driveway. I peek around the curtains to see out the window. I can't explain it, but I have to make sure she gets inside before shutting off my television and pulling the pillow back over my head. Sleeping through the yelling has never been a problem, but I would rather be prepared for the beginning of the battle.

The screaming and yelling never comes. There are no slammed doors or vases crashing to the floor, nothing breaking.

It's absolutely quiet.

So quiet, in fact, that it only takes me ten minutes to realize that there is no logical explanation as to why I would know who Sarah Crocker or Brent Wilkes is. There's no reason why I should know what the interior of her car looked like, and there's absolutely no reason why I should know what her last thoughts were before her car slammed into the barrier. Or that it did for that matter.

I pull the blankets around me, afraid to move from their safety.

What the hell is going on with me?

Does that mean the three girls from my school are going to die because I saw it on the newspaper?

Why is this happening?

And how do I make it stop?

Chapter 18

One o'clock, Saturday morn... er, afternoon.

It sucks that going to bed early can have an adverse effect on the body. Instead of waking up refreshed, I'm ready to slide back into a coma for a couple weeks. Then again, maybe that has something to do with the stress I've incurred over the past few days.

Either way, I have five hours to kill before going to Brady's house. The party doesn't actually start until nightfall, but Brady texted me late last night and asked that I come early. Being January, that means the guests should start showing up around seven-thirty. Give or take.

I glare at the reason why I'm awake. I could still be asleep if my cell phone wasn't so persistent. I ignore the call for the fourth time and pull the covers over my head. Just as soon as I fall back asleep, it rings again.

I finally give up and put the phone to my ear. "Yeah?" I growl into the receiver.

"Good morning, sunshine," Alex says from the other end.

That's not right. The ringtone was generic. As in: not his. I look at the number. "Where are you calling from, Alex?"

"Jen's cell. Mine died."

I roll my eyes, trying really hard not to combust with irritation. "What do you want?"

He clears his throat. "Sorry I didn't call you back last night."

I stay silent. I may be awake now, but I would rather not be.

"I, um...," he sputters. "Are you alright?"

"Never better," I lie. It sounds fake even to me.

I mentally pen "Don't Want to Talk About it" to the end of my list titled "Acceptable Reasons to Lie."

"Good." He doesn't sound like he believes it's good. "I mean, great. Did you need something?"

"Nope."

Silence opens like a chasm between us. I almost ask if he's still there, but realize how little I care if he is or not.

But then he says, "Great, so I'll see you tonight?"

When did it get so hard to have a nice friendly conversation with Alex? Yeah, I know. It happened when I broke the cardinal law of friendship and developed feelings for the bastard. It probably doesn't help that he's talking to me on Jen's phone. That alone makes it feel like she can hear everything we say.

"Yep."

"Good," he says.

"Great." I click the phone off.

My mind vibrates with irritation. Might as well get up now and get some cleaning done or something because there's no way I'm getting back to sleep now.

***

Just after dinner, I tell my parents about the party.

"You'll be safe?" my dad asks.

I wonder if he's talking about drinking and driving or carrying protection. Well, I don't have a car and I don't think we need to worry about boys throwing themselves at me so doesn't really matter either way. I shrug. "Of course I'll be safe."

"When will you be home?" my mom chimes in.

"Um. When do you want me home?"

She pushes her chicken around on her plate. She hasn't eaten much. They probably haven't made up after the fight. It's hard to eat when your sole focus is killing my father, I gather. She forces a bite into her mouth and chews thoughtfully.

"Well, as long as Brady can bring you home, I don't see why you should need a curfew," she says.

My mouth falls open almost comically. No curfew? What kind of sick dimension have I stepped into?

My father covers my hand with his. "You've been so responsible," he tells me. "Your grades are up and you haven't been out late in so long."

I don't remind him about my three o'clock entrance on New Year's. I'm not that stupid.

"I think you're old enough to decide when will be best to come home," he adds.

"Is this one of those parenting things?" I blurt out. "Where you tell me not to worry about it, but it's really a test, and if I don't show up at nine o'clock then I'm grounded for a month?"

My mother giggles. It's the most emotion she's shown all day. "No. It's not one of those parenting things."

That's when I get it. They aren't telling me to stay out all night. They're telling me not to be home too early. The fight must be over. Ew. Glad to.

"You should go out more often," my mother says, driving her point home. "When was the last time you went on a date?"

And there it is. "Mom," I whine. "Please."

My father jumps in. "You are a gorgeous girl, Colette. You should go on dates."

Now I know he's serious. That's the only time he ever calls me Colette. It's the nickname used by every relative before me. He tried like hell to stick me with it when I was little, but I'm just not a Colette. Hell, I'm hardly even a Nicoletta.

"Yes," my mother says. "You should do more than homework and basketball games. I know you hang out with Alex and Brady, but there must be some boy you like, hmm?"

Do they really want me to share the angst-ridden thoughts of teenage romanticism? I'm so not doing that. Not with my parents anyway.

"I have a date," I tell them, excited for the first time about Alex's little ploy. It may be an embellishment since I haven't actually agreed to the date, but if it will make them happy then I'm fine with letting on like this is all a good thing. "Alex set me up." I cringe, realizing that's exactly how I feel: set up. In the most foul use of the words.

They both grin. "That's great," my father says. I notice there's a twitch at the corner of his right eye like he isn't completely convinced this is a great thing. "When?"

"I don't know. There are still a few details to iron out." I place my fork on my half-finished plate. "Well, I better go." I get up from the table, scooping the remnants of my food into the garbage. The dish clangs in the sink as I turn on the water to rinse it off.

"I'll do that," my mother says. "You just go have fun."

I turn off the water, suddenly as eager to be out of the house as they are to have me gone.

"Love you," I call. I don't even bother to get my coat all the way on before I'm out of the house.

Brady's house is all done up like a haunted house by the time I get there. I have to duck under a black sheet just to get through the door. Not that I can see where the door is since all light bulbs have been replaced with black light.

I can't honestly say I'm scared. Not until Jac looks up at me from the couch anyway. The whites of his eyes and his hair glow in the light projecting an illusion that he's some sort of ghostly creature. He inclines his chin at me in lieu of a greeting then turns his focus back to the television.

The TV is already on, playing and replaying the title menu for the first season. The sound has been turned off, but I can hear the ominous theme music as if the volume were up to maximum decibels.

"What d'ya think?" Brady asks, gesturing around at all the decorations.

Unlit candles glow neon in the black light. Every bottle of liquor he selected for the evening is either clear or colored. Luminescent greens, blues and pinks announce the presence of at least thirty bottles.

"I see you're cutting back," I say when I see them.

Brady laughs. "Hardly. This is just what was left over from the last party."

I roll my eyes and turn, almost smacking into Jac who snuck up behind me. I let out a yelp. At least it wasn't a scream. Point one for me.

"I think the atmosphere in here has the desired effect," he says to Brady while focusing on my eyes so intently it feels like they might catch fire.

In an attempt to divert my eyes, I focus on Brady's attire instead. Wherever there is a particle of anything be it dust, ash, or liquid, it glows. My clothes do the same. He and I look like we've been standing in a snow storm, but Jac has no glowy orbs clinging to him. Only his hair, skin and eyes reflect the light. How does he do that? He must use really good detergent.

Jac catches me staring and a predatory smile splits his faced. I look away.

Black streamers hang from the corners, criss-crossing the ceiling. White-sheeted ghosts with shadow mouths in oval shapes cling to the walls. There is even a skeleton standing guard at each door. Brady must have pulled all the Halloween decorations out of the attic. I just hope he hasn't displayed any fake bugs. I really hate those.

Brady looks up from the punch bowl where he is mixing some crazy Witch's Brew-like concoction. "So how late are you here for, Kitten?"

I debate on informing him of my lack of curfew since doing so could be like tying my own noose and handing it to the hangman. I can't count how many times Brady has begged me to stay the night. Guaranteed he would try once more so he wouldn't have to take me home in the middle of the night.

"A while. Until I get tired or my curfew hits, whichever comes first."

"You want a drink then?" he asks, perching behind the counter in his kitchen. It's set up like an honest-to-god bar. The seats even swivel.

I sit in one of those seats and push off with my feet so I swing from side to side. "Sure. I'll have to switch to coffee soon, though."

"Of course. Wouldn't want you falling asleep. Already got it programmed."

Brady has one of those newer coffee makers. The kind I lust after. It's huge, metallic looking, programmable, has an espresso maker built in, and hooks up to the faucet so you don't ever have to fill the reserve yourself. If it could make dinner for me, I'd be in love. His parents don't skim on the coffee either. No sir. No generic brands for the McGowan's. They import their beans from Columbia and grind them personally. When I found out they did this, I asked them to adopt me. They laughed. I wasn't kidding. My parents don't believe in coffee.

"Great," I say, my mouth already watering over the wonderful aroma.

Brady hands me a bright pink liquid sloshing around in a glow-in-the-dark green cup. I take a drink and flinch.

"No good?" he asks, clearly offended.

I cough once, which does nothing to help the burn searing its way down my throat. "Strong. No worries, though."

He looks me over, his eyes pausing on my arms. "You alright there?"

And that's when I notice the scratches on my arms. I must have scratched the hell out of my arms when I wasn't paying attention. Some of the nail marks are really deep, too. I guess the brace wasn't enough of a hindrance to stop me. I sit on my hands and shrug.

Jac drops into the barstool next to mine. My skin reacts before I really notice. It feels like I've been standing outside in the cold too long only to step into an oven. I swivel the seat a little away from him. When that doesn't offer any improvement, I get up and walk around.

"Is there anything I can help you with?" I ask, turning circles on the carpet.

Jac and Brady are staring meaningfully into each other's eyes. I almost ask if this is pay back for making Brady the fifth wheel the other night, but I don't. I also don't ask how Brady can stand to be so close to Jac. The memory of his handshake makes me shudder.

"Nope," Brady says. "Just make yourself comfortable."

Which is worse: Being around my parents giving each other the "look" or Brady and Jac? It's a toss-up.

Just then, a dark-haired figure ducks under the black sheet and stands blinking in the new light. To me, he looks like an angel of mercy.

"Nice decorations," Asher remarks appreciatively.

"Thank you," Brady says. He smiles then looks at me and winks.

Good god. Is he going to be like this all night?

Asher strides over to me looking cool and kind of arrogant. I've noticed he always walks like that. It's as if the world around him doesn't even touch his radar.

"So you actually came?" He stops too close to me. His body heat swims over my skin, refreshingly warm after Jac's chill.

"I said I would."

"I still wondered."

I pretend to be offended, though he's probably right. I had a few moments when I thought about not coming. Like when I found out that Jen and Alex were invited and again when Brady told me that Jac would be here.

Brady walks around the bar and takes Jac's hand. Every nerve under my skin prickles again as if I were the one touching him.

"Well, you two have fun. We'll be back," he tells us before they breeze out the door.

I turn back to Asher. "Is it mating season or something?"

He laughs, but sobers when he realizes I'm serious. "Why?"

"Everyone has sex on the mind."

"Full moon?" he offers.

"Maybe."

"Would explain a lot." Asher walks into the kitchen, opens the fridge, and pulls out a Red Bull. Popping the top, he takes a nice long swig.

Too late, I catch myself smiling.

He stops mid-motion. "What?"

"They call us Caffeinds," I inform him. "You know, the people who can't go two full hours without some."

"Good name," he takes another swig. The knob in his throat bobs up and down with each swallow. "I like it."

For the first time, I notice Asher's clothes look tie-dyed with different shades of black under the light as if his shirt was some ragdoll creation of other black shirts at various stages of wear down.

Since I can't picture him wearing tie-dye, it seems odd.

He catches me eyeing the smooth expansion of his body.

Embarrassed, I cover myself by asking, "You not drinking?"

He shakes his head. "Not if I'm driving."

"You drank on New Year's," I point out.

He points a finger of the hand clutching the can at me. "But I didn't drive."

"Okay. So why tonight?"

"Aren't you the inquisitive one?" he says with a smirk.   "Maybe because I have a feeling that you'll want to leave early? This way, if you do, you don't have to walk."

Don't get me wrong, I'm flattered. But…, "What makes you think that?"

He shrugs and takes another drink. "Call it a hunch."

I let out something between an exaggerated sigh and a laugh before shaking my head and beginning the daunting task of rummaging through the kitchen. A strange look overtakes Asher's face when he sees me searching through the cupboards. There are a lot of spices, marinades, soups of all variety, and boxes of muffin and cake mixes. On top of the fridge is a line of cereal boxes. I take two turns in the kitchen. If I were a pantry door, where would I be?

"What are you doing?"

I stop mid-turn and resign myself to peeking in the fridge and freezer. "Looking for munchies. There's a lot of alcohol and no food. People need food when they drink or they get sick."

I yank a bag of bagel bites out of the freezer along with some potato skins, taquitos, and some frozen pastry things. Then I drop my findings onto the counter. In the light of the fridge, they looked appetizing. Now they just look cold and stale. I turn to flick the light on and run straight into Asher, who was standing behind me. For a moment, I'm stunned. He grabs my wrists so I won't plow through him. Even in reflex, he's gentle with my wrist splint. I am so caught off guard that my breathing hitches. My chest rises and falls against his, the line of his body matching mine.

He looks down at me and smiles, releasing his hold at the same time. "Sorry."

I use both hands to point around him like a moron. "Just getting the light so I can see."

He moves out of my way deliberately and bows with a flourish.

I step around him and flip the switch. The kitchen bulbs appear to be the only ones that haven't been replaced, I notice. The harsh white light spills around the room, blinding me. I stand there for a second, hand on the wall, blinking.

"Need some help?" he asks from too close behind me.

"Yeah. Can you help me find the damn pantry? There's got to be chips or popcorn or something in there."

I hear a creak and turn around. He holds a door open. It's so close to the refrigerator that the doorknob is hidden. Not where I would have been. You know... if I were a pantry door.

"Thanks," I tell him and step inside. A chain attached to a swinging bulb hangs high in the air. Too high for me to reach.

"Allow me," Asher says, reaching up to pull the chain.

When the room is lit, I almost gasp. The shelves are full with more cereal boxes, rows and rows of canned goods, and buckets labeled with names of generic cooking items – flour, sugar, yeast, rice. It looks like Brady's parents have stocked up for the apocalypse.

"Either these people like to shop or they aren't coming back," Asher muses.

"It's food storage," I explain. I select two boxes of microwavable popcorn, the good kind with butter, and shove them at Asher. Then I grab two bags of potato chips. There's a year's supply of Girl Scout cookies, too, so I toss a box of thin mints and the little peanut butter ones on top of the pile. Who doesn't like those?

I jostle the items in my arms to indicate that we are done in the pantry, which is actually more like a small bedroom. He pulls the chain again. Everything turns dark.

While arranging the items and preparing them, I realize I can feel Asher's shadow right next to me. It's like he's never heard of personal space before. I don't complain because his heat is comforting and I'm afraid that if I say something, he might back off. Yet every time I turn, there he is.

When the chips and popcorn are in bowls, the frozen food in the oven, and the cookies set out strategically on a platter, I relax against the bar.

"Tell me the truth," Asher says. "Are you keeping busy so you don't have to be alone with me?"

I stare at him then shake my head slowly. "What do you mean? We are alone."

"But," he drawls as he glides along the floor. When we are face to face, he props a hand on either side of the bar behind me. His breath stirs my hair. I look into his brown eyes glittered with gold and hesitate. His face hovers just above mine. If I breathe, we could touch.

"This is the first time you've stood still for almost an hour," he continues. His voice envelops me like smoke.

I blink against the effect. "I was getting snacks ready."

"No you weren't." His eyebrows arch accusingly. "You were avoiding me."

Honestly, the thought hadn't occurred to me. What reason would I have to avoid Asher? Well, aside from that hungry look in his eyes.

My stomach twists a little. Not in anticipation, but something more like need. What could I possibly need from him?

"Really, I'm not," I whisper. He's so close he could probably hear my thoughts if I was thinking really hard.

His face moves a little closer, his lips just above mine. I take in a deep breath. My lips brush his from the motion, and just like that, his body presses into mine and he's kissing me. It's not like I've never been kissed before, but not like this. Never like this. It's soft, yet furious. My stomach clenches tighter.

Asher is the first to pull back. His forehead presses against mine, his shoulders heaving up and down with each breath. In the dim light, I notice for the first time that there's a dark line just above Asher's eyebrow.

"Did you scratch yourself?" I ask.

And that's when Alex and Jen walk in.

"Nic," Alex says. Then he realizes what he walked in on. "Oh my god."

With my good hand, I nudge Asher's chest until he steps back. My lips feel bruised, marked from his. Carefully, I run my fingers across them. They even feel full. Great. That's not embarrassing at all.

"Where's Brady?" Alex asks, his words clipped with anger.

"Upstairs," I respond quietly. "We were just making snacks."

"Snacks? Is that what you're calling it? In that case, I would love some 'snacks,'" Jen says, covering her mouth to hide her giggles.

Asher hasn't even bothered to glance at them. His bemused look is fixed on me. The dark line is gone now, as if he just brushed it away.

The oven dings. I shake myself out of the situation and go to retrieve the munchies. A pot holder doesn't fit over the brace so I have to try to pull them out with my left hand without being burned.

Jen and Alex walk into the kitchen holding hands.

Maybe a little burn wouldn't be so bad.

Asher is at my side, taking the pot holder from me. "I'll do it," he says.

"I can…"

He holds his hands up. "I'll have better balance. No hospital visits tonight, remember?"

I know Asher's reference is about the last party. But by the red coloring in Alex's face, I assume he thinks the reference is to something else entirely. Like my wrist.

I close my eyes, willing the whole situation to go away. Unfortunately, when I open them, things are worse.

Brady and Jac have come into the hallway. Brady's face holds a glow unlike any I've ever seen on him before that has nothing to do with the black light. Jac is moving to the back door. For someone Brady met at a party, he sure is antisocial.

Alex stares daggers at Asher, who is purposely ignoring him.

How is this worse, you might ask?

The answer lies in what Jen is doing. She's turned toward Alex, putting her perfect ass toward me. Her arms are around his waist and her mouth at his ear. The whole situation has changed, yet at the same time, nothing is different.

At least I have the fortune of seeing that Jen took Asher seriously. Both she and Alex are in costume. Twin vampires. Oh joy. They both have fake plastic fangs. Alex is wearing a red ruffled shirt, black cape, tight black pants and boots. It's a new costume. I hope it cost a lot. Jen is wearing an old Victorian style dress. The kind you buy at a gothic clothing store for a hundred dollars. It's pretty, but it doesn't fit her well. She is a pink and yellow girl. The black and purple washes her complexion out. She doesn't look sexy; she looks sick.

I glance at Asher, who is trying extremely hard not to look at them. A smile pulls at his lips, though. He noticed, too. It's too much to hope that he may be smiling because of me.

"Nice outfit, man," Brady says, brushing past him. "What's the occasion? You going to a costume party after this?"

"I was under the impression that this was the costume party," Alex replies, eyes still glued on Asher.

All of the cookable items are out of the oven and Asher is setting them out on large pans. It's frustrating not being able to help.

Brady chuckles. "No, but that would have been awesome."

Alex's face pales, but his glower remains intact.

"What's this?" Brady says. He's finally noticed the buffet table we've made.

Asher waves at me, still not looking up from his task of arranging taquitos and potato skins.

I explain, "People drink without food, they get sick."

He nods in agreement. "Great idea. I'm kind of sick of girls puking on my floor and passing out in my bathroom."

I nod. That's the only movement I can bring myself to make. It may sound like I'm overanalyzing things, but it seems that if I move toward Alex, I'm rejecting Asher and vice versa. It's better to just stand still and hope they forget about me.

People arrive at a steady pace. I take the opportunity to greet Jessica and remove myself from the situation. First thing I notice is that she is with Dave Kelly, captain of the football team. If we were in the nineteenth century, she would be considered a fortunate girl to land a man of such status. But we aren't. And Dave is a bonafide jackass. I hope they're just friends. If not, I hope she breaks his heart.

Second thing I notice is that everyone is wearing jeans and t-shirts or sweatshirts. Except Alex and Jen. I smile.

Jessica's personality is too quirky to be annoying. She doesn't obsess over herself like most other girls. I'm sure she spends less time on makeup, hair and clothes than most girls – like Jen – do brushing their teeth. Not to say she is plain, because she isn't. Anything but, actually. Her corkscrew curly brown hair is highlighted. Not blond, but blue, and her face has that natural shine so many girls work for hours to achieve. But her eyes are what grab you. They are crystal clear and bright like blue diamonds.

Dave Kelly is neither cute nor funny in my opinion. But when he looks at her, you can see he wants to be. Unfortunately for him, beauty, intelligence and personality are not contagious.

"Hey Jess," I call out, booking it out of the kitchen.

"Hey," she responds with a bright smile. "Looks like Brady's reliving Halloween."

"Yeah." I roll my eyes theatrically. "He sure does go all out."

"Apparently." She laughs, and even her laugh is unique to herself. Feminine, but more like the alto strum of a guitar. That part of her is contagious. "You know Dave, right?" She gestures a hand between us. "Dave. Nicoletta."

"Sure." I smile. "Hi Dave."

He looks me over once. "Right. Nicoletta. You're the foreign exchange student, right?"

While I get that my name makes me sound like I am of French descent (which I probably am somewhere down the line), do these people – my classmates and peers – really not recognize my face?

Shaking my head in disgust, I open my mouth to say, "Um, no."

But Jessica beats me to it. "Yeah, something like that." Then she leans into me, out of Dave's hearing range, I guess. "Sorry," she whispers. "He's not too bright."

I almost laugh. "It's alright."

"No it's not. But after that many blows to the noggin'…" She shrugs, pointing to her own head.

This time I do laugh. "Why are you with him then?"

Dave excuses himself to get a drink. I watch him walk away and understand immediately.

"Yeah." She laughs. "He does look good in those jeans."

"Yep, I get it."

After a few jokes about tight jeans and loose genes with a capital "G", we separate. Asher has left the kitchen. Now he's lounging on the couch, and when I say "on," I really mean he's stretched across the couch, taking up every single cushion. His ankles are crossed on one arm and his hands prop his head up on the other. His eyes are closed as if he's already asleep.

"What are you doing?" I ask.

He gives me a lazy smile. "Perching."

"Okay. Why?"

"Because I really don't want to sit next to Alex and Jen," he answers quietly.

"Alright, scoot over," I say, nudging his leg. Because honestly, it's such a good answer that there's no way I could argue.

Chapter 19

As it turns out, Asher's diabolical plot to monopolize the couch was not necessary. As people show up, the majority of them filter back outside with drinks in hand. Brady's parents have a separate building back there. They call it the pool house. I call it a sauna. We don't have pool houses in Utah as far as I'm concerned. Anywhere that drops down to nine degrees in the winter is too cold for anything like that. It does house a pool, though, heated to seventy degrees, and a hot tub. Next to that building is a gazebo. Judging by the smoke billowing out from the sides, it's a designated smoking spot. I glance out at the people huddled there and hope the druggies found somewhere more secluded.

As I move through the room, I feel like I'm standing in the presence of a painting from a haunted house. Alex's eyes shift slowly in his head, regarding me everywhere I go. I wonder if he's trying to find a good time to talk to me or if he's thinking about the kiss he walked in on. His expression doesn't offer any answers.

The only people interested in watching the show are Brady, Jac, Jessica (Dave Kelly has joined the rest in the pool house), Alex, Asher and me. Jen sits in the crook of Alex's arm, begging him to go upstairs. The least she could do is be quiet about it. There are three couches so everyone gets a seat without having to sit on the floor. Asher and I scooted over so Jessica could sit by us. I was kind of hoping Alex and Jen wouldn't get one.

Since everyone present has seen most of season one, we jumped ahead to season two. Jen hasn't seen it, but none of us care what she thinks.

"So this show doesn't have opening credits?" she asks with distaste.

"It doesn't need them," Brady says, turning to wink at me.

I nod in agreement. "Why take time out of the show for opening credits? Lame."

"Alex," she whines, only five minutes in. "I'm bored. Can't we...?"

"Oh for the love of god, Berkley," Asher exclaims. "Take her upstairs or shut her up. We're trying to watch the show."

Jessica laughs which sends the rest of us over the edge. Like I said, her laughter is contagious.

Alex glares at me. I might as well have been the one who said it for all the hatred he projects. In honesty, I wish I had been me.

Alex stands up. I expect him to take Jen upstairs, but instead, he says, "Nic, can I talk to you?"

"But Alex," Jen whines. She wipes her nose with the back of her hand and sniffs hard like she's getting a cold.

I nod and get to my feet, but Asher grabs my hand.

"You're gonna to miss it," he warns.

I smile. "I'll be right back."

"Hurry. It's about to get good."

With a nod, I follow Alex out the front door. It's a bad sign when he wants to talk to me alone without witnesses. When I get outside, I remember that I forgot my jacket. The cold hits me like a brick wall.

"You and Asher," he says without preamble.

"Are friends," I cut in.

"Right. You and I are friends. But we've never..."

"Wait." If it were warmer, I would hold up my hands. But since it's colder than sin out here, I keep my arms tight around me, hugging my chest. "We've never what?"

"I don't like him." He's pacing now. The cape billows out around his ankles like some live thing.

"Okay." What else can I say? So what if he doesn't like Asher? I don't like Jen. Of course, Alex is dating Jen. Asher and I are... what?

Alex stops mid-turn and fixes his blue eyes on me. "I just don't want to see you get hurt."

"Hurt?" I repeat. "Like calling you last night when I needed you and getting brushed off? Like that kind of hurt?"

"No. You know what I mean."

My fingers are starting to go numb. "Do I?'

He nods, continuing to stare.

"Look. It's cold. So unless you have a point, I'm going back inside," I tell him.

He acts like he doesn't hear me. "He's different, Nic. Haven't you seen that?"

I stop shivering for a second. My stomach does a little turn. Anger warms me. I would never tell Alex who he could hang out with. I'm not his mother. My fists clench reflexively.

"He is different. He cares."

He throws his arms up in the air. "That's not what I mean. I don't want you around him."

"Good thing you aren't my father then," I spit out at him, then turn on my heel and stomp back inside. The door bangs shut behind me.

The cold has bitten into my arms and back. I grab a blanket from Brady's room before heading back to the group.

Alex is already there. "Come on Jen. We're going," he demands.

I try to ignore him while settling back into the cushions of the couch. But I know he's glaring at me. So does Asher, who puts his arm around my shoulders and slides closer. His natural body heat is almost excruciating to the touch.

"Are we going upstairs?" Jen asks, brightly.

Alex doesn't look at her. "No. I'm taking you home."

"But...," she protests.

"I'm tired."

I fixate on the show with all my might. I don't hear them leave. I'm too busy watching Dean befriend a girl who is also awaiting death. This is one of my favorite episodes. She turns out to be a Reaper. It's only a matter of time before he realizes she is there to collect his life.

The hospital room reminds me of Spencer and Mrs. Adams. Is she still awake hoping tonight will be the night her son finally wakes up or is she fast asleep?

I glance over at Jac only to find him staring at me. I wonder if he can tell that I'm thinking his presence in the hospital is as coincidental as the Reaper meeting Dean. I force myself to look away from his cold gaze by snuggling further into the warmth of Asher's chest.

The blanket fell slightly over Asher's stomach. Somehow, his hand finds mine under it. His thumb absently crosses over my palm in a thick line of heat.

Two episodes later, when people start realizing that we weren't kidding about this being a *Supernatural* party, the crowd starts to disperse. Dave tries to talk Jessica into going, too, but she tells him that she can drive herself home. She doesn't drink. He protests mildly before sitting on the couch Alex left open and settling in for whatever the show has to offer. Jessica goes to sit by him. I think about moving over into the empty space, but that's as far as the thought goes. If Asher acts crowded, I'll move. Until then, I enjoy the heat of his body flush against mine. His hair has that clean shower fresh scent and his clothes smell like earth and camp fire. I close my eyes to take in the scent and don't open them again until after midnight.

"Well, I better go," Jessica announces. Her voice startles me awake. I even do one of those half jumps like you do when you have the dream where you are falling.

Asher's arms tighten around me reflexively.

Dave has already gotten their jackets. I'm sure he's been pestering her for a while.

"You really have to go?" I ask sleepily. I was looking forward to spending time with Jessica. She's so much fun in Math.

She nods. "Yeah. I've got to get up in the morning."

"Church?"

"No. Work," she says in a way that implies she would rather be at church if it would get her out of it.

"Oh. Alright." I stand up, throwing the blanket into Asher's lap. If she and I were better friends, I'd hug her. But the least I can do is be polite and say my goodbyes while standing.

Dave helps her with her jacket. Who says you can't teach a monkey tricks?

She thanks him with a smile then says, "See you Monday."

"Yep. Later."

After they're gone, it seems like Asher and I are alone. Completely alone. "Where's Brady?"

He smiles mischievously. "They ducked out an episode ago."

"How did he manage that?" I ask, wishing I could have seen the masquerade myself.

Asher laughs. "Jac pretended to go home. He offered for you and me to stay. Apparently the guest bedroom is pretty cozy."

I flop back on to the couch, leaving a few feet between Asher and me. I feel like I should be cleaning up or something, but half of me is still asleep. My head rolls to the side so I can see him.

"Yeah." He smiles. "He said the couch was cozy, too."

The show is still playing on the flat screen TV. It takes me a minute to realize we are on disc three. "How long was I out?"

He shrugs. "A couple episodes. Do you need to go home?"

"Not yet," I tell him. My parents probably won't go to bed for a few hours yet. Only then will it be safe.

"So, what did Berkley want?" Asher says.

The question throws me off. It's not that I don't want to tell him about the conversation. I'm just not sure what to make of it. Finally, I chuckle. "He thinks you'll hurt me."

His lips purse like he's considering. "He's probably afraid you'll ask me to the dance and I'll turn you down," he shakes his head, laughing, "which would be ridiculous."

"Seriously. What is it with you and that dance?" I ask him. A part of me wants to follow up with a question about the kiss, but the rest of me doesn't want to know the answer.

He slouches down a few inches. "My sister is going. I want to keep an eye on her. But I'm not going alone."

I look at him sideways. "I don't know if I believe you have a sister."

He smiles with such warmth my heart melts. "She doesn't believe you exist either."

"You talk about me?"

He nods. "A little."

Shaking that off so I don't seem too eager, I clarify, "So your sister is going to the dance and you want to be the protective brother so you ask the only girl you know to go with you?"

He laughs dryly. "Something like that. And you aren't the only girl I know, but you are the only one I could see myself going to a Valentine's dance with."

My heartbeat kicks up a few notches. "Why's that?"

The light from the T.V. outlines his features in blue as he slides a few inches closer to me. His hand reaches out and slides along my cheek. "Honestly?"

"Honestly."

He clears his throat. "I like you, Nicoletta, and I want to go to the dance with you. Not just because you are the only girl I know who hasn't been to a dance or whatever, but because I like being around you."

My back arches when he says my name like that single word is a new skin just waiting for me to slip into it.

"I don't plan on hurting you." He smiles. "And you can tell Berkley that."

The look on his face is so sincere. A blush burns my cheeks making me thankful for the dark. "Fine," I say, faking exasperation. "I'll go to the damn dance with you."

He scoots over, closing the distance between us. With his lips to my ear, he breathes out a heated, "Thank you."

The air catches in my throat. When I start breathing again, I say, "Anything to help you keep an eye on your sister."

His cheek nuzzles mine, warming me all the way down to the core. "I thought you didn't believe I had a sister."

I shrug under his touch. "Maybe I do."

Asher's hand slides down my jaw to my neck. All of the fine hairs tingle as if begging to be touched. "When do you have to be home?"

I hesitate, and when I do, he leans back to look at me. His lips are so close I can see the shadow of facial hair growing there.

"Since we are being honest," I say. "I don't."

He lifts his eyebrows just before he kisses me. His mouth tastes of cinnamon and Red Bull. Much better than mine, I'm sure.

***

Sleeping in a coiled mess of limbs next to Asher is nice. Waking up next to him is a tad awkward, though. And yes, all we did was sleep. I promise. I don't know him well enough to give him my V-card. I have standards.

My eyes open to the sound of the front door banging closed. My first reflex is to jump up and make sure I'm decent. I'm still considering it when I hear Brady fumbling around in the kitchen. The smell of coffee curls out toward me.

We'd fallen asleep with the TV still on. There's no menu music, which is probably the only reason why I didn't dream about hunting supernatural beings with Sam and Dean. I've had that dream before. Many times. And it's never a disappointment.

Brady walks into the room to turn the TV off and stops mid-step. His eyes rake over Asher and me lying on the couch. We're both dressed, which seems to surprise him more than us being there.

"Well, hello there," he says.

Asher startles awake. When he does, his arms grip me protectively. I wonder if he was dreaming about the show. After assessing the danger, his head falls back against the arm of the couch, his dark hair spilling in waves around him.

A sense of something builds in my chest. Pride maybe? Perhaps it's something more. Whatever it is, it's feeding itself on the fact that Asher likes me. This beautiful creature likes me. No longer do I feel like a shadow, that's for damn sure.

"I'm making coffee," Brady says, as if the smell of freshly ground coffee beans hadn't already announced it for him.

I look at my watch. It's nine o'clock. "Good."

"So how was your night?" he asks in a sing-song voice. His eyebrows flutter up and down his forehead suggestively.

Something flies over my head and tags Brady in the face. A couch cushion. I glance back at Asher who is smiling innocently.

Brady laughs. "Glad you had fun."

I call my parents while Brady and Asher fix up the coffee. Their church doesn't start until noon, if they even go.

My mother answers on the second ring. "Hi honey. Where are you?" Her voice is too mild. If my daughter stayed out all night, I'd be shrieking. I guess they do trust me.

"I spent the night at my friend Jessica's," I lie.

"Oh good. When are you coming home?"

"In just a little bit. We're having breakfast."

Breakfast, as my parents well know, is coffee. For me, that's all the nutrition I need.

"Okay, dear. No need to hurry."

I don't want to consider those implications. I tell her that I love her and hang up.

"She's not pissed?" Brady asks, incredulous.

"Nope." Grabbing a mug, I begin the ritual of mixing up my coffee. "They told me in no uncertain terms last night not to come home."

Asher smiles at his cup, enjoying the expensive roast.

Brady's face twists up in disgust. "Ew, gross."

I agree.

Brady doesn't mind that Asher and I stayed since we help him clean up the mess left behind. The bitter side of me wonders why Jac didn't stay to help, but then I remember how creepy he is and rejoice that he's gone. The inside takes hardly any time to get back in order. After putting the bottles away and dumping out any leftover food, all we have to do is wipe down the counters. The whole procedure takes twenty minutes, tops. The outside of the house is a different matter entirely.

Even in the morning sun, it's only thirty degrees. I wonder how many people went home with hypothermia.

"You've got to give them credit," Asher says, bagging some empty plastic cups. "They have stamina to be able to withstand the cold."

I'm sitting on the gazebo floor collecting cigarette butts. "I don't have to give them anything. This is gross. Hasn't anyone ever heard of an ashtray?"

Brady, who is gathering trash from inside the pool house/sauna, calls out, "I have." Then he curses a few times.

"You alright in there?" Asher calls back with a laugh.

"Yeah. Remind me to lock this up during the next party, though. It's going to take hours to get the pool the right color."

I grimace. "Gross."

When most of the work is done, Asher offers to drive me home. By this point, my cheeks are permanently colored from the cold and my throat is starting to hurt. Walking wouldn't help so I accept the ride. If my parents see him, I'll make something up. I'm getting pretty good at this lying thing. Or as I like to call it: creative truth telling.

Brady looks sad to see us go. I ask him if he's alright and receive a subdued nod.

"What's wrong?" I ask him while Asher steps out to warm of the car. He only brought a hooded sweatshirt and no jacket. Evidently he is a reptile or something and doesn't ever get cold.

"Nothing."

"Don't lie."

"It's just really quiet around here after a party, you know? I plan for it all week. Sort of anti-climactic, I guess." His eyes are heavy lidded and his mouth painted into a thin line.

I never thought he might hate being alone. Makes sense now that I think about it. All the parties and get-togethers are a way for him to break through the silence. Brady thrives off of being around people. I wonder if it's any better when his parents are home.

"Being an only child sucks sometimes," I respond thoughtfully.

He glances at me with a guarded expression. "Yeah, sometimes it does."

"Is Jac coming back?"

He shakes his head. His hair is still wild from sleep and swishes across his forehead in heavy locks. "I don't think so. He said he has to work."

"Where does he work?" I ask, half-shocked. "Not much going on in Provo on a Sunday, I would imagine."

The look on his face tells me he hadn't considered the thought. He shrugs. "I don't know specifically."

I don't know about you, but one of the first things I want to know about a potential boyfriend is where he works. Of course, Asher was a different story. But he wasn't exactly a potential boyfriend at the time either. Kind of makes you wonder how serious Brady and Jac are.

But seeing how Brady's face brightens whenever he hears Jac's name says multitudes about the gravity of the relationship. At least on Brady's end.

"Hey." I nudge him in the side with my elbow. "Why don't you come hang out tonight?"

"I don't know. I don't want to...," he begins to protest.

I cut him off by rolling my eyes. "Please. Like I want to be alone with my parents tonight."

"You sure?"

I nod emphatically.

He smiles and the room brightens with it. "Okay, cool. I'll text you when I'm ready."

"Deal."

Something, I can't say what, is still bothering him when I get in the Jeep and head home. I watch him stride toward the house with deflated shoulders and hardly even notice when Asher takes my hand.

"What's up?" he asks. "You are somewhere else entirely."

A metallic taste fills my mouth. That's when I realize I've been so tense that I actually bit my tongue. I swallow back the acrid saliva with force then turn toward Asher who looks just as good as he did last night. One thin dark eyebrow is cocked in my direction. In the closed confines of the car and in broad daylight, I finally make out the cut above Asher's eyebrow. There also appears to be a dark bruise disappearing under his hairline.

"Did you get into a fight last night or something?" I ask, pushing his hair back to get a better look.

Asher catches my hand and holds it tightly. "That's nothing. I just slipped on the ice. Don't worry about it. Continue."

My eyebrows pinch together in speculation. I've fallen enough times to know that it takes a particular talent to slip on ice and end up with a neck bruise and a cut above your eyebrow. In other words, those are not accident wounds, but fighting wounds. Who was Asher fighting, though?

"Nicky, what's up?" Asher says, coercing me with his softest voice. Oh well. I guess he'll tell me when he wants to talk about it.

"What do you think of Jac?" I ask from out of nowhere.

Asher doesn't look shocked. He looks curious. "I think Brady likes him a lot. So I don't know. Why?"

"I don't know." With my free hand – the bandaged one – I prop my head up so I don't have to swivel my head back and forth. "Something about him gives me the creeps. I don't know how to explain it."

Asher takes his hand back to shift to a lower gear then takes it again. "Can you try?"

"When I shook his hand the other day, I got this really weird feeling. Like my bones were turning to ice or something. I know it sounds dramatic, but every time he looks at me, it's like my skin wants to crawl away." I take a moment's pause in an effort to organize my next words. If I say whatever I'm about to say wrong, I could come off as crazy. Or worse, jealous. And I'm not jealous. I want Brady to have other friends besides me. I want him to be happy.

"And then seeing him at the hospital," I continue. "There's something not right about the whole situation. Something not right about him."

He glances at me sidelong. I can almost feel him speculating. "It's probably nothing."

Asher pulls over to the side of the road a full block before my house. I half-expect him to tell me to get out and take my craziness with me. Instead, he puts his hands gently on either side of my face and leans in. His lips brush mine in a gentle kiss. My stomach flips like a free-flying acrobat.

"What was that for?" I ask through the shock.

Still holding my face, he whispers, "Everyone is born with instincts. So while it might be nothing, it doesn't have to be. Your instincts may very well be telling you something."

"Yeah," I say wryly. "That I watch too much *Supernatural.*"

He breathes out a laugh. "Maybe. Then again, maybe you just sense when something is off." Taking my hands between his, he continues, "You know, there was a time, a long time ago, when people believed that those who had two different color eyes were gifted with a sort of insight."

"Insight?" I scoff. "Are you serious right now?"

"Dead serious." His thumb traces along the lines of my palm. "In a sense, people believed they were psychics. They would come from miles around just to hear what the woman with mismatched eyes had to say."

The way he says, "woman with mismatched eyes" sends a chill down my spine.

"I'm not saying that's what this is, but maybe you shouldn't give up on your instincts so quickly."

For a long minute, our eyes lock, and I believe him. I believe that my natural instincts might be telling me something beyond worry. Then he releases me and the resolve vanishes.

He gives me a crooked smile. "Ready to go home?"

I shake my head no, but answer, "Yeah, I guess."

Chapter 20

I fall asleep waiting for Brady to come over. I blame my parents and the honey disposition they've been in all day. The dream, I have, however, is not honey flavored at all. It is downright scary.

Through the halls of the hospital, I shuffle. My chest is tight and my eyes water from the exertion of moving. The walls are cold and damp when I touch them to regain balance. A few times, my hands actually slip. I pull back to stare at my palms. They are painted crimson. Blood.

A loud ominous voice echoes over the PA system. "Code blue. Code blue. Two-fourteen."

I gasp. I don't know the codes, but blue has never been good on the medical dramas on T.V. And that's my room, I think to myself. Then I remember that two-fourteen isn't my room; it's Spencer's room. Using all the speed I can gain, I stumble down the hall into a huddled group of doctors. When I reach out, nothing is tangible anymore. Standing next to Spencer's bed, where his mother stood the last time I saw him, is Jac. His pale eyes are turned down to where he clutches Spencer's hand, and when he looks up, his eyes are empty, bottomless. I stop in my tracks, clutching my chest. Why can't I breathe?

I plead with the cold, dead, white eyes as I fall to my knees. I hit the floor. Not the hospital floor, but a dirt one.

Suddenly, I am outside on the ice packed dirt. Snow drifts around me in all directions and I am dying. The pain from my chest travels through my veins, burning every nerve on its way through my body like poison. I cough and a spray of blood paints the ground.

Jac's head looms over me with a sour expression on his face. The fine lines of his jaw and cheekbones seem sharp enough to cut.

"Why?" I try to choke out, but with the blood in my throat, it sounds more like a gurgle.

He smiles at me then and the smile is truly horrific. His lips turn red as the blood on my hands, on the snow.

"You are becoming a huge pain in my ass," he says, and the voice sounds strange, like two people speaking instead of one, double-toned and double-edged.

"Nicky," a voice growls next to my ear. Two hands clutch my shoulders, shaking me. "Nicky, wake up!"

My eyes fly open then shut tight. Brady. It's just Brady. I breathe in a long deep breath expecting it to pierce my lungs like a fiery rod. It doesn't. It's just air.

"Nicky, you okay?" he asks, his voice saturated with concern.

I manage a nod without opening my eyes. "Just give me a second." Slowly, I take a mental survey of my lungs. Everything is in working order, if not sore. My throat still hurts, though.

"Want me to get you some water?" Brady asks.

"Yes, please." The pillow under my head seems too soft, the blanket too warm. I kick both of them off my bed and roll onto my stomach.

Brady comes back into my room with a tall glass of ice water. He offers it to me as he sits on the edge of my bed. His weight shifts the mattress, making my stomach turn. The taste of blood mixed with bile climbs up my throat. I swallow it back.

"Bad dream?"

I nod, my face scratching against the starchy sheets. I remember my normal sheets still in the dryer with a physical longing. "The worst," I tell him.

"Wanna talk about it?" He reaches over and rubs my back like my mother used to do when I was sick. The contact is reassuring. My stomach settles a bit, but I don't move to get up.

"No, not really." I mean, what am I supposed to say? I guess I could tell him that his boyfriend is evil. Yeah, that would go over as well as a monkey tap-dancing into a hungry lion's den.

"Okay, but if you change your mind, I'll listen."

I nod. "My throat hurts."

He eyes me curiously. "I would say so. You were screaming bloody murder when I came in. I'm surprised you didn't wake yourself up."

I rub the base of my throat. "Was I? I don't remember screaming."

He nods slowly. "Yeah. I could hear it all the way outside. Good thing I know where the spare key is. Otherwise, I might have broken down the door. I thought you were being attacked in here."

Shocked, I respond with, "Where are my parents?"

"They had to go to the hospital. They left a note for you. Hang on." Brady leaves the room and returns with a white piece of paper.

I struggle to sit up and take the note from his outstretched hand. It reads:

Nicoletta,

Mrs. Adams called. Spencer isn't doing so well. The doctors are working to get him breathing again. Went to offer support and blessings. Call me if you need anything.

Mom.

My stomach rolls again with vengeance. I manage to launch myself off the bed and make it to the sink before retching. Hoping for the toilet would have been asking too much.

I'm too pre-occupied with the burning in my throat to notice that Brady has come into the room. He's smoothing my hair back and away from my neck.

"Good god, girl. What did you eat? You didn't even drink last night, did you?" He gasps and turns the faucet to cold. It swirls and dissipates the bright red color from the sink. Blood.

"Nothing," I croak. My voice echoes off of the porcelain basin, reminding me of my dream. My stomach rolls again.

"I hope you aren't getting sick," he says, more to himself than me.

"I'll be fine."

"Sure you will. What did you drink that was red?"

"Nothing."

Brady stiffens. "Do I need to take you to the hospital?"

"No... well, yes. But not for me."

"Nu uh," he responds sounding all authoritative. "We are getting you back in bed. You might have a bleeding ulcer or something. I'll make you some potato soup."

"No." I raise my head, catching my grey complexion in the mirror. It startles me for a second. "No. I need to go to the hospital. I need to see Spencer." I wash my hands and face in the sink, rinse my mouth out, and turn to see Brady staring at me.

"You can't go see Spencer," he tells me. "You were throwing up a second ago. You need to get back in bed. Besides, I don't know what the rules are precisely, but I'm pretty sure they don't like sick people visiting other sick people in the hospital."

I push past him and head to my room. I strip off my sweater and replace it with my Rangers hoody. Much better.

"They probably won't let you in," he continues. "You can visit tomorrow."

"Look," I say, turning narrowed eyes on him. "I'm going. You can come with me or I can get another ride. What'll it be?"

Brady hates losing a fight. So when he rubs his face with his left hand and groans loudly, I know I've won. "Fine," he says. "Let's go."

Spencer has been moved to the Intensive Care Unit, but he's alive. Since only one person can see him at a time, the waiting room is full of their friends and neighbors. I'm not even shocked when I don't see anyone from school.

My mother grips me by the shoulder and then pulls me into a hug. "Honey, you didn't have to come down here."

I glance over at Mr. Adams talking to their bishop. His face is whiter than any I've ever seen. His eyes are rimmed red and crazed.

"Yes. I did," I say.

Brady paces the room slowly. I wonder if he's made the connection yet. Not alcohol poisoning. Heart failure. Furthermore, I wonder if he realized that this all started at his stupid New Year's Eve party.

"So what happened?" I ask my mother.

My father is standing next to the bishop and Mr. Adams. They're trying to figure out how to get permission to file in for a blessing. He still insists on giving me blessings when I'm really sick. The elders can be very persuasive. The hospital will let them do it. They have to. Even though I may not believe in it, I find myself hoping it will help. Something is better than nothing.

"Well, they said that Spencer was doing better. They thought he might wake up today. Then out of nowhere, he had a seizure and his heart stopped. Deb won't leave his side," she explains.

"Wow." I wish I had something more to offer, something more eloquent to say, but I don't. All I can think about is that awful dream.

"Yeah. That's all any of us can say." She wraps an arm around my shoulders. Her hand moves up and down my sleeve with a whispering sound.

My phone rings, making me jump. The whole room turns to look at me. Some hospitals still don't like cell phones. I shrug out of my mom's grasp and go to the corner of the room to answer it.

It's Asher. "Hey, what you doing?"

Quietly, I say into the receiver, "Sorry, I'm going to have to call you back. I'm at the hospital."

"You okay?" he responds automatically. His voice is so tense you could play it like an instrument.

A smile creeps across my face in satisfaction. Nice to know he cares. I wave my hand even though he can't see it. "Yeah, well, no. But, it's not me. Spencer took a turn for the worse. I came to see if I could help."

Silence.

"Asher?"

He clears his throat. "Yeah, I'm here."

Something about his voice makes me ask, "What's wrong?"

"It's just, I'm wondering if you are getting too close to this thing. I know you feel bad for him and all because his friends are assholes, but would Spencer really care that you're the one there for him? You said you weren't friends."

"We aren't," I clip off. "But someone needs to be here for him. Someone who knows him, and if no one else is going to do it, I will. Because I care."

"Sorry, I just worry… you know what, never mind. I'm on my way. I'm coming to you now."

"You don't have to."

"I'll be there in five." The line goes dead.

I know I shouldn't be excited to see him. Not with everything going on, but I am. I look around the room at all the bodies milling around. Brady found a chair in another corner and sits staring blankly at the wall. I walk over and sit in the chair next to him, pulling my knees to my chest. I hug them as if they are the only solid thing on this earth.

"Long day," I say.

He nods. "So what's wrong with him?"

I shrug. "Heart defects. I wasn't supposed to tell anyone, though."

He doesn't look at me. I wonder what's so interesting about the wall. It looks like any other wall to me. "How long have you known?"

"A few days."

"You could have told me," he says through tight lips. "I could have—"

"No you couldn't," I cut in. "He didn't want anyone to know. Besides, it's not like we're his friends."

Brady looks at me then. Guilt is tearing him up just behind his eyes. "He's in here because he drank at my party."

So Brady finally put two and two together.

I nod.

"This is my fault. If you hadn't been there…"

Unconsciously, I finger my shoelaces. "It's not your fault. He shouldn't have been drinking. What could you have done? Not invite him?"

"That's just it. I didn't invite him. I didn't even know he was there. Not until you told me." His whole body is taut as a guitar string. I reach over with my braced hand and touch his arm.

"Brady, we can sit here and play 'What if?' all day long, but none of us knew. We couldn't have done anything. If Spencer wasn't so damn secretive about his condition then maybe… but, he's a big boy. These are his consequences. Not ours."

Brady lays his hand on my splint. "You're a good friend, Nicky."

I fake a smile. "And don't you forget it."

Asher ducks into the room and heads straight toward us. For a second, I don't know how to respond. Partly because of last night and partly because of how he looks. His wet hair clings to his ears and cheeks. He's wearing a leather jacket that fits him like it was cut just for his body. It's an almond brown – almost like the color of his eyes at this moment. At least I know now that he owns a jacket.

He slides into the chair to the left of me then leans over and kisses me on the cheek.

I'm glad he doesn't feel awkward like I do.

Immediately, I want to tell him about my dream, but I bite it back. I'll tell him when Brady's out of earshot.

"What did I miss?" Asher asks like he walked in on the middle of a movie.

I tell him what I've heard so far. He listens intently. When I'm finished, he says, "So no one can see him?"

"Not yet. Only one person at a time, but Mrs. Adams won't leave his side."

"Can you blame her?"

"Nope."

Brady agrees, "Not at all."

The nurse comes in, calling attention by clapping her hands once. "To all who are here for Spencer Adams," she says loudly, "he's stabilizing."

"Oh thank you," Mr. Adams says, stepping forward with his hands clasped together in front of him. "Do you know when we can administer the blessing?"

Asher whispers to me, "Does this include salt?"

I giggle. The worst is over so giggling is acceptable now, I figure. "No. But it does involve holy water."

He flashes me a wide grin.

"Yes," The nurse says. "As soon as the doctor is done with his exam, we will take you back."

"Good. Thank you," Mr. Adams replies. He turns to gather the elders, and when he moves, I see a face behind him I hadn't noticed before.

A pale blond head of hair falls back to reveal faded blue eyes glaring right at me. My breath catches in my throat.

Asher and Brady both turn to see what startled me.

"What is it?" Brady asks.

I blink a few times slowly. With each blink, the face changes a little more. The hard lined jaw turns round and the white hair turns golden. Suddenly, Jac's face isn't there anymore. Instead, a woman sits, looking at me quizzically. I glance away.

"Nothing. Just… nothing." My dream must have really screwed me up.

My mother walks over to us. She stops when she sees Asher. It takes a moment for her to recover. "Well, it looks like no one will get to see Spencer today. So if you kids want to go…"

I get to my feet. "If you're sure."

She hugs me the way a mother does when she remembers how mortal her daughter is. "Yes, I'm sure." She glances over my shoulder. "Will you boys make sure my baby girl gets home safe?"

Brady says, "Of course, Mrs. Dubois." He stands up and looks as surprised as I am when she pulls him close, her arms squeezing him tight.

"Brady, dear. How many times do I have to tell you? Don't call me that. It makes me feel old." Then she turns to Asher, hand outstretched to shake his. "I don't think we've been formally introduced."

"Mom. This is Asher Rowan," I say for him. When she continues to look at me, I wonder what else to say. Should I introduce him as my friend, my boyfriend, what? I settle with, "He's on the basketball team with Alex."

She brightens as he shakes her hand. "Well, anyone who is friends with Alex is fine by me."

Asher smiles curtly and I wonder if he's going to correct her. He doesn't. All he says is, "Nice to meet you."

Between the two of my parents, I would have been happier introducing him to my dad first. He's easy-going. But what can you do?

I give her one last hug before we go. Maybe the situation is getting to both of us.

On my way out the door, I almost run into someone. It takes a few blinks before I realize that I just about mowed Jessica down in the hospital.

"What are you doing here?" I ask, taking a few steps back.

Her eyes move from me to Brady to Asher. "I could ask you the same thing."

Surely, she couldn't be here visiting Spencer, could she? I didn't think they were friends. Then again, the three of us aren't friends with him either and look where we are: wasting a Sunday away in hopes of hearing how he is doing.

"We came to check on Spencer," Asher answers for me. "It's pretty full in there."

Jessica gets a look on her face like someone just reminded her that the ground is hard. "Oh, that's right. How is he doing?"

I give a half shrug. "He's stabilized. They don't know much more yet."

"That's good."

I'm not sure if I should ask again why she is walking into the waiting room at the ICU or not. I glance at Brady. He shrugs to tell me that he doesn't know either.

Jessica's eyes look tired. Her hair is pulled back into a tight pony tail with frizzy curls escaping toward her face. Seeing her like this makes me a little sad. I want to hug her and tell her everything will be okay.

"Jess, you alright?" I ask.

She looks startled. Did she forget I was there? "Oh, um, yeah. I'm just tired. I didn't get much sleep."

"Anything we can do?"

"What?" She says quietly. "Oh. No. I don't think so. It's Dave. I guess he had too much to drink or something. He got into an accident. They admitted him last night."

"Is everything alright?"

"I don't know. The damn doctors won't tell me anything because I'm not family. Technically, I'm not even his girlfriend. But I was the last one to see him so…"

I know what she's going to say because I feel the same way about Spencer. "You feel responsible," I finish for her.

She pushes her hair away from her face with the back of her hand. "Yeah, I guess so."

Without thinking, I pull her into an awkward hug. She's tense and rigid but doesn't push me away.

"Hey, do you have your cell phone on you?" Asher asks her.

She nods and pulls it from her jacket pocket. "Yeah, why?"

"I'm going to put mine and Nicoletta's numbers in there. If you need anything, I want you to call one of us. Can you do that?"

She nods and relinquishes the phone to Asher who expertly enters our numbers and saves them to the contact list. I'm a little surprised that he already has my number memorized.

"Thank you," she says in a small voice before taking her phone back and ducking around us into the waiting room.

I wonder if she's cried yet or if she needs to. It feels like I've left something of me behind. Like maybe, if I went back, she would let me help in some way. Then again, maybe she just needs to be left alone. With that thought, I let Asher and Brady usher me out of the hospital.

***

Brady, Asher and I sit in my kitchen discussing what to make for dinner. Brady told Asher about how he found me screaming in my

192

sleep (Thanks so very much for that, Brady) so both of them have resolved to wait with me until my parents get home. I thought it might be nice if they could come home to dinner on the table. Now we just have to figure out what to make. I'm not much of a cook, but I'm willing to try.

Asher has been giving me piteous looks since we got here. I wish I could explain so he would stop. But that will have to wait until Brady leaves.

Brady opens the fridge and pokes his head inside. "Well, let's see what we've got here. Steak, chicken, ground beef, and a lot of leftovers. Name your poison."

I think for a second. "Chicken. That's a comfort food, right?"

Brady pulls out my carton of Cashew Chicken from the other night. He sniffs it, makes a face, and puts it back. "From the looks of it, Kitten, Chinese is what makes up comfort food around here."

"Shut up." I shake my head, feeling slightly embarrassed. I like Chinese food. So sue me. "Just get the chicken out please."

"Okay." He retrieves the chicken and sets it out on the counter. "How do you want to cook it so I can pick the sides?"

I give him a wry look. "I should have guessed you can cook."

"Why? Because I'm gay?"

Asher feigns astonishment. "You are?"

I ignore both of them. "No. Because your parents are always out of town. Eventually, you get sick of take out, right?"

Brady laughs. "From the look of your fridge, you don't actually believe that."

I glare at him, but he doesn't seem to see me.

"So, are we grilling, baking or frying?"

"You choose," I tell him.

He taps his chin. "Well, then. Grilled it is. You'll want something your stomach can handle after today."

"After today?" Asher asks. "Did I miss something?"

I open my mouth to tell him how much better I'm feeling, but Brady gets there first. "Nicky was puking up her existence before we went to the hospital."

Blood rushes into my cheeks. I put my head in my hands, hoping to hide it. "Thanks for that," I say sarcastically.

The pity on Asher's face thickens. "You're not getting sick, are you?"

"No. It was side effects from the nightmare, I think. All that screaming must have induced vomiting or something."

He gives me an inquisitive look. I mouth the word, *Later*.

Brady pulls out the George Foreman grill and some spices then unwraps the chicken. As I get ready to stand up and help, he tells me to stay put. Of course, he adds, "In case you feel sick again. We don't want you throwing up all over dinner."

I shoot another glower his way.

It takes Brady twenty-five minutes to make chicken, corn, green beans and French bread. My kitchen smells better than it ever has and despite the previous state of my stomach, I'm starving.

Like a good little housewife, he serves our food.

"You know, Brady, if you would do this every day, I would marry you," I tell him while stuffing a piece of bread into my mouth.

He laughs. "I'll keep that in mind."

Asher looks at his plate appreciatively. "Make that two of us."

I stare at him. He's slowly moving the food around his plate with a fork. When he feels me watching him, he stops, fork in mid-air and returns my glance. "What?"

Brady laughs again. "I think she's afraid you're going to switch teams on her. I find it kind of refreshing myself. It's nice to be around a no-phobe."

"No-phobe?" Asher repeats.

"Yeah," I explain. "That's what Brady and I call people who aren't homophobic."

"Huh. Makes sense. I haven't heard that before," he says, taking a bite.

Brady points his fork at Asher. A piece of chicken is skewered on the end. "That's because there aren't many of them around."

I shrug in agreement, take another bite of bread, and then say around it, "It's true." Yep, that's me: Miss Manners. My parents would be so proud.

Asher stops chewing and wipes his mouth with a napkin. "Not many gay people around here, I take it?"

We both stare at him. I shake my head. "Not many who will admit it anyway. Not at our school, at least."

"Oh." His expression turns kind of distant as if he's remembering something from another lifetime. Slowly, he shakes his head. "People suck."

Brady lifts his glass of water in a salute. "I'll drink to that."

For a moment, everything feels so warm and natural. Like fifty years from now, the three of us could still be sitting at a table eating a dinner much like this one. My heart swells at the thought.

"Something on your mind, Kitten?" Brady asks.

I look at him and respond at the exact moment I think the thought, "I could get used to this."

Asher glances at me sideways, a ghost of a smile forming on his lips. "Yeah. Me, too."

Brady chuckles. "Not me. It's weird being here with the two of you. All those secretive looks, it's disgusting." But his words are edged with sarcasm. "Now if Jac was with us then maybe…"

Unconsciously, I give Asher another of our "secretive looks," hoping I don't look as horrified as I feel. In all actuality, I've probably been thinking about Jac more than Brady has, but I'm sick of hearing about him. Sick of seeing him everywhere. Sick of him appearing in my dreams. Life will be easier when he's gone. Because there's no way he will stay around forever, right? Brady's gone head over heels for guys before and it's never lasted. Of course, most of them were straight, but still.

So why does his tone make me worry that Jac will be the dagger through my happy visions of the future?

Asher's left hand disappears under the table and squeezes my leg gently.

"Nic, I was just kidding about the awkward thing," Brady says, reading me all wrong. "It's not that bad hanging out with you guys. In fact, it's nice to see you happy for a change."

"I know," I say, staring off into nothingness. Now that the subject has been broached, it's like Jac stepped out of my dream and is sitting in the kitchen with us. It feels like he's everywhere. Even my chest hurts. I try to take another bite of bread. My throat convulses as I swallow. Great. Just what I need. I didn't even get to eat the meal and now the sight of it is making my stomach churn. I stand up, excusing myself and tell them that I'm going to lie down.

The couch is cool against my skin. I lay with my cheek pressed into it and listen to the murmured conversation in the kitchen.

"What's going on with her?" Brady asks.

"Your guess is as good as mine," Asher lies. I know he can see how Jac's presence affects me. "She might just be getting sick."

"Better not be. I don't know what I'd do without her to keep me in check every day."

Asher laughs. "Me either."

The acid in my stomach slowly dissolves. Maybe the bread soaked it all up. I'm still not hungry, though, so I close my eyes and skate around the edges of my pulsing consciousness.

Then Brady's voice directs me back to the conversation in the next room. "Did you get her to agree to the dance?"

Asher laughs and it sounds like he spits water at the same time. "Yeah. I feel kind of bad about how I did it, though."

There's a moment of silence during which I imagine Brady urging him on.

"I told her I wanted to go just to keep an eye on my sister."

When Brady answers, there is a new appreciation in his voice. "Good man."

"I should tell her the truth."

My brain snaps to attention. The truth? What?

"The truth doesn't really set you free, Ash. My dad taught me that."

"Oh? What's your dad do?"

Brady replies with a low chuckle. "He's a lawyer. But never mind that."

A roll of laughter fumbles out of the kitchen. The two deep voices mingle together. It sounds like bass thumping.

I close my eyes to block out all other distractions and focus on what they're saying.

"You know Berkley's trying to set her up on a date?" Asher asks when the laughter dies out.

"God. That's so…"

He doesn't get to finish his sentence because at that moment, my parents walk through the door. My mother heads for the kitchen while my father, seeing me lying corpse-still on the couch, makes his way toward me.

He kneels down in front of the couch and touches my forehead with his cold hand. "You didn't have to wait up if you were tired."

His hair is mussed from the wind. Snowflakes cling to the dark ends. He looks tired and worn out, yet strong, if that's possible. But my father always looks strong and ready to take on the world. I figure it's a job requirement for being with my mother.

"We made you dinner," I say, ignoring his words. "How's Spencer?"

My father pushes his hair out of his face and rubs his eyes. "He's stable. I'll tell you, Nicky. Your mother and I are so lucky to have you. I know Spencer would have really appreciated you and Brady being there today."

Actually, from what I know of Spencer, he would have berated me for nosing around in his business. Now I know why. He had a secret he didn't want getting out.

Everyone has secrets, I think to myself. Then I wonder where the thought came from. I don't have a secret, do I? Sure, my feelings for Alex are kept under wraps, but for obvious reasons. A real life or death secret, though? Not that I know of.

"You look tired, honey. Why don't you say goodbye to your friends and go to bed?"

I nod. Probably not a bad idea.

No, not a bad idea at all. A horrible idea, actually. After I said goodnight to Asher and Brady – who left together, giving me no opportunity to talk to Asher alone – I got in my pajamas and practically fell into bed. Where I am now, listening to the wind pick up outside my window sending branches scraping against the glass like claws.

I've checked my clock three times, hoping the constant changing minutes would make me tired. It hasn't and now it's one o'clock in the morning. Five and a half hours before I have to get ready for school. I curse and roll the other way. I wonder if it's possible to give myself the Vulcan sleep pinch. Doesn't matter, it probably doesn't work in real life anyway.

Every time I close my eyes, I see Jac's face staring back at me, waiting for me to fall into a vulnerable sleep so he can pounce. I don't see what Brady finds so attractive about him anyway. His features are so plain and generic. And his eyes, talk about lacking any color or compassion. Even something about his mouth bothers me. Though, I don't know why. His lips are too thin and pale. But every smile is supposed to be beautiful in some way, right? So says Mrs. Haskins, my first grade teacher anyway. I've seen a lot of smiles I didn't think were beautiful. But Jac has a horrifying one: malicious with evil undertones. You think the description is redundant? Well, you haven't seen him smile.

God, why am I thinking about Jac again? If a man has to be my last thought of the night, couldn't it be Jensen Ackles? Now that's a dream I'd sign up for in a heartbeat. I shut my eyes tight, trying to redirect my thoughts. "No more Jac," I chant to myself. He doesn't exist right now. Tonight, it's just me and Mr. Ackles.

I finally fall asleep at about three o'clock. I don't dream about Mr. Ackles, but I don't dream about Jac either. Score one for me.

Although, for some reason, I do dream of Melinda Carter… or her funeral anyway.

Chapter 21

Three hours of sleep is evidently all it takes to zombify me. I barely remember getting to school, let alone getting up and dressed. As evident by my choice in clothes, I realize while looking over my attire. In the dark, I must have grabbed the only clean pair of jeans I had: black and silver pin-striped pants that match only a certain color of shirt. I have three matching ones at home. None of which ended up on my person before leaving the house. No, I had to grab a dark blue long-sleeved thermal shirt. Luckily, since I knew it was snowing, I grabbed my beloved Rangers hoody for the insulation. It doesn't match either, since it's red and blue, but with sweaters it's less noticeable.

When I approach my locker, there's a girl leaning against it. She's a few inches shorter than me and has flaming red hair with golden streaks framing her face. That's the first thing I notice. The second is how her clothes match. Great. Good to know I'm the only one who wasn't ready to be alive this morning.

Upon seeing me, she pushes off the locker, revealing Asher crouched down on the floor. He glances up, his hair falling into his eyes. Then slowly, as if making a theatrical production of it, he rises to his feet.

Apparently Asher and this girl have been sitting here chatting it up for a while. Wonderful. Just what I need on a Monday morning.

I pause, not sure what to say and regard him with a pointed look.

"Nicoletta," Asher says, feigning a smile. He walks over and wraps an arm around my shoulders as if we've been buddies for years. "I'd like you to meet my sister."

My jaw drops. Usually siblings have some sort of resemblance, but in this case, there's nothing. Well, not nothing. They both carry themselves with the same undeniable confidence. In looks, though, they have nothing in common.

"Acacia," he continues. "This is Nicoletta."

"Acacia?" I ask, cocking an eyebrow. "That's a unique name."

She rolls her beautiful green eyes. "Yeah, yeah. Our parents were hippies. Hug a tree. Love nature. All that crap. Call me Acey."

"Acey." I nod. "I like that. But why not Casey?"

She snorts in disgust. "Never met a Casey I liked. Besides, Acey seems to fit me better, don't you think?"

In fact, it does, and I know a lot about disliking your name. I smile at her in the way I hope you are supposed to smile at your potential boyfriend's little sister. "I think it's great," I tell her. "Call me Nicky."

Asher gives me a disconcerted look, but doesn't say anything.

"Well," Acey says, "It's nice to see Asher didn't make you up."

Asher reaches over and ruffles her hair. "Get to class, troublemaker."

She smiles mischievously before turning on her heel and bouncing down the hall.

While retrieving my books from my locker, I become very aware of Asher's hot breath on my ear. I stop, hold still, and let the air wash over me.

"Would you rather I call you Nicky?" he whispers in low tones.

I barely shake my head. "No. I like how you say my name." With a smile directed somewhere into my locker, I add, "Among other things."

***

I've been looking forward to lunch all day. After getting the cold shoulder treatment from Alex, I need some time off campus. Too bad Alex ends up walking into the same Taco Bell that Brady, Asher, Acey and I are at. Our lunch group appears to be expanding.

I like Acey and not just because she is Asher's sister. She's loud, funny, and doesn't have a filter either. I can't help but laugh when Alex and Jen walk by and she says something along the lines of Berkley's pet having nice shoes. She and I happen to share the same distaste for ballet flats. The only girl I know like that. The sarcasm is strong in this one.

As I'm putting a cheese drenched chip into my mouth, a shadow falls across the table. By way of habit, I glance at Asher. His face is hard as stone and beyond unhappy. That's how I know who it is.

I swallow the chip and turn. "Alex, what's up?"

He looks around the table, pausing to eye Brady. "Can I talk to you for a second?"

Acey waves a hand in front of her face all Southern Belle mockery. "Nicky," she says through her fake panting. "The captain of the basketball team wants to speak to you. Oh my god."

Alex glowers in her general direction. I wonder if I should stick up for him. Nah. As far as I figure it, if he can't handle the words of a spritely little sophomore, then he has bigger problems than whatever he wants to talk to me about.

"Make it quick," I say, standing up to follow him out. Because he's going to want to go outside. I'm not lucky enough to have this conference where it's warm and dry.

We have to force the big glass doors open against the swirling wind. Fat snowflakes rush me, chilling my face.

"God, it's cold," I remark, pulling my jacket tighter around my chest.

I expect Alex to stop outside the door. He doesn't. Keys in his hand, he walks straight to his car. The lights flash as he unlocks it.

I stop walking. His blond highlights seem to glow in the white snowy atmosphere.

"It's warmer in the car," he says, motioning for me to get in.

After deliberating for a cold second, I climb into the passenger side. It is warmer in the car and it feels like home. The scents of his cologne, shampoo and air freshener overwhelm me.

"Nice friends you've got in there," he says dryly.

I turn a little in the seat, propping my wrist on my knee where he'll be sure to see it. His eyes drift toward the brace and he recoils.

"You and Brady are friends," I remind him.

He nods, looking at the stereo to avoid meeting my eye.

I wonder why he brought me out here when I could be spending my precious lunch hour eating. I didn't eat much yesterday so I was looking forward to filling my stomach with warm chips and grilled taquitos.

"Alex, what is this even about?" I ask, sounding more irritated than intended.

He hesitates. "I miss you. I miss hanging out."

His words are so unexpected that I find myself unsure of what to say. He misses me? Have I been neglecting him? Thinking back over the last week, seeing him at school and nowhere else, I think it may be possible.

A few long moments later, I respond, "I miss you, too."

He smiles a little and looks at me through the dark curtain of his eyelashes. "What are you doing tomorrow night?"

I think about it. "Nothing. Why?"

"Jen has dance class so I was wondering if you wanted to go see a movie or something. There's a new horror flick out. Right up your alley."

Without reason, I think of Jac. "I think I've had enough horror for a little while. Any comedies?"

"You bet," he says, still grinning.

A weight I hadn't realized I've been carrying lifts off my shoulder so suddenly I almost gasp. It would be nice to spend time with Alex again. Carefree, fun-loving, easy-going Alex.

Light rapping echoes through the glass on my side of the car. Brady stands outside, shaking the falling snow out of his hair. I roll down the window. A gust of frigid air whips me in the face.

"Hey guys," Brady says, leaning in the window. "We're all done. Time to go back to the hell that is our wonderful school."

"Okay." The disappointment of missing out on my taquitos is overshadowed by the anticipation of hanging out with Alex again. I shoot one last smile in Alex's direction before getting out of the car.

"See you tomorrow then?" he calls out.

"Yep." I shut the door. For a humorous moment, I think he's going to leave Jen in his excitement about tomorrow night. He doesn't, much to my dismay. She runs out of the doors toward the car, mumbling something about her shoes getting all wet.

I laugh all the way to the Jeep. Asher doesn't look at me, but Acey says, "What?"

"That's what the bitch gets for wearing ugly shoes," I say quietly. In the cold and snow, words echo off of everything. For instance, I can hear Jen's exclamations about her feet being cold as if I were standing right next to her.

And she can probably hear Acey's hysterical laughter as if someone turned her volume up.

The drive back is so silent I can make out the commercials on the radio in the next car over.

Asher shuts off the engine and gets out of the car. He's gone before I have the chance to thank him for bringing my leftover lunch along. Acey shrugs and follows him, her coat billowing out like black wings as she runs.

"So what's tomorrow?" Brady asks me as we crunch through the freshly fallen snow.

"Alex and I are going to a movie. Want to come?" We've invited Brady along so many times that I don't even have to wonder if it would be okay to ask.

He watches Asher enter through the school doors with calculated interest. "No. I'm good."

"You don't think that's what has Asher all bothered, do you?"

He shrugs. "I don't know. You'd have to ask him. One thing's for sure, though," he says, holding the door open for me. "Alex Berkley is going to be the bane of your existence if he isn't already."

"The bane of my existence?" I repeat. Then, without warning, I burst into a fit of giggles.

"Mark my words, Kitten. There's a whole world out there. You just choose not to see it. Alex is like the sun blotting out the sky." He glances toward Asher standing at his locker. "But the moon is just as beautiful, and not quite so blinding, you know? You can see it and all its perfect imperfections."

I feel my eyebrows knit together. "No, I don't know. What the hell are you talking about?"

"You'll see soon enough."

203

I have a theory that cold shoulders are contagious. The few times I saw Asher for the rest of the day, he pretended not to see me. What did I do? If he's going to act like this every time I hang out with a friend, I don't think I want to be his girlfriend. If there was even a chance of that. On my walk home from school among the ice and slush, I decide to text Asher. It's a Monday so he works, but I'll try anyway.

I open the phone and type out a text saying, *You alright?* Then hit send.

My phone rings immediately after. My heart rate speeds up. Was he thinking of me at the same time?

No. It's Brady.

To which, I answer with a disappointed "What's up?"

"So here's the deal. I came home because Jac and I were going to hang out, but he's slammed at work. I guess the weather is keeping him busy."

"The weather?" I ask suspiciously.

"Yeah. So anyway. What do you say we go bowling? That's a nice, warm, indoor sport."

I slip on a patch of ice and curse as I regain my balance. "I don't know. You know how my parents are about Monday nights."

"Right," he says, tapping something on the phone. "Family night. Well, bring them along. Tell them my parents are still out of town and I need some family lovin'."

"Wait. I thought your parents came home today." And I'd remember because Brady has no plans to get me to another party.

"They did. Why do you think I want to go out?"

I laugh. Brady's parents never had an awkward stage in their marriage. Maybe because they have never had any problems to speak of. For them, there has always been enough faith, money and work: the three keys to happiness. Four if you include the well-stocked wine cellar.

I turn the corner to my house, careful of my footing. The driveway is empty, but a red Jeep sits at the curb. My stomach flips, my heart goes pitter pat, and it's all I can do to keep from running to the car.

"I'll ask," I tell him, sounding a little too excited.

"Okay. I'll be awaiting your call."

I hang up without saying goodbye. My strides are purposeful now. I am determined to make it to the Jeep without falling on my ass.

The driver's side door opens and Asher puts one booted foot to the snow hesitantly. Then he climbs out.

Even though I mean to put a few feet between us, I hit a patch of ice and slide. Strong arms catch me as I'm going down. The warm security of them makes me forget all else. When I look up, his face is just above mine.

"You alright?" he asks. "That was —"

I don't let him finish. "Are you mad at me?"

He lets out a breathy laugh. "No. Why would you think that?"

"You were angry at lunch."

"Not because of you."

That's good enough for me. I nod once then I plant my lips firmly to his. In the midst of my strange day, it's nice to kiss Asher. No, more than nice. I feel oddly comforted by the warm tingles that pass from his lips to mine.

In fact, I'm so lost in the kiss that I almost don't hear the passenger door open.

Chapter 22

A man – at least I think he's a man and not God's gift to woman – climbs out of the opposite side of the Jeep. His hair is dark, wavy and just a few inches longer than Asher's. The ends of it kiss his shoulders as he moves. He's dressed in a black thermal shirt, boot cut jeans, and a dark duster jacket that swishes around his ankles as he walks. His boots are heavy black leather. He, unlike Asher, I notice, is dressed perfectly for the weather. My breath exhales in a puff of white air as I right myself. He can't be much older than I am, maybe only a year or two.

He smiles in light of the awkward situation and my heart melts involuntarily. His lips are full and perfect as they draw back into his fine cheekbones. His eyes, perfectly spaced under his dark eyebrows, are a beautiful grayish blue. Like the sky during a raging storm.

"Nicoletta," Asher says, pulling me out of my trance. "This is my cousin, Kaleb."

Kaleb, the God, steps forward and takes my hand in a lingering embrace. "Very nice to meet you."

Oh god. His voice is pure seduction. It reminds me of silk, buttery and smooth. I nod, unsure if my voice is up to the task of speaking.

Asher, in my peripheral vision, rolls his eyes. "You still have that effect on all the girls?" he asks Kaleb.

Kaleb's eyes shift to the side, I assume to look at his cousin. He releases my hand. "Not all of them, no."

For a minute, all I can see is the color of slate, all I can smell is the whispering winds on a quiet fall night, and all I can feel is the feather light caress of a gentle rain. A gentle calm embraces me. I don't ever want to let it go.

"You busy?" Asher asks, snapping me back to bitter cold reality. "Can you come over?"

For some reason, I can't think of anything I would rather do than go with them. There were no plans I'd be breaking as far as I can remember. So, "Why not? Let me drop my bag inside and leave a note."

"I'll come with you." Asher offers then shoots his cousin a narrowed look. "I imagine you'll be fine out here?"

Kaleb waves an elegant hand dismissively. A ring on his right forefinger glints red with the movement.

Asher guides me inside with his hand on the small of my back. I drop my bag next to the door and head to the kitchen to draw up my note. But there's one already there.

Nicoletta, it reads. I wonder if my parents and I ever converse without paper anymore. *Went to the hospital. No need to come down. Will be home late. We'll make family night up to you. Promise. Love Mom and Dad.*

I unhook the note from the magnet and crumple it into a ball. "Well, I guess there's no need to leave a note then," I say to no one in particular.

Asher blocks the doorframe, his arms crossed over his chest. Standing there, imposing in the open space, I notice how big he actually is. He looks like he wants to say something but isn't quite sure how to word it.

"What's going on?" I ask on impulse.

His jaw flexes a few times. "Do you trust me?"

"Of course."

"You didn't hesitate," he observes. "You should hesitate."

"Why?"

"So I know you thought about it."

I pause for a minute before saying, "Yes, I trust you."

He crosses the kitchen in three long strides. His hands creep up to cradle my face.

"Asher, you're starting to freak me out."

He brushes a kiss across my forehead then pulls me to his chest. Something rumbles like he's speaking. I think I make out the words "I'll fix this."

Fix what? My heartbeat thumps steadily in my throat.

"What did you break?" I ask into his shirt.

He doesn't answer, just pulls me tighter into him.

"Asher?"

He cradles my face between his hands. "Don't worry. I'll protect you."

I explode into laughter. "You'll protect me? From what? Your cousin?"

I may be mistaken, but from the looks of Kaleb, I assume the only protection any girl needs from him is a bucket to catch the drool so they don't drown.

Asher closes his eyes and shakes his head. "Glad you find this funny."

"Oh, I find this hilarious," I inform him.

Kaleb is right where we left him, leaning against the Jeep, when we return outside. At least it stopped snowing. He eyes us knowingly before cocking one single dark eyebrow.

"We ready then?" he drawls.

Asher gives a tight nod. "Just get in the damn car. Back seat, Kaleb. Nicoletta gets the front."

"Of course," he responds, popping the seat forward and climbing into the back. His coat clings to him like a second skin. I would probably trip if something was dragging at my ankles like that.

I climb into the front seat, a little embarrassed. Then I fumble with the seatbelt until it clicks in good and tight. Snow plus twenty degree weather equals black ice. Carry the two, and that equals a very scared Nicky. Who says I'm not good at math?

"I don't get it," I say dumbly.

Both of the boys turn to look at me with inquiring expressions.

"Well, your sister and you look nothing alike. You have dark hair. She has red. But I can see the resemblance in you two."

Kaleb laughs. Even his laughter has a sexual undertone. He leans forward in his seat and says to Asher, "God, you haven't told her anything."

Asher shakes his head. "Not supposed to, remember?"

I stare at them confused.

"Yeah, but there's some things you *can* tell her. Some things you *should* tell her. Like—"

Asher cuts him off, his voice dripping venom. "Thanks, Kaleb. Now, shut up."

What all *hasn't* Asher told me? I mean, I'm sure it's a lot. We haven't known each other that long. But it's been long enough for me to confide in him. For me to have revealed the disturbed feelings I get from Jac.

Asher's house looks exactly the same as the last time I was here, only now there's a symbol across his red door. I recognize it as the symbol from the sword downstairs. I make a mental note to ask Asher about it when Kaleb isn't in earshot.

Spilling out of the Jeep, we head into the house. His room will always surprise me, I think. It's just so much space for one teenager. Instantly, I notice the sword is no longer pegged to the wall above the bed. It's been moved to the wall behind the TV. A huge improvement, I must say.

Kaleb stares at the blade as if it is the answer to all universal questions or something. His eyes trace every inch of it like he is memorizing every detail.

And I'm staring at him. A fact I'm only aware of when Asher steps down the stairs after me.

"I brought you a Dr. Pepper. I hope that's good enough," he says only to me. His eyes don't move from my face. It appears someone has issues with their cousin.

I take the already opened can from him and sip at the carbonated sweetness. It freezes my throat on its way down. My dad used to tell me that was the sign of a really good can of soda. I tend to agree.

Without looking, Asher's arm extends out. A can sails through the air toward Kaleb's head.

"What the hell?" I say, my words fading somewhere in the air between us.

Kaleb whirls around faster than I've ever seen anyone move and plucks the can out of the air. Did that really just happen? Talk about reflexes.

He smiles blindingly at Asher and nods his head graciously.

What I don't get is why he offers a show of respect when the airborne can could have easily pegged him in the skull. Asher grabs my elbow and leads me over to the couch. Honestly, hanging out with the two of them may confuse me to the point of vertigo.

I plop down before asking, "Did he really just catch that?"

"Yep," Kaleb answers, but might as well have said "duh" for all the inflection he has in his voice. "It was a pussy throw," he continues. "If he wanted to tag me, he would have tried harder."

Asher seems unmoved. "You feeling alright?"

It takes me a second to realize he's talking to me. "Yeah, I think so. Just disoriented."

Kaleb sits on the corner of Asher's bed. His elbows press into his knees as he leans forward. His fingers flip the tab on top of his soda can and release it with an echoing Pop!

"Will you stop that?" Asher snaps, shooting a nasty look over his shoulder at Kaleb. He's taken to kneeling on the floor in front of me.

"What am I doing?" Kaleb responds.

"That incessant noise, squash it, please."

The noise stops.

My head falls back against the cushion of the couch.

Asher's eyes drop to the floor. All his dark luscious hair falls in a waterfall across his face. With one of his hands on my knee, he squeezes me gently. His face lifts to meet mine again and his eyes seem deeper, darker somehow.

"There's a lot I need to tell you. But first, I need you to tell me about yesterday," he says with such sadness that I almost don't want to say anything at all.

"What's going on?" I reply.

"Please, just tell me why you were screaming when Brady got to your house."

I glance over his shoulder at Kaleb, who is still perched on the bed, mechanically flipping the tab on his can again. He stops when he sees me looking at him and sets the can on the floor. He shrugs innocently. "You can trust me, remember?"

I didn't expect to have an audience when I told Asher about my dream. It was hard enough to accept that Asher might judge me, but Kaleb seems like the type who would tease me all the way into next year. "You'll think I'm crazy," I say, shaking my head. "It was just a scary dream."

Asher turns his head toward Kaleb. I can't see his face, which makes me a little nervous. Maybe they already think I'm crazy. But Kaleb isn't looking at him. He's staring off into space somewhere, his eyes focusing on something I can't see. Then he looks at me, a whole untold story in his gaze.

What he says next silences my thoughts.

"Crazy is for the weak-minded. Only people who can't handle the truth call it a lie. Don't convince yourself that your mind is misinforming you. The only thing you can truly trust is yourself."

"Oh god," Asher sighs. "Where the hell did you get that from, a fortune cookie?"

Kaleb clears his throat and scrubs at his face with his hands. He glares at Asher and says with narrowed eyes, "Nope. That was all me and it's true." A smile forms on his lips. He winks. "Trust me."

"But you just said that the only thing I can trust—," I counter.

He holds a hand up to stop me. "Yes, I did, and I stick by it." He pushes himself off the bed and drags the computer chair over. He turns it backwards and straddles it right next to Asher, who looks annoyed. "Listen, I want you to trust me enough to believe that I won't judge you or think you're 'crazy.'" His nose wrinkles at the word. "Tell me what I need to do to make that happen."

Asher's head turns to the side, his face a mask of alarm. I wonder what has him so high-strung.

"Do you trust Asher?" Kaleb adds.

I nod, but say, "I'm not sure anymore."

Before Asher can react, Kaleb says, "And it's fair for you to wonder. I imagine you're curious about what secrets he's keeping from you."

"Yeah, I am." It's surprisingly easy to admit. Either because I can't see Asher's face or my drink was spiked with some sort of truth serum.

"What I will offer you is two truths for one. Do you agree, Asher?"

Asher sits on the floor. He props his elbows on his knees and rakes his fingers through his hair a few times. Finally, he nods, but not without telling Kaleb, "I hate you so much right now."

My interest is piqued. "Two truths?" I clarify.

Kaleb smiles warmly. I can almost feel the heat of it passing along my skin. He nods. "One for me, one for my... cousin. In exchange for one from you."

I think about that for a moment. Even if they do tell me something, how do I know what's truth anymore? There's no telling what has Asher so panicked. What he's been keeping from me. "How do I know you won't lie?"

"Interesting question. Truthful answer? You don't. There's no way you can understand what my word is worth. I will give my most solemn vow to you that I won't lie to you. Not now. Not today. Not ever."

In the course of his words, Asher has curled into himself on the floor. He rocks back and forth, hugging his knees to his chest. Would it be cruel to demand an oath from him as well or just redundant?

I let out an exasperated sigh. "Here I am alone in a room with two guys and all they want to do is play the worst game of 'Truth or Dare' ever. Go figure."

Kaleb shakes his head. "That's not all one of us wants from you." His eyes shift down toward his cousin curled up on the floor. Then he winks at me. "Consider that a freebie."

"God," Asher groans from the floor.

"Is it true?" I ask.

He nods. "But you already knew that. It's nothing new."

I fight the urge to smile while my ego inflates faster than a balloon hooked up to a broken helium tank. "Actually," I say, "I didn't."

"Do you agree to the terms?" Kaleb says, steering us back to the conversation.

I take a deep breath, considering my options. I could either give them what they want and, in turn, satisfy the curious side of me that is so intent on learning what their secrets are, or I could... what? Leave? No way.

I nod, decisively. "I agree. But you first."

"Fine. What would you like to know?" Kaleb crosses his arms over the back of the chair and rests his chin on his forearms. The muscles under his jacket strain against the seams. Before he did that, I hadn't realized how big he was. Now I wonder if it was tailored to look that way. Unconsciously, I glance at Asher to compare, but with him curled into a ball like a lost child, it's hard to judge.

What could I possibly want to know about Kaleb? I just met him so it's not like he has any secrets he can surprise me with. Nor would his secrets be of any consequence. It's his cousin I want to get at. His secrets affect me on a more personal level. But if I only get one truth, which one would I want?

"You choose," I tell Kaleb. "Tell me something about you. Like, why are you here? And remember, you swore to the truth." I wonder if I should have made him swear on the bible. If I had, would I have trusted him more? Probably not. Nothing can stop a lie except the liar.

"Why I'm here?" he asks with a chuckle. "That's it?"

"Yeah."

"Easy. I'm here for the sword." His tone is so nonchalant I almost don't think I heard him correctly. But why would he tell a lie about that? What would he gain?

Arching an eyebrow, I say, "Can I ask why?"

He shifts, propping his head up with his hand. "You can, but you might not like the answer."

"Try me," I tell him.

"Revenge."

Oh. God. Did I just hear him correctly? The only kind of revenge I can think of that includes a sword is the bloody kind. I imagine all the awful scenes where teenagers use violence as revenge. It's not a pretty scene in my head.

"Before you start thinking the worst," Kaleb says, cutting into my thoughts.

Too late.

He clears his throat to hide some emotion I can't read. "My mother died recently. She was murdered." Before I can offer condolences, he continues in the same breath, "Her murderer is now after me. They have my father. I intend to get him back before he becomes a corpse, too."

"Oh my god," I breathe. "I'm so sorry for both of you."

"Both of us?" Asher says quietly.

"Yeah. I mean, they are your aunt and uncle, right?"

He pauses before nodding his head reluctantly. I would have thought he'd be more upset. Then again, maybe he wasn't close to his aunt and uncle. After all, Kaleb and Asher don't seem to have any sort of connection. If anything, it seems like they only exist on the same planet to irritate each other.

"So you plan to kill these people?" I'm proud of myself for how calm I sound.

"Kill, yes. People, no," he responds.

"Is that supposed to make sense?"

"Not yet. But it will."

I'm getting really sick of hearing that particular explanation. "Um, okay. Aren't you scared, though?"

He shakes his head. "Why would I be?"

"Maybe because you aren't invincible," I suggest.

He laughs. The sound surprises me. It doesn't match the faraway look in his eyes at all. A smile tugs at the corners of his mouth. "You sound like my girlfriend."

I want to ask him more about the girl who won someone who looks like him over. She must be the most beautiful thing under the sun. Though, she probably knows it, too. Instead, I ask, "Is that good or bad?"

"Good. Very good." His shoulders exhale some of the tension at the thought of her. That's what love is like, I imagine: a drug that sedates all the wild emotions you can't control otherwise. "Any more questions for me?"

"Yeah. Why kill them? Why not just turn them into the cops?"

Am I really having this conversation? This all feels like a dream that I keep expecting to wake up from. But why would a dream be so awkward? Kaleb has all the makings of a fantasy: hot, steamy trysts with heaving bodices and sultry kisses in the rain. Am I really so unlucky that I would have the dream where we talk about his girlfriend and plan vengeful acts of murder? Of course I am.

It feels so surreal, though. No one talks about murder with such cold detachment unless they are bad people, right? So why does every nerve in my body recognize how good Kaleb is?

"Because nothing is as you believe it to be. The cops cannot offer justice in this case. In fact, to them, my enemies don't even exist," he responds, matter-of-factly.

"Enemies," Asher scoffs. "God, you sound just like –"

"One thing at a time, cousin mine," Kaleb says, holding up a hand.

"I just don't think you should do this alone." Asher stretches out of his ball and tosses his hands up in the air.

"Are you offering to help me?"

"Well, no. But…"

Kaleb stares at him with a look that would have sent shivers down my spine. "Then shut your hole. We made a deal. I help you then I take the sword. No interferences. You gave me your word."

Asher flinches like a beaten puppy when the sadistic master comes home. "Yes, I did," he says, mechanically.

"Now," Kaleb says, turning back to me. "I'm sure many questions will rise later. I, for one, would like to know what we are up against. So shall we move on?"

I straighten and my heart beats hard against the cage of my ribs.

Asher's turn. Goody. Just what I've been waiting for.

Chapter 23

"Do I only get one?" I ask. "Because I have many."

Asher looks at me, shock raising his eyebrows.

Kaleb says, "That would be up to him."

"And will he tell the truth?" I ask Kaleb. This is the closest I can bring myself to demanding a vow from Asher himself.

Turns out I don't need to. He sits up, all innocent and trustworthy. "I give my word. Ask away."

Kaleb clears his throat.

Asher rolls his eyes then amends, "I swear to you, I will be trustworthy and honest."

Kaleb smiles at me, nodding in encouragement.

There are so many questions I could ask. Asher's obviously afraid that Kaleb is going to tell me something. I could ask about that. I could ask why Asher and Acey don't look alike. I could even ask why he has the damn sword in the first place. But, somehow, my first question ends up being, "Why did you ask me to the dance?"

His whole body goes rigid as steel.

Kaleb chuckles. "Of all the things you could ask, why that question?"

My eyes still on Asher, I tell Kaleb, "Because if I don't like his answer, I'm not sure the rest of it matters."

He presses his lips together. A dimple dips into his right cheek. I know girls who would swoon over that dimple. "Fair enough," he says, gesturing with his hand. "Asher?"

Asher's hand tightens into a fist. "The first or second time?" he asks through clenched teeth. His eyes are closed and it looks like the answer is actually painful.

"All times."

He shakes his head and lets out a long breath. "Brady is worried about you."

"Okay?" I urge. "And what does that have to do with the dance?"

"He told me to ask you."

My blood runs cold, freezing my confidence and deflating that ego. My chest burns. I pull my knees up against me to keep from shattering apart.

"Nicolet—"

"Continue," I say shakily. My hands fidget against each other.

"At Brady's New Year's party, he asked me to 'keep you busy.' He wanted to give you some sort of distraction."

"From what?"

"From Berkley."

"What did he offer you?"

Asher looks at me like I am the one digging the metaphorical knife into his back instead of the other way around.

"What. Did. He Offer You?" I demand louder.

He passes a hand over his face as if he can remove the redness from his cheeks. "His dad is in high standing with a lot of Ivy League schools." When he sees the horrified expression on my face, he adds hastily, "You have to understand."

"I don't have to understand anything," I respond, indignantly.

"It was the only way to get out of my life. My one shot."

A hot lump swells in the back of my throat. I close my eyes and will myself not to cry.

Asher continues, "It was only supposed to be the dance. Nothing more. I didn't think I would feel anything for you. I may have started hanging out with you because of Brady, but everything else was me." There's a long pause. "I'm sorry," he whispers.

A heavy hand touches my knee. I jerk back. *Please let this all be a dream. Please let me wake up. Wake up. Wake up. Wake up!* All I have to do is open my eyes. I peel my eyelids back and face the harsh reality: I'm not dreaming. My best friend really did have to bribe someone to ask me out. A single hot tear slides out of my right eye and burns its way down my cheek.

"Damn it," I choke out, wiping it away with the back of my hand.

Kaleb's hand rests on my knee, trying to console me. I bat it away. I don't want consolation. I want the hell out of here. I want to go home and crawl back into my bed where I can cry myself stupid.

Still shaking, I climb to my feet. I'm glad I didn't take my jacket off. Now leaving will be so much quicker. Maybe I can get out with some semblance of my dignity left.

"Where are you going?" Asher asks, his voice following me to the stairs.

I don't turn around. I can't see him right now. If I do, I might break down, and I refuse to give him that. I've given him too much already.

"I'm going home," I say in a quiet voice. "Goodbye, Asher."

When I get to the top of the stairs, I hear a string of loud exclamations, most of the words beginning with the letter *F*. Then there's a loud thump followed by glass shattering. I jump at the sound. The floorboards reverberate under the soles of my boots.

Careful not to let the knife sticking in my back impale my heart, I walk through the house and out the front door, letting it slam behind me.

I've been holding back the sobs for so long now that my throat feels like it's on fire.

Just make it home. One foot in front of the other. Breathe in, breathe out. I don't remember why breathing is important, but I'm sure it is. A cold wind rushes up behind me, sweeping my hair forward. When it all settles back into place, I see a Jeep parked at the curb in front of me: Asher's Jeep with its stupid glossy red paint and six-inch lift. I walk faster pretending not to notice.

"Nicoletta," Someone's voice calls from very far away. No, it only seems far away because of the heartbeat pounding in my ears. A hand touches my shoulder and it's all I can do to keep from running. *Don't run*, a familiar voice in my head says. *Please don't run. It's okay.*

The world around me mutes to a dull blue grey as if the sun passed behind a cloud. Just like Kaleb's eyes.

The hand on my shoulder feels like a cool breeze against my jacket. A few tears escape the dam I built up against them. Soon, it will blow. I turn to see Kaleb instead of Asher, but not before I bark out, "What the hell do you want?"

His hand remains outstretched where my shoulder was. Even with the wind tearing its way around me, he remains untouched by it.

"You okay?" he asks.

And for no good reason, I bury my face in his shirt and cry… and cry… and cry until I'm so exhausted I can barely stand.

Kaleb runs his hand up and down my back. He doesn't complain. Not once.

After letting loose a chain of nonsensical words, I manage to say, "You're girlfriend is one lucky girl." I have to laugh, have to joke. This stranger just saw me at my most vulnerable. All because of his stupid cousin.

Kaleb smiles at something over my shoulder, beyond anything I can see. "We have our problems, too. Not the same kind, mind you, but she has a lot to deal with."

I step back away from him. His shirt is soaked in my tears. If he stays outside, it will turn to ice. Just like I feel.

"Yeah, like what?" I ask, hoping for something to make me feel better. I wipe my face with my sleeve. The cold air freezes my cheeks.

He gestures with his hand toward the Jeep. "Get in. It's warmer."

I stumble toward the Jeep. Opening the door with my left hand is still not easy, but I manage. I also make it into the passenger seat somehow. "I hate this Jeep," I mumble, though it's not true. I love the Jeep. I love the musky smell of Asher clinging to the upholstery and drifting out through the air vents. I love the stupid skull-shaped knob on the stick shift. And I hate me for not being able to hate those things.

"He really does have feelings for you," Kaleb tells me. "He just makes a lot of dumbass mistakes."

"I can't hear this. Please, just tell me about your girlfriend. I need some honesty," I beg.

He looks at the road in front of us wistfully. "You wouldn't believe me if I told you." Then he smiles, but it isn't a real smile. "You'd think I was crazy."

"You swore you'd tell me the truth," I remind him. "Please. I just need something else to focus on right now."

"Okay. Well, I dream about her a lot."

"That's sweet," I tell him.

"You'd think so." He fiddles with the steering wheel cover. "But when I dream about her, she's always in trouble. Like life or death trouble."

"That's normal."

"Then it comes true."

"Oh."

"Yeah. Dreams can be either prophetic or they can be silent fantasies," he says. "My dreams feel like warnings. I feel like they are telling me how to protect her. But sometimes, I wonder if I'm seeing the future or creating it. If I sleep, I dream. If I don't..."

"Then there's no warning and in turn no danger," I finish for him.

He sighs. "I wish. Unfortunately, Kaida – that's her name, by the way – will always be in danger, I think. At least until she fulfills her destiny, whenever that will be."

I stare out the window at the snow covered trees. They look so dead, which is how I feel, ironically enough. "I don't believe in destiny."

"You should. Everyone has one. Mine is to protect her."

"What's hers? Being in danger all the time? The perpetual damsel in distress?" I say bitterly.

"No," he says with a breathy laugh. "I don't know what hers is yet. The future is constantly changing. No one can determine what will happen."

"How do you know that's your destiny then? It doesn't make sense."

"Because, Nicoletta. It's who I am. What I do. Which is also why Kaida and I can't tell anyone that we're together. It's considered wrong."

A small flower of empathy blooms inside of me. "That sucks."

221

"Hard," he agrees. "So, do you want to tell me about your dream or do you still think I'll call you crazy?" Again with the nose wrinkle.

"If you tell me why you hate that word so much," I say.

"It's a long story."

"I've got the time. Apparently I have no one to see since everyone seems to be lying to me."

He nods in understanding. "I'm sorry about that."

"Don't be. It happens." But the words don't match the burning sensation in my throat.

He leans back in the seat, shrinking down to eye level with the steering wheel. "Kaida is a witch." He appraises my reaction before saying, "You with me still?"

I shrug. "Sure. I've read up on witchcraft. I'm kind of intrigued by the whole thing. Which form does she practice? Do her parents not like it?"

Kaleb covers his smile with a hand. "No. See, Kaida is a witch by birth. She comes from a long line of magic. The real kind. When her mother died, she cast a spell on her so she wouldn't remember. It was kind of like a protective bubble. She was eleven when it all happened. Her mother was murdered. Of course, that's not what the police believe. They still buy into the idea that it was an animal attack," he scoffs. "Kaida is one of the strongest, most gifted witches in her line. Though, no one knows."

"About her being a gifted witch?" I ask. I suspect he's waiting for me to argue that magic isn't real, but it's hard to even think of it when every fiber of my being believes what he's saying.

"Either, or. Being gifted also means you are sensitive to unnatural occurrences. While most people use Ouija boards and whatnot to communicate with the dead, Kaida only has to think of her mother to hear her. The connection they share makes it possible," he adds quickly upon seeing my expression.

"Hearing voices? That's rough," I muse.

"Talking to them is even more so. Her sister caught her a few times. Everyone called her crazy. She was put into test studies for it.

Imagine being someone's lab rat because you're different." He shakes his head.

"That's awful."

"It is." He nods. "People are too closed-minded for their own good. They don't want to see anything they would have reason to fear."

Idly, my mind drifts to Brady and Jac. What would anyone have to fear from Brady? Aside from bribery, I guess. Jac is a different story altogether.

"But she's good now, right?" I ask. "She's no longer a lab rat?"

"No. The first chance I got I sprang her from the hospital." He smiles mischievously. "There's a reason why I'm telling you this, though. You are different, too."

"Yeah. Sure," I say sarcastically. But his words send a thrill through me. Who doesn't want to be unique?

He sits up in the seat. "Asher says you have reactions to people. Like an insight to who they are."

"Didn't we just establish the fact that Asher's a liar and a fat mouth?"

Kaleb looks directly into my eyes, searching for something. "You're wearing contacts," he says.

I give him my best look of sarcasm. "Yep. Near-sightedness is a bitch."

"Are your eyes that bad?"

The conversation has taken a sharp turn off of normal on to weird-me-out. "To wear contacts? Yeah. What are you getting at?"

He shakes his head. "Never mind. So tell me about this dream."

I tell him every little detail of that particular dream including the asthma attack in my sleep and the puke fest when I woke up. He nods when appropriate, but mostly stays silent like he is recording me and filing it away for later use.

"This Jac," he says when I'm done. "Does he give you weird vibes?"

"Like bugs crawling into my skin," I admit, cringing involuntarily.

In the thoughtful silence, he turns the ignition which makes the Jeep roar to life. He shifts into first and peels out like a bat out of hell. My stomach jumps into my throat.

"God," he says, barely loud enough for me to hear over the engine. "This is going to be trickier than I thought."

"What is?" I ask.

Either he doesn't hear me or he pretends not to. He continues to drive the roads to my house far too fast for the weather. I'm surprised when he pulls up in front of my house. He's only been there once. How did he remember the way?

"Good memory," I say.

With the index finger of his right hand, he taps his temple. "Photographic."

I struggle with the door handle, wishing I could heal at supernatural speed. Life would be so much easier without the brace.

Kaleb watches me with an amused smirk. "Hold up," he says after a minute. He climbs out of the Jeep and heads around to help me open my door. The air is a slap of ice after the warm car.

As soon as I'm planted safely on the sidewalk, Kaleb grips my shoulders with his strongly elegant hands. "Promise me something."

I try to look at his forehead to avoid his eyes, but fail miserably. The color sucks me into a world beyond reality. I nod, completely transfixed.

The voice inside my head assures me that it will all be okay.

"I promise," I say without meaning to. I'm more surprised than I would have been if my house had been uprooted and moved two blocks north. Alright, maybe not more than that, but equally so.

"I know you don't want to talk to Asher – and I don't blame you – but if anything weird happens or if you have more dreams, text him my name and I will call you back," he instructs.

"Don't you have a cell phone?" I ask, cocking one suspicious eyebrow. Who doesn't have a cell phone?

He shakes his head. A lock of dark hair falls from behind his ear and licks his cheek. He and Asher really do have some similarities. "Cell phones and I don't get along. Besides, where I live, there's no service. If there's an emergency, call him. I will give him instructions to hand the phone to me until you tell him otherwise."

"Okay. Are you sure he'll listen?" I wish he would stop talking about Asher. Every time I hear about him, the hole in my stomach grows wider.

"Yeah, he will."

"Do people always listen to what you say?"

Kaleb's eyes close slowly. When they open again, I notice the blue has swallowed up the grey. The calmness of the color flows through me like a warm breeze. "Usually. I try not to give them reasons not to," he says. "Though, in some cases, they don't. And then they die."

Chapter 24

After Kaleb leaves, taking his ginormous bag of problems with him, I'm hit by the arrow of betrayal all over again. It tears at my heart strings and stings in my throat.

As if it isn't enough that Alex so obviously thinks of me as "one of the guys" and nothing more, let's add Brady's pity bribes to the melting pot. Does he really think I am so pathetic that he has to bribe someone to date me?

And what about Asher? I confided in him. I've never told anyone about my bizarre dreams or the strange readings I get from other people. So why did I tell him? Because I was really starting to like him. Now all I feel is the urge to punch him. Hard. In the jugular.

Well, there's something I can do to retaliate, I remind myself.

I hang my jacket on the hook by the door and stroll through my house. There's no better medicine for heartbreak than coffee and Chinese food. Both of which are situated in my favorite room of the house: the kitchen. Once the coffee is brewing, I take my phone from my pocket and call Alex. He answers on the third ring.

"What's up, Nic?"

I'm so broken inside that I can't even feel the rush I usually get when I talk to him. "Where are you?"

"Just finishing up practice. Hey, I'm glad you called. I'm gonna have to cancel our movie."

Tears that have nothing to do with Alex sting the corner of my eyes. I wipe them away with my sleeve and clear my throat.

"Look, I'm sorry. Dave's not doing so good and the coach wants me to try out for his position on the football team. I really think I can make it."

"I don't care about the movie," I tell him.

"Are you okay?" he asks. He even sounds like he cares a little bit. Bonus for him.

"Yeah. I mean, no. I don't know."

"Wanna talk about it?"

My first reaction is to spill every tiny detail of what happened onto Alex so he can help me deal with it. Just as I'm about to, though, I get a strong sense that I shouldn't.

"Not really," I say. "I was just calling to tell you that I'll go on the stupid date with Tyler."

"Taylor," he corrects me.

I wave my hand around like it doesn't matter even though he can't see me. "Whatever."

"Really?" Alex exclaims. "That's awesome. Thank you, thank you, thank you!"

"Just set it up before I change my mind."

"Done, Thank —"

I don't hear what else he has to say because I've hung up.

I pour a cup of coffee, mix in enough creamer and sugar to classify it as a treat, and sit down at the kitchen table. The newspaper is still spread out over the table where my father must have left it this morning. Trying to make room for my over-sweetened coffee, I flip the paper back to the front page and move it to the side.

And that's when the headline catches my eye.

On the front page of the newspaper are three familiar looking yearbook photos just like my hallucination at the gas station. Only, instead of being girls I vaguely remembered, they were all girls I recognize.

With shaky hands, I push my coffee cup to the side. A little spills over the top onto my wrist brace. I barely notice.

"'Three local girls found dead from possible epidemic,'" I read out loud. The sound of my own voice sounds loud in my ears. But I have to keep reading. That's the only way I know it's real. "'Ashley Marinello, Lisa Tannis, and Stephanie Baldwin, all current students at Olympus High School, have died of complications from viral pneumonia, according to doctors. Autopsy results will show whether there were any other variables that may have attributed to their unexpected demise. Until then, it is recommended that anyone displaying a high grade fever, troubles breathing, and a scaly rash, seek help immediately.'" I trace the girls' faces with my finger. I may not have been close with any of them, but that doesn't mean I don't feel awful about their deaths. I can only imagine what their poor families are feeling right now. "What the hell is going on?"

Unconsciously, I pick up my phone and select Asher's number. My finger hovers over the call button before I realize what I'm doing. I toss my phone back on the newspaper.

There has to be someone I can talk to about this.

The only people I can think of are Alex, Brady, and Asher.

None of whom I can confide in right now.

I cross my arms on the table and drop my head onto them. Stupid dating life ruins everything.

For the second time this year – and it's only January eighth – I ditch school. Sure, I could have just ditched my two favorite classes to avoid Asher, but how would that help me avoid Brady? I don't have any classes with him. He just always seems to find me.

I wake up an hour before my alarm clock and stare at the wall before deciding today will be a sleeping day. I lie to my dad and tell him I'm sick. He looks me over, taking in the redness of my eyes and my raw nose from tissue after tissue and finally agrees that I should stay home.

"Are you okay?" he asks, resting his hand on my forehead. "You don't feel hot, but maybe we should take you to the doctor."

"I'm fine," I assure him.

"Are you sure? I hear there's some nasty virus going around."

"I hear that, too," I say, rolling to my side.

He sits on the edge of my bed and rubs my shoulder through the blankets. "You saw the paper?"

I nod.

"Did you know them?"

I nod again. "I knew of them. They didn't really know me. I used to be friends with Stephanie's brother, though."

His careful expression crumples. "I'm so sorry, honey. Do you want me to stay home? We could have a daddy daughter day like we used to."

I remember one time when my dad took me to the amusement park instead of school. Neither of us got sick very often so he decided we both needed a sick day. I'm not sure my mother ever knew that we went. Anyway, it was warm enough that I think it was May. We ate junk food, rode rides, and played games all day long. I still have the giant gorilla he won for me at the archery game. I kept it as a reminder of how safe I felt that day with my dad.

I smile at the memory. "It's okay, Dad. I think I'm just going to go back to sleep."

His shoulders deflate. It hurts to watch. No little girl wants to disappoint their father.

"Rain check, though?" I ask him.

The corners of his mouth lift slightly. "Sure. Anytime. Will you call me if you change your mind about going to the doctor?"

"Absolutely."

I close my eyes and don't open them again until one o'clock in the afternoon when my phone alerts me to a new text message. It isn't the first. I've been ignoring them and the calls all day. If I have to feel alone then why not be alone, right? At least I don't have to pretend to be okay when I'm by myself.

I put my glasses on and check my phone. My stomach does a little flip then drops straight into a vat of acid. Asher. He's been trying to contact me all day. I'm a little surprised he hasn't shown up at my doorstep.

Out of some masochistic curiosity, I check the message. It says: We should talk. Call me when you get out of school.

I close my eyes, trying to fabricate a response I think might hurt him because that's what I want to do most. I want him to feel the same drowning despair I feel. I want him to feel the pain he has caused me. My head feels like someone has been sitting on it for hours. All I get is a dull thumping of blood into my brain: a side effect from crying all night, I'm sure. The rhythmic beat of my pulse pounding in my head draws me back into unconsciousness. I don't even take my glasses back off.

"Nicky," a monotone voice says. It's thin and not quite real. "Nicky."
I try to open my eyes, but it feels like they're sewn shut.
"Nicky, come here, girl."
"Grandpa?" I say, my voice resonating in my ear drums like I said it out loud.
"Yes, it's okay. It'll all be okay."
I give up, letting myself fall backward into the dream. Darkness closes around me then slowly dissipates.
I'm in a room. My grandpa's room, I realize. From before he died. The bed is huge in the small space. A mirror hangs from the right wall above a black rectangular dresser. On it is a picture my grandmother: Nicoletta Cheri, the sixth. She died when I was too young to remember her. The picture is old, probably from the forties. Her hair is pinned up in a chignon, her face delicate and feminine. The grayscale colors give the illusion that her lips were painted scarlet. I love that picture. It sits in my parent's room on their dresser now.
The room has gold and red striped wallpaper with crimson carpet. I don't remember there being so much red. On the opposite wall is a picture of my father and his brother, Uncle Max, in overalls. It's a painting, though you'd never know it. The detail is so intricate you'd think they could talk to you. The closet in the left hand corner of the room is open. The door stands at a forty-five degree angle. The mirror hanging on it reflects back at me.
But it can't be me in it. I'm too small, too young. I raise my hand to my face and she does the same. Okay. Weird.
"Come here, baby girl," my grandfather says from where he sits on the bed. Pillows are propped up behind his back. He was sick. Everyone knew it, even me, and I was never told.
My legs move and before I know it, I'm climbing up on the bed. "Grandpa," my little voice squeals.
Two thin emaciated arms envelop me into a weak hug. "I missed you so much."
He smells of so many different things that my little nose can't pick them all out. All I can make out is his brand of cologne, the sweet smell of baby powder, and something acrid like rot. Death maybe? But people can't smell death. Not before the body is actually in a state of decay.

230

I freeze, letting the little girl take me along for the ride as she settles in next to her grandfather on the bed. I've been here before. Do I really have to be here again?

"So what's my little girl up to? How is second grade?" Grandpa asks.

The little girl spits out everything that happened at school that day. I can't control her, can't tell her to stop and see what's really going on.

"Cancer," I try to say. "He has cancer. He doesn't want to hear about a stupid spelling bee."

The old man watches us with an intrigued expression, but there's something else in his eyes: a longing only someone can feel when they know it will be the last time they see a loved one, the last time they will get to ask such mundane questions about school.

I watch him, memorizing the pallid color of his lips, the dark bruises under his eyes, the single black streak remaining in his thick grey hair. Under his ear, I notice for the first time, is a birthmark. From this angle, it looks like a two dark, curvy lines crossing over each other. I have a similar one.

"Grandpa, I love you," I try to say, but the little girl is still rambling on. When she looks up, so do I.

A man has come into the room. He stands next to the bed in what I then thought were green pajamas, but I know now are scrubs.

"Little girl," he says to me in a raspy voice. Even then I was scared of him. "Grandpa's tired. It's time for you to go."

"I want to stay," she whines.

Grandpa looks at me with a smile. "Of course you can stay honey. Why wouldn't you be able to?" But his voice has gone weak and he's fighting to keep his eyes open. He glances around to see what I'm staring at and looks right through the man as if he isn't there.

He can't see him, I realize. He has no idea anyone is in the room with us.

"Grandpa, are you going to get better?" she asks. I cringe because I know the answer. He's not going to get better. He's going to die. Just as soon as we leave the room.

He looks at us with a wistful smile. "I sure hope so, baby girl."

"You should go now," the man with the raspy voice says. "Go tell your mother to get some water. Grandpa is thirsty."

I remember feeling like all would be okay if grandpa just had some water to drink. She wraps her arms around Grandpa's neck, her hands rubbing against the rash that had consumed him. Then, with a kiss on the cheek, she bounces off the bed.

"I'll send mommy in," she squeaks.

"Yes, dear," he responds in his paper thin voice. "I love you."

"Love you, too." She turns and skips out of the room.

Somehow, I stay. In a form that is no longer real, I stand in the doorway, staring at the pale-haired man leaning down over my grandfather. My shoes feel stuck to the floor and when I look down, I see that I'm standing in a pool of blood. Thick crimson sucks at my ankles as if it were mud.

I look back at the two men. My grandfather is looking directly into the pale eyes of the nurse. "You came for me, didn't you?" he asks. And he's not scared.

But I am.

"This won't hurt," the man says. "Not much, anyway. Close your eyes, it will be over in a moment."

Then he rests a hand over my grandfather's heart, closes his eyes and inhales deeply.

And that's when I scream.

Chapter 25

I jolt awake, throwing the covers half-way across the room. My cell phone sits beside me as dead as my grandfather in my dream. I scramble to find my charger. The cord has fallen behind my nightstand. I jump up from my bed faster than should be physically possible and plug it in. It takes forty-five agonizing seconds to turn back on.

I scroll to the last message and hit reply.

KALEB, I type in capital letters. Then I hit send.

For two whole minutes, I sit, squeezing the phone in my uninjured hand, willing the breath in and out of my lungs.

When the phone rings, it's Asher's ring tone: *Rejection* by Social Offense. A change I felt necessary after last night.

I take in a deep breath and hold it when I answer.

I don't say anything.

If it's Asher, I'm hanging up.

"Nicoletta, you there?" the voice on the other end of the line says. It's most certainly not Asher. I would have known by the way he says my name. This voice is all velvet and chocolate, sweet and smooth, and a little bit deeper.

"Kaleb?" I choke out. My throat hurts from screaming and my eyes have started to water.

"Yeah. What's going on?" Muted by his voice is the familiar roar of an engine.

"You in the car?" I ask weakly.

"Yep. I'm almost to your house. Will you let me in?"

"Give me a minute."

The phone goes dead. Not much for conversation, I imagine. Or maybe he's just not one for cell phones.

I climb out of bed on shaky legs. My hair is greasy and lumped in a ponytail. I pull it into a new one and glance at my clothes: same pin-striped jeans and mismatched blue shirt as yesterday.

I pull out a new pair of jeans and a black ribbed t-shirt then change quickly. Just in case Asher is with him, I don't want to look like a homeless person. I need my pride. It's all I have left.

When I open the door, Kaleb is already on the other side, shifting his weight back and forth. His slate blue eyes catch mine for a second before he steps inside. When he moves, I see another figure in the Jeep. So Asher did come. I shut the door quickly. He can stay out there for all I care.

"So what happened?" Kaleb asks, leaning against the wall. He crosses his arms over his massive chest. With his hair pulled back in a ponytail, he looks downright frightening. Fit for a fight.

I shrink back against the door. "I had another dream."

"Okay."

"When I first met Jac, I had this weird feeling like I knew him from somewhere. I kept guessing, thought I figured it out, but I was wrong."

The muscled in his jaw twitches. I wonder if he wants me to hurry the story along. But what he says is, "So you had a regression dream."

"A what?" My head feels light and grainy. I lean back against the door to keep from falling over.

"A regression dream," he repeats. "Most people's memories age as they do. As the memories become too much for it to hold, the brain starts pushing parts of the past into a section of your subconscious. That's why you may get a feeling like you remember something, but when you try to get to it, there's nothing there. It's like a hole. Sometimes, those memories will turn into dreams when you're actively trying to access them, and sometimes you don't even have to try." He pushes off the wall and paces the length of the room. "What was the dream?"

"The day my grandfather died," I tell him.

"That would explain why it was one of the first memories 'backed up,' as it were."

"Why's that?" Watching him dance back and forth makes me dizzy. I slide down the door and end up sitting against it with my knees curled up into my chest.

"Because no one wants to remember losing someone they love."

"Makes sense."

He stops pacing and turns to look at me. His shoulders are tense. "But that's not why you called me."

"No, it's not."

Kaleb kneels down in front of me. "What did you see?" The contrast between his eyes and his hair is startling.

"Jac," I respond. "He killed my grandfather."

He rests a hand on my shoulder, a very non-intimate gesture. Something you would do to a stranger who just lost someone, which is exactly what I am. "Can you talk about it? Can you tell me what you saw?"

I rub my hands over my face. Even my skin feels oily, like I have been sweating. "My grandpa couldn't see him. He came in, told me to get my grandpa a glass of water, and after I left, he put his hand on my grandpa's chest and inhaled. My grandpa went limp like his whole life had been sucked away. It looked peaceful, but wrong, you know?"

He nods slowly. His eyes shift up as if he is trying to read something out of his brain.

"Can you handle seeing Asher?" he asks. "I would really like him to hear this."

I want to tell him no. I really don't want to see Asher and yet, I do. Hating myself, I nod. "As long as he keeps his distance."

"Deal." He takes my cell phone out of my hand and relays the message while I go to sit on the couch. Normally, I would let them talk to me in my room while I lay back down (it's not like my parents are home to care), but everything I've ever imagined doing with Asher in my room was blown to hell last night.

Besides, I don't want to risk anything of mine smelling like him.

The door opens and they come into the living room. Asher, refusing to look at me, sits on the loveseat to the left of the couch while Kaleb perches next to me.

I smile in satisfaction when I see Asher. He looks like he hasn't slept in days. He also looks like his dog just died. In other words, he looks how I feel.

"You didn't go to school?" he asks, finally meeting my eyes.

"Nope. Did you?"

He shakes his head. "Why didn't you call me back?"

Kaleb sighs. "Just shut up for a minute, Ash. This isn't about you."

"But—," he begins to protest.

Kaleb glowers at him. "Do you want my help or not?"

Asher folds his arms and sinks down into the couch like a scolded child.

Kaleb has me repeat every detail of my dream. It hasn't gotten any easier the second time around. Then he has me recount the dream before. Probably in case I'd forgotten anything, which I didn't.

They sit in silence while I start to get nervous.

"Anyone care to tell me what the hell is going on?" I ask. "What is all this?"

Asher leans forward. "Well—"

I cut him off with a pointed finger in his face. "Not you. I can't trust you."

He flinches, but settles back into the couch without argument.

Kaleb takes a moment to glance between Asher and me. When he's sure we aren't going to kill each other, he turns his back on Asher and faces me. He rubs his right eyebrow with his thumb. "I'm not very good at this."

"I find that hard to believe." I mean, he seems to be good at everything he does.

A snort comes from the loveseat. When I look at Asher, he glares back at me.

"I wish you would let Asher tell you. He's known you longer," he continues. "He knows how to say it better."

"Not that much longer," I counter. "And he's lied to me, whereas, you haven't."

"I didn't lie about everything," Asher interjects.

I glare back at him. "Just everything that matters then?"

"Look," he says, standing up.

Kaleb holds his hands up as if he's breaking up a knife fight. "God, why don't you guys get a room?"

I turn on him. "What the hell's that supposed to mean?"

"It means," he says with a smile, "that fighting is like foreplay to Asher. If you guys keep this up, I'm out."

Asher says, "Shut up, Kaleb." Then, without denying it, he sits back down.

Kaleb shrugs. "I speak only the truth. So," he says, turning back to me, "anyway. Which do you believe more, your eyes or your ears?"

I think for a second. What a weird question. What a simple answer. People lie, but my eyes will tell me the truth. "My eyes," I confess.

"No one ever believes what they hear anymore," he says with a low chuckle. "I wonder why. Okay. Well, this should be interesting." Abruptly he stands up and walks out of the room with his coat swirling out behind him.

I glance at Asher. He doesn't look at me. Instead, he slowly combs his fingers through his hair like a girl would do when looking for split ends. To be fair, I guess I did tell him to stay out of it.

Kaleb comes back into the room and sets my mother's ceramic salt and pepper shakers on the table. Next to it, he places a small white candle. I stare at the objects like they might offer up a clue to their purpose. They don't.

First, Kaleb upturns the salt shaker and dumps a pile of white crystals onto the coffee table. Then, he shakes some pepper over the top and mixes it together with a lazy finger.

"Wait, I've seen this before. These are my sins, right?" Back in nursery school, when I still went to church, they used something similar to this as a technique to explain baptism. The black on white was a depiction of how impure actions can tarnish the purity of your soul.

Kaleb stares at me as if I'm speaking gibberish. "Um, no. The average person would be half and half depending on what they believe is wrong. But that's a different discussion entirely." He retrieves a cinnamon shaker from his pocket. Less than an eighth teaspoon of rust colored particles fall from the top, covering the white, black and grey.

"This," he begins, "represents every creature on this planet right now."

Okay. When put that way, it's not very impressive. Actually, I see it as a representation of a mess that needs to be cleaned up before my parents get home.

"Let's say that the pepper is all animal and insect kind."

"Seems like there would be more. Especially the spider population," I respond with a shudder.

Kaleb holds up a finger. "Wait for it. The cinnamon represents all human kind."

Okay. I think on that for a second. Isn't that everything?

"So what's the salt?" I ask, confused.

"Everything else."

"I… I don't get it," I sputter. "What do you mean everything else?"

"Do you honestly believe we are the only life forms capable of intellectual understanding?" Kaleb asks me. "That would be like saying we are the only intelligent life form in the universe."

As it turns out, it's not my eyes I trust the most, it's the feelings deep inside of me. And right now, it feels like I swallowed a scorpion. I make a conscious effort to keep my butt on the couch. It's harder than it sounds.

I glance back and forth from him to Asher. Both sets of eyes watch me with a sort of wariness.

"What Kaleb's trying to say is that both of these scenarios would be like saying the Americans are the only intelligent force in this world when in fact, the Italian and Japanese citizens learn on a scale much more intense than ours," Asher explains.

Kaleb tacks on, "Have you ever seen pictures of the universe, Nicoletta? It's a greater amount of space than the human mind can imagine. To think we are the only intelligence out there would not only be wrong, but undeniably selfish."

I'm halfway up the back of the couch now. Despite the fact that there is no immediate threat, my chest heaves, my stomach turns, and my blood thunders in my ears. "So you're telling me that those," I say, gesturing to the salt scattered on the coffee table, "are aliens?"

"Not all of them, no," Kaleb says with a smirk.

I'm glad someone finds this amusing.

"There is a world out there you don't even know exists yet. How can I explain a flower to someone who has always been blind?" Kaleb pulls his hair out of the rubber band and rakes his fingers through it in an effort to keep his hands busy.

"We are not the top of the food chain," Asher suggests in an attempt to help. "There is so much more than just the species that we know about. Scientists find new fossils and remains every day. Do you remember in Science class when we watched that video about how there are thousands of layers to the ocean? How they said no one will ever know what lives at the deepest level?"

I nod. That was one of my favorite discussions for that class.

"It's kind of like that," he says with a shrug. "Only, we aren't talking about the ocean. We're talking about the whole world. There are creatures so good at hiding that they may never be seen."

"But there's more than just other species," Kaleb cuts in. "They don't all have to be alive. When someone dies, the energy has to go somewhere."

"Ghosts?" I ask, my voice sounding a little squeaky. "You're telling me that not only are E.T. and Bigfoot real, but so is Casper?"

"Every story has to come from somewhere," he says, leaning back against the couch.

I feel bad for being difficult, but even though my physical reactions agree that all of this is possible, my mind can't wrap around it. All of what they're telling me sounds like a horror flick or a TV show with great graphics. Maybe even *Supernatural.*

I force deep breaths before saying, "This is a joke, right? Please tell me this is a joke."

Asher drops his head into his hands while Kaleb looks at me with one single raised eyebrow. After a while, Kaleb finally speaks.

"How can you believe me when I tell you that my girlfriend is a witch, but you have a hard time believing that this guy, who killed your grandfather and visits you in your dreams, might not be human?"

Well, that puts things into perspective, doesn't it? "Because people still practice witchcraft? There was a whole group of witches who got killed for their beliefs. Hell-o, the Salem Witch Trials?"

Kaleb snaps back, "And millions of people have undergone exorcisms. So what's the difference?"

I feel his voice as he speaks, slithering along my skin like an electrically charged snake."

"Kaleb," Asher says calmly. "Chill. You can't force it on her."

Kaleb closes his eyes, but not before I see the red in them, and I'm not talking figuratively. I mean the color red like his pupils ignited into flame. When he opens them, it's gone.

I hold my hands out in front of me like I'm trying to calm the lion before it strikes. "Alright, say I believe you. That ghosts and aliens and whatever exist. What does this have to do with the two of you? What does it have to do with me?"

"Every species has a way to protect themselves. The mama bear for her cubs. The lion king for his pack. The most fierce and ferocious are in charge of fighting their battles," Asher explains. "We were born and bred to protect the human race. We are the silent guardians keeping watch, fighting to keep the human race from extinction."

"You're welcome," Kaleb adds.

I look from Kaleb to Asher and back. Then I burst into laughter. I know my reaction is probably the last thing they expected.

They both give me identical looks of confusion, which only fuels my laughter.

"What just happened?" Kaleb asks without emotion. "Did I miss something?"

Asher shrugs.

Through the laughter, I say, "So let me guess." I point at Asher. "You're Sam." Then I point at Kaleb. "And you're Dean."

Kaleb turns his puzzled look to Asher.

Asher grins back. "It's from her favorite television show: *Supernatural*. Go figure."

Despite my best efforts, the laughter turns to giggles, which bubble up my throat and make it hard to concentrate. Who could blame me, though? I spend a good deal of my life watching a television show where two brothers hunt all sorts of supernatural creatures. Now, all of a sudden, I have two cousins in my living room trying to tell me that they were born to do the same thing? There may be a thin line between fantasy and reality, but I think this is pushing it.

"I think she's lost it," Kaleb says, shaking his head.

"Try to remember what it was like for you to learn that the boogeyman was real," Asher responds. He runs a hand through his hair. "I know I freaked out."

I still don't know if I believe the whole thing, but I'm finally able to get a hold of myself. Maybe I can start taking things seriously. Suddenly, the hysterics stop and the blood drains from my face.

"You alright?" Asher asks. "Are you going to be sick?"

I wave him off. "Wait. Maybe I was onto something with the whole *Supernatural* thing."

"What the hell is this *Supernatural*?" Kaleb asks.

Asher stares at him. "Don't you ever watch T.V.?"

"Nope. I'm usually out fighting the forces of darkness who intend to take over our planet. You'll have to forgive me," he quips back. "Those of us who don't run from—"

241

"Enough," Asher growls back. "I didn't run."

"What would you call it then?"

"A sabbatical."

"Some sabbatical."

I do my best to ignore them, which isn't easy since the tension has ramped up to nuclear status. Any moment one of them might blow. "Do you think Jac could be a reaper?" I remember the episode we watched at Brady's house and how Jac looked at me when he caught me staring. The look in his eyes was so cold, so unnatural.

"A reaper?" Kaleb asks, turning to Asher who responds with, "A grim reaper. You know, a spirit who guides the dead to the other side?"

"I know what a grim reaper is," Kaleb retorts.

"Do you have any weapons?" I have to know.

Kaleb stops to look at me with surprise. "Weapons? You mean aside from the sword?"

I nod. "Yeah. Like guns and flares and knives made of silver."

Asher rolls his eyes, but Kaleb kneels down and says, "Watch." With one finger, he reaches out and touches the wick of the candle. It sparks to life.

I squeal in surprise. "How did you do that? That's insane. Can you do that?" I ask Asher.

He shrugs. "I'm a little out of practice."

"So what are you? What do you do? Are you magic?" I watch as the candle grows to a tall dancing flame. Kaleb twitches his finger back and forth, changing the direction of the tip.

Kaleb's head snaps up and the flame dies as if it was sucked back into the candle. "Everything has a little magic. You just have to find it. But, no, we are not magic. We are different, sure. I'll save you the history, but we are like you, just further evolved." He meets my eyes for a second. "Well, maybe not you. But further evolved than humans."

"Huh?" is all I can say.

Kaleb sits back on the couch. "Humans are all born with a talent or gift. Some have a way with words, others with song. Few, and I do mean few, are born with a sensitive third eye. Like you."

"Like me?"

"You wear contacts to hide the color of your eyes."

"Yeah. So?" I say, reaching for the extinguished candle. The wick is still hot, but the wax is cold.

"A long time ago, people believed that you could discern a psychic by the color of their eyes. If they had mismatched eyes then they were certain to know the future." Kaleb cants his head to the side. "I bet your right one is green and your left one is blue."

I place the candle back on the coffee table. "So what?"

"Our kind is gifted with the basic senses as well as our natural talent. We just have a stronger affinity with our talents. It may not make sense now, but it will."

"I am so sick of hearing that," I snap. "When will it make sense? Today, tomorrow, maybe the next day?"

"I can't tell you that," Kaleb says. "That's up to you."

I stare at the pile of spices sitting next to the candle. Here are everyday objects that have officially turned my world upside down. "Then tell me how you did it. How did you light the candle?"

"Easy," he says. "Energy and concentration."

"What else can you do?"

Kaleb's eyes shift to the floor. He looks at our beige carpet with a wistful look in his eyes. "A few other things." He makes a face like there's a bad taste in his mouth. "Anyway, to answer your question: There's no way Jac can be a reaper or whatever you called it. See, while there are some spirits who will sit with a loved one while they die, in the end, we all leave this world the way we came into it: alone." His voice is the sound of heartbreak.

"So what is he then?"

"I don't know yet, but I'll find out. Can I borrow your phone for a minute?" He holds his hand out to Asher, who immediately surrenders his cell phone. Not without a roll of his eyes, though.

Kaleb punches in a phone number and executes the call. "Iz," he says into the phone. Then he gets up and walks out of the room. I hear him ask about Kaida like a good boyfriend, but then his conversation is muted by the walls.

"It's a good thing I have free long distance," Asher gripes.

I turn around and give him the full weight of my glare. "So why didn't you tell me?" I accuse.

"Oh, are you talking to me now?"

"Shut up and answer the damn question."

"Wait," he says, planting his elbows on his knees and leaning into them. "I'm confused. Do you want me to shut up or answer the question? You can't have it both ways."

"How about you answer the question and then you shut up?" I sneer.

He seems to tense. "You couldn't handle it."

"I think I get to decide what I can and can't handle, thank you very much." I'm not really in the mood to fight, but now that we're there, I can't help myself. I want to scream at him. I can't say why, but the idea of reaming him a new one makes something inside me burst into flame: a very hot, intense, intimate flame. And suddenly I understand what Kaleb was saying about foreplay.

Asher pushes himself up off the loveseat and sits next to me on the couch. As he moves, I notice how great his jeans look on him. I shake myself out of it. I'm supposed to be angry.

"I didn't tell you about this," he gestures to the mess in front of us, "because I've sworn off my station. Even if I hadn't, though, there are rules."

"Why would you swear it off?" I ask numbly. "Kaleb seems to enjoy it."

Asher blinks slowly. "Yeah, well, that's how Kaleb is. He's the Messiah, just ask anyone. If there is some wrong to right, he will fight to be the first to do it. I know you don't understand. How could you? You only know a small amount of what we are about. But I want to live my own life and I eventually want to die for good. You know?"

I shake my head. Everyone dies eventually, and after that, there's no coming back. Not unless you believe in reincarnation, and I don't take Asher for a New Age believer.

"If we survive this, I'll explain it all."

"Promise?"

He smiles. "I swear upon my father's name."

I stare at him.

"Yes, I promise." His smile fades. "Now, can we talk about Brady for a second?"

I look at my hands rather than meet his eyes.

"You should know that there were other reasons why he wanted me to take you to the dance. He really thought we would have a good time."

"So why all the false pretenses?"

"What false pretenses?" he asks.

I let out a long breath of air. "Pretending you like me. Always hanging around. How about the other night at the party? Were you just grooming me for the dance?"

"Grooming you?" he asks, amusement lighting his face. "No, I was not 'grooming' you." His forehead creases in discomfort. "Well, maybe I was at first. But I really do like you, and if it wasn't for Brady's asinine plan, I may not have seen how much. I'm really sorry."

"So am I."

Kaleb walks back in then. He eyes Asher sitting next to me on the couch. "All forgiven?"

"Not yet," I say.

He looks almost giddy as he hands the cell phone back to Asher. "That's too bad. Because I think I've got a lead."

Chapter 26

It seems that when big badass demon hunters get a lead, they retreat to some secret lair that human beings (like me) are not allowed in. It kind of feels like hearing about a secret club in elementary school and then being told in the next breath that you aren't allowed to join. Stupid rules.

Not that I would have wanted to go. I mean, I did just find out that real life is more like what's on the T.V. shows than I originally thought. That's enough to give anyone heart palpitations. Some normal time might be just what I need.

After locking Asher and Kaleb out, I head to my room in search of something normal. Halfway there, my phone rings. I don't even have to look at the caller ID. I already know it's Alex.

"Hey," I say into the receiver.

"Well, you don't sound sick at all," he says. You can almost hear the smile through his voice.

"Yeah, well... what's up?"

"What's up?" he repeats. "What's up? I'll tell you what's up! You're talking to the new star quarterback! Please, hold your applause."

There's a sound like someone's yelling outside my window. I open my curtains and see Asher and Kaleb talking with animated gestures.

"Okay," I say, distracted.

"Okay?" he scoffs. "It's better than okay. The coach said I was the best he's ever seen. He told me that if I had tried out at the beginning of the year, he would have picked me over Dave. Over a senior, Nic!"

Kaleb looks like he wants to hit Asher and Asher looks like he wants him to. I open the window a couple inches to see if I can hear what they are saying.

"This is going to open so many doors," Alex rambles on. "Not only will Jen and I be a shoe-in for prom king and queen, but we're talking scouts. We're talking possible scholarships, Nic! Can you believe it?"

"I..." Really, I just want him to shut up. "I don't know what to say."

"You don't know what to say? Congratulate me, Nic! You were the first person I called. I wanted my best friend to know first."

"Congratulations then, I guess," I say, moving my ear closer to the window.

Alex's patience is wearing thin. "You guess?"

"Yeah. I guess."

The sound of a locker slamming echoes over the phone. "Is Brady with you? I've called him like ten times. Maybe he will show some enthusiasm for me."

My ears perk up at the sound of Brady's name. It's been a few hours since I've heard from him, I realize. No call, no text, nothing. "Wasn't he at school?"

"Nope. I figured the two of you ditched school again."

I shake my head at nothing. "I've been home all day."

"If you see him, tell him to call me. I'm going to call Jen with the good news. At least she'll congratulate me for real."

I smile because his little tantrum seems so strange after everything I've learned today. Imagine hearing that aliens are on their way to enslave earth, but your best friend is bitching about a broken nail. Yeah, it's kind of like that.

"I'm sorry," I tell him. "I didn't mean to sound distracted. You're absolutely right. Congratulations, Alex. Congratulations on becoming a high school cliché."

The silence over the line sounds like what you expect before the firing of gunshots. Only, I don't care anymore.

"Tell Jen 'Hi' for me," I conclude, hanging up the phone and shoving it in my pocket.

That's when I realize that I can't really hear Asher and Kaleb fighting through my open window at all. Furthermore, it's damn cold in my room. I shut the window and decide I need to go for a walk.

With one last look at my text messages – just in case I received one from Brady and didn't realize it – I leave the room to get my coat. Just because I haven't heard from Brady in a while doesn't necessarily mean anything wrong, but with everything going on, it doesn't feel like a bad idea to go check on him.

Especially since Alex hasn't been able to get in touch with him. I realize I could try calling him, but I'm not really ready to talk yet. At least this way I can go by his house, see if his car is there, maybe peek in some windows, and leave before he knows I'm concerned.

When I step outside, I see that Kaleb and Asher still haven't left yet, and it seems that I can hear perfectly well from my front step.

"You don't need me," Asher says. "You can do this on your own." He leans back against the door of his Jeep, his arms crossed over his chest.

Kaleb growls in frustration. He points a finger at Asher, inches from his face. "This is so like you. Do you fight for anything anymore?"

A drop, like a tear shed from the sky, falls on my forehead and slowly trickles down my cheek. It startles me. The air may be a little warmer, but I doubt it's warm enough for rain.

Asher's eyes flick to me for a brief second. Then he drops his head. "I'm sick of fighting, Kaleb. Don't you ever get tired of dying for a race that doesn't even know you exist?"

"No," He snaps back. "Because I know I exist and you used to feel the same way. What happened to the Asher I knew? 'We'll go down fighting and take as many as we can with us.' Remember that? You were a great warrior. But look at you now. You're just a... teenager." His nose wrinkles in disgust like teenagers are the worst thing he's ever come in contact with.

Asher pushes off the Jeep and takes a step forward, glowering at Kaleb. "What's the matter, Kaleb? You jealous that I get a life? That I can date and go to school and be normal?"

Kaleb laughs bitterly.

The wind picks up and blows cold rain drops against my skin. I shiver and pull my jacket tighter around me.

"I can date. I go to school. I have a life. But we are not normal. And since when did you consider normal a good thing anyway?" He pauses while Asher stares at him. Then he says, "Shit, this is about Acacia, isn't it?"

"Leave her out of it," Asher warns. "This has nothing to do with her."

"Oh it doesn't?" Kaleb steps back a few paces. "Of course it does. I can't believe I didn't see it before. You're trying to protect her. But you're only hurting her more by quitting. You see that, don't you? You can help me, we can get this thing. Otherwise, there's no telling how many of us it will take out."

I'm afraid to move, to make any noise. They both seem so angry, and when you see two huge boys on the brink of killing each other, you stay out of the way.

"You don't know what—," says Asher.

And right then, my phone dings with a new text message.

Kaleb tenses and turns around.

Without showing any remorse, I pull the phone from my pocket and check the message. It's not Brady like I had been hoping.

It's from Alex. *Taylor will pick you up Friday at 7. I already gave him your address*, it says.

I shake my head and shove my phone in my pocket. I honestly forgot that I agreed to go on this stupid date and after the last phone call, I hoped he had forgotten, too. Suddenly, I feel ill. My stomach hurts and my skin burns.

"You okay?" Kaleb asks, a concerned crease in his forehead.

"Just going for a walk," I tell them. "Carry on. But do me a favor and clean up any blood you spill. My parents are a little particular about crime scenes."

With that, I turn and head South down the sidewalk. The crisp air, clean from the tiny bit of rain that has strangely dried up, feels so good in my lungs. It's strange how you can go so long barely breathing without notice, but once the air clears, you realize how little oxygen you've actually been living off of.

The sound of boots on cement follows me for a few moments before Asher slows down next to me. He's not even breathing hard.

I glare at him and keep walking. "God, can you say 'stalker?'"

"I thought you might like some company," he says. "I guess I was wrong."

"I guess so." But, that's not exactly true. As much as I hate it, when Asher's around, the pain in my stomach ebbs and I feel safe. It's almost like his presence makes my skin fit better.

"You're still mad," he observes.

"You think?"

"Listen," he says. "I know I can't even begin to tell you how sorry I am—"

"No, you can't," I say, cutting him off.

He steps in front of me and stops. It's all I can do to avoid running into him.

"Let me make it up to you." His eyes look so unnaturally gold in his pleading. Like the flecks of his irises have inflated until they burst open and bled all over the almond color with its ink.

I shake myself mentally out of his gaze. "I'll think about it."

He smiles and steps aside. "That's all I ask."

I stare at him for a minute before I start walking again. He falls into step beside me.

"So, where are we going?" he asks.

I glance around the neighborhood I've grown up in. Down the street from my house is where Spencer Adams lives. Brady lives two blocks South and one block east of that. My grandfather used to live two streets to the West and Alex lives five houses down from that. This is my area, my home, and somehow, Asher has made himself a staple here in the short amount of time he's lived here.

I'll be damned if I let Jac do the same thing.

"I'm going to see if Brady is home," I tell him. "I haven't heard from him in a while. It's like he called me a million times and then just stopped."

Asher shoves his hands in his pocket and shrugs his shoulders. To anyone else, he might look cold, but I'm starting to wonder if his thermostat is broken.

"Maybe he decided to give you space," he suggests. "Or maybe he's busy."

"Yeah, okay," I say. "Or maybe he's in the hospital dying of some crazy virus no one can seem to get under control like those three girls at school."

Asher stops walking. He grabs my sleeve and pulls me around to look at him. "What are you talking about? What three girls at school?"

"You didn't see the news? Three girls from school died." I tick their names off on my fingers, "Ashley Marinello, Lisa Tannis, and Stephanie Baldwin. You remember that guy we saw at the hospital? Seth? Stephanie was his sister."

He presses his hands into either side of his head. "They all died at once?"

I nod. "Two days ago."

Asher's eyes shift up like he's trying to remember something and can't. I guess he doesn't have the same photographic memory Kaleb does. "So all in all, we know five people who have all been admitted to the hospital, three who have died, right?"

I hesitate.

"Who else?" he prods.

"It may be nothing, but that accident we saw coming back from Provo, you remember?"

He cocks an eyebrow and bobs his head once.

"I didn't actually know her, but I saw her on T.V. the night before. Her name was Sarah Crocker. I also had a dream where I was driving in the car with her. Well, actually, I was her. Anyway, there was someone in the back seat. He touched her – me – and I – she – couldn't move. It was like his touch sucked the life out of me. At least long enough to distract her."

Asher runs a hand through his hair. "Why didn't you tell me this before?"

I throw my hands up. "Because, Asher. I have strange dreams — always have, and sometimes those dreams come true. It happens and I deal with it. Normally I don't run around sharing that information with strangers."

"I thought you trusted me," he says, sounding hurt.

Something dark unfurls inside me. In a low, menacing voice, I challenge, "Do you really want to talk to me about trust right now?"

He takes a step back, a surprised look on his face. "Fair enough."

"Now, if you don't mind," I say, turning around and stomping off.

Asher follows a few feet behind me. The silence between us is awkward, yet comforting. I wish he'd say something to fill the void, but appreciate that he knows when to shut up.

I wish it were easier to make up my mind.

Once we get to Brady's, Asher steps up next to me, hands in his pockets again. "Well, his car is here."

"That doesn't mean much," I tell him, waving my hand at the Lexus parked next to it. "That's his dad's car. It's a strange occurrence he usually tries to avoid."

Asher shrugs. "Okay, so what do you want to do?"

"I'm not going to do anything," I say, grinning. "You are."

"Excuse me?"

"Don't look so surprised. You owe me a great many things. Talking to Mr. McGowan is just the beginning of that list."

Asher looks like he wants to argue, but thinks better of it. He groans. "Fine."

If history is any indication, Mr. McGowan, if he sees me, will invite me in for coffee. And I believe we have already established that only a moron could turn down the delicious roast Mr. McGowan can brew. Since I am not a moron, I take three steps to the left and lean up against (read: hide behind) the tree in their front yard.

I tip my head forward so I can see what Asher is doing.

The front door opens and Mr. McGowan, dressed in his suit, fills the door frame. He's a tall man, about six-foot-one, with distinguished gray streaks on either side of his auburn head of hair. He's still wearing his glasses like he was in the middle of reading a deposition.

"Hello, is Brady home?" Asher asks.

Mr. McGowan removes his glasses and rubs the bridge of his nose. "You just missed him. He was going out with his friend, Jac, I believe."

Even from here, I can see Asher's shoulders tighten. He stands up straight and nods. "Thank you, sir. Will you tell him that Asher Rowan stopped by?"

Mr. McGowan puts his glasses back on and gives Asher the once over. "So you're Asher Rowan? My son's told me good deal about you. I hear you are interested in going Ivy League."

I growl beneath my breath. That coffee is looking awfully good all of a sudden.

"Yes, sir," Asher says with a respectful nod of his head.

"It's good to see a young man like you striving toward more in life." Mr. McGowan beams. It's like he can see something in Asher that reminds him of himself. He's never looked at Brady that way. "We should set up a time to meet. You can bring your parents," he says.

"Actually, it's just my dad," Asher says. "My mom died a long time ago."

"Sorry to hear that, son."

Son? Good thing Brady isn't home. This might just kill him.

"It's been a long time. I think it's made me a stronger man in the long run."

Mr. McGowan gives Asher a light punch to the arm. "That's what I like to hear." He pulls out his wallet, extracts a card, and hands it to Asher. "Call my secretary and we'll get something on the books. I'll tell Brady you stopped by."

"Thank you, sir," Asher says as the door closes.

I abandon my hiding spot behind the tree and start walking home before Asher is even off the steps.

"Nicky, wait up."

"Can't," I say. "I'm so disgusted by your flirting with Mr. McGowan that I might puke if I stand still."

Asher snorts. "Flirting, really?"

"Absolutely," I say, turning my nose up in the air for what may be the first time ever. "Tell me you weren't flirting with his power and status. I dare you."

"I was not."

"Sure you were. But who can blame you? I mean, school is the most important thing to you, after all."

Asher catches up to me and falls in stride. "Will you stop?"

I do as I'm asked, but not without irritation seething from my pores. I cross my arms over my chest and wait.

He scrubs a hand over his face. "I'm not going to ask you to try to understand what it's like to live my life. What I am going to ask is that you try not to read me as if I'm black and white. Because I'm not."

"Don't you get it?" I say, my voice cracking. "This has nothing to do with your life. This has to do with your blatant disregard for mine."

Asher takes a step forward, his hand hovering near my face. When I don't pull away, he tucks a lock of hair back behind my ear. "I don't...," he trails off.

"In my world, it doesn't take a bribe for a guy to ask a girl out. In my world, people don't lie to their friends."

He tilts his head to the right as if he's thinking about it. The space between his lips and mine is decreasing by the second. "See, that's where we enter that grey area," he says. "Because in my world, people you care about are cannon fodder and telling the truth will get you killed. Sometimes worse."

"Maybe one day you can make me understand," I tell him. "But sadly, today is not that day." I step out of the circle of his energy and immediately feel frozen to my core.

I turn on my heel, hunch into my jacket, and slowly walk back toward my house.

Asher doesn't follow. Or if he does, his demon hunting resume must include master ninja, because I don't see him once.

My phone rings with Asher's ring tone as I step inside my house. I stare at the screen, my jacket half on, half off, and debate on answering.

Just before the song ends and sends him straight to voicemail, I pick up the call.

"Nicky, don't hang up," Kaleb says. "I want you to do something for me."

I lift the phone to my ear. "Frankly, Kaleb, I'm tired of doing things for other people right now. Why don't you do something for me instead?"

He chuckles. "Rough night?"

"Not as bad as yesterday," I tell him.

"At least there's that. How about a little quid pro quo? You do this thing for me and I'll do something for you. You're choice. The sky's the limit. From ice cream to helping you hide a body." He laughs to let me know he's kidding.

I think about it. "Okay, fine. What do you want me to do?"

"All I want you to do is meditate before you go to bed. Then when you wake up, write down whatever you saw in detail. Pretty easy, right?"

"Sure," I agree. "Except that I'm not very good with detail."

"I'm sure you'll do fine," he replies.

"No, I'm serious. Ask any one of my English teachers."

There's a long silence. "Just try to write down whatever you can remember."

I look at the throw blanket tacked to my wall and pray to Dean, the God, that I can do this. "Okay, but when I do, you're going to tell me whatever I want to know."

"Agreed. *Cureieuse fille.*"

I roll my eyes. "I don't speak French."

"But you knew what I was saying," he points out.

"Only because my grandfather used to call me his petite fille to drive my father nuts."

He whispers something soft and in the same tongue. The words roll together like a ribbon tying itself into a beautiful bow. The sound of it caresses my eardrums.

"What was that?" I ask in amazement.

"A blessing. I'm amazed Asher hasn't spoken to you in his native tongue."

"Asher's from New York. Last I checked they still speak English." Though, to be honest, I'm not sure what to believe of Asher anymore. Hell, I'm not even sure his name is Asher.

Kaleb laughs. "Sure he is. Whatever you say. Goodnight."

The phone disconnects into silence. I pull it away from my ear and stare at it long and hard.

"What the hell does that mean?" I ask myself.

Myself doesn't have the answer either.

Why the hell does Kaleb have to be so cryptic all the time? Are all of them like that? If they are, I don't know if I want to meet any more of them.

I put the phone back on my dresser, trying not to think about the recent radio silence from Brady and what it might imply. I also try not to think about how I'm going to dodge him at school tomorrow.

When bed time rolls around, I take off my glasses, sit up and fold my legs into my body. I've read about meditation before so I know you don't have to do it in the Lotus pose, but that's as far as my knowledge on the topic goes. Closing my eyes, I imagine myself slowly brushing black paint over a wall of my thoughts. It takes a while, but finally, I see nothing but a clean slate, and of course the multi-colored lightning strikes that appear behind my eyelids when I close them too tight.

Breathe in deep.

Hold.

Breathe out.

Hold.

Just as I'm reflecting on how calming the sensation is, I hear a blood curdling scream, and then another. It reverberates through my bones and echoes in my ears.

My eyes fly open. The room around me is dark save the light from my alarm clock, which is blinking. Weird. It's not like the power went out. At least not that I know of.

I sit very still in the pitch of my room, my senses on high alert. Even the pipes sound like banging on the walls.

After a few minutes, I figure I imagined it.

I close my eyes again, but I'm too tense to relax and my breathing is impossible to pace. I make a mental reminder to thank Kaleb for that brilliant idea and flop down on the bed. I pull the covers over my head and am surprised to find that being trapped between the blanket and mattress offers an appreciable amount of comfort. It feels absurdly safe.

Slowly, I breathe in and out again. At first, it feels like there's a large weight sitting on my chest. My breath rattles on its way out and whistles whenever I breathe in. Then, it slowly starts to lift.

My thoughts have all returned, written across the back of my eyelids in glow-in-the-dark ink. Beyond those thoughts are phantom names. Some I recognize. Others I have never seen before. But one thing's for sure: they are all connected.

As I read through them, I know, deep within myself, beyond a shadow of a doubt, that each and every one of these people was murdered. And Jac was the one who did it.

Chapter 27

I have successfully ducked Brady through the majority of the day. Not to say I didn't think about taking another sick day, because I did. But the day is almost half over and I'm eating a nutritious lunch consisting of Doritos, a Dr. Pepper and peanut M&M's on the stairs leading to my next class. I'm probably being ridiculous. Knowing my luck, he ditched school today anyway, and I would have wasted all this time avoiding him.

Footsteps echo on the stairs behind me just before someone sits down a few steps up. I turn, half expecting to see Brady because that would be my luck, too.

"Oh it's you," I say when I see Asher.

"Wow. Thanks for that." He puts his hand on his chest theatrically like it's all he can do to keep his heart from breaking.

"You know what I mean. What do you want anyway?" I pop a Cool Ranch Dorito into my mouth and immediately chase it with my drink. Cool Ranch isn't my favorite, but it's all they had in the poorly stocked machines.

"Do I need a reason to want to talk to you?" he asks.

I shrug. "Guess not."

"Good."

"Fine."

I go back to chewing my chips and swallowing them before the taste registers. I have the book from English on my lap, but I couldn't read it right now even if I wanted to, which I don't. Actually, I just want to go home and catch up on sleep. It was impossible to fall asleep after hearing that god-awful scream.

"So what are you doing in the stairwell?" he asks after a minute of awkward silence.

"Avoiding everyone."

"You mean Brady and me."

"Whomever," I say dismissively.

He leans in close enough to smell my hair. "You don't really mean that, do you?"

Right now, I don't know. The natural scent of his shampoo and the campfire smell of his skin are clogging my senses. But I did a few minutes ago, before he leaned in. "Yeah, I do."

I'm awarded with an offended look.

"Want me to go?"

"No. It's fine. You can stay. But why aren't you out to lunch with Brady?"

Asher passes his hand across his face to hide his expression. "He went to lunch with Jac."

"And you let him?" I snap. The sound of my voice reverberates up and down the stairs.

"Nic, there's nothing I can do. He has to make his own choices."

Consciously lowering my voice, I reply, "But you know better than I do that Jac is dangerous."

A defensive block goes up over Asher's eyes. They turn from warm brown liquid to something cold and hard like stone. "Truly, I didn't think you'd care."

"Of course I care. Just because I'm mad at Brady doesn't mean I want him thrown to the demons."

Asher shakes his head and rolls his hand around in the air like he could rewind the situation. "I'm sure he'll be fine. He's a big boy."

"With a deranged psychopath," I tack on.

"Maybe. But we don't know that yet."

I think of the three girls who all checked into the hospital and never checked back out. I'm not sure what I would do without Brady in my life. "What if it's too late when we do?"

He sits quietly, watching my face. I wonder if he is mentally recording me like I do him sometimes. When it looks like he isn't going to answer, I say, "Kaleb said you quit all this. Why?"

He closes his eyes. His dark lashes shadow his cheeks perfectly. But everything about him is perfect, isn't it?

"Truthfully?" he asks, opening his lids to reveal golden irises. I've heard of people's eyes changing color with their moods, but never so instantaneously.

"Is it possible for you to tell the truth?"

He nods, his eyes clouding over. "I've been doing this for an extremely long time. While the experience is good, the consequences can be, well, fatal."

"What do you mean... fatal?" I swallow hard past the word.

"Come to my house today and I'll explain it all," he responds.

His house? Seriously? If I go over there then I might get answers, but how will it strengthen my resolve to stay angry at him?

"Please," he says through my deliberation.

"Fine."

"Deal." Then he gets up and walks away. Just like that.

And I'm left with the word "fatal" burning in my brain.

***

Mrs. Jarvis' usual uplifting mood feels damp today. She stands at the front of the room, her cardigan pulled tight around her shoulders. I've never seen her wear a cardigan before and it makes me wonder if this is another experiment. If she were to ask me right now, I would say that she's dressed in a way that represents protection.

I don't feel protected, though.

"Before we begin class, I would like to make you an offer," she says."

The class is silent. Some of us are looking right at Mrs. Jarvis while the rest of us focus on anything but her.

Mrs. Jarvis sighs. "Being a teenager is hard. In fact, it downright sucks at times. There are so many feelings and illogical thoughts floating around and it's impossible to make sense of it half the time. Don't even get me started on hormones."

At this point, I expect a few of my more immature peers to giggle. No one does.

Mrs. Jarvis continues, "I'm not sure, nor will I ask, what each of you believe about death. Whether you believe in reincarnation, heaven, hell, or an empty black space, the fact of the matter is: death is permanent. It's a change that your young minds are not prepared to handle yet. When you reach my age, it's a different story entirely."

I look around at my fellow classmates. I've never seen so many of them transfixed by a teacher before.

"I want you to know that the death of your friends, loved ones, and enemies come as a shock to us as well." She places her hand over her heart. "So please, if you feel lost or depressed, maybe like you are unable to gain control over your thoughts and emotions, come to one of us. I'm available any time after school and for those of you who won't take advantage of it. I'm even listed in the directory. Of course, for those of you who would take advantage, the number listed isn't really mine." She winks. "Can each of you promise me that you will reach out before you do anything... permanent?"

Everyone nods their head in agreement. Everyone except Asher and me. I'm still in awe over Mrs. Jarvis' offer. Seriously, what teacher does that?

"Alright, then," Mrs. Jarvis says. "That being said, today is our final day 'fighting' our disorders. You should have already submitted your interviews and final diagnoses."

I look at my team. If we were still doing the assignment, I would wonder if we were all suffering from depression. Jen and April sit in complete silence with wide, bloodshot eyes. Funny, I didn't think they were that close to Ashley, Lisa, or Steph.

"What we are going to do," Mrs. Jarvis continues, "is discuss your 'disorders,' symptoms, and possible causes. Some of you might be surprised to find that your diagnosis was wrong, but the majority of you did quite well. Next, we are going to suggest treatments. By the end of the semester, I expect you to be able to answer the age old question, 'Is the treatment worth the side effects?'"

We are released to our group. I notice how quiet our pep squad counterparts are and ask, "Is there something wrong, ladies? Do you not like the assignment?"

When they don't answer, Asher says, "I, for one, like the assignments. They're different and invigorating."

"It's not that," April responds quietly. "It's Melinda."

Asher sits up a little straighter, his interest piqued.

"What about Melinda?" I ask, having to watch the pronunciation of her name.

Jen sniffles. "Melinda is in the hospital. You didn't hear?"

I shake my head. Another person in the hospital?

Asher leans forward, dropping his head into his hands. "What happened?"

Jen wipes her eyes the way girls do when they are worried about smearing their make-up. "No one knows. She left work and walked out to her car and then —"

"They found her," April finishes for her.

"What? Where?" I ask.

"In her car outside the movie theater. We didn't hear the whole story, but —"

Jen jumps in, "They think she had a seizure. She's in a coma right now. I went and saw her last period. Weird thing is, she's two doors down from Dave."

April nods. It's as if it takes both of them to form one coherent thought.

Asher looks up then. His eyes meet mine with a knowing look. I turn to avoid his gaze.

I feel awful because now I know that the scream I heard last night was real.

And to whom it belonged: Melinda Carter.

Chapter 28

I half expect to see Kaleb playing some ironic game on the computer like *Resident Evil* when we get to Asher's house. I mean, what else would you expect some big badass demon hunter to be doing while everyone else is in school? But to my shock, he sits at the counter in the kitchen with three black leather-bound books spread out in front of him.

He nods his head by way of greeting before returning to his task of flipping pages back and forth comparing notes. At least I assume that's what he's doing given the presence of a yellow legal pad, a pen, and a pink highlighter. He looks like he's studying for the SAT's.

Asher grabs a Red Bull out of the fridge for him and a Dr. Pepper for me. He tells a distracted Kaleb where we'll be and leads the way down the steps.

"What's he doing?" I ask as my boots sink into the shaggy carpet.

"Research." He yawns. "We've been up all night."

"Any progress?"

"A little. Unfortunately, his lead is all hearsay. Before we can even begin to investigate, we have to prove whether or not the lead is even credible."

I pop open the can and find comfort in the sigh of carbonation. "Wait, I thought he had a photographic memory."

Asher eyes me as if I just told him that Kaleb and I exchanged friendship bracelets and created a secret handshake. "He does. So do I, but when you have as much memory to sift through as we do, it doesn't hurt to refresh them."

"And how much is that?" I start walking toward the bed to sit down and immediately do a U-turn to the couch.

"I don't know." He smiles. "Hundreds, maybe thousands, of years' worth."

I pause in mid-motion of taking a drink and cock one eyebrow. "Huh?"

I'm sure he meant to say he has memories of literature that old.

He sits down on the floor in front of me where he was curled up only two days ago. This time is different, though. He sprawls out instead of tucking himself in. It's as if his body language is trying to tell me that he has nothing to hide.

He sighs. "Where should I start?"

"From the beginning please."

After taking a long pull on his drink, he says, "Which beginning? Christian, Buddhist, Greek? No? How about further back? Well, in the beginning, there was a black void, better known as chaos."

I laugh. "How do you only have a three-point-eight if you have a photographic memory and extensive knowledge of religious myths?"

"Formulas," he says with a grimace. "I suck at formulas. Remembering them is easy. Applying them is stupid."

I smile. "Alright. How about you start at the beginning of your story?"

Asher leans backward, bracing his weight with his hands behind him. This is what he tells me:

"I was born to a poor merchant and his wife. In my village, women weren't allowed to work. They were housekeepers, caretakers, and that's it. My mother found a way to put her talents to work. She'd sew the items my father would sell. We weren't rich, but we were happy, comfortable. We lived in what is now known as Bordeaux. Sometimes, I even miss it. But that doesn't matter anymore. One day, while we were having dinner, a fire was set to our house. We got away, but everything was burned to ash. The people of our village were kind, don't get me wrong, but kindness can only take you so far.

My father was getting anxious. He wanted to find a place to call our own. There were other fires of the same mysterious kind. No one knew who started them. But that was just the beginning.

The whole village was befallen with misfortune. The neighbor to the North, a healthy young woman, was diagnosed sterile. I know that doesn't seem like much of a reason to believe disaster was on its way. One woman unable to bear children is hardly a sign of dark times. Not yet anyway. Not until she had a child one year later. The others believed she made a deal with the devil in order to have the child. I never believed it until I saw him. He was the scariest thing I've ever seen. At the time, that is. I've seen scarier since.

Then the neighbor to the South was murdered in his sleep. His wife was beside him in bed. She knew nothing until she awoke covered in his blood.

Things progressed.

Soon, there were tales of beasts who stood upright like men, but would rip your heart out like a lion. Children would disappear, never to be found. Shadows would overtake the sun, casting us in darkness for days. For those who were religious, this was believed to be the apocalypse.

My parents were scared. My father actively helped create a new society. Men and women, who wanted to combat the evil, rallied together. They discussed strategy. When I turned sixteen, I joined the war. It seemed natural. It was the right thing to do.

We called ourselves the Sentinels of Light, loosely translated. Many of us patrolled the streets at night, waiting for the opportune time to strike, but we were so weak in comparison.

My father went for help. He left my mother and me for close to a year. For a while, we wondered if he was dead. But when he returned, he had thousands of men and women with him. It was a sight to see. Our salvation had come.

But we were still weak. You see, our blades were not made of fire or iron. They were steel. We had no guns and many of us were not built to withstand such violence. Not only that, but my village was not the only one terrorized by malicious things.

They built an encampment out in the fields since there were so few houses to contain us at this point. I spent days at that camp training with swords and learning hand to hand combat. We still weren't safe, though. Not by any means.

I left for a while to care for my mother who had fallen ill and when I returned, I found nothing but ash and bones. The men had fled when the shadows came. Well, most of them. Those who remained found me as I was sifting through the pieces left of their kin. My father returned last. His face was red with anger and frustration. He fell to his knees and cried out to the heavens. He screamed to the God. When he didn't answer, he turned to the Goddess.

And she heard him. She came to see the destruction of her land and children. I wish I could describe the beauty of her. It's nothing like the new age pictures depicting Gaia. Those could never do her justice.

She told the survivors that she would aid us in our battles if we retreated to her protected land. You don't say no to the Goddess. You just don't.

So we went.

It felt like an endless journey, lasting days upon days, but when it did end, we came upon a place more beautiful than you can imagine. The clearing looked like something out of a story book with millions of wildflowers, trees so tall and old that their branches tickled the sky, and streams that glittered like jewels. We held our ground for weeks, feeding off of grain and water. We were starving when she finally came back to us. She asked for our vow to never harm those we intended to protect. Then she consoled each of us personally for our losses. I remember her arms embracing me and the warmth of her touch. I want to say she smelled of ginger and lilac, but that wouldn't be accurate.

No, she smelled of life, of ineffable beauty.

As she clutched each member of our army to her breast, the ground began to quake under our feet. She hugged my father last, holding him and caressing his long dirty hair, and when she let go, the ground opened up and swallowed us whole."

A gasp, which can only be my own, breaks through the silence. Not because of his words, though the story was fantastical in its own right, but because for a second, it was as if I was there and the earth was closing over me.

"When was this?" I ask, surprised I believe him at all.

"There's no way to tell. We didn't run off of calendars at the time of the Dark Wars and any record we would have kept was destroyed."

"But if you were buried alive...," I trail off.

"Then how am I here?" he offers.

I nod.

"Each of us received a gift and then we were all reborn."

I stare blankly at him. "That sounds ridiculous."

He presses his lips together in thought. "I can see that, but tell me how it feels."

Casting around inside myself, I realize that it feels like the truth. "Even if it does feel true, it's not like you've been completely forthright with me so far. How can I trust that?"

"I can't argue that." He hesitates then smiles. "Okay, so you remember the fight Kaleb and I had yesterday? And how it started raining?"

I nod. "That was Kaleb?"

"Sure was. Kaleb has been given gifts so few of us can even dream of. You don't want to see him get really angry. Though, if he sticks around much longer, you just might." He winks. "I'm not sure if you've noticed, but we tend to push each other's buttons."

"So I've noticed." I spend way more time taking a swig of my soda then necessary. "So," I hedge. "What was your gift?"

He smiles mischievously. "Nothing quite so intense."

He holds his hand out, palm up. The air seems to move in a breeze around him. His hair lifts at the ends and swirls around his cheeks. Then he takes a piece of paper from his pocket and sets it in the middle of his palm, pinning it down with one finger so it doesn't fly away. He looks at me, an amber glow in his eyes, and then he closes them. The paper flares up briefly before it turns to ash and drifts through his fingers.

I shriek involuntarily and jump backwards, up, and almost over the back of the couch. "Wha... what the hell was that?" I stutter.

He looks at his hands and wipes the brown dust on his jeans. It leaves a dirty streak on the denim material. "That's my gift. Like I said, we all have something."

"So," I say, stroking my nerves to calm them. "Let's see if I have this straight. Kaleb makes it rain when he gets angry—"

"Nope." He interjects, popping the P. "Kaleb inadvertently makes it rain when he's irritated. And he doesn't really make it rain, it just happens. I remember thinking that the Goddess was crying for him when he was upset." He shrugs. "You really don't want to see what he can do when he gets angry."

"Okay," I drawl. "So Kaleb does what he does and you can turn things to ash?"

He grins. "How do you think I got the name Asher?"

"Asher isn't really your name," I observe. Why do I feel like the slow kid in an advanced Trigonometry class? Can't they just come out and tell me anything without all the dramatizations? Maybe they think that if I figure things out on my own, I'll believe them more.

"Not originally, but it is in this life. My name was Damien – a family name. After a while, though, the name Asher stuck. It seems to fit me, I guess," he says, looking over the soot on his hands.

"That's for sure."

I sniff the sulfur still permeating the air. A chuckle escapes before I can contain it.

"What?" he demands.

"In *Supernatural*, sulfur is tied to the demons."

He closes his eyes for a long while, pain twisting his features like I just called him some unforgivable racial slur. "Thanks for that," he whispers.

I hold up my hands in mock surrender. "Hey, you asked."

"I did." He shakes his head before slowly opening his eyes. "Besides, demons don't smell like sulfur. Demons smell so much worse."

"Have you ever met one?"

He smiles. "Millions. So, do you think we're all crazy now?"

"No," I tell him, shocked by the truth in that one word. "I kind of feel like I've *been* crazy. Or at the very least, confused. But now, it feels like things are starting to clear up. Like I suspected, but never knew."

"Does it?"

I nod, watching him carefully. It's pathetic because he's touched me before with no ill effects, but now that I've seen what he can do, I'd be lying if I said I wasn't a little bit scared. "Yeah. It's like I've been in the dark, but this makes sense. Well, some of it does anyway. I'm still confused about you. Are you trying to tell me that you're immortal?"

He laughs out loud. "No. I live. I die. I'm human. Or at least I am in all the ways that count. I was born. Just like you."

"So how were you around before the French Revolution?"

He scowls as if he can remember the French Revolution. Who knows? Maybe he can. He scrubs his face with his hand then takes the last few gulps of his drink. "It's a form of reincarnation. Only, instead of our energy being recycled into a new life form, we are kept intact. We are an army and in exchange for our service, we are given life after life to defend what belongs to the Goddess." He lets out a long breath. "There's so much you don't know and it would take forever to tell you."

"That's fine. You have time." Then a thought occurs to me. "Is your sister, Acey, one of you? Is she a 'Sentinel,' too?"

He looks away, but not before I see the pain tearing at his face. "Yes. She's not really my sister, though."

"She was adopted?"

"Something like that. You'll have to ask her about it sometime."

"Why?"

"Because," he explains, "I can tell you my story, but I can't tell you someone else's. That would be a betrayal of their trust. I've told you before: I *am* trustworthy, despite all conflicting evidence."

I cock my head to one side and say mockingly, "Of course you are."

He flinches like I threw a lit match at his face. "The majority of the time, I am. Then there are times when I have to lie. But I promise you, I will never lie to you again. You have my most solemn vow."

"Sounds solid, but how solid is it, *Damien*?" I say, trying to link Asher to the name. As far as a physical reaction, though, I get nothing. It doesn't sound like it could be him at all. If anything, I liken it to how it feels when my dad calls me Colette.

I guess Asher could have been Damien at one point, but he's not anymore. He is Asher through and through. I smile apologetically when I see the disgruntled crease in his brow.

He stands up, making his way toward me. When he reaches the edge of the couch, he drops to his knees, taking my hand, and bowing his head over it. "To swear to the Goddess is the most solemn vow I can make. I hold to it. Can you say the same about swearing to your God?"

"No," I reply. "I can't say that at all."

His hair tickles the skin of my palm. It's reassuring rather than uncomfortable. After everything I've learned about Asher, his subservience at this moment feels like an honor. This must be how Cinderella felt when the prince knelt before her. You know, if Cinderella had worn boots and Prince Charming was a demon hunter.

Chapter 29

A loud noise pounds through the ceiling.

"What the hell is Kaleb doing up there?" I ask, glancing at my cell phone for the time. It's a lot later than I thought.

Kaleb peeks at my cell phone screen. "I don't think that's Kaleb."

"Your dad?" I suggest.

Asher shakes his head. "I don't really have parents. It's just Acacia, one of the Elders, and me."

"The Elders?"

He nods, watching the ceiling like it might cave in. "Every good army has its leaders. The Elders are ours. Six men were appointed to find and train us. They protect our secrets and are as close to immortal as you can get."

I run my fingers along the micro-suede material of the couch. The fibers turn a pale cedar color then back to chocolate brown. "So you live with one of them?"

He smiles. "Yes. We live with Gabriel, the third of the chosen, and according to the time, it's a good possibility that's him."

I draw a star on the fabric. "Why does Kaleb have parents, but you don't?" The thought of growing up with no parents is disconcerting. Even if they are stuck in a vicious cycle of hatred and lust like mine, it still seems wrong to be denied paternal leadership.

"I had parents. They died when I was in training. It's actually really common. The good ones don't even last a full lifetime. For Kaleb's parents to have lived this long, it's like a miracle."

"I'm sorry."

Asher waves one hand dismissively. "It happens. I'm sure they've already been recycled. Some of the really lucky ones can even find their mate from a prior lifetime. I hope they have. They were good together," he says wistfully.

I feel that same sadness creeping up into my eyes. "So nothing is ever over for you? Not like it is for us?"

The sound of a door creaks open then there's a soft whisper of movement on the carpet of the stairs. I look over my shoulder to see a man, huge and broad shouldered, standing at the bottom of the stairs. His button up shirt is tight over his chest making him look like The Hulk in mid-transformation. He doesn't look like he could be older than thirty. His face is all soft lines and curves. That is, until he clenches his teeth. The muscles jump and flex against his hard jaw. His dark, spiky hair is cut short. If I saw this man on the street, I would turn and walk the other way despite how sophisticated he looks.

Everything about him is intimidating. Maybe that's because there's only one exit and he's blocking it.

"Kaleb said you were down here," he says, a hint of an accent to his voice. "I brought pizza home. Oh, I didn't know you had company."

Asher nods from where he is standing. He must have moved away from me while I was busy taking stats like I was filling out some sort of Superhero score card. Six-four (maybe six-five), black hair, coal grey eyes, and about two-hundred and fifty pounds of pure "I can kick your ass and I know it" muscle. Just for starters.

"Gabe," Asher says respectfully. "This is Nicoletta Dubois."

Gabriel's eyes flick to me. His hard gaze softens and the corners of his mouth tug upward as if we were old friends. "Colette?" he says.

Doing my best to ignore the cold rush in my veins, I stand up and fake a smile. "Actually, it's Nicoletta. Nice to meet you."

He closes his eyes and shakes his head. Then he looks at me again.

"She's my friend from school," Asher says. "She's helping us with an investigation."

And just like that, the Elder's expression transforms into something dark and cold. "You know better, Asher," he scolds, pinching the bridge of his nose with his thumb and forefinger. "This is too dangerous. Besides, we're retired, remember?"

The tension building between them is enough to make me choke. I debate on ducking below their sight line and hoping they forget about me or slithering between the couch cushions. In the end, I go with the former because, frankly, I'm not sure I could fit between the cushions.

"People are dying, Gabe. What do you expect me to do?" Asher demands.

Gabe passes a hand over his face. "I knew Kaleb coming here was a bad idea. Now you've endangered a human. I sure hope you boys know what you're doing."

"We do," Asher snaps. "And after this, I'm done. Back to retirement."

"Right." Gabe hangs his head. "All that work for nothing." Without raising his head, he turns, and stalks back up the stairs.

When I'm sure he's gone. I step out of my hidey hole behind the couch. "Nice guy," I say wryly.

"He's just stressed," he tells me, his eyes focused on the door Gabe just disappeared through. "He gave up more than I did."

Asher's posture has changed dramatically in a matter of moments. Instead of standing tall and confident, he looks like a puppet with loose strings. Unable to help myself, I walk over to him, and wrap my arms tight around his waist. His chin rests on my head as his fingers find my hair.

"You hungry?" he says quietly.

Truth be told, I am hungry, but while pizza may have sounded good a half hour ago, the thought of eating with Kaleb and Gabe makes my stomach churn. I nod against his chest anyway.

"Good. Let's go get something. Pizza doesn't sound appealing anymore."

I look up at him with a smile. "Are you sure you can't read minds?"

He blinks. "A gift like that would be amazing. I would love to know what you're thinking." He hesitates. "Well, most of the time."

***

The answer is: Steak and mashed potatoes. The question? What do you eat after an awkward first meeting with your would-be, could-be boyfriend's father figure?

Obviously, I can't ask him any of the questions I want. Risking exposure is a huge no-no. So dinner ends up being more of a get-to-know-you affair than a history lesson. It's a shame really. I have a lot more questions.

Though, I guess it's kind of nice having a moment of normalcy with someone who is anything but normal. I get to learn his favorite color (green), subject in school (history, go figure), and movie (Fight club, never would have guessed).

He, however, gets to ask me more intrusive questions. After all, I'm not part of a secret army sworn to protect all human kind. I'm just me.

"Whatever happened to that date Berkley was trying to set you up on?" he asks me.

I raise my head high, pretending to be all gung-ho about it. "I agreed to go out with him on Friday."

Asher leans into the table. He makes a visible effort not to yell. "What? Why?"

I sip on my straw and get only air. My soda has been gone for a while. "Well, at the time that I agreed, I didn't have any other prospects."

"What about now?"

I shrug. "I don't know. What about now?"

"I don't think you should go."

The waiter passes by the table to drop the check. Whenever he comes by, the hairs on the back of my neck stand at attention. Then my arms begin to itch. I start scratching as Asher removes two twenties from his wallet and sets them on the receipt. The waiter stares at me and something in his gaze that makes me itch more.

"You alright there?" Our waiter asks. Something in the way he stares at me makes my skin feel like it's on fire.

He has one of those haircuts that covers his forehead and frames his cheeks. It looks like a helmet and it looks stupid on him. But that isn't what's irking me. It's something else. I give him a quick nod and will him to go away.

"What's wrong?" Asher asks, when he finally leaves.

"I don't know. I just got really itchy all of a sudden."

"You aren't just trying to get out of the conversation, are you?" he jokes.

The light in the restaurant is dim. The candle in the center of the table burns just bright enough that I can make out the gold flecks in his eyes.

"I don't think so?" I reply, making it sound like a question. I lean forward, the heat of the flame waving at my cheeks. "I think it's the waiter."

"The waiter makes you itch? You think you're allergic to him?" he asks, nothing humorous about his tone.

"I know. Ridiculous, isn't it?" I scratch my arms through the sleeves of my sweatshirt, marveling at how much worse an itch can get after you scratch it.

"Here's your change," the waiter says from behind me. I nearly jump out of my chair and run for the door. "You have a great night."

"Thanks, we will," Asher replies, his eyes fixated on me, his brows forming a perfect arc.

My neck itches almost as badly as my arms. I scratch it lightly, trying not to look like I want to shred the skin from my body. The waiter abandons our table to attend another one at the other end of the room. I drop my hands on the table, relief washing over me.

My arm burns from the intense scratching session. I remove my brace and roll up my sleeve. Five long gashes stand out against my pale flesh; thick beads of blood well up from them. I inhale sharply.

"Oh my god," Asher breathes. He takes his napkin, dips it in his ice cold water, and pats the wound gently. It comes back crimson.

"Did I do that?" I gasp. Turning my hand back and forth, I scrutinize the short clip of my nails. They could never cut that deeply into, could they?

Asher shakes his head. Not in response, but in disbelief. "I'm not sure. They look deep. Do they hurt?"

"A little," I admit. My arms feel like I've been scratching them, but they don't feel mutilated. It doesn't even hurt as much as my hand did when I went down on the cement last week.

He pushes his chair back and stands up. "Come on. Let's get you home and we'll clean that up."

I agree, but fake like I'm tired and need to go to bed. If my parents are still gone, I don't want to be alone in the house with Asher. A fleeting thought of kissing him on Brady's couch flips through my head like a still-life motion picture. That's how I play it when I go back over the memory: nice and slow so I can revel in the sensation. Yeah, he is definitely not allowed in my house tonight.

Chapter 30

In Psychology Friday, I learn that two more people have been hospitalized: Derek Stafford and Chris Reynolds, both members of the basketball team with Spencer, and both juniors.

Jen strokes April's hair in an effort to soothe her.

April unsurprisingly used to date both of them. At different times, but still.

I received a text from Asher just before class informing me that he would not be at school. At the time, I was so distracted by the promise of results that I hadn't considered that he was leaving me with these two.

I send him a text from underneath the table stating: *I hate you so much right now.*

Mrs. Jarvis returns our interviews and diagnoses.

As it turns out, I was right when I diagnosed Jen as Obsessive Compulsive. Okay, so maybe Asher helped me with that one. Personally, I didn't think she was that good of an actress.

He must have experience with diagnosing crazies filed away in that photographic memory of his. Not that I'm saying Obsessive Compulsive Disorder is a form of crazy, but… well, you know what I'm saying.

Asher was a narcissist. No surprise there. I wonder if he even had to act.

April was the easiest of all. I had her pegged from the get-go: Paranoid Schizophrenic. Given her incessant shouting about little green men, I gather she hasn't met many paranoid schizophrenics. Her acting was as unoriginal as it comes.

Along with our original assignment, we each receive a copy of what our team members diagnosed us with. It was a two part assignment: how good you are at smelling out the disorders and how well you portray them.

April said that I showed signs of Post-Traumatic Stress Disorder. I chuckle to myself. She must be clairvoyant.

Jen diagnosed me as a Sociopath. She also suggested I treat my symptoms with high doses of valium. Exactly what you'd want to give a suicidal person, right? Wrong. I mentally fail her from the class. Here's hoping she doesn't go into medicine.

Asher was dead on: depression with suicidal tendencies. I can't help but wonder if he was talking about inside or outside of class. He suggested a little excitement under the watchful eye of my doctor. I can just imagine Mrs. Jarvis' reaction when she reads that.

"Do you know what happened?" Jen asks April.

My ears perk up and I get a brilliant idea. While Kaleb and Asher peruse over *The Satanic Bible* or whatever *Demon Census* they have at their disposal, I can find out more information about the initial attacks. After all, isn't that what a real life demon hunter would do?

April looks up. Her eyeliner is smudged across her eyelids and down her cheeks. She looks like something straight out of a horror movie. I don't tell her that, though.

"From what I hear, Chris passed out after practice and wasn't breathing. When Coach found him, he wasn't breathing." April runs a finger under her left eye. She looks at the black smudge across her fingertip as if her make-up has committed the ultimate betrayal.

I wonder what she'd do if she saw a mirror right now.

"Anyway," she continues, "it's so weird, you know? I mean, he's, like, the healthiest person I know. He doesn't even eat gluten."

"How awful," I say before I can stop myself.

April gives me a look, but rather than show me the door, she actually includes me in the conversation.

"Yes, it is," she says, nodding emphatically. "I remember thinking he was invincible when we went out and now he's on life support."

I nod in understanding. "Must be the body's natural starvation for gluten. I mean, who could live without it?"

Jen and April give me identical looks of disgust. Then they return to their conversation without me.

I take out the notebook I've been doodling in and write down what I've learned: *Chris was gluten-free.* Then, just in case there is any confusion, I add: *Probably not what's killing him, though.*

Look at me. I'm Nancy Drew incarnate.

I cover the page with my right arm. "Hey, April," I say.

She turns her head slowly. "What?"

"What about Derek? Do you know what happened to him?"

April's face crumples into a sobbing mess. Jen wraps an arm around her shoulders and glares at me. "Maybe she doesn't want to talk about it, *Nicole.*"

I let that one slide out of respect for April. For now. But she'll pay for it later.

April wipes at her face with the back of her sleeve. She glances at the white cotton, which is now smeared with black and purple, and drops her hands in her lap like there's no choice but to give up.

"Oh, honey," Jen says, pulling her closer. "Don't worry; we'll fix you right up."

April shrugs her off and turns her attention to me. "Why do you want to know?"

I realize that with straightforward questions like that, I might actually grow to respect her one day.

I always have tissues in my bag because my nose tends to run when I have to walk home in the cold. I remove them from the front pocket and hand them over to April as a peace offering.

"Thanks," she says, yanking one free from the package, and blotting her eyes with it.

"Why do I want to know?" I repeat.

She bites her lip and nods.

"Honestly, I don't think any of this is coincidence and I intend to find out what links everything together."

April's kohl-smeared eyes roam across my face. At first, she looks like she's going to spit at me, but then one side of her mouth turns up in a half-smile. "I hope you figure it out," she says.

"I do, too."

She takes a deep breath as if she's trying to gain strength. "They think Derek tried to kill himself. Ridiculous, right?"

My jaw unhinges. "What?"

"Yeah," her fingers fiddle with the tissue. "Derek would never try to kill himself, by the way. He had plans, you know?" She leans forward and whispers, "We were getting back together."

I'm not sure that's enough evidence for me to confidently rule out suicide, but I don't tell her that.

"Can I ask how?" I hedge.

She nods once. "They think he tried to run his car off the road."

A chill runs up my spine. I remember hearing the crunch of Sarah Crocker's car as it slammed up against the freeway barrier and hearing her scream. There was no way she was trying to commit suicide. I know because I was there.

"See? Ridiculous, right? That car was his baby. He worked on it all summer with his dad."

I scratch my nose to distract her from whatever expression I have on my face. "Is he going to be okay?"

She drops her head, shaking it back and forth. "They don't know. He was pretty messed up. I'm going to the hospital after work."

I rip off the corner of my notebook paper and write my number at the bottom. "Will you text me updates?"

She stares at the piece of paper as if it might be venomous.

The bell rings so I set it on her desk and stand up, shouldering my backpack. "Just in case you want to talk or whatever."

As I leave the room, I hear Jen say something to April about how I'm not their friend and how, if April needs to talk, she should call Jen. I turn around one last time to catch a glimpse of the green monster riding Jen's back. It's nice to have her jealous of me for once.

***

Jessica is more than willing to tell me what she knows about Dave when I see her during Math class. Apparently, he drove Jessica home that night. Before she got out of the car, she asked him if he was okay to drive, to which he laughed and assured her that he only had one beer.

I may have been asleep off and on, but it sounds accurate enough to me. The official story is that on his way home, he hit a patch of black ice and swerved into a telephone pole. When they found him, he was unconscious. MRI's and CT scans haven't shown any internal bleeding. In fact, as far as they are can tell, there's no reason why he hasn't snapped out of it.

I could probably come up with a few reasons myself.

"Was there anything weird about the accident?" I ask her, trying to sound as sympathetic as I can.

She thinks about it for a second. Her eyes seem permanently etched with red these past few days like lightning strikes trying to warm the ice blue of her eyes. "You know, there was something I found kinda weird, but no one believed me."

"Oh, yeah?" I lean toward her, diminishing the distance her words have to travel. "What was that?"

"Well, Dave isn't the smartest person in the crowd, but he's not stupid either. He had all-weather tires and the streets were freshly salted. I saw it on our way home. And, Nic—"

I nod in encouragement.

"He wasn't anywhere near his house. He told me he was going straight home, but he was up by the freeway. He lives a mile the other way."

A shudder runs through me. "I believe you, Jess," is all I can say.

I decide to talk to Alex after that. He's always been privy to any information involving the "popular" crowd and it appears most of the victims are part of that group.

I have to wait by his locker after school since he no longer uses mine. It takes ten minutes after the bell for him to show.

"Hey, Nic, what's up?" he says. "You ready for your date tonight?"

I totally forgot until he brought it up. Absently, I itch at my wrist.

"It itches the most when it's healing," he tells me.

"Yeah, I'm sure." I bounce up and down on the balls of my feet, waiting for him to close his locker. Once it slams shut, I say, "Hey, Alex, can I ask you some questions?"

"Sure, what's up?"

"What do you know about all your friends ending up in the hospital?"

He seems taken aback by my question. Either he didn't think I'd care or he didn't expect me to ask him. He rubs the back of his neck. "What do you mean?"

I smile innocently. "Well, it seems weird, doesn't it? I mean, like eight of your friends have all ended up in the hospital. I heard three of them even died. I was sorry to hear about that, by the way."

He hesitates before nodding. "Four of them actually," he amends. His shoulders deflate and expression weighs heavy with devastation.

I reach out to hug him. Once I realize what I almost just did, I pull my hands back and shove them in my pockets. "Four?"

"I'll take you home and we can talk," he says, leading the way to the parking lot.

I climb into the passenger side of the mustang. Already the car is starting to smell of cheap body splash and hairspray. I cringe from the smell.

"Well," he says, starting the engine. "When we got out of the movie the other night, I swear I saw her car right out front. She drives that blue VW Beetle."

I stare at him in silence until he turns his head to look at me. "What?"

"We didn't go to the movie. Something came up, remember?"

He doesn't even have the decency to look abashed. "Oh, it must have been a different night."

"And a different movie with a different girl," I tack on.

He nods. "Something like that. Anyway, her car was out front that night, but when they found her, the car was moved to the back lot. It's weird, you know? The movie got out pretty late. I just don't see any reason why she would have moved it."

"Maybe they had a delivery or something," I suggest. For some reason, I'm not as upset about Alex ditching me as I thought I would be.

"Maybe, but I don't think she would have moved it to a dark corner of the lot and the doctors say she had an asthma attack and passed out." He looks at me with raised eyebrows.

He knows how many asthma attacks I've had in the past: too many to count, and some have been really bad, but I've never passed out from one. So why would Melinda Carter, cheerleader minion and member of the volleyball team have an asthma attack worse than me?

He watches as the truth of his words sink in. Then he says, "Weird, right?"

"Totally. I thought they said she had a seizure, though."

"There've been a lot of stories. I've even heard that she was mugged," he says.

That little extra sense deep inside me tells me that she wasn't attacked. Not like that anyway. "It seems like their grasping at straws," I agree.

He glances at me, barely able to stifle a grin. "Listen to you, Detective Dubois." I shake my head. "Nah. Well, thanks for the ride, see you later."

He waves at me as I get out of the car and go inside. I make a mental reminder to call Kaleb and Asher after my date to relay all the new information. Writing it down doesn't seem like a bad idea either.

Chapter 31

I groan as I look through my closet for what feels like the fiftieth time. I'm having a really hard time trying to figure out what to wear. On one hand, I don't want to look like one of the guys, but on the other, I don't really want to look like one of the girls either. I look to the picture of Dean on my wall for guidance. He gives me the same seductive smile he always does. That's what I love about the picture: all seduction, all the time.

Finally, I dive into my closet head first, resolved not to come out until I have chosen something. After a lot of digging, I end up with a black gypsy skirt and a red peasant top, complete with ties cinching just underneath my chest. Alex told me to dress up.

The shirt makes my boobs swell out of the neckline. They look huge and sculpted. I turn in the mirror, making sure they won't fall out. Everything seems to stay in place. I plan to wear my soft leather jacket most of the night so as long as the girls stay tucked inside, we're good. Now for shoes. Since my mother has a shoe fetish, I don't need to look too far. My closet is a breeding ground for sneakers and boots, but hers has everything else. I put my Doc Martens away with a pang of sadness then pull out the black Mary Jane heels I stole from her bedroom.

I have a charm bracelet I bought online from a *Supernatural* fan site. It's a hunter's bracelet. All the major religious symbols used to ward off evil beings dangle from a silver chain. It doesn't fit my wrists, though, and it most definitely doesn't fit around the brace on my right hand. I bend down and snap it around my ankle. It glitters in the light beautifully. The strap of the sandals sits perfectly below the cross and the heels add enough height to bring me to five-seven. Score.

I wonder if Kaleb and Asher would make fun of me if they knew I wore this thing.

The brace has been on for over a week now. I'm usually a fast healer. So I shuck it off and turn my hand. The pain isn't intense enough for me to bother putting it back on yet. Besides, it doesn't really go with the outfit.

I don't feel like messing with my hair so I leave it down. I've always kept it long. It's about to my waist now. Sometimes, it's more trouble than it's worth. I pin my bangs back at the crown of my head with two bobby pins.

After a little eyeliner, mascara and shadow, I wrap a thin choker around my neck. A single ruby tear drop sits at the hollow of my throat. While I'm admiring my transformation from one of the guys into a full-fledged girl, my mother comes in. She stops two feet away and covers her mouth with her hand.

"You look stunning," she tells me.

I smile as I mentally roam back over my outfit. The peasant top has bell sleeves that engulf my wrists and the skirt goes to my ankles. It's all perfectly modest except for the foot of flesh over the top of my shirt, but I don't think she'll notice. Not with my hair resting along my shoulders.

"You're date's here," she says. "He's cute."

"Thanks mom. I'll be there in a second."

She holds up a finger while walking toward me. I half expect her to fix my hair since it's sitting nearly untouched, but she doesn't. She reaches under it and I hear a snap.

I turn my head to see her brandishing a tag in the air.

"I can't believe you've never worn this. It's beautiful." She smiles.

"Never had a reason to." I turn back to the mirror, studying my new look. It's not so bad being dressed up. I bet Asher would tease me if he saw it, though.

I follow my mom out of the room and down the hall to see my father talking to a boy in the living room. He's about six feet tall, his shoulders are square in his leather jacket, and he's wearing jeans. So much for dressing up. Although, the back of him is nice to look at.

"Honey, you look beautiful," my father exclaims, bringing their conversation to a dead halt.

My arm burns under the jacket where I nearly scratched my skin off a few nights before. I shrug the jacket off and check the marks. They were mostly healed and healing involves itching, right?

"Nicoletta, I presume," a deep voice says. I have a sense that I've heard it somewhere before, but I can't remember where.

I look up into the hard-lined face of Taylor, who apparently works a popular restaurant after school. Taylor... is... the... waiter. Just great.

I shrink back unconsciously, almost falling over my heels.

His hair is done differently tonight, arranged in a type of faux hawk, coming up in the front. He's cut off the nasty sides, but something still bothers me about him. Maybe it's his washed out, pale blue eyes. I never was a fan of dull colored irises. If the eyes are the window to the soul, then his soul must be shallow because I feel like I can see right through them.

He smiles, revealing how thin his lips are over his less than pearly whites.

I can do this, I tell myself. For Alex, I can do this. After all, he's done so much for me over the years. Like taking me to the doctor when I sprained my wrist or sitting up with me all night when he made me watch a scary movie in seventh grade. Of course, those were both his fault, but... oh, who am I kidding? I don't know if I can do this. I contemplate faking stomach cramps, but I went to so much trouble.

Instead, I make up an excuse about how I forgot my keys and go back to my room to get my cell phone. I open it up and realize for the first time that I haven't heard from Brady in two days. He hasn't even been at school. I'm a bad friend. I stomp my foot once. So what? So is he. Friends don't bribe people to date you. Even if it is Asher, whom I miss with a physical pain I try not to acknowledge.

I check the phone's charge. Full. Proud of myself for remembering to charge it after school, I slip the phone in the pocket of my jacket and grab my purse. After realizing that I've never used it either, I check it over for tags. Apparently, I remembered to disembody all signs of purchase, though, so I slip it over my shoulder.

I clench my teeth to keep from itching as Taylor ushers me out of the house.

The night is clean and frigid. On the air is the smell of fireplaces all around the neighborhood. The smell reminds me of Asher. I push back the thought. No, I'm not going to think of him. I'm going to have fun tonight with Taylor.

Taylor doesn't open my door. He climbs in and unlocks it from the inside. I realize that I haven't opened my own door for a while now. It's funny how quickly you can get used to something like that. Since I didn't wear the brace, the handle only causes mild discomfort. Otherwise, it would have taken me forever to get into the car. Ahem, the 1967 Ford something-or-other. All I know is that the car looks like it could have potential if it weren't rusted out in areas, painted maroon, and dented on the front and back bumpers. The upholstery is torn in places, too, which makes my skin itch worse.

"Nice car," I say, trying not to sound like a snob. It's not like I have a car, but compared to the Jeep, this is a trash can on wheels.

"Thanks." He beams. The ignition switch sends the car into sputters before it roars with an unhealthy growl. The music kicks on, playing a Social Offense song.

If he likes Social Offense then maybe this date won't totally suck.

Just as I am about to declare my undying love for the band, he pushes in a tape.

A *tape!* I thought those were extinct.

"Sorry," he says. "What a shitty song."

I narrow my eyes at him in disgust. Who doesn't love Social Offense? They didn't get to be number one on the charts by being a second rate band.

The music kicks on. I cringe when I recognize the hip hop love ballad from around the time I was born. If he isn't the only person out there who still has a tape player, I guarantee he's the only one out there with this exact tape.

I lean over and roll down the window, hoping to free some of the noise. The handle turns and turns, but nothing happens.

Taylor looks at me sideways. "Broken!" he yells over the music.

The car speeds down the street at unyielding speed. The winter grey sky has already turned dark. The black void presses in on me. I take shallow breaths as my throat closes.

"Where are we going?" I ask, disdainfully. Loudly, too, I might add.

"What?" he yells.

"Where are we going?" I holler back.

"Oh. To a party!" He grins and bobs his head in excitement.

I let out a long gust of air. The beat pulses painfully in my frozen ear drums. Of course it would be a party. It's not like it could have been anything else. Like, oh, I don't know. Dinner and a movie could have been fun. But, no, it has to be a party because his idea of fun would have to be my idea of torture.

I scoot down in my seat and count the streets we pass. If my calculations are correct, and I'm positive they are, the party is at some house in a dark and secluded neighborhood close to Cottonwood High School.

It seems everything in my life has to revolve around the creepy side lately.

My hand is on the door handle before the car can come to a complete stop. The music, if you can call it that, cuts off.

"The handle is broken, too. I'll have to let you out," Taylor tells me.

Thoughts of Ted Bundy come to mind. I palm my cell phone and consider calling anyone to get me out of here.

Just then, my door opens. I step out onto the gravel driveway. The house has close to twenty cars parked at the curb and on the lawn. The bass beats its way out the front door. The music is not much of an improvement from what was playing in the car. I should have brought my iPod. This group could use some culture. Then I decide I'm not being fair. I should give them the benefit of the doubt. It could be the radio, though, I doubt it.

I have to watch my footing to avoid stepping on smashed beer bottles and cigarette butts. These shoes were not meant for traipsing through loose gravel and debris. Taylor drapes an arm over my shoulder. My stomach clenches involuntarily.

"You look hot," he drawls. His eyes are pinned to my cleavage. I wonder if he's talking to me or my bra. Tonight is such a waste of my outfit. But what did I expect? An opera?

But Asher would have taken me…

Enough about Asher, I remind myself.

We aren't even two steps into the house when someone hands Taylor a beer. He takes three long gulps before he catches me staring at him.

"What?" he says, complete with flying spit. He wipes his mouth with the back of his sleeve.

I glower. "How can you take me home if you get wasted?"

"God, Nicole. Don't be such buzz kill," he says, smacking my ass with his free hand.

I jump. Not in a flirty way, but in a *DON'T-TOUCH-ME-AGAIN* way. Images of breaking his hand off play against the back of my eyelids. I need to get away from him. Problem is that I don't know anyone else in the overstuffed living room.

People of all shapes, sizes and genders mill around. It's hard to breathe in the darkness. That, I realize, is because of the marijuana smoke poisoning the air. My lungs tighten up and refuse to budge. I wish I'd thought to bring my inhaler.

What the hell possessed Alex to set me up with this douchebag?

For every minute spent sitting in the corner watching Taylor drink more, and more, and more still, my anxiety level doubles. I can't breathe. I feel like I've come down with the worst case of chicken pox ever and Taylor isn't slowing down. Furthermore, the music is not from the radio, but from an mp3 player owned by someone who has a very specific (read: awful) taste in music, and the only time someone talks to me is to ask if I've had my boobs done. I shake my head, but imagine pummeling him to the ground.

When did I sign up for the lead role in Utah's worst back to school special?

"Taylor," I say, grabbing his arm. A lit joint sits perched between his fingers. I hope he hasn't smoked it yet. "I don't feel well. I want to go home."

He laughs, which dies abruptly when he sees my expression. He sighs. "Alright. Fine. Let me say goodbye. I can't believe we're leaving."

I shrug and go to wait outside. The chilly air is like a savior to my lungs. I take in deep breaths until it gets too cold. My teeth chatter. I pull out my cell phone and check the time. I've been standing outside for ten minutes. Shaking my head, I type out a message to Asher asking him to come get me. Just as I hit send, Taylor stomps out of the house. Suddenly, I'm not cold anymore; everything burns.

It's almost over, I tell myself.

I send Asher a message that says, Never mind, and go to the car.

Taylor is fumbles with his keys. They fall from his hands into the debris. He curses loudly and bends over to retrieve them.

"I can call someone to pick me up," I offer.

"No. I brought you here. I'll take you home," he responds, coldly.

When we are finally on our way, I focus on anything, but him. As long as I don't have to look at him, I can almost ignore the disturbing feelings he instills in me.

I almost feel guilty for making him leave. Maybe I am a buzz kill – a stupid, stuck-up, buzz kill.

At least the music fills the silent void so we don't have to talk.

The car zips through the streets at a speed I didn't think it could reach.

My arms feel like they've been torn apart by dull teeth. I rub at them with the pads of my fingertips. Don't want to make myself bleed again.

All the while, visions of accidents and gore dance in my head. I see Sarah Crocker lying on the side of the freeway, thrown from the driver's side of her car. Her face is bruised and swollen, her eyes dull, and blood trickles from the corner of her mouth. The worst part was who she was with when she died. Please God, don't let my last minutes be spent with this worthless garbage (meaning, the car and the driver).

When he should turn left, he continues straight.

"That was the turn to my house," I protest.

He pretends to ignore me.

"Where are you taking me? I want to go home." The music is so loud that I have to yell just to hear myself.

"You'll get there, babe. Just one more stop," he yells back.

"No. I want to go home. I don't feel well."

He smiles. It's not a pretty smile. If the car door could open, I would throw myself out. I don't care how fast we are going. My hand finds its way to the pocket of my jacket and clutches my cell phone for dear life.

"One more stop" turns out to be a quiet and abandoned parking lot surrounded by nothing.

I'm sure the lot must have belonged to a building long since razed to the ground. If I close my eyes, I can almost smell burnt coffee forgotten in the pot and see people sluggishly walking toward the elevators with the memories of the weekend slowly trailing behind until they fade to smoke.

The lot feels cold. Like a mortuary, a cemetery, or a prison.

That's exactly what Taylor's car feels like, I realize with a jolt. That uneasy feeling that's burrowed its way into my skin and raised my hackles is my body's reaction to feeling trapped.

I'm trapped.

"I want to go home," I tell him for what feels like the millionth time. I've really only told him four times at most, but like my dad always says: Once is enough.

The fingers of my injured hand twitch around the phone in my pocket. Due to the sprain, I've lost my expert ability to decipher where numbers and letters may be.

I remember Asher telling me not to go on this date and wonder how smug he will be when he finds out he was right.

The engine dies with one last sputter. Taylor turns in his seat to look at me.

"Just relax, babe," he says coolly, reaching out to touch the collar of my jacket. "I'm not going to hurt you. Not unless you want me to."

I jerk out of his reach. "I want to go home," I tell him again. My voice shakes. I curse myself for not being stronger.

"I'll get you there," he assures me.

I don't feel assured. I turn my head to the window and jump when I feel something sliding down my neck.

Taylor has leaned into me. His mouth burns along my skin. One hand wraps around my hair and pulls while the other tugs at the front of my shirt.

With as much force as I can muster, I push him away. His shoulders meet the resistance and he moves closer.

My throat burns. "Please, take me home," I cry out.

He moves up to my ear, licking along the lobe. "Come on, baby," he whispers. "It's nothing you haven't done before."

"What the hell are you talking about?"

"Jen promised me a sure thing. We made a deal."

Tears are welling up in my eyes. I don't know any self-defense moves. I don't even have mace. Hell, I've worn my nails down to the quick with all the scratching I've done over the past few days.

Taylor's hand slides up my back and grips the collar of my jacket. He yanks so hard that a clump of hair rips from my scalp. If he tugs any more, the jacket will have to come off, otherwise, my arms will.

"She said you like it rough. Is that how you like it?" he says in what I imagine is supposed to be a seductive voice, but reminds me of fingernails on glass.

"No. I don't like it at all." My voice is broken shards of hysterics. "I want to go home."

"Right after you give daddy what he wants." His teeth clamp down on my neck hard enough to bruise.

I push away, scrambling up against the door.

He clutches a fistful of my hair and pulls me back toward him. I try to lunge forward, but he has a good grip on my long hair.

I wonder if I screamed would anyone hear me?

Taylor releases my hair and grabs my arms with brutal force. When I jerk back, his nails dig into the skin of my forearm. Five red gashes scream across my skin.

"Oh my god," I gasp.

"You like that?" He pushes himself into me, pinning my back against the door by my wrists.

"No!" I scream into his face. I wish I wore my brace. The pain in my wrist is enough to make my vision checkerboard. My breaths are ragged and shallow from the world's worst asthma attack. My whole body shakes with terror.

His arm presses into my neck while his free hand slides my skirt further and further up my thigh. Futilely, I struggle against him.

Lightning tears the sky wide open. I focus on it, begging for it to hit the car. I'd rather die than live through this. Heavy rain drops beat against the windows.

The front of my shirt is ripped wide open, my skirt bunched up around my waist. The monster touches me with no real goal other than to expose me. His hand leaves my thigh to fumble with his belt.

Another flash of lightning. *Please God.*

I take in a deep breath and scream. Scream for my life. Scream for all I'm worth.

Chapter 32

Muffled by the sound of heavy rain and Taylor's heavy breathing, I can almost hear something inside me change. My vision is no longer black and white, but four different shades of red.

Nothing hurts anymore.

A dangerous mixture of fear and anger burns through me, starting with my fingers. I jerk hard against his grip. In surprise, he releases me, his weight falling forward.

On instinct, I slam the heel of my right hand hard into his nose. There's a satisfying noise of cartilage snapping and bone breaking. It echoes in my ear drums. While I feel strangely happy playing that track over and over again, my stomach churns at the noise.

Taylor falls into a heaving lump across my chest, pinning me to the seat. I'm not even sure he's still breathing.

I reach around me, trying to open the door, before I remember that it's broken. The door is unlocked, though, so if I could get break the glass somehow, then I might be able to open it from the outside.

That is, I could, if this huge monster wasn't on top of me.

There is one thing I can reach. My jacket was shoved down to the floor boards during the scuffle. I fumble with the soft leather, hoping my wrist will hold out.

Before I have a chance to reach my phone, the passenger side door opens. I nearly fall backward, but am caught by two strong arms. They haul me back, wiggling me out from under Taylor's dead weight. In all the excitement of being free from that prison, I kick off the door frame and send both of us tumbling to the wet asphalt.

The body under me shifts to the side. First, the person pulls my shirt back together and smoothes out my skirt. Then he says, "Nicoletta. You alright?" in that beautiful way he pronounces my name.

My response? I cry. Hot stinging tears cascade from my eyes, mixing with the cold rain. I struggle to sit up. The arm behind my back urges me into a warm embrace.

He doesn't say anything. He just holds me for as long as I need.

Asher's head lifts from my hair and whips around just as the sound of a Jeep rolls up next to us.

"Kaleb," he says, his voice reverberating through his chest and wrapping around me like a cocoon. "Don't let him leave yet. I would like to make his acquaintance."

"No worries there," Kaleb responds, his voice more menacing than I've ever heard.

"You'll have to beat me to it," a female says, her voice so pretty and girlish, I figure it must be Acey.

"Fine," Asher says, cuddling me in tighter. "Just leave him alive. We have business to discuss."

The engine dies and a car door slams before I can warn them about the handle.

Wait, why am I worried about them? Aren't they trained to kill? Truth is: I'm not worried about the boys. I'm worried about Acey and all her petite beauty around those meaty hands. The same hands I can still feel crawling on my flesh.

I pull Asher tighter around me as if I could climb inside of him and disappear.

"Asher," I whisper.

"Shh," he coos, stroking my hair. "I'm here. I'm not leaving you." Turning his head slightly away, he calls out, "Kaleb, cut the water works, could you? It's getting cold over here."

Kaleb grumbles something, but the fat water drops on my face lighten to a drizzle. Then a long black coat drapes over me, which reminds me that my favorite leather jacket is still in the car. I breathe the smell of lavender deep into my lungs. The sweet herbal scent calms me somehow.

"Ace. I mean it," Asher warns. "Alive."

"Yeah, yeah. I know," she replies in a sing song voice from inside the car.

"Is… is he al…alive?" I chatter.

Asher looks down into my eyes. His irises look like they are on fire, tinted with a red orange glow. He nods slowly, tracing my cheek with his thumb. "Why wouldn't he be?"

I don't have it in me to explain right now. Besides, I'm not even sure how to explain the feeling that came over me just before I hit him. It was almost like I was possessed. Like I was someone else entirely. My clothes are soaked in the thin frigid air. After the shock wears off, I might have pneumonia served to me on a big shiny platter. As it is, I'm numb. The only thing I feel is Asher's warm arms.

"I… I don't know," I say, shaking my head.

"Well, if he is, I want to be the one to handle it." He turns his head and yells, "You hear that, Ace? If he's alive, he's mine."

Any one of them probably would kill this monster, and yet, the thing that scares me is I'd be disappointed I didn't do it myself.

A scream shatters the night. A dark, baritone scream that rises higher and higher until it cuts of completely.

"He's alive," Acey hollers out the open door.

"Damn it! Kaleb, could you please watch her?" Asher yells.

"Sure," Kaleb says, only a few feet away. I wonder what's so intriguing about watching me cry.

Asher whispers something in my ear. It's quick and quiet in a voice more angel than human. I recognize the language, but not the words.

"I don't speak French," I mumble into him. The cold has embraced me for so long it's a part of me now. "What did you say?"

Asher clears his throat. "I said, 'My heart, my soul, my dearest one. Be at peace.'"

These are the times I wish I wasn't numb. My heart would surely kick wildly and my whole body would react to his words like a caress inside of me, no matter how corny they are. But I can't feel. Taylor made sure of that. For a brief moment, I consider getting up to help Acey torture the son of a bitch. I know. I shouldn't feel that way. It's wrong and blah, blah, blah.

I nod. "That's what I thought you said."

He chuckles, pulling me tighter into him.

"Maybe we should take this somewhere a little less conspicuous," Kaleb suggests, a good ten minutes later.

My nerves can process impulses again. They tell me that during the struggle, my wrist was re-injured and probably broken now.

"Where do you suggest?" Asher asks, clutching me to his chest. His shirt is soaked with my tears.

Kaleb shrugs. "There's a training center downtown. We could go there."

Asher hesitates. "I don't know if I should go there. I'm not a part of that world anymore."

"You may not want to be, but you are. You can't fight it, Asher. It's a part of you, and right now, for everyone's sake, it will do you good to accept that."

Asher sits up a little straighter and clears his throat. I don't know exactly what he's going to say, but I know it isn't going to be good.

"Can you please not fight right now?" I beg. My limbs and butt have gone numb from the cold despite how warm Kaleb's coat is.

Asher releases me so he can look into my eyes quizzically. I wonder how bad my face looks. This is why I don't wear mascara on a daily basis: it tends to run. I'm sure I look like a train wreck.

"Will you be okay here for a second? I'm going to talk to Acey," he says.

I nod. In a small voice, I manage to tell him where my jacket is. I sure hope it wasn't ruined. I like that jacket.

While Asher stomps over to the car, his back a solid line, Kaleb helps me to my feet. I wobble on my heels.

"You alright there?" he asks me.

"Yeah. Do you think Acey –?"

"She's fine," he assures me before I can finish and damn him if there isn't the smallest of smirks pulling at his mouth. "There are times Acey scares even me. I'm more worried about you."

Acey, scary? Not likely. Not unless beauty is a terrifying trait, which I guess it sometimes is.

"To be honest, Kaleb, I thought I was going to have to take you up on that offer," I tell him. "You know, to hide a body. I for sure thought I killed him." Something cold rushes through me and I shiver.

He laughs. "I have to admit, I wondered if you would need to take me up on that offer. Lucky for you, he's alive."

"Why's that lucky?" I ask.

"Because. Now you can cash that one in later and I have a feeling you might need to."

"What makes you say that?"

He cocks an eyebrow. "Have you met Asher?"

I chuckle, which feels weird given the current situation. "How did you find me anyway?"

Kaleb regards me with wary eyes. "Asher is pretty good at sensing when people are in distress, you in particular. We were already in the car, on our way to get you, when you told us not to come. Then we followed you." He focuses on Asher and Acey, who are dragging Taylor's body from the car, and shakes his head. "Not close enough, it would seem."

"Then what took you guys so long?"

He lets out a snort. "Asher was very clear. He didn't want to disturb your date so long as you were safe. A bad date happens to all of us. But this," he gestures to the car, "is unacceptable."

My body has grown accustomed to the cold now so I try to give Kaleb back his coat. His shirt may be layered, but I've dealt with Utah's frigid winters longer. He refuses.

"It's okay, really. I'll have my jacket back as soon as they're done," I say, holding it out to him.

"I'm from Landon, Montana. Do you know what that means?" he asks.

I shake my head.

"Negative temperatures. I'm used to it. Please, take it. When we get you in dry clothes, I'll get it back."

Shrugging my arms into the coat, I realize how much bigger he is than me. The bottom hem drifts along the ground and the sleeves swallow up my hands.

"Thank you."

"My pleasure." He glances over to the car, putting his profile in the glow of the neon light. A small brown freckle dots his left temple, making him look the most human I've seen him. His wavy hair is now thick, wet curls. As the wind lifts and swirls around us, I see a mark just under his ear.

Unconsciously, I reach out to touch it.

He steps back.

"What is that?" I ask.

He glances around, avoiding my eyes. "What?"

"That mark on your neck. It looks like a tattoo or something."

He touches the skin under his ear. "It's nothing. Just a birth mark."

"Can I see it?"

He deliberates a few moments while I wonder if he's ignoring the question, but then he lifts his hair and offers me his neck. "Not many people see it," he explains.

I trace the shape of the mark. It looks identical to the silver symbol from Asher's sword. Only, when I see it on Kaleb's skin, it doesn't look like a symbol. It looks like a real life story.

"I've seen this before," I say in a daze.

Kaleb chuckles. "I'm sure you have. Acey and Asher have one, too. And it's on the sword."

"No," I say, still touching it. The darker is raised compared to the smooth skin of his neck like a tattoo. "I don't mean that."

"What do you mean?"

A memory of something I think is important dances just outside of my mind, but when I try to snatch it, it turns and disappears. "I don't know. Thanks for showing me."

He shrugs and drops his hair. The curls fall back into place as if knowing where the mark is and how to hide it.

"You know, Kaleb, your girlfriend is one lucky girl," I remark before I catch myself.

"So are you." He turns his head, casting himself in shadow. "I know I give Asher a lot of shit, but he's a good guy. He'll take good care of you."

"I'm starting to sense that," I reply.

As if talking about him triggers some universal switch, Asher struts over, my jacket in his right hand.

"Acey'll meet us there. Let's go," he says, waving an arm toward the Jeep. Kaleb insists on driving. I imagine he likes to be in control when he can. Asher exchanges the keys to sit in back with me.

"I'm not going to cry anymore," I assure him.

He smiles. "I know."

Heat blows across my cheeks, burning me. The pores of my skin scream in agony as the frost thaws out of them. I lean into Asher, who takes up most of the back seat with his long legs, and bury my face in his shoulder to slow down the process. He smells smoky like a chimney fire would. It reminds me of calm winter mornings at home, where everything is safe.

"How's Acey getting there?" I ask. "She's not driving with him, is she?"

"Don't worry." He rubs his hand along my arm. "She'll be fine."

After a half hour of lights dancing through the car in turn with my heartbeat, we pull into an underground parking lot. It's empty. I blink a few times frantically. The harsh lights sting my eyes.

Acey's ride, a 1967 Ford P.O.S., pulls in behind us. She's in the driver's seat while a very unconscious looking Taylor slumps up against the window. A line of blood smears down the glass from his nose.

"What did she do to him?" I ask, mostly out of curiosity. I heard him scream in the parking lot so I know I didn't kill him, but he doesn't necessarily look alive either.

"What Acey does best. He's not dead, though, he probably should be." Asher says.

We climb out of the Jeep. Acey is already out of Taylor's car. She leans against the hood with a smug look on her face.

"At least I hope he's still alive." Asher says through clenched teeth.

"Oh chill." Acey tells him, rolling her eyes. "He's breathing. Want to check?"

"I believe you," he says, but sounds like he doesn't.

My stomach slowly twists itself into an intricate cluster of knots. "Why is he here?" I sniff hard, trying not to cry again. The gashes on my arm have finally stopped bleeding, but they still burn like the fires of hell.

"We need him," Kaleb says, jostling Taylor's weight out of the passenger door. When his legs are free, Kaleb purposely lets go. Taylor's body falls to the floor in a limp heap. "Oops," he says with a malicious smile.

Asher walks over and lifts Taylor's lifeless legs. One of them could probably carry him alone, but by the way they're holding him, it seems neither of them wants much contact with the body.

Acey leads us over to a big metal door. She fishes out a white plastic card and swipes it through the reader. Then she enters a code into the keypad. The lock clicks and whirs for longer than necessary before the door pops open.

"Nicky, be a dear and get the next door," she says.

I walk into a highly air-conditioned hall. The next door is five feet in. I pull on it, but it doesn't budge. "It's locked."

"Right," she says like I should have expected it.

The boys move through the last door with ease. Taylor's head bumps against the doorframe.

"Please be careful," Acey scolds. "If there are any dents in the door, Gabe will have our heads. The code is two-five-one-three-one-seven."

I punch in the code and the door breaks free. I shoulder it open to avoid using my wrist. The guys move past me into the next room. Acey follows, calling out something about an elevator.

The elevator is glass with metal bars outlining the room. We shuffle inside. Asher and Kaleb immediately let go of Taylor. His body hits the metal bottom with a thud.

"Isn't that going to hurt him?" I ask.

I'm awarded with identical looks of astonishment from everyone.

Acey touches my arm. I flinch from the unsuspected contact. "I'm sure he'll be fine. He can't feel much of anything right now. He might wake up with a headache, though." She smiles as if that's the happiest thought she's had all day.

The elevator also has a code lock. Acey punches in another four numbers then pushes one of the two buttons on the panel. The elevator whirs to life. The scene on the other side of the glass is disconcerting as hell. Walls made of silver concrete stare back us all the way down. Three stories later, the elevator stops and the doors sigh open.

Acey bobs her head toward the open doors. "After you."

The elevator connects to a large room, which appears to be the size of a small football field. Weapons ranging from medieval maces to modern day firearms hang in glass cases along every wall. It's like some sort of macabre trophy room.

I take a deep breath, surprised that the air down here is thin and easy to breathe. I never thought I'd see the day when my lungs would be happier underground than outside.

"What is this place?" I ask.

Acey leans against the frame of the elevator door to keep it open while Kaleb and Asher struggle to lift Taylor with the least amount of contact necessary. "The training center. The hallways over there," she gestures with her hand to the right, "lead to the infirmary, the library, specialty rooms and a sort of sanctuary housing. The ones over there," she gestures to the left, "lead to the weapons, sparring, and interrogation rooms, and cells."

"Cells?"

"Yeah. Sometimes we have to keep… things here for a while before they're willing to talk. They don't get used much anymore. No one usually survives long enough to be questioned."

It's not lost on me that she includes herself in the explanations.

Asher and Kaleb carry Taylor off the elevator and to the left. I have to say, the hallways to the right sounded much more appealing. I follow them across the foam pads and down a dimly lit hallway.

"For some reason, I didn't think you were a demon hunter," I tell her.

She giggles. "A demon hunter?" With an eye roll and a shrug, she says, "Actually, that's not too far off. Anyway, I'm not really. At least not anymore. Gabe says it's too dangerous."

"Because you're a girl?" I say sympathetically. "They're afraid you'll get hurt?"

She laughs. "Nope. It's not me they're worried about."

I laugh, too, because I assume she's kidding.

Asher hits a switch on the wall with his elbow, dropping Taylor's legs in the process. Somehow, he manages to catch the flailing limbs, but not before they hit the ground.

The room sparks to life as harsh neon light floods the hall.

"Do you miss it?" I ask.

"Sometimes." Her red and gold hair bounces around her shoulders as she shakes her head. "Then others, not so much."

The second room on the left is our stop. In order to get inside, there is a number of codes that have to be entered then reprogrammed. Acey punches in twelve numbers then licks her finger and presses it onto an impression reader. The door snicks open.

Kaleb positions Taylor's body into a regular office chair. If an office chair was used for electrocutions, I realize. Leather straps weave through a metal fastener that looks heavy and cold like iron. Asher works furiously buckling them over Taylor's wrists. Then he fastens another strap across Taylor's chest.

I want to ask if tying him down is necessary, but I am tired of getting those confused looks. I wonder if I'm really acting that much different from any other girl in this situation. I must be. How would I know? It's not like I've met many girls who have been sexually assaulted then escorted three stories underground to confront their predator.

When it all becomes too much to watch, I turn my back to everyone, and slowly case the room. The walls are made of some sort of shiny metal and iron bars. I reach out and touch it, feeling the warmth leach out of my fingertips.

What the hell is this room made of?

By the time I turn back around, Taylor has been wheeled over to a large metal table bolted to the middle of the floor. Like something straight out of a cop drama.

Acey leans down and says loudly into his ear, "You can wake up now."

His head lolls to one side then the other. His eyes open wide then wider. "Where... where the hell am I?"

Asher and Kaleb position themselves in front of me, blocking me from view. I duck to the side to see around Kaleb's elbow. Acey leans back against the table, only an inch away from Taylor's bound wrists.

"Judgment Day, Asshole. This," she spreads her arms wide, "is your trial. We are your jury. How do you plea?"

He zeroes in on her, his eyes revealing how weak he thinks she is. "What are you talking about?"

Acey laughs. The sound of it makes him flinch. As well it should. Even I feel the sharp edges of the noise. "You have been a very naughty boy." She walks her fingertips along the back of his neck, just under his collar.

He shudders.

"Care to tell me what you were doing tonight?" she continues, canting her head to the side.

Taylor makes a snorting sound and spits at the ground, narrowly missing Acey's feet.

Asher moves forward like he might tear the head from his body, but Kaleb holds him back with one arm. "Easy," he says.

Acey bends at the waist, putting her mouth right up to his ear. A low growl emanates from her throat. "The next time you do that, it will be the last thing you do. I will personally make sure of that."

"Bitch!" he snarls.

I reach up on tip toe and whisper into Kaleb's ear, "I want to say something."

Asher looks over his shoulder at me and shakes his head once. It's the look my dad used to give me when I was younger and got bored at church. I'd ask to leave and he would shake his head just like that. I had to listen to my dad, though. I don't have to listen to Asher.

"Please, Kaleb," I beg.

Kaleb takes one step to the right, which wins him an acidic glare from Asher. "She said please."

"Is that all it takes?" Asher says. "All I have to do is say please if I want you to go away?"

Kaleb grins and crosses his arms over his chest. "You only wish it were that easy."

I toss a daring look over my shoulder. "Would the two of you like to take this outside?" Once I'm sure they are done bickering like an old couple, I tack on, "That's what I thought."

Taylor's eyes narrow at the sight of me. "Shit," he says, dropping his head. "This is the last time I let Jen set me up. You broke my nose! You're all crazy!"

I take a step forward, trying to remember what I wanted to say. A million unprintable things that might win me a one-way ticket to the pit come to mind. Those are quickly erased by the repetitive sounds of his nose breaking playing in my ears. But what comes out of my mouth is: "Who the hell do you think you are?"

A muscle in his jaw jumps.

Gathering strength from the two men behind me, I stand my ground. "When a girl says no, Asshole, she means no."   He laughs. It seems oddly out of place considering the situation he's in. "I know girls like you. You whore yourself out to everyone. To you, no just means try harder."

In a blur of motion, Asher jumps the table. His fist cocks back and shoots into and through Taylor's jaw with an emphasized cracking noise.

Taylor glowers up at him. A ribbon of blood runs from his mouth to his chin.

Asher leans down and clutches Taylor's jaw in his hand, forcing their eyes to meet. "When you speak to the lady again, it might do you good to show some respect."

Taylor glances around. "I don't see a lady."

This time, Acey grabs him by the hair and jerks his head back. Her face hovers above his, close enough to kiss. "I'd watch my words if I were you, Big Boy. We don't like your kind around here. And you just stepped into our world where I'm not only the judge, but the executioner." A flash of red light crosses her eyes.

I blink twice, unsure of what I saw.

Taylor's expression goes vacant. He stares off into some unseen world, mouth moving mechanically as if he can no longer control it. "Jen made me a deal. She said she had a girl that was loose, easy, a guaranteed lay. So I went for it."

Acey releases his hair and pats his head like a dog. "And why would she do that for *you*?"

"She and I have been doing business together a long time. I am her sole provider. She owed me money. This was payment."

"Sole provider?" I repeat, sounding confused.

"He's her drug dealer," Acey confirms.

I'm less surprised by this revelation of drug abuse than I would have been if someone told me that Jen goes to church every Sunday. It all seems so fitting.

Taylor prattles on in monotone. "She owed me. She still owes me. She said, 'Do me a favor and take the slut out. She'll for sure give you some. Put it toward my payment.'"

"A favor?"

"Yeah." He blinks once, but there's nothing behind his blank stare. "She said that the girl was trying to steal her boyfriend."

Asher tenses. He glances at me sideways.

"It's not true," I assure him.

Kaleb leans a shoulder against the wall. "Why wouldn't you stop when the pretty girl said 'no'?" he asks, his voice rough.

"It's all part of the game. Jen said she likes it rough, likes a man to be in charge."

"I'll show you rough," Asher mutters, stepping up to the table and leaning toward Taylor, the robot.

"So she offered you a 'guaranteed lay' for what?" Acey asks, ignoring her brother.

"I told you, she owed me."

"What else did Jen say?" I demand.

He blinks once slowly. "She said you were a sure thing. That her boyfriend had you every which way to Sunday. The boyfriend said you had a body just waiting to be ravaged. I didn't believe him until I saw you."

"Liar!" I shriek, lunging toward him. Asher turns and catches me with one arm around my stomach and hauls me back before I make it over the table. "Alex would never say that!"

"Nicky," Acey says, shaking her head, "he can't lie. He is incapable of anything but the truth right now. I'm sorry."

"No." I push Asher away and walk backwards until I can feel the door. "I can't hear anymore." Then I turn on my heel and stomp out of the room.

Once outside, it's as if every last minute since that damned party weighs heavy on my shoulders. I lean against the cement wall. This place feels like a gigantic maze and I'm the mouse searching for the block of cheese that never existed in the first place.

Chapter 33

My eyes peel back breaking the seal of my dried tears. I must have cried myself to sleep on the cold cement floor. For a dizzying moment, I wonder where the hell I am. My head rests on something hard and warm, and it's moving.

"Nicoletta?" Asher asks close to my ear. "You awake?"

In the darkness, I realize that I must be lying on his chest. Fingers stroke through my hair.

"I need to go home." I tell him. Though, I don't make any effort to move. "My parents are probably worried."

"Shh. Acacia called them."

I sit up, scooting backwards so I can make out his face in the dim light. "What?"

"You've been asleep for five hours. We didn't want them to go file a missing person's report or something, so Acey called and told them that she ran into you at the party. She said you didn't feel comfortable with all the 'debauchery' so you went to her house and ended up talking until you fell asleep."

"Seriously?" I reply. "They bought that?"

He scoots up on the bed until his back is up against the wall. His hands fold together in his lap. "Your parents are very impressed that you didn't stay in a situation you felt uncomfortable in. There are a lot of awful people out there, you know?" His lips turn up in a smile. "So, you're sleeping at Acey's house tonight."

"My parents would never agree to that," I explain, rubbing my eyes. I realize I'm no longer wearing my skirt and the torn shirt. Rather, I'm dressed in a black nightgown. "Where are my clothes?"

"They were still wet. Acey got you something dry." Upon seeing the mortified look on my face, he adds on, "Don't worry. She changed you. Your clothes are hanging on the shower door in the bathroom and I wouldn't be too concerned about your parents. Acey can be very persuasive." He chuckles.

I feel like I'm missing out on a joke. "Huh?"

He reaches out and runs a hand down my back. My nerves stand on edge, ready to be touched by someone I trust.

Then he lifts a blanket and wraps it around my shoulders. I notice for the first time that he's changed, too. Instead of wearing jeans, he's wearing grey pajama pants and a black shirt.

"Acacia is a plant, did you know that?" he asks.

I didn't, but nod anyway.

"It's the base ingredient in some of the strongest mind-altering drugs."

Something in my brain clicks into place. "What's her real name?"

He laughs. "In another life, it was Ariana."

I think back to the vacant look in Taylor's eyes when Acey demanded he tell her the truth. It was as if someone spiked his drink with a truth serum. Only, the truth serum was a short girl with red hair and green eyes.

"Kaleb called her terrifying," I muse. "Now I know why."

"We're all terrifying," he admits.

A laugh startles out of me. "That's funny."

His expression says he thinks it's anything but. "What is?"

Canting my head to the side, I say, "I'm not afraid of you."

Asher remains silent for so long that I'm not sure he hasn't fallen asleep sitting up with his eyes open. The only indication that he might be awake is the confused look on his face. "Nicoletta," he says, shaking his head.

"What?"

He turns until he is sitting on the edge of the bed, facing the other side of the room. "Why wouldn't you be afraid of me? Don't you realize? I could have killed him. I really, really wanted to kill him, and I wouldn't have even flinched as I did it. In fact, I probably would have reveled in the feel of taking his life."

"You didn't though," I counter. There's no way he means any of that, right?

"That's because I wasn't entirely sure *you* hadn't already."

I stare at his back, willing him to turn around. "He's still alive, isn't he?"

Asher stands up and paces the space between the bed and the wall. After his third turn, his eyes meet mine. They shine gold. I can almost feel myself falling forward into their depths. "Yes, he's still alive. Though, I'm not sure how long that will last. Acey put him to sleep... for now."

I crawl across the bed in a rustle of satin and silk. At the edge, I reach out with my right hand to push an errant black curl behind his ear. A white hot flare shoots up my wrist and I wince.

"Your wrist," Asher says, all concerned. "Does it hurt?"

I stretch the muscle, gritting my teeth. "Like a bitch."

"When you feel up to it, we'll go cast it in the infirmary."

"Fine, whatever," I say, waving him off. "Look, Asher, please don't feel bad for anything. If I weren't so weak, I would have had it taken care of way before he ever put his hands on me."

"You aren't weak," he argues.

A nasty feeling crawls through my stomach. My chest burns. I feel... broken inside. "Yes, I am. I feel like a traitor to my gender for not being able to break his hands off. And that's another thing, I want to. I want to make him hurt and writhe and cry out in pain. Don't you understand? It's normal to want vengeance."

"But is it normal to act on it?"

I shrug. "I don't know. For you guys, maybe it is." I take a deep breath through the pause. "What I want to know is why it's okay that I almost killed the little bastard, but you beat yourself up for feeling like you could."

He thinks on that for a while before rubbing a hand down his face. "Because if you had killed him, it would have been an accident. If I killed him, I would've enjoyed it."

I focus on an empty space somewhere between the wall and the infinite expanse of the universe. This world is so different from the world I live in. In my life, if I were to (almost) kill someone who attacked me, I would have to prove that I was defending myself. In Asher's life, though, it would be expected of me to hurt him like he's hurt me. An eye for an eye, as it were.

I think I like his philosophy better.

Maybe that makes me terrifying, too.

Asher pushes his hands through his hair abruptly and says, "Kaleb asked me to go back with him. He needs help tracking down the things that killed his mother."

"To Montana?" My chest constricts and my heart feels like paper burning down to ash.

He nods. "After the issue here is resolved, he's going right back to it. He invited Acey as well."

"What did you say?"

"I told him I'd think about it. I'm not sure how I feel, but I have to admit, it felt nice to make a difference. And...," he trails off.

"And what?"

"It would be safer for you." He shrugs. "You were never meant to be a part of this."

I blink at him a few times, trying not to cry. "What are you talking about? What about college?"

"I never should have given up, Nicky. I should be out there doing what I was born to do. It's unfair to leave my family out there alone."

"What about me?" I whisper.

His fingers trace the line of my face. He tries to smile, but fails. "You will live a long and beautiful life, and eventually, you'll forget all about this."

A single scalding tear runs down my cheek and kisses his fingers.

The door to the left of us opens, casting a bar of light across the room. Before that, there was only the dim, crackling glow from an electric fireplace. Now I can make out the simplicity of the room: all bed and floor. Must be one of the sanctuary rooms.

A fiery, red halo forms around a dark shadow. "Good you're up," Acey declares. "Can I talk to you for a second?"

Asher nods and offers me one last mournful look before stepping out of the room, taking all my hope with him. The door shuts, cutting me off from the last person I have left to trust in this world.

My head falls into the pillows and I cry. Logic has left the room and what feels like clarity burns like heat waves through my brain.

Asher is trying to let me down easy. He doesn't want someone so weak, someone who's been tainted by the hands of another.

Infuriated, I launch myself off the bed, rushing into the bathroom. There, on the floor, are my clothes where Asher said they were. I pick up the pile and stomp back into the bedroom. They've had plenty of time to dry. Now they are stiff and ruined. I almost wish they were in better shape for where they are going. If they are already destroyed, I may not get the kind of closure I need.

With one deep breath, I toss them into the fire and watch as the flames consume everything right down to my underwear.

I stare, my eyes burning from smoke and tears. I don't feel better. Phantom hands crawl along and under my skin. I shudder violently.

Sitting back on the bed, I curl into the tightest ball I can manage. Sobs rock through me. At first, they are soft and weak, and then they become hard, then harder. And finally, when all tears have been shed and I am empty, I drift off to sleep.

Jac stands at the far end of a darkened room. The walls are painted red: the color of blood. He stares at me, his pale grey eyes unmoving.

"What do you want?" I call out in frustration.

He smiles, his lips parting to reveal sharp white teeth. "More to the point, what do you want?"

"I asked you first." I say, at the risk of sounding like a five year old.

He takes a tentative step forward. "It seems that since I hold more cards than you do, it would be fitting for my question to come first."

Then I see it. There's a motionless lump in the middle of the floor. A wisp of auburn hair catches my eye. "Brady." I gasp. "What have you done to him?"

"Nothing, yet." His smile widens, making me feel cold and nauseous. Under that, there's a part of me that feels uncomfortable, vulnerable and violated. Like someone's hand caressing me in places I don't want to be touched – places that Taylor exposed for the world to see.

"Let him go." I plead in a voice far too shaky and broken to be my own.

A pale eyebrow arches up Jac's forehead. "For free?" he asks out loud, but sounds like he didn't mean to. Then his voice pitches louder. "For free? You've got to be kidding."

I smooth my hands down the black silk I'm still wearing. Even in the dream, my palms feel moist. "I already asked what you want."

His grey eyes roam over every bit of my exposed skin. "There are many things I desire. You must be more specific, Ma Petite."

And there it is. Through all my vulnerabilities, a tiny flame of irritation ignites, warming me. "I don't speak French! It's just a name!" I yell. The words reverberate in my ears and I know I spoke out loud, even in my sleep.

"Pity that. With your lineage being so pure…," he trails off, clucking his tongue. He hesitates for a moment and lifts his chin higher in the air. His nose twitches as if he smells something foul. "You're confused," he observes. "I like confused. Don't get me wrong, confusion isn't nearly as delectable as fear, but I enjoy it nonetheless."

"Good for you. I don't."

"Maybe you should ask your new friends to translate. Nice choice by the way." He claps a few times just to mock me. "Much stronger than your poor Brady. He's too trusting. Too caring. He'd do anything for you, you know." He sneers. "In fact, if our dear Brady didn't prefer boys, I'd think he was your ardemwah."

"My what?"

"Ardemwah," he repeats as if it will somehow make me understand. "I'm surprised your little warrior friends have not told you. You should ask them. I'm not here for a vocabulary lesson. Though, with as clueless as you are, maybe I should be." He waves one hand around like he's shooing away a bug. "Anyway. You should hear how he cries for you. Pathetic, really."

It's hard to remember that this is a dream. I feel so exhausted. "What. Do. You. Want?" I enunciate.

His expression turns cold and malicious. "You know what I want. You've kept it from me for far too long."

My feet feel warm and wet. That's when I realize that the walls aren't painted crimson. They're bleeding. The fat drops cascade into the thick pool gathering on the floor.

"Spencer." I whisper.

Jac tilts his head to the side and gives me an unimpressed look.

"You've had plenty of chances." I tell him. "How would I have been able to stop you?"

He steps forward, sloshing through the puddle at his feet. "You have no idea, do you? It's not just a boy. Nor is it a couple of boys. It's everything. How can you stop something when you have no knowledge of what you're doing?"

My fingers tremble the closer he gets. When he keeps coming, I flinch. It looks like he's about to plow right through me. But then he stops, his face inches from mine. I turn my head as he breathes in through his nose.

"You will learn. Quickly," he whispers. "Tomorrow night, you will know exactly what I want and how to give it to me. Or…" He snaps his fingers and a scream pounds against the walls.

It takes a few moments after I'm awake to realize the scream was mine. The darkness of the room bears down on me as I try to catch my breath.

The door opens and two dark haired figures rush in.

"Nicky," Asher exclaims. He sits on the bed next to me and pushes my hair back with both hands. Then he cradles my head between his palms. "What's wrong?"

My shoulders shake violently in reaction to my sobs. "He… he…," I sputter.

"Shh." He pulls me into his embrace. "It's okay now."

"No, it's not," I cry out. I push him away and focus my eyes on Kaleb. "He's got Brady. I have until nightfall before he kills him."

"Until nightfall for what?" Asher asks.

Kaleb's face has drained of all color, though it may be a trick of the light. "He needs to eat," his mouth says mechanically. "He's getting weak. This may be our chance."

"Chance for what? Didn't you hear me? He's got Brady." I grip the material of Asher's shirt and try to shake him. He barely budges. "He's going to kill Brady, Asher."

Then I fall into a crumpled mess, sobbing into his arms. He slowly runs his hand down my hair to my lower back.

"No, he won't. We'll get him back." He whispers. I feel his head turn toward Kaleb. "Right?"

Kaleb lets out a long breath. "We're sure going to try."

Chapter 34

After Asher puts my wrist in yet another splint, he declares that I've officially broken it. I would ask him how could be sure, but I'm over all the strange looks I've been getting. As it stands, I guess I should just assume that they've had experience with anything and everything.

Acey left some clothes in my temporary room. I make a mental note to thank her later. While sleeping in a skimpy nightgown doesn't necessarily bother me, walking around a training center in only that and a thin robe is beyond embarrassing. I run my fingers over the tight black pants. They're made out of some thin stretchy suede-like material. The black tank top is a thin cotton-like substance that reminds me of a leotard. My favorite part, though, are the black combat boots sitting on the edge of the bed. They aren't Doc Martens like I'm used to, but some expensive brand I've never heard of.

Acey must have measured me while I was sleeping because everything fits perfectly. Right down to the black satin underwear. I go to the bathroom to put them on while she sits on the bed and waits for me.

"Wow," she says when I come out in my new threads. She is dressed in similar clothes. Although, she wears a utility-type belt slung heavy with shiny objects. Weapons, I realize. She said she got them from the weapon's area so I guess they must be some kind of fighting garb.

I grin at her. "What? Does my ass look big?" I gesture to my back end. "Because my ass feels like it might look big."

She shakes her head. "No. It's fine. It's just, not many people can pull an outfit like that off. How's it feel?"

I shrug. "It feels great actually." I'm not lying, either. The materials may hug my body a little tighter than I'm used to, but I like it. It makes me feel strong and secure.

315

She unties a leather thong from her wrist and uses it to tie her red and gold hair back into a ponytail. "You look like one of us. Asher is going to die."

I twist my hair into a tight braid starting at the base of my skull. A few tendrils of hair escape the knots and drift into my face. This is what happens when you're hiding underground: static electricity. "Why is Asher going to die?"

"Have you looked in a mirror?" she asks.

"No."

"You should. You look like a badass."

I wave off the comment since I'm not sure if it's meant to be a compliment or what. Acey jumps off the bed and is already holding the door open as I finish tying a rubber band into my hair.

We step out into the hallway and turn left. Everything here looks so cold and barren in all its concrete glory.

Asher and Kaleb are engaged in an animated conversation. Asher is motioning around with his arms, speaking in hushed whispers, and Kaleb is leaning against a door frame with his arms crossed over his chest. Their conversation must be pretty intense. It takes two and a half minutes for them to notice we're there.

When Asher catches me out of the corner of his eye, he stops talking and turns slowly to face me. His eyes widen and his mouth falls slack.

"My mother would kill me if she saw me dressed like this." I tell him, gesturing at the outfit.

Asher's eyes slide up and down, taking in each curve and swell of the material. "Why?" He smiles. "You look fantastic."

Asher's dressed in black cargo pants made of the same suede-like material, a tight black long-sleeved shirt and a pair of heavy boots. Along with his glimmering belt stocked with weapons, he has the sword hanging vertically down his spine. Leather straps cross his chest and connect with shiny buckles.

Dressed as he is, he looks dark and dangerous.

"She'd think I was going goth and would probably want to put me in therapy." I pause, glancing around the hall. "Then again, I might need it after this."

Kaleb chuckles.

"Why don't you have to wear this?" I demand, slapping him in the shoulder.

Kaleb's lips stretch into a wide grin. He makes a show of looking down at his boot cut jeans, black hooded sweatshirt and boots. He shrugs. "I'm just special, I guess."

"Yeah, short bus special." Asher remarks. He reaches over and smacks Kaleb on the back.

"I save you a seat, don't I?"

Acey rolls her eyes and steps between them. "Boys, boys, boys. Haven't we had enough?"

I ignore all of them. "So where are we headed now?"

Acey moves next to me and wraps an arm through mine. Her smile glitters. "We're going to get our friends from their interrogation rooms."

"Friends?" I ask. "You mean Taylor?" My stomach turns when she nods. "What is he still doing here?"

"We need him." Asher explains.

"Well, technically," Kaleb corrects, "we need someone who is taking up way too much oxygen with their existence. He just happened fit the bill. Surprising, isn't it?"

I turn the full weight of my stare on him. His reaches out and rests his hands on my shoulders. I shrug out of his grasp. "Why would we need him, Asher?"

He gives me the looks he gets when he doesn't want to tell me something. I know this look well.

"Why?" I demand again.

Kaleb laughs. "Bait. We need someone no one will miss. You know, in case something goes wrong."

"Wrong?" I ask only Kaleb.

He nods. "There was no choice, Nic. We'll probably get there in time, and if we do, then nothing will even happen to him."

Asher's face is blank of emotion, but Acey and Kaleb share identical grins of amusement.

"Probably," Acey says.

"Yeah, probably," Kaleb tacks on. "In fact, I'm about thirty-two percent sure."

She nods. "And rising."

Kaleb mimics her. "And rising."

"Was this your idea?" I ask Asher.

He puts his hands up defensively. "I swear it wasn't. That doesn't mean I don't think it's the most brilliant idea so far, though. We need someone worthless. He just happens to be, you know, worthless. Besides, it doesn't really matter as long as we get Brady back, does it?"

"Wait." I cut in, realizing what they said. "You said we were going to get our *friends*. As in, plural. Who's the other one?"

Acey touches my shoulder and turns me around. "You're gonna love this."

My feet move like they are on auto-pilot. Behind us, Kaleb and Asher take small digs on each other. I wonder if this is how they always are. I haven't been around them together enough to know. If the exasperated look on Acey's face is any indication, this must happen a lot.

Just as Kaleb sticks out a foot, which Asher trips over, we come up on a window. Inside is a girl. Her head is down on the table, her blond hair spilling around her face.

"Oh my god." My heart pounds against my contracting chest. I cover my mouth with my hand in order to hold all expletives in. "You brought Jen here?"

Acey smiles. "Surprise."

"No. No. This is not a good surprise." I say like I'm scolding a child.

Her face falls. "It's okay. She won't remember being here. She thinks it's all a dream."

"Can you do that to me?" I ask, sarcastically. "Make me think all of this is a dream?"

"No." She giggles. "We'll return her. Besides, we haven't done the interrogation yet. We were saving that for you. Aren't you just the tiniest bit curious?" She nudges me with her elbow. "Come on, have some fun."

"I have –" I glance at my watch with feeling – "fifteen hours and forty-six minutes to save my best friend. I don't have time for fun."

But Acey already has the door open. She leans a shoulder against it. "There's always time for fun," she says. "Besides, the boys will continue to work on the plan. No time will be wasted."

I glance over my shoulder at Asher.

He nods and says to Kaleb, "To the bat cave?"

"This whole place is a damn bat cave. Be more specific," Kaleb replies as they head down the hall.

"Right. Like Montana isn't?" Asher's voice trails away.

I hear Kaleb say something about a "Badass Cave" before they disappear completely. Before I know it, I'm shoved inside the room with Jen, who is sitting up, looking around.

Her eyes narrow on me. "Nic? God, when will this dream end?" The disappointment in her voice is as comforting as a warm blanket.

"Soon," says Acey. "Very soon. You'll wake up and all will be good again in your boring little life. But first…," She urges me on with a wave of her hand.

"How could you?" I ask, realizing that I'm not very good at this. Acey said to have fun, but none of this is fun for me. In fact, I wonder what makes Acey think I could have while my best friend is missing.

"God," she says, exasperated. "I thought you needed a little help getting over Alex. He's mine."

"I don't want Alex," I tell her, realizing for the first time that it's the truth. I don't want Alex. I want Asher. Asher, who is going to leave me to join some crusade against some demonic warlord. I wonder if I should just diagnose myself with "Want What I Can't Have" syndrome now rather than later.

"Whatever." She rolls her eyes. "You should hear him talk. It's always Nicky this and Nicky that. I'm his girlfriend. Not you."

Well, this is news to me. I stand across the table from her, stunned into silence.

Acey jumps into the conversation feet first. "I will never understand girls. Wouldn't it make more sense to punish Alex instead of Nicky?"

Jen blinks. Obviously she hadn't thought about it from that angle. "He wouldn't want her if she wasn't so pure and innocent."

"He doesn't want me." I protest.

She doesn't hear me. Why would she? As far as she's concerned, this is *her* dream, which means she'll be completely honest for what may be the first time in her life. Because we don't have to lie in our dreams and we aren't even really here, right?

Right.

Maybe this *could* be fun.

Acey nods in encouragement as if she could hear the puzzle pieces click together in my head. Her grin widens.

"Who's Taylor?" I ask. "Is he really your ex?"

"No," she scoffs. "He's my dealer. I wouldn't be caught dead dating someone like that."

"Like what exactly?"

"Hello," Jen says in the most annoying way possible. "Taylor should, like, be behind bars or something. He's got a reputation at his school and it's not that he's Prince Charming, if you know what I mean. I swear, even in my dreams you're a retard."

That stings. I mentally tick off all of my alleged traits. Not only am I stuck up and a buzz kill, but now I'm a retard. I try not to smile when Acey walks around the table and yanks on the back of Jen's hair. Jen yelps.

"So you set me up?" I demand to know.

Acey crouches down on her haunches next to her and hisses in her ear, "She didn't set you up. You heard him, she used you as payment."

"I offered a deal," Jen corrects. "But he said it would be a pleasure after seeing the picture Alex keeps of you in his wallet."

When Acey yanks on her hair again, she throws her head back, begging. "I would like to wake up now, please?"

Blame it on my wardrobe or on everything I've just learned, but a switch has flipped inside me. I feel powerful, like I could take Jen on and leave her bloody and bruised with no remorse. The feeling kind of scares me, to be honest. I want to throttle her, make her cry out in pain. I want to be downright evil. I want to hear her scream like I did in the car when Taylor's hands forced themselves on me. The tide of confused emotions tears a rift in the world and threatens to swallow me whole. It's all a bit overwhelming. I clench my fists to keep my hands from trembling.

"Take her home," I tell a confused Acey.

"What? Come on, Nicoletta, you don't want to let her go yet, do you?"

I nod. "I want her out of here. I really need to focus on what's really important, and that's definitely not her. Knock her out, or whatever, but get her the hell out of here."

Jen's eyes widen like saucers. She glances from me to Acey and back again.

"It's almost morning, Ace. Get her home. She's just not worth any of my attention right now."

Acey nods, leans over, and kisses Jen on the cheek, frowning all the while. Jen sags in the chair like a puppet cut from its strings.

I turn my back on them, open the large metal door, and walk right into Gabe. That's right, Asher and Acey's guardian. He shoots me a horrified glance.

"What are you doing here?" His eyes roam up and down my clothes disapprovingly. It's a relief to see that his gaze doesn't linger anywhere longer than needed.

"You know, I've been wondering the same thing." I respond. This may be the longest night of my life. I hook a finger at the door I just came out of. "Acey's in there."

As I turn to walk away, Gabe grabs my elbow. "Collette," he says softly.

321

I glower back at him. "Why do you keep calling me that? I am not Collette. I am Nicoletta. Nicky. Nic."

His hand falls as if my skin is suddenly too hot to touch. He apologizes under his breath. "I'm sorry. I must have, I thought you were somebody else."

Then he turns and disappears into the room.

The only person who has ever called me Collette is my father. He liked it because it was the name my grandmother went by. I stare at the doorway, wondering how he knew that. It's not like anyone has ever thought to abbreviate my name that way before. I make a mental note to ask Asher later.

There's an eerie silence coming from the room I just left. I expect yelling. After all, it's not like we've been good, law-abiding citizens tonight. It feels like the last twelve hours have been scenes from the longest Lifetime teen drama ever.

I wonder what will piss Gabe off the most: the kidnapping or the torture of a drug dealer.

Probably best to warn Asher and Kaleb.

I find them fifteen minutes later in what is labeled the "Reference Room."

The library – and I use that term loosely – has rows upon rows of leather bound books lining the shelves. There are large plush chairs sitting in a circle around a long rectangular table and the lighting is so low that I can't imagine anyone using it for research.

Asher sits in one chair leaning over a dusty tome open on the table. His elbows perch on either side of the book while his fingers tug unconsciously at his hair.

Kaleb sits a few chairs to his right. Flipping back and forth between his fingers is a glinting dagger.

"Done already?" Asher asks without looking up. "That must be a record. Acey usually takes her time. She likes to make 'em squirm."

I plop down in the chair to his left. The stretchy material of my clothes slithers along my body. It surprises me. They look so stiff and constricting, but in reality, I could probably do acrobatics in them if I knew how.

"I cut it short," I tell him. "I didn't want to hear anymore. She's just a crazy, jealous girl. By the way, Gabe's here."

Asher's head whips up and around to stare at me. He massages his unshaven chin with his hand.

"Gabriel? Here?" Kaleb asks. "Well, this just gets more and more interesting."

"Or something like that," Asher quips back.

I pull my feet up onto the chair and hug my knees. "I ran into him on my way back from the interrogation rooms. I think he was going to talk to Acey first."

Asher nods once then turns back to his text. It looks like a journal of some sorts. Cursive writing scrawls across the page put there by a careful hand. The curls and dashes of the letters look familiar.

"Can I help?" I ask, startling both of them.

Asher hesitates then says, "Sure. It might make this faster. Let me show you what we're doing." He flips the book closed over his hand, marking his place, and runs a reverent finger over the insignia burned into the cover. It's the same design from the sword: two hooks crisscrossing with what looks like the curve of a snake intertwining them. There is a four-point starburst embossed just below the design.

On the spine is a name: Asher Rowan, then a dash.

"It's yours," I observe.

"Was," he agrees. "Now it belongs to the library. Every active warrior keeps one to document their discoveries. It's like building our own encyclopedia. When we fade, copies are made for each of the centers."

"What's the dash mean?"

He clears his throat. "Our last names change all the time, but we usually keep our first and middle names. For research reasons, it's all alphabetical by first name."

"So why Asher Rowan? Isn't Rowan your last name?"

He shakes his head. "Actually my birth certificate says my name is Asher Rowan Donorio. We dropped the last name when we moved here. Acey took on Rowan to avoid confusion."

I nod, pretending to make some sense of it all. "So what's Acey's middle name?"

"Her books can be found under the name of Acacia Gardenié."

"A French name?" I say, raising my eyebrows.

"We don't really have time for history lessons, but our library was destroyed sometime in the fifteen hundreds. Acey and I were living in France at the time. That was when we changed our names," he explains.

"What about Kaleb? What was his real name?"

Kaleb snorts, reminding me of his presence. "Don't you dare," he warns.

Asher whispers close to my ear, "I'll tell you later."

"Hell no, you won't," Kaleb cuts in. "And if you do, I'll tell her about the battle in sixteen-oh-four."

Asher's smile fades. A darkness shutters over his eyes. "Fine. You win." Then he mouths the word "later" to me.

I can't help but laugh out loud. "So, how do I do this? Do I just grab any book and start skimming?"

"You could." He shrugs. "But we'd be here all day. Why don't you grab Gabriel's? Gabriel Monet."

"Like the painter?"

He nods. "Just like."

Reluctantly, I get out of my comfy chair and stand staring at the first oversized bookcase. I feel like a little kid looking for a clear bouncy ball in a toy store. Who knew there were so many people fighting in this invisible war? I sure didn't.

The books smell like dust and age. I run a finger across Acey's journal. She has seven thick volumes under her name alone. I move on, trying to read the names as I go. Some of them are written neatly, while others look like they were scrawled down in the middle of a seizure. Some of the stories inside would for sure put the Fiction section at Barnes and Noble to shame. My eyes are incredulous, my brain unwilling to process. There are just too many names. How is it possible that so many of these people exist and no one knows about them?

Finally, I come upon the name. It's one single volume thick as a dictionary. I wiggle it free and look at the cover. Underneath the insignia lie three stars. I wrestle to keep the weight of it off my wrist and plop it down on the table sending puffs of dust billowing from the pages. I cough.

"What are these?" I ask Asher who is back to perusing his own text. Tracing the stars with my right hand, I realize they are branded into the leather.

"Gabriel's an elder. Or was anyway. They have a different life span. The stars indicate that there are only three of these volumes in existence. Two of them were destroyed," he explains, staring off into the space just over my shoulder as if he can see something there.

Just to be sure, I glance over my shoulder. Nothing.

I flip open the cover. Inside, there are a lot of French words scribbled into the pages. I try to make sense of it, but am finally forced to accept that there's nothing sensible inside. I shake my head and shut the book. "I can't read this."

Asher glances over and smiles. He takes three inches of pages between his fingers and flips it halfway through. "Don't worry about the beginning." He says. "I'll glance through it when you're done. It's probably just history."

"What am I looking for anyway? Am I even allowed to read this?"

"Technically," Kaleb interjects, "we aren't even allowed to talk to you, but here we are."

"You aren't what?"

He sighs. "Never mind."

Ignoring him, I set upon trying to research, but find that the light is too dark to read. "I don't know how you guys can read in here."

"There's more light over here," he says, leading me to a desk hidden in shadows. I hadn't noticed that there was anything else in the room before now. When he flicks on a lamp, I see that there are actually three large wooden desks lined up along the wall. Light spills out of a reading lamp and illuminates the whole corner.

"What am I looking for in here?" I ask, taking one of the desk chairs. They aren't as comfortable as the table chairs, but what can you do?

Asher touches my cheek with his fingertips. I close my eyes to revel in the contact.

"Just look for anything that might jump out at you," he whispers. He leans in and brushes my lips with his tentatively. He's so warm and soft. "Call me if you need anything."

My nerves sing. "Sure," I say sarcastically. As if I can focus on anything now. I'm reminded that Kaleb is still in the room when he clears his throat. I give him a look that borders on begging.

"How much more time do we have?" Kaleb asks point blank.

His words are like a cold shower.

While my best friend is missing, here I am mooning over a guy. What kind of friend am I anyway?

I mumble something that may have sounded like a "thank you," droop my head, and head to the corner with a book large enough to be considered a deadly weapon in at least three states.

I will save Brady, and when I do, God help the demon who dared take him in the first place.

Chapter 35

"Holy shit. Gremlins exist?" I exclaim. "I thought they were just a movie." I flip a few pages. "And fairies?" Then a few more. "Vampires and werewolves, too?"

"There are more were-animals than just wolves." Asher looks up at me with an amused expression. At least I think it's amused. It's hard to tell with the light from the desk lamp blinding me. "I told you," he says, "everything comes from somewhere."

"Apparently," I muse, glancing over the description and prophecy of the Werewolf. I've had to remind myself three times already to keep focused.

In all reality, it wasn't hard for me to believe in witchcraft and other forms of magic. How else would you explain some of life's natural mysteries? But blood-thirsty undead humans? Those are just tales told by Bram Stoker, Poppy Z. Brite, and Anne Rice, right? It's science fiction, that's all.

Even if they did show up in *Supernatural.*

I bite my lip to keep all other outbursts to myself. I'm not even tired. This book has so much action it could be a best seller.

Gabriel has a keen sense of detail. He draws you in to the description and paints a picture in your head.

I pause on one paragraph, re-reading it over and over again until the words blur. "Asher," I say, my voice trembling. "Can you come here?"

He turns the book upside down to save his page then lopes over. Placing his hand on the desk, he leans over me and reads out loud. "And it is to my belief that this woman will be the cause of my demise. I swear unto the Goddess herself, she will be my undoing. Collette, my ardemwah." He turns curious eyes to me. "Okay? So?"

"Two things." I raise the first two fingers on my left hand like a dork. "First, Jac used that word. What was it? Avamdah?"

He chuckles. "Ardemwah?"

"Right. He said that if he didn't know any better, he would think Brady was mine."

His eyebrows knit together in a disconcerting line.

"What does it mean?" I ask.

"Literally? It means 'the blood of my soul.' It's a term of endearment used by our people. It's like a kindred soul or a soul mate. Someone intertwined with your creation. You know, blood of my blood, flesh of my flesh and all that?"

"I don't believe in soul mates," I say quietly, lowering my fingers and resting my hand next to the book. Asher covers it with his own, his fingertips skating over my skin.

"If you had been brought up in this life, you'd be amazed what you might believe in," he whispers, searching my face with his eyes. I assume he finds what he's looking for in them because he quickly turns away. "What's the second thing?"

"When I saw Gabe earlier, he called me Collette."

"Another version of your name," he says, thinking that over. "Could be a coincidence, but I suppose you don't believe in those either."

I shake my head defiantly. "Not anymore."

He scratches his eyebrow with his thumb. "Well, keep reading. We'll ask Gabe when he finds us, which he inevitably will." He takes a lock of my dark hair and fingers it thoughtfully before walking away.

Gabriel, I find, is quite the romantic, which makes me wonder if all of them are. I can see the contentment behind Kaleb's eyes when he speaks of Kaida. And well, I know what Asher is capable of. I guess it makes sense when you think about it. They come from a time when there was no instant form of gratification. You worked hard for what you had. It's kind of sad that things aren't like that anymore.

From what I've read so far, Collette didn't know Gabriel. He knew of her, watching her from afar, but she never knew him. Not until fifty pages – or three years – later when Gabriel stumbled upon her being attacked... by a human man. I'm not as surprised as I probably should be. My skin burns all over and my stomach churns with each rapid beat of my heart.

Collette fought hard against her attacker. In fact, she almost dispatched of him herself when Gabriel wandered along.

"My awe fueled by my great desire." I read quietly to myself. "A woman who possesses such power is most certainly capable of possessing me."

"What's that?" Asher calls from the table.

"Nothing."

Some time later, Kaleb drops a bagel and a cup of coffee off at my desk. I rub my eyes. Words swim behind them in pink and green lines. I've been so wrapped up in Gabriel's love story that I must have lost track of time.

"What time is it?" I ask, testing the coffee. It's a tad sweeter than I like, but caffeinated enough for its purpose.

"Nine." He responds. "Do you need a break? You've been at it most of the morning."

"No, I'm good. This is really interesting."

He nods. "Have you gotten to the part where Collette leaves him for another man?"

I gasp. "How could she? He lives for her."

He shrugs while taking a sip of his own coffee. "Some people can't handle waiting for their lover to come home in a body bag," he says, his voice weighed down with guilt.

I blink slowly to clear water from my eyes. "I guess I hadn't thought of it that way."

Kaleb hooks a foot around the leg of another chair and pulls it over. He slumps into the seat. His hair is dried in curly locks framing his slate blue eyes. He looks like a fallen angel.

"You see, Nicky," he begins, leaning back in his chair. "There are many reasons why we aren't supposed to take humans for our mates. While one reason is to preserve the bloodline—"

I cut him off. "The bloodline? What does that have to do with anything?"

His eyebrows arch in surprise. He must not be used to getting cut off. "Well, it's hard to explain, but basically a child of our blood line would need certain nutrients that only a woman of similar genetic make-up could produce. Any other child would be lost." He rubs his chin with his thumb. "In theory."

"You don't know for sure then?" I demand to know. Poor Gabriel may have lost the love of his life to a theory.

"History is all we have to work with. The funny thing about history, though, is that it's ongoing. When you look at the available data, it's not possible. But in my experience, there's often new data that hasn't been taken into consideration. Look at us, at what we do. Scientifically speaking, there's no way we should be able to do any of it. How could anyone retrain memories and attributes beyond death and rebirth?" He shakes his head. "It should be impossible, and yet, there it is."

I take a long draw of coffee, letting his words sink in. "What are the other reasons?"

Kaleb clears his throat. With a glance over his shoulder at Asher, he says, "It's dangerous. Not only for us, but for you as well. We will always have a target on our backs. And the few times we have taken humans as our mates, it hasn't ended well. You see, our life spans aren't as long as yours. We die, just like you, but we aren't gone forever. If one our mates die, the side of us that is more human gets reckless."

I pick apart my bagel slowly, turning it to crumbs. Only a few bites make it into my mouth, the rest ends up in my lap. "But Kaida is human," I remind him.

He nods wistfully. "That's true. No matter how powerful of a witch she is, that won't change. But you see, I'm a lost cause." A smile splits his face. "No one knows what to do with me."

My eyes fix on Asher as he slowly turns a few pages before turning them back. A wrinkle forms between his brows. I remember our first kiss and how good it felt to have his heat surging through me. A blush creeps up my neck.

"And so are you, it would seem," Kaleb continues. He leans forward and pitches his voice lower. "You know he can't stay. He'd never be able to live with himself if something happened to you."

My heart thuds uselessly in my chest. A tear slides down my cheek and leaves a dark wet stain like blood on my shirt. "But how am I supposed to live without him?"

He taps the desk next to the book. "You'll have Brady. Good friends are hard to come by."

"That seems highly unfair."

Kaleb pats my head. "Are you alright?"

I nod unconvincingly.

"Okay then. Let's get back to it. We're close. I can tell."

***

"Maybe we are looking at this the wrong way." I say, slamming my fist into the old book an hour later. I've read over a hundred pages of pure heartbreak and still have nothing. It's beyond irritating.

Collette married a man named Jean Bouliver. Gabriel followed her for months, watching and waiting at the sidelines. Though, when Collette got pregnant, he gave up.

Luckily, Kaleb had napkins. Otherwise, the words might have bled with my tears.

Asher walks over to the desk and takes my good hand in his. "Calm down," he says quietly. "We have no other leads right now. The answer is in here. I know it is."

"Maybe there's something we're missing," I say. "Like, why is Spencer so important? Why doesn't he just feed off of another accident victim?" I wince at the coldness of my words. Dave is an accident victim. The woman in the car accident on that ditch day so long ago was an accident victim.

Kaleb's eyes narrow on me. "What?"

"I saw him at the scene of a car accident a couple of weeks ago. There was an ambulance, but the papers said that the victim didn't make it. I have a strong feeling that he targeted her." I turn to Asher. "And all of those other people actually. Answer me this: how do a

331

bunch of jocks end up with sudden onset asthma? Furthermore, how does that asthma turn into fatal pneumonia within hours?"

Asher shrugs, but the look in his eyes says he already thought the same thing.

"Why wasn't I informed of this?" Kaleb asks.

I shrug. "It was before you came into town. I saw him at the hospital a few times, too. I think he was there for Spencer though. Which brings me back to the question: why is Spencer so damn important?"

"Why any of them?" Kaleb stands up and paces the length of the table. "Maybe Spencer is too strong for him."

"He's just your run of the mill asshole," Asher remarks over his shoulder, shooting down that logic.

"Well," Kaleb says thoughtfully, "maybe because he's an asshole then. Vengeance is the number two reason people kill as far as I can tell."

"What's number one?" I ask before I can stop myself.

Kaleb's eyes shift to the book where my fist is still pressed into the pages. "Love."

"That's not the case here, though."

Both of them look at me skeptically. "Are you so sure?" says Kaleb. "When he took your grandfather, it was as you left the room. He was probably brimming with love at the time. How do you know it doesn't give him some sort of high? Maybe he's addicted to feeding on people who have something to lose."

"Like Asher said. Spencer's an asshole – a bonafide douchebag." I shake my head. "No, it's got to be something else."

Kaleb focuses on the text where it sits on the table. He walks over and flips a few pages absently.

Asher's eyes bore into mine. In the light, they look darker, a liquid gold flowing hot and molten. "Think," he begs. "Is there anything else from the dream you might have forgotten to tell us?"

I think back, trying to remember the nightmare. I spent so much effort trying to forget, but as soon as I try, the images rush back. In my mind, I recreate the images beginning with the bleeding walls.

Asher turns abruptly when the door opens. He groans. "Gabriel."

"Just in time," Kaleb announces. "Sit down, we're hoping for a breakthrough."

Gabriel glances from me to the book on the desk to Kaleb. "No thanks. I prefer to stay out of this."

"Oh come on," Acey says, shutting the door quietly behind her. "This will go so much quicker if you help. Besides, due to recent developments," her eyes fix on me, "you may not want to leave us on our own. *Someone* might get hurt."

Gabriel drops into one of the chairs next to the table, his hands scrubbing roughly at his face. "Fine. What do you have?"

"A whole lot of nothing and a deadline," Kaleb responds. He holds his empty hands out in front of him to emphasize the lack of information we've found.

"Not true." Asher says, turning around and hopping up to sit on the table. "We can't discount all the 'maybes.'"

"Is that it?" Gabriel asks. His accent gets thicker the more irritated he gets.

"We know it's evil. Probably a demon." He chuckles to himself. "One who apparently likes to gamble."

Gabriel looks at him with a quizzical expression. "Gamble?" he qualifies.

"Well, barter is more like it," I correct. "He has one of my friends. But he's willing to trade for someone else."

When no one responds, I go about telling them everything I remember about the dream all the way down to my sweaty hands. I may have left out the detail about the silky black nightgown, but can you blame me?

"What did you say he looks like?" Gabriel asks. He walks over and retrieves his book from the desk.

I suddenly feel like a voyeur to his darkest secrets. I pause for a second wondering if I've offended him by pawing through his personal journal. Honestly, I would be upset. When he sets the book down and flips past my bookmark further into the story, I let out a long breath.

"He's pale," I tell him. "Like, *everything* about him is pale. His grey eyes, that blond hair. And something about him makes my skin burn like I've been holding dry ice." That last detail may not have been necessary, but something tells me not to leave anything out.

Gabriel stops fingering the pages and looks at me a little sideways. "Your skin burns?" he asks as if he hadn't really been paying attention to me until that moment.

"Did we forget to tell you?" Acey asks with a smirk. "Our dear Nicoletta Dubois is an Empath."

Why would she use my full name like that? She's never called me Nicoletta. Just like I've never called her Acacia. At least not to her face.

Gabriel's head whips around until he's looking right at her. "I guess you did." His voice sounds urgent, almost like a warning.

Her head bobs up and down emphatically. "With psychic tendencies. Isn't that just a-ma-zing?"

He turns back to the book, slowly skimming each of the pages from where I left off.

I wonder if I look as confused as I feel. Acey has never acted so strange in front of me. It sounds like she's trying to pass a secret message.

"Here," Gabriel exclaims. "You're right. He's a demon."

"You're kidding," Asher says, hopping down from the desk. "The answer really was in your book?" He strides over to read whatever passage Gabriel's finger points to.

Kaleb walks up behind Asher and smacks him upside the head. "Of course it was. What better place for our answer to be than in the only book thick enough to kill someone with?"

Asher ignores him. "It says: From the belly of hell was born a demon with a thirst unsatisfied by food. Fair haired, pale eyed, he seeks out that which could satiate his thirst."

Gabriel continues where Asher left off, reciting from memory, "Victims range from those who battle illness to those who can aid him in vengeance."

"Wait," I say, my voice dull and unfeeling. "That's me. He seems to think I'm the only thing in the way of his feeding." A sick feeling swells in my stomach. "Which means –?"

"Which means," Asher says, continuing my thought. "Brady may not make it home after all."

Chapter 36

"Wait," Kaleb says. He holds up a hand like he is expects to be called on. He flips further and further into his own book, the lines of his forehead creasing with the intensity. "I know I... yeah, here it is." He jabs a finger into the book mid-page. "'...where I found a demon brandishing the name Jac as if he were human. I recognized him first by his non-descript features. No human would try so hard to be unnoticed as he. Upon further investigation, I found him to be the seed of a disease breather with the flesh of a fallen angel. Certainly, this would explain his abilities to inflict illness and even death to those he seeks vengeance against.'" His eyes light on Asher, who has been strolling around the room. "We've seen this guy before, remember? The battle we shall not speak of. Sixteen-oh-four? The bastard slipped right through our fingers."

Asher's face turns a sick shade of green. "Oh, Goddess. I knew he looked familiar."

I lean into Acey and whisper, "Should I be this confused?"

She nods and whispers back. "Yes, I think the 'WTF Response' is quite acceptable right now."

"Kaleb, what's a disease breather?" I ask.

He stares at me, rubbing his forehead with his palm. "It's a demon that can make someone sick, even comatose, just by breathing on them. They can also feed off of a body's will to live."

"What do you call them?"

He smiles. "We call them assholes."

I smile back. "Good name."

"So how do we kill him?" Asher asks. "If he's half angel then we can't kill him like a demon. His flesh alone will be like steel."

Gabriel, who has been sitting quietly staring off into some land we can't see, says, "There are ways. We just have to find them."

"Thanks for the false hope there, Gabe," Kaleb replies.

Pressure builds behind my eyes. The room spins around me, faster and faster until I have to grip onto a chair to keep upright. I hear a shrill scream cut through my ears then all is silent save the pounding in my ears. I see Asher's mouth moving frantically, but no words escape his lips. It's like someone has punctured my ear drums. The lines of Asher's face blur until he looks like a smudged charcoal portrait. That's when my vision breaks into puzzle pieces of black, blue, grey and white.

I must have lost consciousness because when I come to, the first thing I notice is a pain knifing through my neck. If I didn't know any better, I would say I was hit with a blunt object.

"It's okay. Just a seizure," Gabriel says, sounding like he's a mile away rather than right in front of me. "Give her a minute."

"Not a seizure," I try to say, but the only sound I can make is a low gurgle. My heart rate picks up, fueled by panic. Why can't I talk?

"That wasn't a seizure," Asher states from somewhere near my head. His hands absently trace over my moist forehead. He must have lifted me into his lap after I passed out. "She crumpled, Gabe. Since when is that sign of a seizure?"

A cold hand presses against the beat of my pulse just under my jaw. I smell rain and lavender: Kaleb.

"She'll be fine. We just need to get her to somewhere she can rest. God, I wish Kaida was here."

"I think I've only heard you say that about a million and four times." Asher sneers.

My vision clears enough to see Kaleb glare over me at Asher. "Kaida is a healer, dumbass."

"Whatever. Just move. I'll get her to her room. She can rest there."

"No," I manage to choke out. Flames lick at the inside of my skull. I only have god knows how many hours left to figure this thing out, and I'll be damned if I waste all that time trapped within my own nightmares.

Asher cocks an eyebrow at me. "Nicoletta, you need to rest." He sounds worried and a little out of breath. "There's nothing you can do to help in this condition."

"Fine," I snap, "but I'm not going to sleep."

Asher passes a hand over his eyes. "Fine. We'll get you Tylenol, Ibuprofen or whatever. Just please lie down for a little while."

I push myself off the ground to stand on my shaky legs. How the hell am I supposed to walk there if I don't have any strength?

Asher answers my unspoken question by sweeping one arm under my legs and catching my back with the other. He lifts me with such ease that I feel weightless. Wrapping my arms around his neck, I lay my head on his shoulder.

Silently, he walks me down the hall to my room. It feels so good to be in his arms that I feel the absence of them immediately when he rests me on the satin sheets.

"Where are you going?" I groan when he walks to the door. "Don't go."

One side of his mouth lifts into a gentle smile. "I promised you pain killers. You hit your head hard on the way down. It's got to be killing you. How's your wrist?"

I wince. "It was fine before you reminded me." The pain in my neck throbs with every beat of my pulse, drowning out all other feeling.

"Then I'll get four," he responds. The door clicks shut behind him.

I don't bother taking off my boots since doing so would require more effort than I have to spare. Instead, I roll onto my side and curl into a little ball.

Judging by the short time it takes Asher to return with the meds, I can only assume he ran all the way there.

He sets an ice cold can of Dr. Pepper on the nightstand then helps me sit up. I lean listlessly against him. The pills go in my right hand and the drink in the other. I take two long swallows and hand the can back before curling up to the pillow again. By way of habit, I check my watch to see how long before relief will hit. Then I realize that the twenty minutes it will take for the pills to numb my system is just another twenty minutes where I'm completely useless.

"Asher," I say quietly as he sits on the mattress next to me. "My episode was at noon."

"Okay," he says. "You want lunch?"

"No." I wave my hand at him. "Not that. My deadline is half over. I think that was my warning."

"Warning?" he repeats, his voice thick with doubt.

"Is it awful that I wish Jac would just kill Spencer? Then maybe he would just go away. Or I could focus all of my energy…"

"On protecting Brady?" he finishes for me.

"Exactly."

"You know Jac isn't going to just go away, right? There's a reason why he's here. Besides, you can't block everyone you love from him. You don't have the strength. He's a demon. If he can't take Brady, he'll go after someone else, unless we kill him."

"I know," I say as my argument slowly deflates. "It was just a thought."

Asher leans back against the wooden headboard. A sigh of frustration escapes him. We are both so wound up that neither of us breathes with regular precision.

"So, you're going back with Kaleb, huh?" I hedge. Might as well talk about it now since the pain in my head might overshadow the hurt I will most certainly feel when my heart shatters.

He nods in response and I realize that I can still feel my heart break.

"As soon as this is all over, you're leaving?" I continue.

"Nicoletta," he says on a breath. "I've been fooling myself. I can't live among people like you. Kaleb was right. College was never a viable possibility. I mean, come on. What if one of my professors turns out to be a vampire? I'd probably consider an 'F' as a declaration of war. Then I'd stake him, take his head, and the whole thing would be a bloody mess."

I stare at him, no longer sure whether is being serious or not.

"It was a joke," he says when he sees my face. "Just trying to lighten the mood. But, seriously. Everything I thought I wanted was just a pipedream. I think deep down, I always knew that."

"What if it's not? It's not like you've ever tried."

"It is." He strokes my hair back over the pillow. "Look what knowing me has done to you. Here you are: dressed like a fighter, having something like seizures, but not, and being assaulted."

I scoff. "I wasn't assaulted by a demon, if you remember. That was all because of an annoying little human girl named Jen, who was afraid I might steal her boyfriend."

His eyes flash amber in the soft light. "I know how she feels," he whispers. "You know, you *could* have him. The two of you could grow old together and have thirty-four kids, or whatever is average in this state. It kills me to say this, but you'd forget about me someday."

I laugh. "Thirty-four kids?"

He smiles in response.

In the silence, my mind wanders to thoughts of Collette and Gabriel. The comparison is weak, even I know that. I haven't known Asher all that long, and in that short amount of time, he's already lied to me at least once. I have no idea what I mean to him. Hell, I don't even know what he means to me. His very presence confuses me. But then there's what he said as he consoled me in that abandoned parking lot. A part of me wants to believe he meant it while another part of me thinks he would have said anything at that moment. Still, I wonder if Collette ever forgot about Gabriel. Could she forget him after everything they shared?

"Yeah, I don't think so," I say, rocking my head back and forth against the pillow. "First of all, there's no way in hell that I'm popping out thirty-four kids. And second, you don't get to determine what and whom I remember."

"Nicky," he warns.

"Asher," I challenge back and if I sound like I'm mocking him, well, who cares?

"You can't have the life you want with me around."

"Third, you don't get to tell me what kind of life I want."

"It's not safe."

"It's not safe anyway. Don't you get that?" I sit up abruptly and am surprised when my head doesn't fall off. "Just stay," I say, hating how much I sound like I'm begging. "I can protect myself. You won't have to worry about anything."

"I can't," he snaps. "Don't you understand? I can't do that to you."

I lean in, hoping to kiss him so he'll shut up already, but he's off the bed and by the door quicker than a rocket. He moved so quick, I barely saw him. He opens the door and hesitates like he's unsure he can walk away.

"You know," I say coldly. "I was under the impression that Kaleb came for the sword. I didn't realize he came for you, too. If I'd known, I probably would've shot him before ever speaking to him."

Asher looks at me through his dark hair. The conflicted lines of his face blur into a bemused expression. "The sword," he repeats. "Holy shit, Nicky, you're a genius." He lunges toward me, his lips pressing against mine in the quickest of kisses, and then he's gone.

I believe this is what Acey would call a "WTF moment."

I swing my legs off the bed and take off after him, singing praises to the God of Ibuprofen the whole way to the library.

"Feeling better?" Acey inquires from the doorway.

Asher, Kaleb and Gabriel stand in a circle. They speak in hushed voices as their hands wave around their heads maniacally.

"It won't work," says Gabriel. "It's a suicide mission."

"It's worth a shot," Kaleb argues. "Besides, if it works, think of the possibilities."

"Assuming your theory is right, Asher. A plan like this puts you within inches of the target. What if he infects you?"

Asher extends his right hand out, palm up. A red glow emanates from his skin. "He'll get one hell of a sun burn."

Kaleb puts a hand on his shoulder. "Maybe a lightning strike would be more sufficient," he says proudly.

I grab Acey's arm. Her red hair looks like a suspended flame caught in mid-dance in contrast to the black fighting gear. She looks so feral. It's hard for me to imagine her being younger than I am.

"What are they talking about?" I ask.

Slowly, she turns to face me. Her lips curl into a grin. "They're having a friendly little debate over who has the honor of slicing our friend, Jac, in half."

"What?" The tightness in my chest has given way to an urgency I can't control. I wrap my arms around myself to refrain from puking.

"Don't worry," she assures me, patting my shoulder. "It'll be me. They just don't know it yet."

"What?" I repeat, with an emphasis on the "huh."

She beams and it's not the first time I question her sanity. "You'll see."

I'm not sure I like the idea of Acey wielding a sword, but the thought of Asher anywhere near Jac makes my throat burn.

"I'm efficient with a sword," Asher argues.

"But you can be compromised," Kaleb says, bobbing his head toward me.

"She won't be there," he counters. "She's going home."

"The hell I am," I call out, surprising even myself. I never imagined myself to be a fighter. In all honesty, I'd be a curl up and cry until it's over kind of girl. I imagine what it would be like to sit in a corner and cry while everyone around me is slaughtered.

For a second, I consider going home, but then I think about Asher. What if he died and I wasn't there?

"I agree with Nicky," Acey says, cutting through my thoughts. "She has to be there. Jac is expecting her."

Gabe nods. "She's right. Even if it's a trap, I have a feeling he would follow Col... Nicoletta wherever she goes."

Asher tenses and steps back a few feet, shaking his head. "No. No way."

"It doesn't matter what you want," Kaleb says. "The vote has been cast. You're outnumbered."

"No," he argues. "What if she was Kaida, huh? I bet you wouldn't be so gung-ho about it then."

Kaleb's face turns ashen. "Not if I had anything to say about it."

"See?" Asher says, pointing a finger.

"She's also never given me a say about it. Do me a favor. Next time you see her, ask her how many times I've tried to leave her behind. Then, after she gives you that mind-blowing number, ask her how many times she's come anyway. I guarantee you the answers will be identical." Kaleb smirks at a memory none of us can see. "Face it, Asher. We probably wouldn't want them if we didn't know how strong they could be."

Gabriel reaches out to Asher, who steps back out of reach. His face is flaming red and a wisp of smoke escapes the corner of his mouth.

"Asher," Gabe says, his hand falling uselessly to his side, "I don't want her involved any more than you do."

"Yes, you do. You want her in the line of fire. It's not like you've ever cared for the humans." His voice is loud enough to shake the walls. "You don't care what happens to her. I saw it on your face when you met her. Why the hell would you care what happens to Collette's offspring?" Asher waves his hand at me. "This is the only way you can still hurt her."

The world around me stills for a moment, the only sound my rapidly beating heart.

Gabriel flinches. "I would never hurt Collette. Not now. Not ever."

"Bullshit," Asher accuses. "You gave up everything for her. You gave up the life, the fight. Why wouldn't you hold a grudge? She. Didn't. Choose. You."

I shrink back against the wall, feeling century's worth of guilt belonging to me only by name. My stupid hand-me-down name. Maybe when this is all over, I'll change it. I could take a page out of Asher's and Acey's books and call myself Jinx. Because I'm starting to feel like that's what I am.

"Shut up, Asher." Acey warns, stepping between them as if her petite frame can stop bullets if need be. "You have no idea what you're talking about."

The look of grief on Gabriel's face is a stark contrast to the fury on Asher's. Kaleb positions himself behind Asher, hands out and ready to hold him back.

"She did choose me," Gabriel says in a small voice. "She couldn't marry me, but she did choose me. Over everyone else."

"What the hell are you talking about?" Asher snaps.

"Kaleb, could you and Gabe go for a walk while I have a nice little talk with my brother?" Acey says politely.

Gabriel shakes his head. "No. This should come from me." He closes his eyes respectfully. "You want to know why I gave it all up and moved here of all places?"

I raise my hand. "I would love to know actually."

It's as if I'm invisible for all the attention I receive.

Asher nods tightly, his eyes still challenging. One of his feet is planted on the floor at a right angle, bearing all his weight. He looks ready to fight.

"Collette was pregnant when she married. With my child," he explains.

Kaleb steps forward abruptly. "Impossible," he says. "We can't have children with their kind. They would never survive."

Gabriel glances at the corner where I'm hiding. "I thought that once, too, but Nicoletta is evidence of a lot of things I never thought possible."

The room goes silent. So silent, in fact, that I can hear the beat of my heart pumping the accused blood through me.

Asher relaxes and rubs his face with his right hand. Then, he turns so suddenly it startles me, and stomps out of the room. Gabriel falls into the well-padded chairs and hangs his head while Kaleb paces, muttering a lot of four-syllable words: impossible, improbable, incredible.

Acey is the first to speak. She jumps up on the table and folds her legs beneath her. "That went well. Now, since that's out of the way. Time for a plan."

I drop to the floor and cover my head with my hands. For being part of an age-old race of demon hunters, I sure suck with conflict. I put my head against my knees, or rather between them, and resolve not to move until the nausea passes.

"Well, what the hell do we do now?" Kaleb asks, his voice echoing the walls of my brain.

My thoughts exactly.

Chapter 37

Learning that I'm not all human isn't the only enlightenment I receive this afternoon. Through the chaos of my thoughts, I realize that my grandfather, Jac's last victim, was also a member of this secret race of demon hunters. I could believe it of him. He was a fighter. Hell, he took on cancer and won. For a while, at least. The one thing I can't wrap my head around, though, is that I'm sitting in the same room with my great-grandfather: an Elder for some unknown army I never knew existed. I'd never met my great-grandparents and it never bothered me. Until now. How many questions would I have for my predecessor, if it were possible for me to ask her? The answer is beyond the point of my comprehension. Would I ask for her help or throttle her? Probably a little of both.

I feel, rather than see, someone sit down on the floor next to me. A wisp of chamomile drifts through the air. The smell is comforting, yet wholly unfamiliar. Slowly, I lift my head and shift my eyes to the right. Gabriel sits with his fingers laced over his propped knees. For the first time, I look at him. I mean, really look at him. It makes sense that there should be some resemblance between us. That is, if he is telling the truth. His eyes are a little narrow, whereas, I've always thought of mine as abnormally large. His nose is sharp and hard-edged while mine is soft and curved. Even his mouth seems like a straight line. Not like mine, with lips too big. The only trait we share is one dimple on the right cheek and I'm sure millions of people have that. His hair is the same color as Asher's and Kaleb's. The same as... mine. He catches me staring at him and looks away.

"You alright, kiddo?" he says, giving me his profile. Just below his left ear is a mark. The same birthmark, I realize with a jolt, that my grandfather had.

"I don't get it," I tell him. "I look nothing like you."

He smiles. His eyes crinkle around the edges, the only sign that he could be someone's grandpa. "You take after your great-grandmother. You look so much like Collette that I almost thought

346

she came back just to murder me." He forces a laugh to key me into the joke.

I don't even crack a smile.

From his pocket, he produces a small glasses case. He flips it open and removes a pair of wire-thin spectacles. Underneath, is a white case identical to the one I have at home. With a practice motion, he removes his contact lenses and places them in the case. Then, after returning the spectacles, he closes it and looks at me.

I blink rapidly at him.

"I overheard Asher and Kaleb talking about you. They mentioned something about you wearing contacts."

I nod.

"They probably didn't remember because they haven't seen me without colored contacts in so long, but as you can see, you and I share another trait: one green eye, one blue. When I first saw you, I thought maybe you were spared the sight. If I had known, I would have up and moved before you and Asher ever had a chance to... connect," he says wistfully. "But when I heard them, I knew. You, unlike your father and grandfather, received my gift."

"Don't you mean curse?" I amend for him.

One shoulder lifts in a half-shrug. "If you choose to see it that way."

I'm so confused. One on hand, I want him to tell me everything he knows, everything about where I actually come from, but on the other, I can't stand the fact that someone else knows more about me than I do.

"What else? What else don't I know?" I say, the accusation sharp as a razor.

"There's so much I could tell you, I don't even know where to start."

Suddenly, I feel exhausted. I'm sick of hearing about how much I don't know, but how no one can give me the answers I need. I push myself to my feet. "Well, when you figure it out, come find me. Where's Asher?"

"Where he always goes when he's angry," he says, staring a hole through the floor.

I circle my hand in the air, urging him to get on with it.

"The training room. When he can't drive, he sweats it out."

A sudden urge overtakes me. I give him a dark look. "Did she know what you were?"

He looks up at me for a brief moment then lowers his head. "There's nothing I wouldn't have told Collette. Not even this." He gestures with his hand to where Acey and Kaleb are huddled in the corner, speaking in hushed tones.

"Was that why she didn't stay with you? Because of this?"

"Yes. She knew she was pregnant. Back then, it was a sin to know a man before marriage. Her father arranged for a husband. She got married before anyone would know. She wanted a husband she could grow old with. I couldn't blame her for wanting that."

"Because you couldn't?" I ask.

"I age," he says in a sad voice. "Just not quite as fast as you. If I could have given it up, I would have. For her, I would have."

"That's why you retired."

"No. I retired because I wasn't able to save her. I plan to make up for that tonight."

"Tonight? How?"

"By saving you and your father. I think I finally figured out what the demon is after. And if it's revenge he wants, he'll have to face my own."

A bitter taste fills my mouth: the taste of nausea. "What is he after?"

He shakes his head, unwilling to tell me.

I push anyway. "What is he after?"

"Not what. Whom."

"Fine. Who is he after?"

"You," he finally says. "He may be reeling you in, but he's going to get me instead."

***

Asher lunges forward, thrusting his blade into an invisible opponent. He holds the blade steady for a three second count, drops down to one knee then turns, drawing the blade back over his shoulder in an arc. His hair falls into his eyes and clings to his sweaty forehead.

"Again," he breathes to himself, barely loud enough for me to hear.

Two steps back, he begins by holding the sword at his side. By the looks of it, that thing must weigh more than I do, yet it seems weightless as he pulls back and cuts a diagonal gash out of the air in front of him.

I watch the silent, graceful movements of his arms as the sword wields wildly around him. The light glints off its speed. Bringing the hilt in close to his body, he drops to one knee again and thrusts the blade outward.

He does this again and again until his breaths are fast and ragged.

"I think it's dead," It's been so long since there has been any noise, my voice sounds like a scream.

Asher turns sharply and levels the sword on me for a three long seconds. Then he relaxes and returns it to the sheath at his back.

"Don't ever sneak up on someone with a sword. Didn't your mother ever tell you that?"

"Sure," I respond, rolling my eyes. "First was potty training, then sword safety, followed by the how-to's of disabling pipe bombs."

His expression is blank. He walks toward the end of the gymnasium, retrieves a bottled water, and drains it. "Aren't we clever? So, has Acey convinced them that she should carry the sword yet?" he asks, surprising me.

"She hasn't mentioned it. How did you know?"

He loosens the straps of the sheath and gently leans the sword up against the wall. Then, he tugs his shirt over his head. The material clings to all the right places. As do my eyes. When he's free of the fabric, he balls it up and wipes his face with it. "I know Acey. She thinks she's invincible. Besides, she has something the rest of us don't."

"Oh god." I peel my eyes from his chest and focus in on his glistening face. "Is this a sexist thing?"

He scoffs. "Hardly."

"Well, what then?" I lean back against the wall and fold my arms over my chest.

"Acey is one of the few who has had the misfortune of being... marked."

I nod, but feel like screaming. "What the hell is with all the dramatic pauses? Will you do me a favor? When this is all over – if we're even still alive – I want you to kick me if I ever do that again."

Asher's mouth twists into a mischievous grin. "Do...," he pauses, "what, exactly?"

"Now who's the clever one?"

He stares at me.

I stare back. When he looks away first, I relax.

Now, if I know Asher, he'll follow up his dramatic pause with a history lesson, all the while ignoring my outburst. I sit on the floor mats, waiting for the lesson to begin.

"What are you doing?" he asks.

"Getting comfortable."

He shakes his head. "Anyway, our blood is pure. Any toxins we ingest dissipate when they go through our system. It's something to do with our blood cells rapidly regenerating or something. No one's been able to pin-point why exactly. We don't get sick and we heal faster than you." He wipes his forehead with the back of his hand. "I mean humans. We heal faster than humans."

It takes me a second to realize that he's including me in "us" rather than "you." I blink at him. That's going to take some getting used to.

"We're susceptible to few things. At least we thought we were. Anyway, Acacia had an altercation with a greater demons a few years back. He marked her before she ever had a chance to fight back."

"Marked her?" I ask.

"Yeah. The demon army grows in numbers all the time. At first, we didn't know how. It was all theory."

There's a haunted look in his eyes. I want to reach out and stroke the muscles of his arm.

Okay, so maybe that's not the only reason I want to pet him.

Asher wipes his mouth with the back of his hand and looks out into the expanse of the empty room. "Somehow, demons have been able to turn humans. We narrowed it down to a series of four marks. Somewhere along the line, they figured out how to compromise one of us, too. Acey bears three out of four of the marks. She's not the first one either. But now, no demon will touch her."

My forehead crinkles. "Why not?"

"Demons are strange things. Once they mark something, it becomes there's. Like they've branded it or something. Then, if another demon encroaches on that territory, it's considered a declaration of war."

I remember the look in Acey's eyes when she stared at Taylor. She seemed so serious and intimidating. I wonder which side that trait comes from: demon or Sentinel? Furthermore, I wonder if I should be afraid.

Though, considering what I've seen Jac do, it's hard to see Acey as anything other than little and lovable.

Asher leans into me. The musky scent of him tickles my nose. "What are you thinking?" He whispers.

Thinking? What's that? Sitting next to a half-naked Asher has derailed my thoughts completely. I close my eyes and force myself to focus on the issue at hand.

I wonder what Brady would think if he knew the lewd thoughts I am thinking while he is missing.

My guess? He'd probably scold me for not acting on it.

My stomach contracts into a knot. Brady. Must save Brady.

I assume he wants me to comment on what he said rather than how we should be packing up the weapons and heading out on a good old fashioned demon hunt. So I clear my throat and murmur, "Poor Acey."

He shrugs. "She deals with it. As long as she doesn't contract the fourth mark, she should be fine. Right now, she's just enjoying the extra power. As you could see." He sits down next to me and takes my hand in his. My skin tingles where we touch. "How are you handling this, by the way?"

"It's just so much to take in, you know?"

He nods. "I know."

"That, out there, was impressive, though," I say, gesturing toward the center of the mats with my chin.

He sighs and leans back against the wall. "Yeah, I guess."

Silence opens up between us. It feels wrong wasting so much time sitting here when we should be devising a plan.

I glance at my watch. "There's only a few hours left," I say finally.

"Yeah," he says, his fingers tightening around my hand.

"Asher, I don't want to be a liability."

"So you're staying home?" he suggests, brightening at the thought.

"No." I feel rather than see his disappointment. "Can you teach me some basics so I can protect myself?"

"Nicoletta," he says, slowly and deliberately. "You can't come."

"The hell I can't. If Gabe is right, it's the only way," I argue, and deep down, I know I'm right.

Asher clucks his tongue, deliberating. Then, suddenly, he jumps to his feet. He takes my hand and guides me to the middle of the room, his eyes locked on mine as if we are engaged in a dance.

First thing he does is fixes my stance by pushing his foot back and forth between mine until they are what he calls "a shoulder width" apart. I feel his height pressing in on me as he walks circles, looking me over.

"You sure about this?" he asks. His hand reaches out and sweeps my braid over my shoulder. I shiver at his touch.

"Absolutely."

"Open yourself up to it. See if you can anticipate my moves. If you are what Gabe says you are, then you'll have an inherited ability to sense anyone who gets near. Follow that reaction."

He continues to circle me like a predator to its prey. When he meets me face to face, he steps one leg behind mine, braces a hand on either of my shoulders, and pushes me to the ground. The breath whooshes out of me as my back connects with the mat. Asher follows me down, his legs straddling my chest and pinning my arms to the floor. His left forearm hovers an inch above my neck.

"If I had a knife, you would be dead." He chuckles. "You didn't even try. You need to focus."

I swallow reflexively, fighting past the pain exploding in my chest. "I did focus. I focused on not hitting my head when I went down."

Asher moves his arm, plants his fist into the mat inches from my head, and pushes himself upright. He extends his hand as a peace offering. I brush him off and slowly climb my way back vertical.

When I meet his eyes, his eyebrow is arched in question.

"What?" I ask.

He brushes my hair back over my shoulder. Every nerve in my arm stands at attention. Why do I feel like I've put my finger in a light socket all of a sudden?

Words trail out of his mouth in a language I don't understand.

"What was that?" I ask, sounding a little out of breath.

His thumb traces a line under my hair and up behind my ear. "No matter how much I didn't want to believe it, I guess it's true. You have the mark," he says, sounding sad and disappointed.

"The, what?" I ask, touching my neck reflexively.

"The birth mark. It's lighter and hard to see, but you have it. Did you honestly not know it was there?"

Running my finger along the skin, I notice a softer patch, like a burn scar formed of puckered circles. A memory of baby pictures comes to mind. Even then, I always had thick, dark hair. Just enough to cover it.

"I must've forgotten," I admit. "I've always had long hair."

He shakes his head and closes his eyes. He lists to a little to the side so I reach out and touch his arm. The muscles are taut underneath the skin.

When he opens his eyes, there's a ghost of a smile forming at his lips, but I can tell it's not a real one. "Ready to try again?"

"Give me a second," I wheeze.

"You okay?"

"You don't happen to have an inhaler on you, do you?"

He shakes his head. "No, but I've got an idea," he whispers to me, moving toward me. His breath is hot on my ear, then shoulder, then my neck, then my other ear. "Try closing your eyes."

"Why?"

"Because it'll help you see better," he says, tapping the center of his forehead with his finger.

I do as I'm told. In the darkness, I try to focus on his progress as he circles around me. Heat radiates off of him, hinting that he is to my right. My whole body tenses seconds before he grabs me by the waist and flings me to the ground. His body lands perfectly over mine as I hit the floor with minor impact.

My eyes flutter open. "I did it!" I squeal. "I sensed what you would do before you did it."

Asher's face is close to mine, his eyes heated. "Then why didn't you stop me?"

Before I have a chance to respond, someone standing behind us clears their throat.

Arching my neck, I tilt my head back on the mat to see Kaleb standing at the edge of the room with his arms crossed over his chest. There's a mischievous grin painted across his face. "Am I interrupting something?"

"No," I respond at precisely the same time Asher says, "Yes."

"Then by all means, proceed. I'll just be, you know, over here. Watching."

Asher hops to his feet gracefully while I stumble there.

"Nicky wanted to learn some self-defense." Asher says, sounding bored.

"Oh, of course. That's exactly what it looked like." Kaleb winks. "But it's a good idea. Especially with her part in the game plan."

"Game plan?" I ask.

"Her part?" Asher chokes out.

Kaleb nods. "While you two were reenacting the rated 'R' version of Karate Kid, we figured out a plan. Please, by all means, join us when you're finished."

"You sure you don't want in on this?" Asher challenges. "For educational purposes, of course."

I glare at him.

"Mine or yours?" Kaleb counters, spreading his arms wide.

My eyes shift to split the glare between the two of them.

"Neither. Nicoletta's of course. Just so she knows that we fight fair."

Kaleb laughs. "Like you fight fair. You invented the term 'fight fire with fire.'"

The tension between them is thick and hard to breathe around. I imagine if they were to fight, they would kill each other.

Kaleb can probably see that, too. He smiles, and it's all teeth. "Later. We'll go at it like old times. I promise."

Asher returns the smile. "I look forward to it." Then he looks at me. "One more time?"

I close my eyes in response and tune into his natural heat.

"Try to stop me this time," he whispers as he passes my ear.

"We'll see."

He circles me once then turns and circles back. The image of the first attack pops into my head. So when he steps in front of me, I step in, wrap my right leg around the back of his, and shove him with all my might. He topples to the ground, but not before he latches onto my shoulders, taking me down with him.

He laughs. "Very good. We need to work on your landing, though."

I glance down at the line of my body pressing against his. "I don't think it was so bad," I tell him. I pull my knees up and plant them on either side of his stomach. "Or would you prefer I land like this?"

He runs his hands up my sides, pulling me toward him. My braided hair falls forward and tickles his throat.

"Perfect," he says in what sounds like a purr. "Just like that."

Bracing myself with the brace on my right hand, I raise my left to his throat, where I gently drag a nail down his jugular.

His breath catches.

I lean into him, my hand wrapped around the base of his neck. His pulse flutters against my fingertips.

I sense his hesitation and breathe against his lips, "What? I won't break."

He strokes my cheek with his thumb. "You have no idea how breakable you are," he manages to say before I press my mouth to his effectively silencing him. Finally.

Chapter 38

"I feel like we should be calling 'break' or something." I say. I'm rewarded with strange looks all around. "You know, like a huddle?"

Asher smiles at me in a way that makes me wonder if he thinks I'm crazy. Everyone else ignores my attempts at humor.

We are back in the library, discussing the new plan. I'm so controlled by this outward pressure urging me to get out there and save Brady that I feel like the runner waiting to start the race. Can we just get this done already?

"How much longer?" Kaleb asks.

I search my brain, but can't remember. So much has happened since I had that dream. "I... I don't know. Just sometime tonight."

"Where do you think he's holding him?" Asher asks.

"Blood on the walls." Acey repeats over and over again. Her eyes light up. "Somewhere people have died?"

"Maybe a lab," Gabriel suggests. "Or a blood bank?"

"No. Too many people would notice," she says, waving the suggestion away with her hand. "It's not going to be a public place."

I close my eyes and try to recall the image of Brady lying on the floor, but all I can think about is the brief kiss Asher and I shared before Asher pushed me away with some lame excuse about how making out was a bad idea. I think it was the best thing we could be doing since it's the only time I haven't been in panic mode.

"Earth to Nicky." Acey says, snapping her fingers in front of my face.

I mentally shake myself. "Sorry. What?"

"I said that the first thing we need to do is call your parents. The last thing we need is for them to come looking for you."

I feel through the strategically placed pockets all over my pants. I presume they're for weapons. Though, I can't imagine they would need twenty-five of them. My cell phone isn't there. It's weird for me not to know where it is at all times. Where could I have left it? My stomach lurches in panic before I remember where it is: in my leather jacket, which is back in my room. I hope it still has a charge.

"My cell phone…," I start to say.

Acey laughs abruptly. "Unless you have some super network, it's not going to work."

"I have Verizon." I say in the snottiest voice I can fake. "*The* network."

She reaches into her pocket and pulls out her iPhone, turning it to show me the screen. "So do I. See? No bars. I guess the network has better things to do today than follow us around. Come on, I'll show you to the landline."

I follow her out the door and down the hall. "The what?"

Acey laughs. "Don't worry. It's re-routed so that any caller ID will see it as a restaurant on the west side."

"Again, the what?" I repeat.

She smiles. "Funny. So anyway, I was thinking you could tell your mom that we went to get something to eat and I asked you to stay over again. When I talked to her last night, they sounded really excited to have the house to themselves."

I shudder involuntarily. "Ew."

"Yeah, well." She nudges a door open. I recognize it as part of the cell they kept Taylor in earlier. It's empty now. "Tonight may be a bit harder so if you need help convincing them, I'm available."

"I'll be fine," I tell her.

She pushes me toward a thick black rotary dial phone on the far wall. My grandfather used to have one of these, but I never really used it. I hope I can figure out how it works. I pick up the receiver. The dial tone clicks a few times before it flat lines.

"I think I'm being recorded," I say before turning the old-fashioned rotary wheel. "I feel like James Bond right now."

She hops onto the metal table, folding her legs under her. "It's re-routing." Then she studies her fingernails before pushing back each cuticle one by one. "After this, I'm going to need a manicure."

"Hello?" My mother asks on the other end of the line. I let out a long breath. Her voice is something comforting in a world I don't know anymore. "Hello?"

"Hi, mom. It's me."

"Nicky. I'm so glad you called. Your cell phone must be dead."

"It is." I twist the curly cord around my fingers a few times. "Sorry for not calling earlier. Acacia and I went shopping and lost track of time."

"That's fine, dear. When are you coming home?" she asks.

"That's kind of why I was calling." I pause for a second. Despite how often I have to do it, I really don't like lying to my parents. I can justify it when it will cause a cease fire in one of their fights, but this seems wrong. So I try to keep it as truthful as possible. "Acey was wondering if I could stay another night. We wanted to see a movie and the only showing is pretty late."

"Oh, I don't know."

"My homework is all done and I promise I'll be home in time for dinner tomorrow," I counter.

"I know, dear. It's not that. It's just, your father and I wanted to talk to you about Brady."

"Brady?" I ask, feigning confusion.

Acey's head snaps up, her eyes trying to convey some silent message.

Too bad I didn't take Communicating Without Words 101 last semester.

"Honey, his parents called here wondering if you've seen him," my mother continues. "They said he hasn't come home for a few days. They're really worried. Especially with everything going on over at your school."

I stop short. I don't know why I hadn't expected this, but I didn't.

"They tried calling Alex, but couldn't get in touch with him. His parents said he was out with Jennifer... something." When I don't reply, she says, "Nicky, dear. You still there?"

"Sorry, I'm here." My chest constricts. I feel like I'm suffocating. "I bet Brady went on a road trip. He loves his road trips and he probably forgot his charger. I bet he'll be home tomorrow. He wouldn't miss school."

Please God, I pray silently, *let us get him back tonight.* I don't know what I would do without my best friend.

"If you think so," she says, though she sounds like she doesn't necessarily believe me. "You know him best. I guess I'm just all worked up over Spencer and the other kids. It's a much scarier world now than when I was younger. You'll be safe, won't you?"

I close my eyes only to see Brady laying in a room with walls the color of blood. My mind finally clicks to attention, working through every clue it can find.

Blood.

Red.

Death.

"I guess it's fine if you stay the night. I'm just glad you finally have some girlfriends. Come home early, though, okay? It's a school night."

Blood dripping at my feet. Pooling around my ankles. Blood in a room. A large room, which seems even larger because of the mirror. Brady lying lifeless in the middle. He looks asleep. I only hope he is.

"Thanks mom. I'll see you tomorrow," I say, mechanically. "I love you."

"Love you, too, honey. Bye."

I hang up the phone and don't move, don't breathe, for a few moments.

Blood like carpet.

Carpet of crimson.

I jump, nearly knocking the phone off the wall.

"Oh my god," I say, clutching at my chest. "I know where Brady is."

Acey jumps off the table and runs to my side. "You do? Where?"

Chapter 39

Two hours 'til sundown.

"I don't see why we have to wait. I know where he is. Just give me the Jeep and I'll go get him," I complain.

The kitchen feels overcrowded with the five of us sitting around the large wooden table. Well, only four of us are sitting while I pace the room like a lab rat that has just been told that the cheese is in a different maze. There is a plate for each of us, loaded up with chicken, fried vegetables, and bread. Kaleb and Gabe drink some French imported wine I can't pronounce the name of while Asher and Acey sip at their Cokes.

Acey cuts into a piece of chicken with a dangerous looking knife and daintily takes a chunk into her mouth. She pats her mouth with a napkin as she chews.

I don't know how she can eat when she knows what we are getting ready to do.

"We can't just go in there half-cocked," Kaleb says, shoving a piece of bread between his teeth. "We need to be at our best, which means, you need to eat."

"Are you seriously talking to me about food right now? Brady is out there. When we get him back, I'll eat whatever you want."

Kaleb grins. Asher points his fork at him and says, "Don't even say it."

Gabe reaches a hand out to touch my arm. I pause long enough to let him. "Nicoletta, please. Starving yourself isn't going to help your friend."

"Waiting isn't going to help either," I inform him. Something occurs to me then. None of these people want me present during the big showdown with Jac. So why not wager a little deal? "I'll tell you what, if we can go now, once we have Brady, I'll get the hell out of there. I'll be vapor, I promise."

Gabriel looks at me over the rim of his glass. There's hope in his eyes.

"No can do. He'll be expecting that. Once you ditch, he'll have something worse waiting for you. Guaranteed," Kaleb leans across the table, his glass pinned between his hands. Red liquid swirls inside, reminding me of a blood bath. "For now, Brady is safe, but if you go storming in after him, he most certainly will not be."

A sharp sensation stings in my stomach. "Safe?" I almost shriek. "He's not safe until he's home."

"I'm sorry to be so blunt, but you could get yourself killed," Gabriel states. "Then where would he be?"

"Jac has had plenty of chances to kill me. If he wanted me dead, I wouldn't be breathing."

"That's just it. Maybe he doesn't want you dead. Maybe he wants to make you suffer."

There's a loud clinking noise at my right. I look over to see that Acey has put down her fork and waits impatiently to join the conversation. "You know what I don't get?"

I turn in my chair to meet her gaze head on.

"I don't get why he would choose the Adams kid. You said he's been sick for a long time, right? So if he died, where would the surprise be?" she says, placing her napkin next to her plate. "Not to sound cold or anything. The other kids I understand, but Spencer baffles me."

Silence all around.

"You know what I think?" she continues. "I don't think this has anything to do with Nicky at all. I don't think there's any revenge," she says to Gabriel. "I don't think he's even put that part together. No," she shakes her head, "I think Nicky and her abilities were in the wrong place at the wrong time."

I feel my eyebrows draw together as my brain digests her logic.

"And maybe, just maybe, we shouldn't focus so hard on killing this demon. Instead, maybe we should figure out how to break her tie to Spencer. If she can release whatever shield she has over him then this could all be over." She raises her glass of coke in salute. "One less asshole in the world." Then she takes a swig and sets her glass down on the table with more force than necessary.

"Acacia," Gabriel warns.

Asher puts his elbows on the table and leans into them. "Maybe she's right, Gabe. Think about it. The Adams kid has been sick his whole life. Maybe he wants to die. Why else would he have been drinking at that party? Besides, wasn't it you who told me that you can't make an omelet without cracking a couple of eggs?"

The room is silent. I might have been able to dismiss Acey's deliberation because of her demon marks, but that's before Asher agreed. Now, I don't know what I think.

Kaleb drops his bread onto his plate. He pinches the bridge of his nose and groans. "I think I just stepped into the goddamn twilight zone. Is everyone here possessed? This is a demon we are facing – a thirsty, disease-breathing, man-killing demon. These types of demons are to blame for half of our epidemics. And what do we do with demons, boys and girls? We take them out. No matter how much we may dislike the victim." He sneers at Acey then glares at Asher. "Or how little chance of survival they may have on their own. I, for one, plan to see him on his way back to hell. Now, who's with me?"

I remember how peacefully my grandfather drifted away in his sleep. From what I've seen, it sure beats the alternative. Though, I can't help but wonder how long he would have lived had Jac not entered that room.

"Gabriel," Kaleb says. "Can you please talk some sense into them?"

Gabriel sets down his glass and licks a drop of wine from his thumb. "I won't force them to fight. They chose to give up this life, but I will be beside you every step of the way." He stands up and leans into his palms on the table. He looks haunted and a hundred years older than he did this morning. "Not for the boy, mind you. I have my own score to settle. As do the two of you," he says, nodding at Asher and Acey.

Asher stiffens in his seat, anticipating whatever might follow.

Another damn dramatic pause.

"This demon has been killing people close to me for a millennium. First, my Collette, then her husband, then my son and his wife. So I doubt it would surprise you to know that while he may not have killed your parents, Asher, I guarantee you he was at the execution."

Asher nods once. There is a world worth of words in that one nod, all leading to the same resolve. He is on board.

And so am I. In fact, I have never felt more on board than I do right now. If this demon has been working his way through my family then it is only a matter of time before he catches up with my parents or me. His actions now may not be against me, but in the future, they will be.

"We will be at the Jeep at sundown," Gabriel announces. "I will understand if you choose not to fight. Now, if you'll excuse me." He tucks the rest of the bottle in his elbow, takes his glass, and leaves. He never touched his food either.

"Think about it. Long and hard. Make sure your decision is the right one," Kaleb tacks on. "Nicoletta, I assume you're in on this suicide mission, right?"

I nod.

"Great. I'll be in the weapons room if you need me." Kaleb's chair squeals as he slides it back against the tile. He stares long and hard at Acey and Asher, who both hang their heads like scolded children. After a weighted five seconds, he shakes his head and walks away.

Acey picks up her fork and takes a bite as if nothing happened. Asher pushes his plate away.

I hesitate a moment before following Gabriel and Kaleb out the door.

"Where are you going?" Asher asks.

I level a stare at him. So many emotions crash through me, I can't sit still: anxiety, fear, anger, you name it, I'm feeling it. "To pack."

"Right now?"

"Yeah. Some of us have to go home when this is over. As long as I'm still alive," I say before thinking my words through. It sinks in all at once. I could die trying to save Spencer tonight. That's something I never thought I'd have to do.

No, not Spencer. I wouldn't risk my life for him, but I would risk my life for Brady.

Asher flinches at my words before averting his eyes.

It's amazing how much a single gesture can hurt. I turn on my heel and stomp out into the hall.

That's when I start to tremble.

***

Back in my room, I gather my few belongings and stack them on my bed. After cursing Acey for being right about my cell phone, I find a black backpack to shove everything into. I take the nightgown, too. Not because I love it or anything, but because it will remind me of Asher when he's gone.

The flames in my chest burns a little hotter. I flop down onto the bed and close my eyes.

"We're coming for you, Brady," I whisper out into the world. "Just hold on tight. I'm coming for you."

I wonder about the impact this is going to have on our lives. Will Brady and I ever be the same? Every time someone dies, am I going to wonder if there is some sort of supernatural play going on?

Worst of all, will I ever be able to watch *Supernatural* again?

I laugh at how that feels like the most painful change I face.

"What's so funny?"

I open my eyes to see Asher standing in the doorway, his hands stuffed in his pockets.

I sigh and look up at the ceiling to keep the tears from rolling down my cheeks. "Nothing," I say. That's the problem. Nothing is funny anymore. What are you doing here anyway?"

He pushes off the wall and strides into the room. He avoids my eyes by fiddling with the lampshade. "I was just wandering. I've never been able to sit still before a fight. It's the anxiety. I like it better when it's not a rescue mission, you know?"

"You?" I ask, skeptically, rolling to my side and propping my head up on a fist. "You've fought a million fights just like this one. Isn't it, like, second nature for you?"

365

He glances at me out of the corner of his eye. "Under normal circumstances, yes."

"Why is this different?"

He paces the room, touching inanimate objects with the tip of his forefinger. I wish I could take all of those things, too, but I doubt I could fit the credenza in my stolen backpack.

He smirks. "It's been a long time since I've had to worry about the safety of someone else. Being back in the chaos, I realize I'm not very good at it."

"I don't think you need to worry about Acey. She's kind of terrifying when she wants to be," I assure him.

"You noticed. Didn't we tell you?"

"You did."

He lets out a long breath. "I told you I wouldn't lie to you again."

"I know. She's just so prim and proper. Anyway, I believe you now." I run my fingers along the suede-like material of my pants. I wonder how much different I would be had I been born into this world. Would these pants still feel like suede? Would everything look, smell, or taste different? Would I be able to abandon a human at the hands of a demon just because they weren't my favorite human?

"Asher?" I ask quietly, sitting up and scooting to the edge of the bed. "Why did you really retire? Was it because you were tired of dying or because you needed to take care of Acey?"

He pauses then sits on the end of the bed next to me.

"Honestly?" He says, clearing his throat as if honesty is the most difficult thing he's had to do in a while.

"Honestly."

His head drops forward. "I was tired of it. It hurts to watch the people you love die over and over again. I knew that if I were to remain inactive long enough then I wouldn't be recruited again. I was prepared for this to be my last life."

"What changed your mind?"

He casts me a sideways look before turning on the bed to face me. "What makes you think I changed my mind?"

The words feel like they are hard-wired to my heart-strings. "I just figured that since you were going back with Kaleb…"

"Right." He nods. "Kaleb has always been there for me so I'll be there for him, but after debts are paid, I'm out."

Heat balls up in my throat. "Why?"

"Well, we've always had these rules, these unchanging laws about how we live. They were simple and precise, but they are changing. First, there was Kaleb. He was recruited sometime in the fifteenth century and some of the shit he can do is unreal."

"Like making it rain?" I joke.

Asher doesn't laugh. "Among other things. And then there's you. In accordance of the old law, you should not exist. It's supposed to be impossible to impregnate a human. Something about how our genetics are mismatched."

"But here I am," I say, trying not to take offense.

"But here you are." He shakes his head. He laces his fingers together in front of him. "I'm not sure if it's an omen or what, but it feels like we were lied to."

I roll my eyes. "I know how you feel."

He laughs bitterly. "Yeah, I'm sorry about that. That's another caveat of running with this crew: the gag order. Think of it this way, though, you have a choice and it doesn't have to be this." He gestures around the room to encompass everything around us. "You can live a long life, get married, become whatever you want to and have all thirty-four of those kids," he says, his voice lilting in suggestion.

I stare at him long and hard. I don't feel capable of much else at this moment.

"You could even go home," he tacks on under his breath, "where it's safe."

Fire courses through my veins. How dare he? "Is it safe, Asher? Is it?" I challenge.

"Safer."

Fury ensues. "Are you that worried that I'll get you or Acey hurt? I'm not that big of a liability!"

"You're untrained," he reminds me.

I get off the bed, not wanting to be so close to him. "But I'm not stupid!"

"No one said you were." He stands up, following my lead. "It doesn't mean you're stupid if you get hurt. Things happen – things beyond our control."

I throw my hands up in the air. How did we get back to this fight again? I hate arguing in circles. It makes me dizzy and frustrated. "I'm going, okay? I appreciate your concern that someone might get hurt because I'm 'so untrained,' but for some stupid effing reason, this involves me."

He mumbles something under his breath. I figure it's a curse and plow on.

"I'll do my best not to put anyone in danger so don't you worry."

Asher moves so quickly, I don't see him until he has me pinned up against the wall with the full force of his weight. I'm reminded of that time so long ago at the hospital when I did the same thing to him.

"You're not listening," he growls into my face.

I breathe in and out, feeling the resistance of his chest against mine. If he were anyone else, I would go into full panic mode. Especially after everything that happened with Taylor. But he's not Taylor. He's Asher. The same Asher who could fling me down on the training room floor over and over again, leaving more flustered than terrified.

"I don't want you there," he continues, his words scalding me.

My stomach drops. All I hear is that he doesn't want me, which would perfectly reflect how he's been acting. My eyes focus somewhere near his collarbone to avoid making contact with his.

His hands take hold of my hips and shove them back into the wall. It doesn't hurt, but it's enough force to make me look at him.

"Don't. Don't shut me out. You need to hear this," he demands.

I blink at him, wordless.

His forehead rests against mine, his hands move up to my waist. His eyes drift shut. "If you got hurt, it would kill me."

My stomach flips. I take a sharp breath.

His eyes flutter open, meeting mine so closely that all I can see is the gold in them.

"I don't care if you put us in danger. Please do. We're used to it. What I'm worried about is you. Only you."

I open my mouth to speak, but when no words come, I shut it again.

"In all my lifetimes, I've never felt anything like what I feel for you. You aren't just a part of me, you're the whole thing." He hesitates. "I'm sick of losing the people I love. Don't you understand?"

My heartbeat is so strong and steady that I imagine he can feel it kicking against him. "Did you just say you love me?"

He rolls his eyes, theatrically. "Good god. What the hell did you think this was about?"

I try to shrug, but his weight is too much.

"Oh hell." He rolls his forehead against mine, skin drawing along skin. The tension inside him shakes its way into me. "You are the most infuriating person I've ever met. How could I not love you?"

"That's why you love me? Because I piss you off?" I tease.

He forces my hips back into the wall again. My shirt rides up between us, exposing my sides and stomach. His thumb slowly moves in circles along my belt line. The nerves under my skin sing a chorus of hallelujahs.

"No," he says, his mouth moving tentatively closer to mine. "I love that I can't figure you out and piss me off. I hate the law because it says you shouldn't exist. I can't live under a law that thinks you are an anomaly."

I lunge forward, closing the space between us, kissing him with such brutal force, my lips come feel bruised. My hands snake their way around his back, pulling him closer as if I could draw him into me.

Somehow he manages to slide his knee between my thighs. He captures my leg and lifts me off the ground with one hand. I wrap my legs around his waist unconsciously as my back slams into the wall. A moan escapes my throat.

"You okay?" Asher whispers into my mouth.

In response, I lace my fingers into his hair and yank his head back hard. When his neck is fully exposed, I draw my nails down one side and nip at the other. He bucks into me in approval.

He reaches back behind his head, grips my wrists, and pins them to the wall above my head. His mouth is hot on my neck. My eyes fix on the ceiling as he moves to my shoulder.

"God, that's so…"

"Wait," A voice interrupts from the doorway.

Asher groans and drops his forehead to my shoulder.

"I'm confused. Who's winning? I mean, this is a sparring match, right?"

I close my eyes and pray my face doesn't look as red as it feels.

"That's what they told me earlier." Kaleb confirms. "But I'm beginning to think that their idea of foreplay is beating the shit out of each other."

I drop my legs from Asher's waist and let him slide me to the floor. He rests his forehead against mine for a brief second for four slow breaths. Then, without opening his eyes, he says, "You just couldn't keep walking, could you?"

"Hey," Kaleb says with a chuckle, "an open door is the same as an invitation."

"Not a chance." Asher turns around. The second his heat is gone, I shiver. We stand side-by-side against the wall like little kids being scolded for playing too rough on the playground.

I touch my swollen lips and taste blood. Oh god, I must have bitten him harder than I thought.

"Well, Acey was going to see if Nicky needed some help, but it looks like you got it covered," Kaleb says, giving Asher a thumbs-up. "Way to go, buddy. Take one for the team."

"Okay, seriously. What the hell do you want?"

Kaleb cants his head to the side. "Just a little pre-battle tradition."

"And it couldn't wait?"

"It could, but the opportunity was too good to pass up."

"Asshole," Asher breathes, shaking his head. He takes my hand and squeezes it once. "I'll meet you in the training room in twenty. This shouldn't take long."

"Okay." I say, one hand covering my mouth. I wonder for a second how bad Asher's neck looks, but there's no way I'll ask him about it in front of these two.

Asher moves slowly out the door. He looks back once to wink at me. My heart melts into a puddle in my stomach.

Acey watches me with a strange grin on her face. She nudges the door shut with her foot and leans against it. "So… what'd I miss?" she asks as if she hadn't just walked in on everything she missed.

I incline my head and say in my best sing-song voice, "He loves me."

She laughs, pushes her golden locks behind her ears, and says, "Oh my god. Honey, you are clueless, aren't you?"

Chapter 40

One hour until sundown.

Since I have a little bit of time before we leave, I head over to the weapons room to see if they have any extra jackets available. Surviving Winter in Utah 101: When it's freezing outside, don't wear leather. I'm not sure why, but that's the quickest way to freeze your ass off.

When I come up on the room, the door is open and the lights are on. At first, I keep walking.

But then, someone inside the room says, "Collette? Come on in."

I freeze before taking three wary steps through the doorway. The room is three times the size of Asher's bedroom, and just like everything else here, it's all concrete. I guess there's no use in sugar coating where you are.

There's a large metal table in the center of the space. On it is Gabrielle's glass of wine, an open backpack, and a thick binder open to a page a fourth of the way through. Weapons line the walls behind glass cases. It kind of reminds me of how Victoria's Secret displays their merchandise. Below every item – ranging from small thin daggers to broadswords and feather staffs – there is a cupboard. I assume that if you open that cupboard you'll find a stock of whatever destructive item is on display.

Gabriel hunkers down in front of the cupboard below what looks like a throwing knife. He flicks a blade with his thumb to check how sharp it is. He looks up, catching me staring at him, and puts the knife back.

· "I used to be a good aim," he tells me. "But now I'm just an old man."

I laugh bitterly. "Sure you are."

He smiles. "You'd be surprised."

The cupboard closes with a click of the lock. "What did you need?"

"A jacket," I say, fiddling with my ear. When he notices, I stop. There's no need to show him how nervous he makes me. "And maybe a long sleeve shirt. It's cold out there and I can't keep myself warm like Asher can."

Gabriel laughs. "None of us can. Come on, I'll show you where they are." He motions toward the far wall before turning away from me.

There's a door tucked away in the corner where no one would notice at first glance. Gabriel opens it and steps inside, flipping a switch on his way in. Light floods the room and I flinch.

"You know, for being so far underground, it sure is bright down here."

He shrugs. "When you deal with shadows every day, you start to crave the light."

Once my eyes adjust, I see that the room is much smaller than the one before it, like a closet. Black pants, shirts, tank tops and jackets hang from metal bars with white plastic cards to separate sizes. Lined up like this, they look like uniforms.

"We only have fighting gear. I hope that's alright." Gabriel says with a rueful smile.

"That's perfect." I walk toward the long sleeve shirts and pull one out, checking the tag. Medium should work. Without removing the tank top, I slide into it. It clings a little tight, but shirts don't fit girls the same way they do guys. It's called boobs and I was blessed (or cursed) with decently sized ones. When I'm all situated, I head over to the jackets.

The jackets are made of the same material as the pants: that soft, stretchy almost suede. The collar doesn't fold down like they do on the jackets I'm used to. Instead, it stands stiffly to cover the neck. I take one out and look at it. The buttons are made of black onyx with a thin silver design on them.

"What are these?" I ask Gabriel, who has been watching me.

He looks over my shoulder at the buttons. "They are symbols of protection in battle. Signs of the Goddess."

I run my thumb across the smooth stone. "They're beautiful."

"Yes, they are."

I thread my arms into the sleeves and pull the jacket on. The hem cuts off just before my thigh. It fits perfectly. I look down at myself and turn back and forth, letting the strange material filter the light.

"Nicoletta, I've been meaning to talk to you."

I wince. The only thing worse than when a girl says she wants to talk to you is when one of your elders says the same thing. "What about?"

Gabriel places a hand on my back and guides me back toward the weapons room. "Perhaps you would like to sit?"

I stand still as a post, unwilling to move near any of the five chairs in the room.

"Or stand, whichever you would prefer."

I can't imagine he would react kindly if I told him that I'd rather not do this right now. I barely know the man so there's no reason why I should feel this overwhelming sense of worry, like he's going to say he doesn't like me or I'm doing something wrong. It feels like I was caught sneaking a cookie before dinner and am about to get a stern talking to from my father. That's who he reminds me of: my father. Maybe I should give him a chance to speak for that fact alone. I move to the chair across from him and sit down. My legs twitch like an agitated cat ready to bolt for the door.

Gabriel takes notice and rubs at his forehead. "I know this must be hard for you. It's hard enough for me to wrap my head around and I've known for a long time." He pauses to think for a second. "A really long time. But it is what it is and I want you to know that if this is the life you choose I will help you."

I interlace my fingers to stop the shaking. It doesn't work. "Look, I don't even know what this life is, Gabe. I'm learning as I go. Everything is happening so fast. All I know is what Kaleb and Asher have told me."

"I know," he says, his eyes dark with sadness. "And I apologize for that. I wish I could tell you everything in a matter of minutes, but I'm afraid a disclosure like that will take years. Maybe I could give you some enlightenment, though."

With my hand, I motion for him to continue. Am I being rude? Do I care?

"You're great-grandmother was a wonderful woman. She was kind, smart, strong, independent, stubborn, and a gigantic pain in the ass." He smiles into the past. "Much like you."

"I'm a pain in the ass?" I retort.

He chuckles. "You know you are so why hide it? It's an endearing trait really. It's what made me fall in love with her and I imagine what made Asher fall for you."

I stare at him open-mouthed.

"I know how Asher feels about you. I knew before he did. You don't know what it was like living with him before." His hand gestures wildly about as if he's trying to catch the right words in mid-air. "It was hell. Watching him tear himself apart every day, not knowing what he wanted to do. He's always had to be the hero. I should have known he couldn't put that aside and function as a normal member of the kind."

"Why do you call us… them that?" I ask.

The side of his mouth quirks up. "It's an inside joke among the dark-seekers, the Sentinels. The human race is the only species we know of who thinks they harbor the only intelligence anywhere. They are *kind* of in the dark, *kind* of lost. *Kind* of, how you say, simple-minded? They believe they are the only ones of their *kind*."

I'm a little offended, but it makes sense. What doesn't make sense is why I feel like I need to defend everyone. I'm not one of them anymore, am I? At least not completely.

"Anyway, I don't want to go into this knowing you hate me."

"I don't hate you," I tell him.

"Don't you?" His accent grows thicker with each word. I lean forward, giving him my right ear, just to make sure I decipher it right.

I shake my head. "No. I just feel lost. It's like everything I knew to be real is suddenly different. It's not normal for a girl to find herself face to face with her great-grandfather. I mean, come on, you look thirty. It's weird."

"I understand."

"But it's not just that, you know? It's more than that. I was raised to believe in one God, not a Goddess, and over time, I accepted that God was too busy to care what I did. Now I come to find that I'm a member of a race I didn't know existed for a Goddess I've never believed in. Weird doesn't even begin to describe that. It's like someone told me to pick a door and I fell through a hole in the ground instead."

He nods. "Yes, I imagine it would."

My voice pitches a little higher, indignation dripping from my words. "And what am I supposed to do now? Pretend none of this ever happened? Go back to my life? Go to college? Or am I supposed to stay here and be something I know nothing about?"

Gabriel reaches out a hand and touches my shoulder. "You can be anything you want to be. Haven't you figured that out, yet? You control who you are. You control what you become. Everyone around you will fade away or die at some point in your life. If you choose to live as one of the ki… as a human, there's no telling how long you'll live. It's the sad reality of who you are."

I wipe at my burning eyes. My hand comes back wet. I hiccup on a laugh. This all feels so silly. Here I am, getting ready for battle with a demon (A Demon!), but talking to my great-grandfather sends me into tears.

Wryly, I say, "Don't sugar coat it or anything."

"If you wanted a lie, I'm sure you would have asked for it."

He's right. I don't have to tell him that, though. "I'm just really confused right now and talking about it isn't helping. I need to save my best friend and waiting for nightfall is driving me insane. This is not how it happens in the movies."

"How does it happen in the movies?" he asks without a touch of irony. It reminds me of when Kaleb asked about *Supernatural*.

"In the movies, the hero would have been in their car searching for the bad guy before we even knew who he was," I explain.

"Hmm. Interesting. I've been on many missions that have started that way, but never when an innocent's life is at stake. That's just asking to get them killed. Besides, this isn't a movie. We have no choice but to work with what we have." He touches my shoulder again. "We'll be ready to go soon enough," he assures me. "I'll tell you what, how about you come over after school on Monday? We'll get Chinese take-out and talk."

"I love Chinese food." I say quietly.

He nods as if he already knew. "So do I. So what do you say? We can discuss your options, the ones your parents don't know about. I can tell you stories, the good and the bad. And if you want, I'll even bring the sugar."

Sniffling, I say, "Sound pretty good actually."

He smiles. His eyes crinkle around the edges. "Good. I look forward to it. And don't worry about tonight, you're in good hands. I know Asher will take good care of you."

**

Forty-five minutes to sundown.

Asher walks into the training room with a mischievous smile leading his way. Acey explained to me what a pre-battle ritual consisted of after they left. Apparently it's a warm-up sparring match. She followed it up with a joke about Asher needing a cold shower instead, which I admit, I laughed at.

"They test their strengths and abilities without any barriers," she said.

That's why I couldn't watch.

Asher's hair is wet and wild like he's been out in a monsoon for the past twenty minutes. His shirt is torn across his stomach and he's bleeding from the mouth. There's a livid red circle on his neck like someone bit him. At least I know that wasn't from Kaleb. There's something different about his eyes, though. They exude excitement unlike any other. In fact, he looks positively giddy like he just jumped out of an airplane with no parachute and survived the fall.

"Dare I ask what the other guy looks like?" I joke.

Cinnamon and Salt

His grin widens as he strides over to where I have propped myself against the wall. He leans down without touching me and presses his lips to mine briefly. He's hot to the touch.

"Where's Kaleb?" Acey asks from her seat on the edge of the mat.

"He's getting some minor burns taken care of," he says, his eyes still glued to mine.

Acey stand up and brushes her hands down her pants. "Shit. I told him to wait until the two of you were done. You're so violent when you're worked up."

"I went easy on him."

"Whatever. I better go help." She holds her hands out palm down. "Do you two need a chaperone or will you be okay?"

Asher waves her away with one hand. There's something else in his eyes: a hunger I hadn't noticed until now.

When we're alone, I say, "God, if I knew how turned on you'd get by a sparring match, I would have picked a fight with you a long time ago."

He plants a kiss at the base of my throat. "Why wait? I could always teach you some more moves."

I nod and follow him out to the middle of the mat. Getting thrown around like a rag doll sounds a lot more interesting than silently arguing with the acidic feeling in my stomach, which is what I've been doing.

Asher holds up a finger. "Wait, I brought you something." He produces a bundle of black straps from his back pocket and holds them out for me.

"I think we might need to work up to the bondage."

He smiles. "Wait for it."

He peels the straps away one by one to reveal an eight inch dagger. I recognize the detail instantly; it's a miniature version of the sword.

My eyes go wide. "What's that?"

"A dagger."

"Yes, I see that. But what am I supposed to do with it? I can't even play darts."

He kneels down on the floor and looks up at me. His eyes are back to his normal coffee brown with gold flecks. Each fleck could tell its own story. "For protection. You'll only need it if someone is close enough to grab you, in which case, I won't be able to help you."

"Well, that's a comforting thought." I say down to him. "Where was this thing yesterday?"

He reaches through my legs and straps the dagger to my thigh with surgical precision.

I hate to admit it, but the weight of it is comforting somehow. I rub my thighs together to make sure I can still move. It's a perfect fit.

Asher laughs at me. "I'll be with you the whole time so you shouldn't have to use it. But if you do, make sure your aim is true. Try it out."

I reach down and grasp the hilt. It slides out easily with a sound like metal scraping metal. I smile at the blade.

Asher shudders and steps around me. His chest presses into my back. "Have I ever told you how much it turns me on to think of you with a weapon?" he whispers into my ear.

I slide the dagger back into its sheath. It sighs as it locks into place.

One arm wraps around my chest while the other goes around my waist. I lean back into him, his embrace the only thing holding me upright.

"You scared yet?" he asks.

I laugh. "Hell no. I do this sort of thing all the time. Not a day goes by when I don't have to fight a demon for my best friend's life."

"So that's a yes?"

"What makes you say that?"

I feel him smile against my temple. "You're rambling."

379

I close my eyes, feeling the mixture of anticipation and anxiety trickle through my blood like ice. "Terrified."

Asher's arms tighten around me like they can offer all the strength I'll need to make it through the night.

"I'll protect you. Goddess help me, we will get through this alive," he whispers before speaking a strand of French words I don't recognize.

I don't stop him. Instead, I close my eyes and follow the syllables as they roll off his tongue.

I have got to learn French.

Chapter 41

Sundown.

The sky is alight with the purple, blues and reds of a winter sunset. All five of us are packed into the Jeep. Gabe drives while Kaleb lounges in the passenger seat, every inch of space filled by his broad shoulders. He has a bandage on his bicep, blood seeping through. I would love to see the damage beneath it. Wisps of curly hair float around his bowed face and his lips move in what seems to be some kind of prayer.

Asher sits between Acey and me in the back seat since we are the smallest of the group. I huddle in my borrowed jacket. It's surprisingly warm.

The sword stretches the length of our laps. It's too big to comfortably sit with it strapped in its sheath, which makes me wonder how it ever came to be.

Not a minute goes by without Acey spouting out some new argument about why she is best fitted to carry the sword. Asher has already conceded and handed over the straps. Kaleb, I can tell, isn't too sure. Between his silent whispers, he glances over his shoulder at the blade with a bonded look in his eyes.

"Alright, Nicky, you know what to do?" Kaleb asks.

I let out an annoyed breath. We've only been over it thirty times. "It's pretty simple. Get in, get Brady, and get the hell out."

"Good. Asher will be your wingman. When you get out, get gone. Don't look back. We'll all meet at the school."

Stupid rendezvous point if you ask me, but it's close to our mark, so who am I to judge? After all, this is my first rescue mission.

"Where do I turn?" Gabriel asks.

I point out the direction and street.

"You're kidding me, right?" Kaleb says with a harsh laugh. "Morning Star Drive?"

"That's right," I tell him. "He's at my grandpa's old house. I'm sure of it."

"Aren't there people living there?" Acey asks.

"Nope. My grandpa left it to my parents. They meant to fix it up and sell it, but something always came up. Why?"

Asher gives me a curious look. "In most religious texts, Lucifer was called The Morning Star," he explains.

"Great. Just great." I mumble to myself. "Now I'm positive he's there. He couldn't pass up that kind of irony."

Kaleb grabs Gabriel's arm. "Pull over."

Gabriel does. "What?"

"You don't feel that? Park the car. We're close."

My skin turns cold from the tone of his voice.

Out of the darkness, a woman seems to materialize. She walks over to Kaleb's window and taps three times lightly on the glass.

I jump.

"It's okay," Kaleb assures me. "It's just Debbie. She's a local witch. She's going to work some magic to keep this whole operation under wraps. We don't need the cops getting called."

Kaleb rolls down the window and converses with the woman in hushed tones. In the fading light all I can see of her is brown hair with thick streaks of blond. Her face is the color of cream and her eyes a bottomless brown. She looks young – barely twenty – until you reach the wisdom in her eyes.

"Here we go," Asher whispers, running a hand absently over the sword in his lap. "Stay close to me. We're going in first."

Gabriel ducks out of the Jeep and flips the seat forward with barely any sound. I stumble out, but don't fall. Yay for me. Asher climbs out noiselessly save the disgruntled comments about having to sit in the back seat of his own car. This is followed up by a gripe about how much he paid for the thing. The price alone reminds me why I don't have a car yet.

Gabriel rests a lingering hand on my shoulder before nodding at me. I don't know Gabriel that well, but from the look on Asher's face, I assume it's a show of respect.

"Like a ninja," Kaleb whispers, reaching out a fist to bump Asher's.

In the process of rolling my eyes, I catch Acey standing proudly with the sword point down between her feet. She grins at me.

"Remember. Get in and get the hell out. Oh, and be careful," Gabriel repeats softly.

We nod dutifully before turning toward the street. The roads around here loop and cross over each other like some misrepresented Celtic knot and each of them has a scientific or mystical name: Solar Circle, Evening Star Drive, and Mercury Way to name a few. We stand at the fork between Evening Star and Morning Star Drive. My grandfather's house is still a ways down. I don't remember this street being so dark, but I haven't been here for a while.

Every sound sends my nerves skittering. I take a breath. I'm too on edge. Not that I don't have a reason to be. We are getting ready to face one of the most dangerous creatures I've yet see in real life. Unless you count Taylor and Jen. They could make me homicidal or run screaming.

Which reminds me...

"Asher," I whisper. "What happened to Taylor?"

He walks upright rather than crouch down like a stuntman. I don't say anything since we are still a few houses away. That's right, folks, just a couple of kids dressed for battle going on a twilight stroll.

"They took him home, as you asked," he assures me. "We wanted to keep him for bait, but didn't want to upset you. Acey had a lot of fun with him."

"A lot of... you know what, never mind. I'm pretty sure that I don't want to know." I grab his hand and pull him back. Our footsteps echo one more time. Why is everything always louder during the winter?

"What?" he asks, startled. His whole body is on hyper alert. His head swivels around, his golden eyes searching.

"That's it," I tell him, pointing to a red brick two-story house. The driveway wraps around the front to the detached garage. One single motion light is on, but it's dim from needing a new bulb for far too long. The rest of the house is draped in an eerie cluster of shadows. If it had snowed recently, we wouldn't be able to make it around. Lucky for us, we didn't miss any snowstorms while we were underground. Though, that means the air is cold enough to bite and sting.

Asher ducks down like I originally expected him to, bringing his six-two frame down my level. "How do we get in?"

I run a mental map of the house. "There's another door around back, but it's probably locked. Some windows, maybe?"

"I need more description."

"I haven't been here in years. That's the best you're going to get," I snap back.

"Think, Nicoletta."

"I am thinking, Asher."

He looks me over before shaking his head in frustration. "Fine. Let's go."

I grab his hand again. "I should go first."

He glowers at me.

"I've been here before. There could be traps."

"If there are traps, they were set recently. You wouldn't know where they are anyway," he whispers furiously. "Just stay behind me."

Against my better judgment, I duck down behind a row of bushes and follow him. Quietly, I hum the theme from Mission: Impossible to drown out the thudding of my pulse in my ears.

"Funny," Asher says sarcastically.

I shrug. "Where to now oh glorious leader?"

He circles his finger in the air then points.

"This is no time for a party," I say with just the right amount of sarcasm.

He looks to the sky. "Goddess help me. Around the hedge. Follow the shadows in and don't lose me."

"Want me to crawl on my belly, too? The house looks empty. I bet we could walk right in," I say, absently itching at my right arm.

Asher looks at me with wide eyes.

"What?" I say defensively. "I itch when I'm nervous."

"That's not why you itch. It's a defense mechanism." He gestures at my arms. "You know as well as I do that it's not empty."

"Then why aren't you itching?" I force my arms down to my sides. It costs me something to do so.

"We all react differently to danger. Apparently yours is scratching the shit out of yourself."

"What's yours?"

He glances back at the house. "Heat. Now let's go."

I hear something behind me like the sound of shifting clothes. My whole body goes cold. As I open my mouth to scream, a hand covers it: a hand with long fingers, a red sparkling ring, and the clean smell of a rainstorm.

"What the hell is taking you guys so long?" Kaleb whispers into my ear.

The sharp intake of breath through my nostrils isn't enough for my lungs. I peel his fingers away, gasping for air.

"Don't ever do that to me," I warn. "You almost gave me a heart attack."

"Yeah, well, speaking of attacks, we're all in place while the two of you sit here bickering."

Asher levels a glare at Kaleb. "We weren't bickering."

"Whatever. Just get to it. We're getting antsy over there." Then Kaleb is gone without a noise or a trace.

I drag large, gulping breaths into my lungs.

"You alright?" Asher asks me.

I shake my head while vowing silently to permanently affix my inhaler to my hand. Some heap big warrior I am. One minute into the mission and I'm already dying for Albuterol.

"Just breathe. In and out. Just like that. You want to stay behind? It's not too late."

I shake my head again. "Let's just get this over with."

Asher takes my right hand, closing his fingers around the stiff brace. I let him pull me slowly around the hedge, ducking down below the vines. When we are on the other side, in full view of the

385

house, I follow his lead in running along the shadows half bent over. The hedge ends abruptly at a chain-link fence. We pause for a second before stepping out of the shadows. My pulse pounds wildly in my ears like a wild animal begging for release.

"Which window?" Asher whispers.

I look at the three windows lining the back of the house. There's a back door somewhere between the first and second windows, but the ever-increasing darkness tricks my eyes into believing that it's not there anymore. The porch light from a neighboring house glints off of something hanging in the second window.

I point at the swinging object. "That one. That's my dream catcher I put in Grandpa's room."

Asher lets out a gust of air. It turns to white smoke and floats upward. "Alright. On the count of three."

One, he mouths, *two*...

And we run, the frozen grass crunching loudly beneath our boots. I have to fight the urge to turn around and make sure no one is behind me, but somehow I keep up. When our backs are against the rear wall of the house, I take in the mangled grass throughout the twenty feet we've crossed. I could have sworn something was right behind us. I force myself to dismiss the thought.

We hold impossibly still, neither of us breathing for ten full seconds. Then Asher turns his head, glancing in the corner of the window. He looks back at me.

"What? Is there...?" I ask, not sure I want the answer.

He cocks his head to the side, regarding me with a gentle look. It's the kind of look someone gets just before they tell you bad news. "You were right. Brady's in there."

My stomach turns to lead.

"You sure you're ready for this?"

I scratch my arm again. This time, they don't itch; they burn. "Keep asking and I won't be."

He turns, facing me head on. His hands cup my face. "You can do this. I'm sure of it."

I bob my head, shaking from head to toe. "As long as one of us is."

Asher reaches up his back. A flat blade about a foot long appears in his hand. I shudder at the thought of how many weapons he might have on him. My parents don't even own a gun because they're dangerous, but here's Asher walking around with an array of weapons in his back pocket like it's no big thing.

He jimmies the tip of the blade into the seal between the window and the frame. The wood crackles in protest.

"Why don't we just use the back door?" I suggest. "There's a key."

"No." His face is drawn into hard concentrating lines. "It'll be safer this way. We just need to get in to where he is." A loud pop shatters the still night. Asher smiles, slips the blade back wherever it came from, and turns his back on me. He slides the window open. "Watch my back."

I watch the empty yard as the shadows of night settle over it. I have to bite my lip to keep from laughing at the irony. Just a few weeks ago, I was sitting at home watching a scene similar to this on *Supernatural*. I remember how little I reacted when they got inside and found the victim lying dead on the floor. I've seen the episode probably about twenty times. Now, I'm the one going up against an actual demon – not the Hollywood kind – hoping to save my best friend. I wonder if – on the off-chance we ever had to do this again – it would feel like a re-run episode.

I realize this is another defense mechanism of mine: the human kind. My mind focuses on mundane topics to keep my focus away from the real questions. Like, what if I can't give Jac what he wants? What if Brady is already dead? What if...? I squelch the thought. If something that bad happened to Brady, I'd feel it, right? Like a piece of my own soul was removed. I run a quick assessment. I don't feel empty. So everything must be okay. For now.

Asher grips onto the edge of the windowsill and by using those magnificent muscles in his arms, flings himself into the room. A soft thud follows him.

A few seconds later, his head appears through the open window. "It's clear," he whispers. "Give me your arms."

I hold out my hands and try not to focus on how much this is going to hurt.

"I'm going to pull you in slowly. I got you. Just walk up the wall. I'll do the rest."

I lean back, giving him the majority of my weight. Then I place one boot in front of the other against the siding. The bricks crumble and slough with each shuffle.

"That's it. You got it. Just a few more…"

When my head reaches the bottom lip of the window pane, his arm snakes out and wraps around my waist. He places me on the floor. Sadly, I still make more noise than he did.

Asher smiles down at me. "Like a ninja."

I ignore him and turn to the body lying on the floor. My heart sinks half an inch in my chest. "Oh god. Brady."

Asher's eyes follow mine to the shadowed mass on the floor. Unconsciously, he shifts his body in front of mine as if he can protect me from the sight.

I sidestep him.

"Nicky, he could be really hurt. Keep your back to the wall. I'll check him out."

I nod, unable to do anything else. Brady, my anchor, is curled up in the fetal position. He doesn't look blue, but doesn't look like he's breathing either. The realization is like poison running in a white hot serum through my veins.

There's something off about the situation, though. As Asher moves forward, my eyes fix on each familiar object in the room: the mirror above the dresser with its rusty gold frame, the lamp, and the closet door, now shut, with an image of me reflecting off the looking glass. The whole thing seems so oddly familiar and yet, so different at the same time. The other version of me stares back. Her left arm moves furiously up her right as if she has a horrible case of poison oak. She watches me with a quizzical look as I do the same. Then she looks worriedly at Asher. Did I just do that, too, or did her head actually turned two seconds before mine did? Her eyebrows draw together. Then her mouth falls open and her eyes widen in terror.

"Asher." My voice is shaky from some unknown horror. I clear my throat and try again. "Asher."

"Hang on," he says. He's only a foot away from Brady now.

"No, Asher. Stop," I snap.

"What? Why?" Still, he inches closer, his head swinging back and forth, seeking out any danger.

"Asher, stop, please," I cry out.

He pauses. Maybe it was the "please." A muscle in his jaw jumps. He's on full alert. "What? What is it?" He looks at me over his shoulder, scratching at the sleeves of my jacket so violently that I could tear the soft material to shreds.

I catch my reflection in my peripheral vision. She looks strong and resolved, but her eyes try to communicate something. I grip onto her strength and pull it into me.

"Leave him," I say.

Asher looks at me like I just told him to hit the world's self-destruct button. He turns his back on Brady and levels his eyes on mine. "We need to get Brady out of here."

"Agreed," I say. "But…"

He takes a hesitant step toward me. "But what?"

"We can come back. Just please, let's go. We need to get out of here," I tell him, urgently.

From the floor, Brady stirs. My heart clenches hard. It's all I can do not to run to him.

"Not until we get Brady out of here." His eyes flash a color brighter than any gold I've ever seen. "What you're feeling is normal. Just breathe through it. We're almost done."

There's a distant muted song coming from somewhere: *The Smurfs*. The theme song plays, each note punctuating my horror. "Asher, no," I cry out again. "That's not Brady."

But it's too late. There's a blur of motion. Asher turns slowly to meet Jac's pale eyes peering out of Brady's face. Brady's hand clamps down on Asher's throat. Asher claws at his hand. Then, with barely any effort, he tosses Asher across the room. Asher meets my reflection head on before crumpling to the floor. A waterfall of glass shards rains down on him.

Chapter 42

I scream, but there's no sound. My voice has dried up along with the rest of my throat.

Brady moves slow and steady toward me. My stomach constricts. My skin burns like I've been set on fire.

"What did you do with Brady?" I manage to choke out.

He cocks his head to one side then the other. "I told you: nothing. This was never about him."

"Where is he?"

The form in front of me reaches up and tugs at clumps of his auburn hair. The image of Brady falls away like a curtain. In its place is Jac. "You're clever, you know," he says. "That was a strong glamour. Even your bodyguard couldn't see through it."

It takes every bit of control I have not to look back at Asher. God, I hope he's still breathing.

"I do hope you brought other friends."

"Just him," I lie.

He rubs his ear with his thumb and forefinger. "You're a horrible liar. I think that if we wait long enough, someone will come. You've made a lot of dangerous friends, Nicoletta. I've been looking for one of those friends for a long time."

I stand tall and puff out my chest. It's all a show. Inside, my organs tremble like the aftershock of an internal earthquake. "You'll be waiting a long time. No one else knows I'm here."

"Time is all I have. Such a waste if you ask me." He grins, his mouth a gaping hole between his lips. His teeth are white enough, but jagged and poking out in every direction.

I shudder. How the hell did Brady kiss that?

Glass scrapes against the ground. My head turns before I can order it not to. Asher is on his hands and knees. His back arches like he's going to get up before he falls again.

Jac laughs. "The least you could have done was brought the demon children. Give me a challenge." His nostrils flare. "I mean, this is pathetic. But of course you'd choose the weak one. It's in your blood. You are certainly your grandmother's child."

If I had known my ancestry would play such a huge role in my life, I would have signed up for the Genealogy course at school.

"History does have a nasty way of repeating itself, doesn't it?" Jac says, as if he can reach my mind.

Maybe he can.

A string of unprintable things unwinds in my head: names, accusations, and even suggestions that Jac do some anatomically impossible things with himself. In other words, things I would never say out loud.

Jac makes a noise like he's scolding me. "Such a foul mind for such a young girl. Your parents would be extremely disappointed. Also, I feel it necessary to tell you that you can't shut me out. Feel free to try, by all means," he says, responding to each thought before I have a chance to finish it.

I throw my hands up in the air. "Great, so you can read minds?"

"Only minds I have connected with. Marked, is the term your little friends used." He pinches the air between his fingers. "Your mind is the perfect representation of teenage angst. Tell me, have you ever worked for what you want or have you always been so scared? Wait, don't answer that." He smiles maliciously. "I already know."

Asher is finally up on his knees. He shoots me warning looks while removing a thin shard of glass from his shoulder. I think he's trying to tell me to forget he's here. It's the only way this plan can be saved.

I close my eyes for a brief second and think of the only other monster I know: Taylor. I need something to piss me off enough to do this and he's the perfect candidate.

One blink is all it takes for Jac to appear directly in front of me. I blink again, trying to refocus my vision, which turns out to be a colossal mistake. When I open my eyes again, his fist tangles in my hair, yanking my head back at an uncomfortable angle. He examines every curve and angle of my face, getting closer and closer as he does so.

Remember that move Asher taught me earlier? The one where I pushed on his chest while sweeping his legs out from underneath him? I resolve in trying that, but the second I think it, he's gone, moved far out of my reach.

"You don't want to do that," he says in mild irritation.

I blink rapidly between glances around the room. If only I had more light. The sliver filtering in through the window isn't enough.

"You have to be quicker, Nicoletta, or you will surely die on your first night out."

"So you don't have Brady?" I say.

There's a maniacal laugh from somewhere – I can't pinpoint where – inside the room.

Asher is up on his feet, pressing a fist into his bloody shoulder. He looks around and shrugs.

"I never needed Brady. Sure, he was fun, but I only used him to get close to you. Same with the little heart victim."

"Why him anyway?" I call out. "I don't get that."

"I saw how you went to his rescue. You were the only one who did and I needed to get your attention. You care for him, even if you don't want to."

"You're wrong," I say with emphasis.

Jac appears in the open doorway. "Am I? Am I so wrong? Then would you waste so much precious energy protecting him from me?"

"Because he doesn't deserve to die?" I blurt out because it sounds better than reminding him just how clueless I am. Of course, as soon as I think it, he already knows.

"Everyone deserves to die eventually. I just expedite the process. Make them useful."

"To who? You?"

"Yes." He says deliberately. "A noble cause, I must say."

Asher remains completely silent, hoping he won't be noticed. I ignore him, trying my damndest to forget about him completely in hopes that Jac will forget about him, too.

"Oh. I almost forgot." Jac says, pretending to be startled. "I brought you a gift."

"A gift?" I repeat. There's a lump in my chest constricting my breathing. A gift from a demon is never a good thing. "Why would you bring me a gift?"

He steps back into the shadows of the hallway. "A gift for both of us then. To show my appreciation, See, you, my dear, have set more into motion than you know."

When he re-enters the thin light of the room, he's dragging something large behind him. His fist curls around what looks to be a thick glob of wet hair. The thing slides along the floor with a sickening ease.

"You'll have to forgive me. I got a little carried away," he says nonchalantly before chucking the thing to the floor. A pair of glassy blue eyes is illuminated by the thin bar of light piercing the center of the room. I inch forward, my heart beat punctuating each step.

What I know at this moment is that the dark hair is really blond. Without being told, I also know that this person was screaming and fighting for her life at noon today. I don't know when she was taken, but I do know that she was free at four o'clock this morning when I last saw her.

I suck in a sharp breath. It's Jen.
"What did you do?" I demand. I focus on her vacant stare while everything else in the world falls away.

"As a personal favor, I fulfilled a wish of yours." He sounds so proud. "I hope you know that favors don't come cheap."

"You killed her!"

"Why, yes. You thought of doing it yourself many times. I've seen it in your mind. Oh don't look at me like that. I did that for you." He cocks his head to the left and chuckles to himself. "That boyfriend of hers is quite the lion. He gave me the best fight I've had in years."

I choke on his words. "Alex?"

"Alex, is it? He made a fine opponent."

Made. My blood boils at a hundred and fifty degrees. Without thinking, I lunge myself over Jen's corpse and aim myself at Jac, only to slam into the wall with my shoulder. I slide to the floor. It takes more energy than I have to force myself back up.

"Struck a nerve there, princess?" He moves from back where I had been standing.

I turn and give him the angriest look I've ever worn. "If you hurt him...," I yell.

"He may live. His life is in the hands of a higher power now: me." He smiles proudly. "Though, I might be up for a trade. What do you say?"

"I say go to hell," I tell him in such a monotone it surprises even me.

A warming sensation crawls up my spine and caresses my neck just beneath my hair. It's just the comfort I need right now. Pity I can't focus on it.

"Don't you even care to know what I want to trade?" he asks, amused.

I stand silent, staring at the mangled corpse on the floor. From this angle, I can see the crack in the right side of her skull. Blood still seeps from the wound, dyeing her hair and soaking the carpet. Just like in my dream. An empty feeling takes me over from the inside out.

Jac lets out an annoyed sigh. "You're wearing on my nerves, little girl. If you can't handle seeing your enemy dead then what makes you think you can bear the death of a loved one?"

"Who says she'll have to?" says a girly voice from somewhere behind me.

"If I were you, I'd be worried about how you're going to handle your own death," says another, this one soft and cool.

A sense of warmth washes over both my arms as Kaleb and Acey step forward, keeping me between them. Acey wraps an arm around my shoulder.

"You okay?" She whispers.

I nod, barely feeling the movement. My eyes never leave Jen's lifeless stare. If I blink or move, she might disappear, and that's no way for anyone to go. No one should be forgotten like that, not even my worst enemy.

"Well, well, well," Jac says, sounding pleased, "if it isn't Voltock's children. To what do I owe this pleasure?"

"Who?" I ask.

"What kind of name is that?" Acey tacks on.

Kaleb shrugs. "It sounds like a venereal cream."

Now that there are two other people to focus on, I take a moment to test how much he "hears" from me. First, I think about Brady, wondering where he is and if he's safe. I don't think Jac would be able to resist making a comment if he could hear me. When he doesn't have any response, I think long and hard about a mental wall, hoping it works. I read somewhere that mental walls could protect you from telepathic individuals. Okay, so maybe I read it in a Science Fiction novel, which isn't that reliable, but I'm willing to try. Then I try to sense Asher much like I did back in the training room. His heat signature is somewhere close by. That's good enough for me. I release the thought and the wall.

Then I have an involuntary thought, one I don't mind saying out loud. "I was never blocking you from Spencer, was I?"

Jac laughs darkly. "Does it matter? I never wanted that weak-hearted boy. I only wanted to get you here, and I have."

"Why?" Kaleb asks. Through his sharp tone, he sounds as confused as I am.

The puzzle pieces in my head slowly slide together, creating the image of this mystery. "It was all a trap. For a greater purpose, wasn't it?"

Jac nods encouragingly, like he wants me to figure it out.

I wish Asher would get on with whatever plan he's cooking up, but try not to think about it.

"You wanted to get us all here for what?" Acey says. "Because you want to die? You do realize you're outnumbered, right?"

Jac's head turns slowly to Acey. His eyes flash crimson in the slice of light. "Am I, little girl? As I see it, there are five people in this room. Six if you count the girl," he waves a hand at Jen, "which I don't. Out of the five of us, three bear the demonic bond. You do the math."

"I am not one of you," Acey growls.

"Neither am I," Kaleb agrees through clenched teeth.

My head swivels back and forth between them, shock plain on my face. They wear identical expressions of fury. I take an unconscious step backwards. Standing in the protection of not just one, but two marked demon hunters is not a place I want to be.

"She's scared of you," Jac says happily. "As well she should be. You reek of evil blood."

Acey turns to reach a hand out to me. I flinch as if her fingers were spiders.

"It's okay," she coos. "We're the good guys, remember?"

My legs ache to run from the room. I plant them firmly to keep them still. After all, this is Acey – cute, fun-loving Acey. Sure she has three of the four demon marks, but she's not evil, is she?

"Good guys?" Jac mocks. "I've never met anyone of Voltock's line who could call themselves that."

"Shut up," Kaleb warns. He looks over his shoulder at me and amends, "We are not of his line."

"Is that so?"

"Yes."

"My, my. Wouldn't your Goddess be so disappointed?" His nose wrinkles when he refers to the Goddess as if it pains him to do so.

"This is getting tedious. Why don't we discuss terms?" Acey cuts in. "I'd like to go home."

"Terms?" Jac takes a deliberate step forward, his face soaking up the light. His skin looks grey and his eyes sunken. He looks almost dead.

"Yeah. It's called 'negotiation.' Maybe you aren't familiar with the word." She places a hand over her heart. "For example: I want your head stuffed and mounted on my wall. Now you tell me what you want."

She's baiting him, buying time, but for what?

He looks at her with a bored expression. "Would it be so cliché if I said that I want you all dead?"

Acey pretends to think about it for a moment. My blood crashes in my veins.

"Yes, it would be," Kaleb responds. "And your request would be denied. Try again."

Behind his back, Kaleb flicks his wrist in a subtle motion. I've only seen him do this once before when he lit the candle in my living room. I shrink back, expecting the carpet to burst into flames. It doesn't. Instead, rain thumps against the open window. Jac turns his head in that direction just as a flash of lightning hits the window pane. Something like a spark shoots through me, setting my nerves on edge. The room illuminates for two seconds and that's when I see him: Asher stands behind Jac with his dagger raised above his head, ready to plunge it right through where his heart would be, if demons even have hearts.

A moan, sharp and jagged comes from that side of the room. Could it be over so quickly?

Another flash of lightning reveals Asher on his knees, his head inches from the ground. Jac looms over him, twisting his arm back at an unnatural angle.

"Try that again, boy, and I will dismember you." Jac says into his ear. "On second thought." He yanks up hard. The sound of a bone snapping rings in my ears followed by Asher's scream.

I cover my face even though they are back in shadow. I can't risk seeing Asher crumpled to the floor again. The only sound I hear for a solid minute is the echo of that god-awful scream. Asher's hurt and there's nothing I can do to help. I imagine what his eyes will look like when all the light has been drained from them. Like my whole world has been squashed by a giant hand, that's what it will look like.

A hand strokes my hair. I recognize that it's a hand, but that's all. I keep hoping that this is all just a bad dream, starting from the party.

Though, some annoying little voice in the back of my head tells me that this fateful night was set into motion long before that stupid party.

"Nicoletta," I hear from far away. It's a rough voice I can't quite place.

I peek through my fingers to see Gabriel kneeling in front of me. Behind him, Kaleb and Acey move in on Jac, circling him like a pack of wolves would a deer.

"Asher," I moan struggling to push myself up off the floor. I have to get to him. I have to make sure he's alive.

"He's fine, but he's hurt. I fear that if we don't get him out of here, though, he may…" He shakes his head as if to kill the thought. "We need to get him out of here. Can you help?"

It takes two ragged breaths before I nod.

"Good. I'm going to bring him to you then you get him outside. The Jeep is around the corner. Okay?"

"Okay."

Acey's hand sneaks up her back with such subtle grace that no one else notices. I wonder if she's going for the sword. Did she finally talk Kaleb into letting her have it? No, the hilt would be at her neck, whereas, her hand eases up the back of her shirt and returns with two metal objects. Throwing stars? Knives? I'm not sure I want to know.

The air around Kaleb changes so quickly that he seems to shimmer in the midst of it. His eyes are crimson, just like Jac's. Something crackles at his fingertips: sparks of silver and blue fall to the floor like a wasted firework.

It surprises me to see Jac back away from Asher, where he lay twitching and writhing in pain. If a big scary demon like him has reason to fear Acey and Kaleb, maybe I was right to back away. No, that's not right. He's evil and they are cavalry riding to the rescue, right? He has reason to be terrified. What would I have to fear?

I follow Gabriel along the far right wall toward Asher. It's almost easy to believe that Jac is so busy defending himself that he doesn't know what we're doing.

Until he says, "Well, hello greater purpose. Nice of you to join us."

Gabriel stops in his tracks and lets his head droop for a second before he regards Jac with narrowed eyes.

A glinting object flies toward Jac's face from Acey's direction. I hadn't seen her throw anything, but Jac flicks it away with his hand as if he were expected it all along.

"I've been waiting for you," he says with an evil grin. "Been a long time."

"Not long enough," Gabriel scoffs. "I'd hoped you'd find something more constructive to do with your time."

"This," he waves a hand at Kaleb and Acey, "is very constructive. What about you? Still stalking your children I see." He gives me a pointed look. "Tsk tsk. Don't you have anything better to do? You know, there is such a thing as personal boundaries."

Gabriel motions with his hand behind his back, urging me to keep moving. I shuffle slowly so as to not draw attention to myself.

"Well, you know me," Gabriel replies. "So what brings you here?"

Their polite banter makes me nervous. I was under the impression that this was a rescue mission, not a reunion. It was supposed to be cut and dry. Get in, destroy the demon, and get out. Why is nothing ever that easy?

Jac glares at Kaleb, who is still moving in. "You know, see the sights, visit a few friends." Then he scowls. "Collect old debts."

Gabriel stiffens. "Well, as you know, I'm retired. So if you don't mind, I will happily gather my children and we'll be on our way."

I crawl my way down to Asher. I smooth his hair out of his face. A mask of pain twists his features, but he doesn't cry out. Silently, I thank the universe for small miracles. I'm not sure I could handle hearing that noise again. My hands flutter over him, taking a mental inventory of his body. I'm not sure what I expected, but his body is completely intact save the one arm, which is hanging at an odd angle.

"Can you walk?" I whisper into his ear.

"Think so," He grounds out. "This sucks."

"What? Broken bones?" I ask. "Of course it does."

"No," he says sternly. "Knowing I won't get to watch them send the bastard back to hell."

I run a finger down his neck. "There is something seriously wrong with you."

He fakes a smile. It comes across as a grimace.

"We can leave," Gabriel argues. "Forget any of this ever happened."

"Now that is a great idea. I'd love to go home and finish that book I've been reading," Jac mocks. "You know how I love doing mundane human things." As he says this, the door swings shut with a bang and the open window drops down hard enough to make the glass shiver.

Asher looks at me in alarm. "Alright, so I probably shouldn't have wished that."

"You think?" I snap back.

Gabriel continues, "I remember how much you love torturing me."

Jac shrugs. "It is my passion."

Kaleb catches my eye and nods once. I'm not sure what he's planning to do, but I know that once he does it, I'm to get Asher up and get us the hell out. He closes his eyes and the shimmer around him spreads. His wrists move in a circular motion at his sides like he's stirring something. The air in the room thickens to a dense fog. My lungs notice before my brain does.

Maybe I should have told him that I have asthma. Reflexively, I gulp in huge lungs full of moist air. It feels like I'm breathing water. However, while it may burn a little, it's also kind of soothing, like having a cold wet wash cloth on a fevered head. Acey smiles at me. The medicinal feel must be her doing. She'll want me to thank her later.

I struggle to get Asher to his feet by throwing his good arm around my shoulder.

The fog thickens.

"I've heard rumors of a boy with talents such as yours." Jac says. His voice is calm enough to fool me if it weren't for the sudden shift of his eyes. "Of course, the stories made you sound like a God of some sorts. I guess I expected more."

I push and pull Asher toward the door, reminding him where Jen's body is. We manage to sidestep it completely.

"I have many talents," Kaleb says. The room gets murkier until it's hard to tell who is where and doing what.

It takes a little jostling, but I somehow manage to position Asher between the wall and my shoulder. I feel along the door for the knob. When I make contact, the metal sears my skin. I curse and shake my hand to cool it down.

"What's... wrong?" Asher groans.

"It's hot."

"Oh," he says like it's no big deal. "Let me try."

I start to protest as he moves his arm from my shoulder to work on the doorknob. After a second, he groans and slumps against the wall.

"Did it burn you?" I ask.

He laughs bitterly. "No."

"Did you get it then?"

He makes an unintelligible noise before saying, "It's locked."

"Of course it is."

Acey screams Kaleb's name, drawing my attention back to the real action. The air around Jac thins as he breathes in and out with deep, unnecessary breaths. Once he can see, he rushes at Kaleb.

Kaleb sticks out his hands nanoseconds before Jac collides into them. A flash like lightning rocks the room followed by a thunderous bang. Jac staggers back, holding his chest and convulsing.

"Impressive," he spits out, "but you'll pay for that."

Acey moves forward, her hand clutching at the back of her neck.

Now this may sound stupid given the predicament we are in and all, but I have a moment of pure astonishment when I realize that Acey really did end up with the sword. Honestly, my money was on Kaleb.

The sword whispers a quite song as she unsheathes it, drawing it out theatrically, probably to avoid cutting her hair with the blade. When it's free, she brings it down in a two handed arc over her shoulder.

"And how do you think that sword is going to save you?" Jac says.

Acey levels it at his chest and fakes a shrug. "I'm going to cut you in half with it."

In an instant, Jac is gone, moving silently and invisibly through the room like a fruit fly. Kaleb sucks back the last of the fog, his eyes searching furiously around the room.

I close my eyes to get a better sense of his location. My heart skips three beats when I realize where he is.

"Asher, Get up!" I yell at him, tugging at his good arm. "Now! We need to move!"

Asher stares at me for a moment longer than I would have liked in normal circumstances, let alone this one.

I grab him around the chest and pull. He doesn't fight me. That's the only way I manage to get him to his feet and moving back along the wall.

But we're too late. Jac materializes as if from thin air right behind Gabriel. He wraps an arm around his torso from behind, as if they were lovers.

"No!" Acey screams, rushing toward the two men. Kaleb shifts back and forth, trying to get the best angle from which to attack.

"This," Jac says just loud enough for the rest of us to hear, "is what I've waited centuries for."

Asher's weight is like an anchor holding me in place. I press him into the wall and hope he can keep himself upright.

"She never loved you," Gabriel says. He doesn't sound angry. He sounds like he's given up.

I search the area, trying to find something – anything – I can use as a distraction. If only my parents hadn't taken the picture of my great-grandmother, I could have thrown that at him.

"She did," Jac growls. "She loved me with a passion you will never know. It was poetic justice that she married another. How'd that feel by the way? Did it burn to know you were cast aside like I was?"

"She couldn't be with either of us. You know that. Collette wasn't a part of this world," he says with such disgust it's a mystery that he ever signed on for this life.

"That didn't stop you from giving her a child: an abomination. You made her a part of this world."

As Acey closes in on them, Jac flings an arm out, knocking her to the side. Her head hits the wall with a thud. The sword clamors and clinks its way toward Kaleb.

My stomach turns. I have to find something. Why is this place so empty? I wipe my sweaty hands down my pants, and that's when I feel the dagger strapped to my thigh. My fingers wrap around the hilt reverently.

The floor starts to tremble. At first I think it's just me and my shaky nerves, but then the empty mirror frame starts to sway.

We rarely have earthquakes in Utah, is my first thought. But it's not an earthquake.

Kaleb is extremely still, standing in the middle of everything, his hands clenched at his sides. His eyes, with their cobalt glow, zero in on Jac.

"I didn't know," Gabriel says over and over again.

"Of course you didn't. Would it make you feel better if I told you she didn't know either?" His words are sharp. "Of course not. That child should have been destroyed before it ever entered the world."

My blood burns white hot. That's my grandfather he's talking about. My grandfather, who I loved and idolized up until the very moment he died, the moment Jac killed him.

I slip the knife out of the sheath. Any attack I make probably won't be very effective, I'm sure, but it might be enough to draw Jac's attention back to me. Then maybe Gabriel will have a chance.

I creep around them, careful not to lose my footing. Knowing my luck, if I fell, I'd end up cutting myself on the dagger.

The ground shudders violently.

"And after I kill you," Jac continues, "I'll take care of the legacy you've left behind, starting with your great-granddaughter."

"You wouldn't," Gabriel says. His tone, though, implies that he believes Jac would do just that.

"Why wouldn't I? Because of Collette? Bah, she's more like you than I'm willing to allow."

I make my way to his back, close enough to feel the cold waves pulsating off of him. I can see Jac's left hand as it stretches and moves slowly toward Gabriel's neck. It presses into skin and a strange gurgle bubbles in Gabriel's throat.

The whole scene transports me back in time. Not to the tainted dream planted in my mind as a clue. Not to where my grandfather closed his eyes and went peacefully, never reopening them again. But as clear as if I were there now, I see Jac standing over my grandfather, his aura glowing red as he places his hand on my grandfather's chest. There is no silent breath drawing the life out of him. No, my grandfather wasn't so lucky.

His ghost looks at me, the light in his eyes diminishing as he opens his mouth in a silent scream. His hands scratch at his chest, his legs popping up to kick at whatever – or whoever – is near him. Then room goes dark and I'm transported back to the present.

No, it wasn't serene at all.

Gabriel's body writhes in Jac's arms.

I lunge forward, plunging the tip of the dagger into the side of his neck. Something dark and wet pours over my hand. There's a phantom feeling in my palm as if I still hold the blade.

Jac releases Gabriel, who crumples to the floor. He wheels around, his full attention on me.

The dagger catches the light and glitters. Blood spurts out from the blade. It's a gruesome sight to be sure. He looks so human, but it's not blood, I realize. It's thicker, like black oil bursting forth from a bottle in slow pumps.

But what really makes my stomach turn is his expression when he moves toward me: anger, hatred and homicidal rage all take turns across his face.

I stumble backward, smacking into the wall.

Jac plucks the dagger from his wound and tosses it across the room. "Now, you die."

Chapter 43

"I shall enjoy this immensely." Jac says, glaring a hole through my head.

A heroine version of me would push him out of the way and run for the sword. A smart person would just run. I'm neither of those things, which is why I find myself wanting nothing more than to curl up and go to sleep until it's all over.

"You shouldn't exist. I hope you understand that your death will put things right. You are the unbalance."

Why the hell is he explaining this to me? Surely, he doesn't feel guilty. He's a demon for hell's sake. They don't feel guilt, do they?

I remember Gabriel calling me Collette back at the training center. What had I done to remind him of her? The only thing I know about my great-grandmother is what I read about her in his journal. I've never heard stories about her. What kind of woman gets emotionally involved with a demon and a demon slayer?

A hard ass, that's what kind.

Fighting the urge to fall to the floor and puke up my own kidney, I meet his eyes dead on. Careful to show no fear, I tilt my nose and chin up into the air.

He watches me with growing suspicion.

"Jac," I say, faking an accent I've never tried. "Don't do this."

The irises of his glowing eyes dull to a soft pink. Then they black out completely. His expression softens to one of careful consideration.

"You don't want to do this," I tell him.

We stare at each other. The oil spills out of his neck, soaking his shirt. I wonder if demons can bleed out.

"Collette," he says, his voice trembling. He steps back two paces and rubs his face.

"This isn't you, Jac," I hedge. I don't know anything about him, but he must have some sliver of decency. How else would my best friend and great-grandmother develop feelings for the monster? I make a mental note to puke over that later.

"This is me," he whispers.

"No. You are so much more than this."

"That's not what you said when you left me."

"You know that's not why."

The words fall from my lips naturally, as if I am her. I say the first thing that comes to mind without consideration. Who am I to deny him his last moments of closure before I kill him?

"I had to settle down. My family needed the estate. You know that," I say.

"The estate! Always with the estate." He's still not looking at me. The soaked carpet is too interesting for that.

"I made my choices. There's nothing either of us can do about them now. You made sure of that when you killed me."

My hand twitches with an absurd desire to console him. I clench my fist, digging my nails deep into my palm. I am not Collette. I am Nicoletta Cheri Dubois. I am the demon's prey, not his lover. My distance is the only thing keeping me alive.

Too bad my heart strings don't remember that. They tug a little too tightly. My breath catches in my throat.

Jac whispers something in French. I don't know what he says, but some of the words sound vaguely familiar. He glances at me sideways with his pale eyes.

I nod, not knowing what I'm agreeing to.

Two things happen at once: my body is slammed sideways into the corner a few feet away, and a bright object comes down in an angle across and through Jac's chest, slicing him in half. Brackish liquid splatters my face and arms as I slide to the floor, gasping for breath.

A range of conflicting emotions wage war inside me. I'm not sure whether to cry or scream, smile or break something. It feels like hours before I can finally lift my head.

When I do, I see Kaleb standing over the two halves of Jac's body. His jaw is tight and his eyes stone cold. I've never seen anything more frightening. He mumbles something under his breath and spits on the body.

Asher has somehow moved to my side. "You alright?"

I'm sore from the impact of the wall and my face burns like I've been attacked by a porcupine. "Bruised, but I'll live."

He gapes at me for a moment. I hide behind my hands. Why is he looking at me like that? He rips off a strip of his shirt, carefully pulls my hands away from my face, and wipes my cheek with it. The cloth feels rough on my skin.

"What are you doing?" I ask him.

"Cleaning off the ichor before it burns through your skin."

I don't ask. I'm too tired to care what the answer is. The only thing I want is to get out of here and maybe a shower.

When he's done, he smiles. "Looks like you will live after all."

"How about you?"

He gives a half-shrug. It looks weird with only one movable arm. "Broken. But I'll survive."

I cast a glance around the room. The lamp and dresser has shifted about into unusual spots. I wonder whether Kaleb was trying to create a diversion or redecorate the place. If all he wanted to do was rearrange furniture, then mission: accomplished.

Four bodies are scattered on the floor – five, if you count the two halves of Jac. I hope only two of them are dead. Kaleb crouches down next to where the top half of Jac landed and retrieves my dagger from the floor. He wipes the blade on his black t-shirt. It leaves what looks like a grease spot down the front. Maybe there are more reasons for wearing black than camouflage.

"God I hate ichor," he complains.

Asher reaches out with his good arm and takes the dagger from Kaleb. Something passes between them as the blade exchanges hands. It's like nostalgia, pride, and respect all wrapped into one. It seems too intimate to watch, so I focus on Acey lying in the corner, her hair a fiery spill around her.

I want to climb over to her to check her pulse, but don't dare move. I doubt my legs are stable enough to hold me.

Her eyes flutter open. She blinks a few times like she's trying to remember where we are. Then she pulls herself to an upright position. "Shit. I miss everything."

My throat is thick. "Kaleb," I choke out, "is Gabriel…?"

He crouches down next to Gabriel's body. Using two fingers, he gently prods the man's neck. My great-grandfather's neck, I remind myself. The victorious look on his face disintegrates. He shakes his head slowly.

And that's all I can take. I mumble something to Asher about needing air and launch myself out of the room. I bump back and forth between the walls like I'm stuck in a pin-ball machine, but I make it out the door. Once outside, I suck the air in hard and quick. It feels like I am suffocating. Good thing I didn't eat. I'd probably be vomiting all over the place, too.

I sit on the grass and push my palms into my eyes. Fireworks spark behind my lids. And I cry. For so many reasons, I cry. For the guilt of never having the opportunity to really know my great-grandfather. For Asher and Acey, who have lost the only parental figure they had. For the battle we won… and lost. Though, it seems now, at this moment, that all victories come with a price. Ours came with many. And finally, I cry for myself. Sure it's selfish, but I just found out things about myself and my history I may have never known if Asher hadn't waltzed into my life all chivalrous and helpful. I cry at the thought of life without him. Then I cry because I know I will lose him. There are so many questions I may never get the chance to ask, so many answers I may never get.

Asher's arms encircle my shoulders from behind. I try not to push into him too hard for fear of hurting him more. It's a feat considering that if I could, I would disappear into him, finding solace somewhere deep inside where it's safe. His warmth seeps into my skin while the cold air presses down on us.

"Shh," he whispers against my hair. "It's over. It's going to be alright."

But it's not going to be alright, is it? I will never know everything I need to know. I will never spend time with the great-grandfather who has lived so close to me for so long. I can never go back to the days when thing I had to worry about most was whether or not I would miss my favorite shows because of Brady's asinine plans.

I won't be able to look Alex in the eye after he hears about Jen's death. And the worst part of it, the thing that burns all the way down to my core, is that Asher is leaving. He'll walk away from this battle, ready to return to the war.

I sniffle. "No, it won't. But I appreciate you saying so."

The door opens and Acey calls out to us.

"Just a second," Asher tells her. He gets to his knees and turns me to face him. My eyes fill with tears that make the light around him shimmer and glow. He looks like an angel. He pushes my hair back from my face. His forehead rests against mine. "Are you okay?"

I close my eyes. "I don't know."

Acey, in her impatience, has come to stand next to us. "Asher, we need you."

He glances up at her, waiting.

"We can't exactly leave this place like this. We need to torch it to the ground, but make it look like an accident."

He looks to me in question I realize he's asking permission.

I wave an exhausted hand in the air. "Do it. It's fine."

After a quick kiss to my forehead, he gets to his feet and follows Acey into the house. Kaleb steps out onto the porch, the sword in one hand and another object dangling from his grasp. He collapses onto the grass next to me.

"Long night," he says.

I agree whole-heartedly.

He wraps an arm around my shoulder. "You did awesome in there. Gabriel would be proud."

"No he wouldn't. He's dead."

Kaleb shrugs. "True, but such is the way with our kind. He may choose to rejoin us. Besides, dying in battle is considered the highest honor."

I rest my head on his shoulder, feeling a weight settle in on my mind. It feels like my head is trapped between two solid walls, and they're closing in.

"Hey, I brought you something." Kaleb says to me. He holds up a hand, the object dangling in his grasp.

"What is it?"

"The dream catcher from the window. It looked important. I didn't want it to burn."

I take it from him, slowly tracing the outline of webbed strings. Red and brown beads dot the leather cord. "I made this for him a long time ago. My mother was big into arts and crafts. He always had bad dreams and wouldn't talk about them. Now I know why."

Kaleb nods, his cheek brushing against my head where it rests on his shoulder. "Don't think of this as a curse, Nicoletta. Think of it as an amazing gift. You could help a lot of people with that mind of yours and if you decide not to go that route then at least you have a choice."

I'm too tired to make anything out of his philosophical fortune cookie garbage. "So, what happens now?"

He thinks on that. "Well, Asher will torch the place, removing all the evidence of Jac. Then you guys will go home to get some sleep. Acey and I will take care of the girl."

"I meant in the long run, Kaleb," I tell him.

He sighs. "I don't think any of us know the answer to that one."

Behind us, the house ignites into high burning flames. Red, yellow, and orange fingers reach out of the windows as the glass explodes. Asher and Acey carry Jen's body between them. They carefully set her in the back seat of the Jeep. I doubt they were that gentle with her when she was alive.

They are quiet as they stride over to where Kaleb and I sit on the grass, watching my grandfather's house burn to the ground.

"You know, I think this is a good resting place for Gabe," Acey says.

Asher nudges her with his elbow. "Yeah, I think he would have wanted to be with his son."

412

My throat burns.

Debbie, the witch we met earlier, appears out of nowhere. I probably just didn't notice her before because I'm mesmerized by the fire. It dances about carelessly, devouring my memories before bursting forth from the house and escaping in smoke and ash.

"Now?" Debbie asks.

Kaleb shakes his head. "Wait until we leave. Then tear it down. We don't want the neighbors seeing us here."

I glance at Asher, hoping he'll launch into one of his long-winded explanations.

He doesn't disappoint. "She put up a glamour, a façade. No one has been able to see anything except what they expect to see for the past hour."

An hour. That's all it took for my world to upturn, scattering all the pieces about like unappreciated objects.

"Come on, Ace, let's go," Kaleb says.

Asher takes my hand and pulls me along. "Let's go home."

Home. Where is that anymore? I feel more lost and confused than ever.

He wraps his still useful arm around my shoulder and steers me away from the heat and flames. We walk in silence to his house two blocks away. My feet move mechanically. The silence around us has me on edge. What else is lurking out there in the shadows? What else have I yet to see?

Eventually we make it to the house and stumble inside. I feel numb and lifeless, surprised I'm still moving. That must be a good sign. There's a heavy feeling in the house like Gabriel might be chillin' upstairs. Strange that I didn't know him all that well, yet I feel like I'm breaking apart while his own adopted children haven't shed a tear.

We go through the kitchen and down the stairs. I strip off the jacket and long-sleeved shirt leaving only the thin material of the tank top. Then I shuck off my boots and fall into Asher's bed.

The bathroom door shuts quietly and the shower turns on.

I close my eyes. I'm barely aware when Asher, smelling a little like campfire and soap moves in next to me. I feel the warmth of him as he presses himself against me. A weak arm comes up to rest around my waist. Already he can move it better than he could twenty minutes ago. It'll be interesting to see if it's healed by morning. It feels like morning is a million miles away.

Chapter 44

When I wake the next morning, Asher is up and moving about the room. I stare at the clock. It's fuzzy. I forgot to take out my contacts. Then again, who could blame me? It takes four long blinks before I can make out the time.

"Asher, do you realize it's only ten?" I ask him.

He kneels down at the side of the bed. "Good morning to you, too."

I grimace. "No. Get your ass back in this bed. It's not morning until after noon today."

He chuckles. "I'm sorry. I wasn't informed."

"You're forgiven. Now move."

I'm almost surprised when he does what I tell him to do. He nudges me over so he can climb in next to me. He's wearing a pair of black and grey striped pajama pants and no shirt. His left arm looks a little bruised, but seems to move fine.

He pulls the covers up around us, blocking out the rest of the world. Then he kisses me softly.

"What are you doing up?" I ask him as I nuzzle into his cheek. Sleep looms over me.

He hesitates before he says, "Packing."

I startle awake. "Why?"

"Kaleb and I head out at noon."

My heart sinks like steel in water. "You're leaving." I observe, choking on my own vocal chords.

"I promised and I always keep my promises."

I don't speak, in part because I'm not sure what to say and also because if I do, I'll cry. I'm amazed I still have any tears left to cry after last night.

He gathers me into his arms and holds me tight. "I never wanted any of this for you, but you still have options. Options I have never had."

"Are you coming back?" I ask, each word sharp as a dagger.

"I... I don't know."

"You don't know?"

"No. If I could promise you that, I would, but I can't."

I throw back the covers and climb out of the bed. I can't be so close to him knowing that he can't – no, he won't – stay, even for me. Each touch is a reminder of just that. I slip my jacket over my shoulders, flipping my braid out from under the collar. Then I sit on the computer chair to lace up my boots. That way, there's no room for him to sit by me.

"Don't leave mad," he says. He shoves the blankets the side and sits up, regarding me with sad eyes.

"I'm not mad."

"Yeah, okay," he says sarcastically. "You're not mad at all. In fact, I think this is the happiest I've ever seen you."

"Don't be smart with me."

He smiles. "I can't help it. You must bring it out in me."

I finish lacing up my boots and get to my feet. Glancing about the room, I realize my backpack is still in his Jeep. Maybe I can get Acey to get it for me. I realize I never heard her come home last night. I hope she and Kaleb are okay.

"Nicky," he says. "Please."

"Please what?"

"Sit down and talk to me."

I place my hands on my hips, but drop them to my sides when I recognize my mother in the gesture. "First, tell me why you want to leave me."

"It's not that."

"Then what is it?"

He rubs his face in what I assume is frustration. "I have to go. Kaleb needs me. I am bound by the law."

"The law? Since when do you care about the law? I thought you were retired."

He releases an exhausted sigh. "Don't you see? I can't retire. Even if I can turn my back on my past, the danger will follow me everywhere and as long as you're with me, it will follow you, too."

"I'm one of you, remember? That means I'll be in danger anyway."

He hangs his head. "Don't remind me."

"Don't tell me. You liked me better when I was a helpless little human girl, is that it? That's why you don't want to be with me."

He doesn't respond.

"Oh, God. That's pathetic."

That gets his attention. He narrows his eyes on me. "Are you done?" he growls.

"Done with what? With us?"

"With this misguided tirade. Are you ready to listen to me yet?"

I sit back in the chair and do a little face scrubbing of my own. "Fine. What?"

He scoots forward to sit on the edge of the bed, facing me. "Nicoletta, I love you any way you are. Human, Sentinel, witch, whatever. Goddess knows, you could be a demon and I'd still love you. You are my ardemwah. There's nothing I can do to change that. But you need time to decide without any outside influence. This mission, though, no matter how suicidal it is, has nothing to do with that. I swore my loyalty to Kaleb long ago. Unfortunately, that's how it goes. That is what this life is about: putting the battle first always. I don't blame you for being upset. I'm not happy about it either. But be sure of this, my will to live lies with you and wherever you are is where I'm going to want to be. If I have to walk through the fires of hell, I will find you again. But I can't promise I'll live through this. Nor can I promise that I'll return. Do you understand?"

I nod slowly. My feelings fight an unending war inside me. I want to revel in his words, feel the warmth of his honesty, but I also want to kick him hard in the head. Because no matter what he says about how he feels, he's still leaving.

"What do you say about that?" he hedges.

I go to him, wrap my arms around his neck. He smells like a warm day. I breathe in deeply, taking his musk into me. Then I kiss him as softly and gently as he kissed me under the covers.

When I pull back, he smiles.

I don't return the smile. I lean my forehead against his and whisper, "Goodbye Asher, and good luck." Then I turn to leave. And he doesn't stop me.

Chapter 45

Three weeks later.

"Honey, you look spectacular." My mother touches her lips, smiling. "Where did you get that beautiful dress?"

I look down myself at the thin satin fabric clinging to any curve it can grip onto. It shows more cleavage than I'd like and the slit is high enough to bear most of my thigh, but it feels good. It slides over my newly toned body like water and falls around my ankles in thick folds of fabric. I've replaced my mother's Mary Janes with a pair of my own. When you're friends with Acey, you learn how to shop.

"I borrowed it," I say with what I hope sounds like nonchalance. "Acey had a few extras lying around."

"That was so nice of her. It looks like it was made for you."

That's probably not far from the truth. When Acey gave me the dress, it wasn't lost on me that I'm three inches taller than she is with at least one more dress size to attend to. Yet, the dress fit with an ease only a tailor could accomplish.

"Well, I'll let you get ready. If you need any help…"

"Thanks mom, I'll let you know."

She ducks out of my room, flashing me a bright smile on her way out.

I lean into the mirror and paint on the finishing touches of my eye shadow.

I cut my hair a week or so ago, hoping to gain some control over my life again. Now, instead of it hanging down my back, it's just above my shoulders. I even took the time to flat-iron it. The layers curl out from my jaw and neck. It shocked everyone at first, but as Acey said, "Short hair is almost impossible to grab onto, which makes it less of a liability." After a week of persuasion, I even let Acey put some red highlights into it. Not an easy thing to do to black hair and I'll probably never let her do it again. But my mother was right: I do look spectacular. I turn in front of the mirror. Nope, definitely don't look like one of the guys tonight.

I look at the glass image of myself. It feels like something's missing and that thing is in my nightstand. I have to move some magazines where Jensen Ackles, aka Mr. Dean Winchester, poses on the cover before I find it.

I unfold the straps and hike up my skirt. The slit goes up my right thigh so I strap the dagger higher up than what I consider comfortable. Luckily, I don't live in a bigger city. If I did, there would be metal detectors at the door. Here, I don't even have to worry about having my purse searched.

Just as I finish smoothing my skirt down over the sheath, my father calls out, "Honey, your date is here."

"Coming," I call back.

I wasn't even going to go to the stupid Valentine's dance. It just seemed like there were more important things to do. Like search out my heritage. I was granted access to the training center shortly after that day three weeks ago. They had to determine my lineage through blood, but as soon as that was complete, I was accepted. Now, every day after school, I go there to hone my – what they call – psychic and empathic abilities. I always thought they were just nightmares brought on by watching too many horror movies, but my link to Gabriel proved otherwise.

My parents think I got a job at a Mexican restaurant on the West side of the city. It wasn't too much of a stretch. It feels like a job. Training is downright brutal. Hopefully, my parents won't get a craving for burritos anytime soon. I doubt they would understand. Sometimes, I hardly believe it myself. So, no, I didn't want to go to the stupid dance, but Asher made me promise a long time ago.

And I keep my promises.

I slip into my training jacket and take three long breaths.

Then I go to meet my date.

My father is busy chatting it up like he always seems to do before I go out, and like always, he notices me first.

"You look wonderful, honey," he says, abandoning all conversation to kiss my cheek.

"Thanks, Dad."

"Now, I've warned your date about the consequences he'll face if he touches you," he assures me.

I laugh. "I doubt it will be a problem."

My date turns around, running his fingers through his auburn hair. He looks a little uncomfortable. "You don't know. I could get frisky," he says.

Brady is dressed in a black tuxedo with crimson stitching and a tie of the same color. He looks like he could be on the cover of this month's *GQ*. Seriously, how could no one know he's gay? No one wears a tux that well.

The joke is lost on my father, who watches us with a crooked eyebrow.
"Ready to go?" I say.

My mother steps in with her camera cocked and loaded. I groan a little, but finally agree to a few snapshots.

As soon as the memory card is full, we sneak out the door with barely a word.

Brady opens the passenger door for me. I try to slide in gracefully, but the dress has other plans. Once the door is shut, Brady jogs around to his side.

It's still strange to see the little blue Saturn Sky in my driveway. What used to be Gabriel's car is now mine. A pang of sadness hits me in the throat. Acey gave the car to me shortly after he died. I wanted her to keep it, but she thought it would be better off in my hands. The first of my inheritances. Evidently, my grandfather left his house to me. That's the only reason my parents never got rid of it. When I turned eighteen, they were going to give me the keys. But after the fire, I received an insurance check instead. The property is still mine to do what I want with. So for now, it's just a piece of scorched land with haunting memories.

I smile at Brady because that's what you do when you get your best friend back from a brush with death, or in his case, a brush with stupidity. Yes, it was stupid for him to cut out without telling any of us. When all was settled down, I got my phone charged and surprise! Guess who decided to take a road trip to Vegas? Brady, that's who. He said there was a band he wanted to see playing at the Hard Rock for one night only.

I almost killed him for two reasons: one, for not telling anyone where he was going, and the other? Because the band was Social Offense. The least he could have done was invite me along. So what if I was five stories underground and there was no way to reach me? For something like that, you send out smoke signals or a homing pigeon.

I may forgive him. Someday. At least he brought me back a shirt and a signed CD.

I suspect he still feels bad about Jac leaving town suddenly to spend time with a sick relative. That's what we told him. I have to hand it to him, though. He's taking it extremely well. When I think about how many opportunities Jac had to kill Brady, I realize something: Jac did love Brady in his own weird way. Otherwise, he never would have left him alive.

"I'm glad you decided to come," he tells me on our way to the school. "I was afraid you wouldn't after..."

"After Asher left?" I finish for him. "Honestly? I probably wouldn't have. But I promised."

"I'm sorry."

"Yeah, me, too."

It's been two weeks, six days, nine hours and twenty-two minutes since I last saw Asher, but who's counting? I tried calling him a few times. It went straight to voicemail. I didn't leave a message. By the way, Kaleb was right. Service there sucks.

I still see Acey every day. She agrees with me that the whole thing is stupid.

The aching hole in my life where Asher had been seems to grow a little more each day. I wonder if it will ever get better. Maybe, if he survives, he'll come back and fill the empty space with his warmth. My problem isn't with the "maybe," it's with the "if."

"Ready?" Brady asks, standing just outside my open car door. I hadn't even noticed the car stopped.

I nod once and climb out, careful not to flash my fellow students filing into the gym. A little leg would be fine, but if they saw the dagger sheath…

I wasn't ready to part with it yet. It's the only thing I have of Asher to get me through tonight. I hope I don't need it for anything other than comfort. So far, all my training has been at the center. No missions for me until they decide I'm ready.

Brady must see it, though, because he raises an eyebrow in question. "What is up with you lately?" he asks, gesturing to my leg. "Now you're packing?"

One of the first things I did after I called Brady was tell him about my blind date three weeks ago. He held me while I cried for a long time. Since then, he's been blaming all my changes on what he refers to as "the episode." That's fine by me, I guess. It gives me the perfect excuse.

"A girl can never be too careful," I tell him.

He smiles that sad smile. I wonder if he blames himself for being AWOL at the time. Not that he could have done anything. "Come on. Let's make 'em jealous," he says, wrapping an arm around my shoulders.

I roll my eyes. "I highly doubt any of them will be jealous."

"We'll see."

The gym has been done up in various shades of pink and red. Tacky little hearts plaster on the wall, and for only five dollars, you can write a message on one. Many of them have been purchased for the sole purpose of paying homage to our fellow students who have passed, but most of them are for Jen. RIP Jen; *We love you, Jen*; and one particularly creative one says: *Roses are red. Violets are blue. Many people should die, but it shouldn't have been you.* Morbid, yet sensitive. The perfect valentine.

The newspaper declared Jen's death as congenial heart failure due to extensive drug use. I imagine whoever performed the autopsy has never seen a demon let alone know what an attack by one looks like.

There have been some rumors running around about the bruises and other violent markings found on her body. Some say she went out on a date to make Alex jealous and when she wouldn't give it up, the guy attacked her and made her walk home. Others say Alex did it. Only Acey and I know the truth: Jac happened to her. Simple as that. Acey tried to clean her up before resting her body on her parent's steps. Unfortunately, that was the only closure we could offer them.

"Nicky," someone calls out from behind me.

I don't respond right away. Not many people recognize me with my new look, but after they say my name two more times, I turn.

Alex stands there, looking me over skeptically. "You came."

"I did."

"You look amazing."

"Thank you," I say proudly. Aside from Asher's absence, I feel amazing, like some missing piece of me has been restored. I have my great-grandfather to thank for that.

Melin-duh hangs on his arm, searching for someone more interesting to talk to. After that night, Melinda, much like the others, started to get better. The doctors call it a medical miracle. One day, they were all in separate comas and the next, they stabilized. Seeing her gives me an odd sense of victory. We saved her life. No matter how big of a bitch she can be.

"Save me a dance?" Alex asks.

I nod, expecting it will never happen. This is how things have been between Alex and me since he set me up with that crazy asshole. It became clear to me soon after the fact that he and I are not as close as I once thought. I'm sure we'll always be acquaintances and maybe one day, we can even be friends again, but no more of this I give and he takes kind of shit. I'm more than just a cure to his loneliness. I have a purpose. I can fight now. I know more about this world than he could ever dream.

"Come on Alex," Melinda whines, pulling on his sleeve. "Dave saved us a seat at his table."

"Catch you later," he says before conceding to let her drag him off to their sitting area.

Brady leans into me. "And so the sun sets, leaving only the night."

"I prefer the night," I tell him. "Only then can you see the stars."

He smiles. "Good girl. You're learning."

Acey has saved us a seat at a table in the corner. We shed our coats, draping them over the chairs. Seth and Jessica are there, too. I guess they really connected during their frequent visits to the hospital.

Spencer and Jessica's friend, Elayne, sit next to them. He got out of the hospital only two weeks ago, but he looks good. And I've always liked Elayne. She has a sweet, sensitive side that may possibly help to drain the asshole out of him. Spencer and I haven't talked much about his secret or about how he got better so quickly after that night. I figure if he wants to talk, he'll find me. I did give him one piece of friendly advice, though. I told him not to lie to Elayne about it. That's it. End of story.

"I hope it's okay that we sit here," Jessica says to me. "I didn't want to sit by the clique."

I smile. "It's perfect."

Spencer nods at me in greeting. I beam at him. Something has changed between him and me. I guess that's what happens when you almost die for a person. It's weird and I won't ever admit it out loud.

Seth waves at me uncomfortably. Jessica somehow got him to wear a tux and it looks amazing on him. The black material compliments his tan complexion. His hair is cut short. I've never seen it free from his beanie. It's a good look for him. I'm not sure why I never thought of Seth and Jessica together, but now that I see it, it makes sense.

Acey breezes up to the table wearing a green velvet dress. It's long and tight, just like mine. Her hair is in red and gold ringlets down her shoulders. She smiles at me before falling into the seat next to mine. I wonder idly if she's armed, too. Not that Acey would need weapons.

"Great décor, right?" she says, a disgusted look on her face.

"Couldn't have done it better myself," I joke back.

I love seeing Acey, I do. But every time she's around, it's a reminder of her brother and how he left me. I try not to be serious when talking to her. If I am, I will undoubtedly break into tears, and I don't want to cry in front of her. She would either snap at me about being a liberated woman or do whatever she does to send me into a deluded state. The latter may not be so bad.

"Dorian," Acey calls out. "Over here."

A boy, who I have recently become acquainted with at the training center, lopes over. He's six-foot two with short spiky black hair and a body like Channing Tatum. Acey pounced on him during my first session and she hasn't let go since.

"Nicky, good to see you again," he says, taking the seat next to Acey.

She mouths the word *yummy* to me then turns a shining smile at him. "Don't get too comfortable, handsome," she tells him. "The first good song I hear, we're dancing."

He stretches an arm across the back of her chair. "Oh, I count on it."

"Have you heard from Asher?" I ask softly.

She shakes her head. "Sorry. They were supposed to be out on an S and R. I'm sure he'll call when he gets back. That reminds me..." She pulls out her cell phone and snaps a quick picture of me. I don't even have a chance to protest before she shoves it back into her shiny green bag.

S and R: Search and Rescue. My stomach turns to stone, but I manage to give her an unimpressed look anyway.

"What? He'll want proof that you came. Besides, I want him to see what he's missing."

"You're evil."

She smiles at the inside joke. "Of course I am. Nothing good could look this fabulous."

Brady excuses himself to hit the refreshment table. After a few minutes of watching the three couples engrossed in each other, I do

426

the same. Only, instead of going to the refreshment table, I bee-line it to the bathroom. Not the one located off the gym. I head to the one by my locker.

My heels click across the linoleum drowning out the horribly sappy song playing in the gym. I really just want to go home, but I don't want to leave Brady. Friends just don't do that to each other.

I'm almost to the bathroom when I hear an echo behind me. I turn to see an empty hall.

I shake my head. Paranoid, that's what I've become. Jules, my training coach, tells me that I will have a specific reaction to anything demonic presence. He thinks it will feel like a wave of nausea and a cold chill deep in my bones. I feel neither of those things, but as I've learned, some of the most evil intentions are human, not demonic. Demons just want to kill you, but some humans want to make you suffer. I still have nightmares about Taylor, but Jac is just a distant memory. Could be that Jac is dead while Taylor is still very much alive.

I push through the door to the bathroom and stare at myself in the mirror for a good while. I'm a different person now inside and out. How could I have gone from what I was to what I am now in a matter of weeks?

I tell myself to go back in there, dance with Brady, and pretend to be normal, even if normal is the furthest thing from what I truly am. Most of all, I tell myself to forget the aching hole burning its way through my lungs. It's not an asthma attack. That I could cure. No, it's something bigger: the edges of my heart feel like they're on fire. This is what it feels like to miss someone so badly it hurts every moment of every day.

I take out my phone and send off a quit text message to a number I haven't used in over a week. I miss you. That's all it says. I read it over and hit send. When Asher gets to his phone, he'll see it. I hope he'll be happy to hear from me, but who knows? Maybe he's moved on.

I slip the phone back into the pocket of my jacket. I couldn't bear to discard it with the other coats. It still smells like him.

I wonder what he's doing right now. Is he fighting for his life this very minute or is he lying somewhere still as a painting?

"Don't think about it," I say out loud. Sometimes it's just better to hear it that way. This is not one of those times. My throat feels raw as if I've been screaming. "Oh, no you don't," I tell myself, "You'll ruin your mascara."

Oh well, back to the dance before Acey comes to find me.

As I step out of the bathroom, someone grabs me from behind. One tight arm crushes my stomach while the other hand covers my mouth, silencing a scream.

The voice in my head says, *Quick, think, remember what you've learned.*

I brace my heels on the floor and shove back as hard as I can manage. The person behind me grunts as their body slams into a locker with a satisfying clank. One more time and the hand falls away from my mouth.

I grab his wrist, bend at the knees, and flip him over my shoulder. He scrambles up off the floor, backing up against the wall. I draw the dagger quick and easy from my right thigh, just like I practiced. Then I lunge at him, pressing the tip of the blade into the hollow of his throat. Only a little. My hair has fallen into my face, obstructing my vision with all its carefully styled strands. I shake my head violently to move it way.

And that's when I see my attacker.

"Asher?" I gasp.

He smiles. "I'm impressed."

I flip the dagger around, blocking the sharp edges of it with my wrist. Then I shove him back into the wall hard.

"Ow," he complains.

"What are you doing here?" I'm not sure if I'm angry or ecstatic. I feel both so I choose to exude anger.

He rubs his neck where I drew blood moments before. "I don't suppose you'd believe me if I told you that I came for a dance?"

I close my eyes, feeling his heat soothe the chill that's taken up residence within my heart. My inner eye registers him immediately. It's Asher, he's really here.

I shove him again, but he catches my hands and draws me into him.

"You left me," I snarl.

"And I came back." He dips his head and brushes his lips against mine. "I told you: as long as I'm alive, I'll always come back for you."

I let my head fall onto his shoulder. "Does that mean it's over?"

He shakes his head. His arms encircle my waist and drag me to him. "No," he whispers. "It's far from over, but I have my own beginnings with you."

"Yeah, you do," I say. Then I kiss him urgently.

***

Acey takes the news of Asher's return a little better than I did. Meaning, she punches him playfully in the arm rather than draw a blade.

"What are you doing here?" she demands. "I thought you were with Kaleb."

"I was," he says mildly. "It's a long story and I kind of wanted to take Nicoletta out for a spin on the dance floor."

Out of the corner of my eye, I catch Brady trying to duck out. I grab him by the arm and yank him to me.

"Actually," I tell Asher, "I'm kind of here with someone."

He looks taken aback.

"Next dance?" I offer.

He glances from me to Brady and back. "Yeah. Maybe I can talk my sister into dancing with her poor rejected brother."

Acey's eyes light up, a smile wide on her painted lips. She pats Dorian on the arm once like she's consoling a pet then she hops up. "Let's show 'em how it's done."

Asher reaches out, takes her hand and twirls her away to the dance floor. People part to let them through. I watch the crowd move to circle them as they take in their elaborate dance steps. It's like something out of a movie. I think about suggesting a dance contest, but decide it would be cheating. After all, they've had lifetimes of practice.

"You didn't have to do that," Brady says. He takes my hand and leads me to the dance floor. It's a simple box step. Just up my alley. My balance has gotten better since I've been in training, but I still like to take it slow.

I squeeze his shoulder. "I know, but I wanted to."

"Well, thanks. I know it must have been hard. You've been missing him a lot lately." He sounds so proud, almost full of himself.

"I never got to say thank you," I say as he spins me.

"For?"

"For blackmailing Asher. I mean, don't get me wrong, I hate you for it, too. But without it, we probably wouldn't have said two words to each other." I think about all the things that have happened since that first day I talked with Asher. All the things I've learned about the world and about myself. Inadvertently, it was Brady who made those things possible.

Brady pauses for a second, losing time with the music. "Oh."

I look at him with raised eyebrows. "Was that necessary, though?"

He thinks about it. "I think it was. Besides, even if you didn't like him, I would have gotten him the recommendation anyway. But let me tell you this, Kitten…"

He spins me again and I catch sight of Asher and Acey dancing away like they are the only two in the world. They move in some extravagant waltz. Asher catches my eyes and winks.

"Do you believe in soul mates?" Brady asks.

It's a question for the ages. The first thing anyone ever wants to know. For me, the answer has always been a big fat negative, but for the first time, I consider it. "You mean, like two pieces of one soul split apart and destined through space and time to find each other, to be together?"

He nods. Then after a long moment, he smiles at my hesitation. "That's what I thought. Anyway, Kitten, I believe you're mine."

"Yours?" I say, confused. "I love you and all, but—"

He holds up our joined hands to stop me. "I'm not talking about the traditional definition. I'm talking about the people who dance into your life and permanently alter you and your view of reality forever. For the greater good and all that."

The song ends and another one picks up with a slightly stronger beat. We stop.

"I was destined to find you," he continues. "When you are unhappy, I feel empty. Maybe it's selfish of me, but I want you to be happy because that makes me happy. That's why I did what I did."

I nod. When put like that there is no hesitation, I can believe in it. "At risk of sounding cheesy, I feel empty when you're unhappy, too."

I don't tell him how it almost killed me when I thought he was in danger. I also don't tell him that with a little bit of effort, I can feel his pain and anguish while he experiences it. That's what an Empath does. I can't tell him that either because I'm not sure he would understand what means. Maybe one day I'll tell Brady everything, but not yet.

Asher pops up behind Brady and touches his shoulder. "Can I cut in?"

I shrug and step aside. "As long as you get him home by midnight. He has a curfew."

Brady laughs and winks at Asher. "But I'd miss curfew for you, cupcake."

Asher sighs. "I missed you guys. Hey, Brady, thanks for making her keep her promise."

Brady is already backing away. "Anytime."

Asher's hand drops down my side and takes mine. Then without warning, he spins me away from him.

"Don't go anywhere, man, I brought you a gift," he says to Brady before pulling me back into him. We shuffle our way out to the dance floor. At this rate, I might have to take dancing lessons. I don't care what they say about letting the more experienced partner lead; someone who doesn't know how to dance can't be led.

Which is exactly how Asher ends up slowing down to my speed. We fall into the familiar box step.

"A gift?" I say when Brady's out of ear shot.

Asher's head bobs a little to the side. My eyes follow. Standing next to our table, dressed in an elegant grey pin-striped suit, is a familiar looking man. I squint, not sure I'm seeing him right.

"Devereux is his gift?"

Devereux is one of my instructors at the training center. He's tall, dark, and handsome. Actually, I've found myself looking at him for longer than necessary at times.

"He's French," Asher says as if that would answer all my questions.

Brady shakes Devereux's hand and smiles shyly.
"Looks like they've connected," I say.

Asher smiles. "I owed him for giving me you."

Something inside my stomach flutters as he twirls me once then again.

"So what were you guys talking about?" he asks, plucking at a strand of my short hair. "Your new look, perhaps?"

I laugh. "I needed a change."

"I like it. It suits you."

"We were talking about soul mates. Pros, cons, beliefs, disbeliefs," I say, waving the hand on his shoulder dismissively.

"Pretty boring discussion for a Valentine's dance."

I shrug. "If you say so. I was pretty intrigued."

"So what's your stance on it?" he asks, moving closer with each word.

"I'll let you know."

His lips graze mine, sending little tingles through every nerve in my body.

"So why did you come back?" I hedge.

Asher looks around at the crepe paper hearts dotting the walls. "I couldn't miss this," he says, sarcastically.

"Seriously," I urge.

"Seriously? Kaleb sent me home. He said that hanging out with me was as bad as spending all his time with a lovesick puppy. His words, not mine. I don't know what the hell he was complaining about, though. After spending a few days with him and Kaida, I wanted to drink liquid Drain-O."

"That bad?"

He smirks. "Worse. I just have a high pain tolerance."

We dance in silence for a moment. I realize then what song we are dancing to. *Lost in You* by Social Offense. My stomach does a little flip.

"Do you have to leave again?" I ask, hoping for a certain answer.

"When Kaleb needs me, he'll call. Then I'll head back up."

That was not the answer I wanted. Something inside me deflates.

He lifts my chin with his forefinger. His eyes have bled to amber gold. "But if we get enough training under your belt and you feel ready, you could come with us."

I roll my eyes at his lame attempt at a joke. "Yeah, right."

"We could. You're pretty handy with a dagger, you know." He touches our conjoined hands to the base of his throat.

I shake my head, chuckling. "My parents would never let me go."

"We could take care of that. Too bad they weren't there in the hallway. Maybe they wouldn't worry so much."

I laugh. "I'd like to try that again."

"Anytime you're ready," he challenges. "Of course, I may not be so easy on you this time."

I reach up on my tip-toes to kiss him. "That's what I'm counting on."

Epilogue

New Year's Eve:

A time for new beginnings, new experiences, and of course, copious amounts of alcohol.

Brady may never change, and I'm alright with that.

I stare at the house from the front walk, thinking over the last year. How I survived it, I will never know. Not only was I pushing to keep my grades up in school, but I also completed three levels of training. My clothes fit differently now after all the cardio, my emotions have been put through the ringer more times than I can count, and I'm exhausted more often than not.

I take a deep breath and head into the brightly lit entry way. Immediately, I can sense where everyone is. At least everyone I have mentally catalogued in my book of auras. Brady is in the kitchen with Devereux, probably mixing drinks. Surprise, surprise.

I head there first. He grins when he sees me and hands me a drink that looks like purple Kool-Aid.

"Glad you made it," he says.

I smile at him. "Wouldn't miss it." This time, I don't even have to lie. I'm genuinely glad to be here. When you almost lose your best friend, you learn to appreciate their silly parties.

Devereux salutes me with his glass. It's filled with the same liquid. "Nic."

"Dev," I say by way of greeting. It's good to see him here with Brady.

That's one thing that's changed about Brady: he doesn't care what people think anymore. Of course, his parents still don't know that he's gay, but everyone else has taken it pretty well. Good thing, too. I might have to kick some ass if they didn't.

I move into the living room. It's crowded with people who probably still don't know who I am, but I know them, and their personal heat signature. I've been using them for research.

I sip my drink as groups of people move back and forth from room to room. I'm pleased to notice that my drink even tastes like grape Kool-Aid.

A familiar bronze head walks toward me, bobbing above the crowd.

"I didn't think you'd come," Alex says, wrapping an arm around my shoulders. I let him hug me for a second before shrugging out of reach. He has a similar drink in his hand, but his you can smell in his pores.

"Why wouldn't I?"

"I don't know. Not your thing?"

I chuckle. "Maybe it's growing on me."

Alex looks me over, from my short dark hair to my soft suede skirt. I'm still wearing my Doc Martens, though. Like I said, some things never change.

"Everything about you is so… different."

"Different?" I ask, fiddling with my necklace. It's a silver cross Asher gave me. You know, just in case those things actually work.

"Yeah. You look, I don't know, happy."

I nod. It's been a rough year, but it's almost over, and I have high hopes for the next one.

"Hey, Nic, I wanted to talk to you about something," he tells me. I recognize the expression on his face. It's the same look I had last year.

"Sure," I say. "First, I'll get us a few drinks. You want champagne?"

He looks stunned. "Yeah, sure."

I turn and glide out of the room. I can't help the smile spreading across my face. I pass by Spencer Adams leaning across the doorframe to the McGowan's study. Elayne is tucked under his arm. In his hand is a bottle of water. Thank God for small miracles.

"What are you smiling about?" a voice from my dreams asks.

I stop walking because my knees are too weak to move. Asher pushes off the wall and envelopes me in a hug. I let myself fall into him. He feels so right, so perfect, pressed up against me.

"Justice. It's a wonderful thing." I say, giggling as he kisses my cheek.

He brushes my hair aside and nuzzles into my neck. Just then, his cell phone rings.

I look up into his eyes, pleading with him, "Don't get that."

He kisses up and around my ear. My stomach flips wildly, my heart racing. I wonder if Brady's room is open.

The phone cuts out and immediately starts ringing again. Asher groans. Then without moving away, he puts the cell to his ear.

"What? I can't hear you," he says curtly, his mouth working its way along my skin.

He tenses, every muscle hard as stone. Lifting his head, he leans back against the wall, taking me with him. I turn my back to him, pulling his arms around my waist.

"Yeah... but... alright, alright. Yep. Fine." He disconnects the call and locks his phone.

"What was that about?" I turn and bury my mouth into his collarbone. He smells like campfire smoke.

He runs a hand through my hair, his breathing unsteady.

I stop. "What?"

"I love you?"

"Don't avoid the question."

He passes a hand over his face. "That was Kaleb."

Unconsciously, I scratch at my arm. It's not a warning itch, it's a nervous one. Who ever thought I'd be nervous about a phone call from Kaleb? "What did he say?"

Asher rests a hand on my cheek. "We leave in three days."

My heart drops into my stomach. Am I ready to go back into battle again? I've been training for the better part of a year, but last time I was actually in battle was when we faced Jac, and I don't think that turned out so well. Two people died, and that's just the ones we know about. After perusing the newspaper, I realized it could have been more like twenty, maybe even more than that. I swallow through the burning lump in my throat.

Asher peers at me through half closed lids. "Nicoletta? You in?"

I answer with a hesitant nod.

Fear, I've learned, is a driving force, much like anger or hate. It's the cause of war, the reason why people kill each other.

If Kaleb is scared enough to call for backup, I have to embrace my fear. I don't fight it when my heart races, or when my stomach churns.

I can do this.

I am a Sentinel.

My blood says so.

To the reader:

I hope you enjoyed reading Cinnamon and Salt. These characters stepped into my life and made an impact the size of a crater. That was five years ago. We've gone through many stories together and I hope to be able to share them all with you.

That being said, I need your help.

As a writer and perfectionist, I understand that errors are going to slip through during the editing process, and as an avid reader, I understand that there is nothing more frustrating than running across the same silly error every time you read a book. So, this is my proposal: as you read through Cinnamon and Salt, if you find any errors, discrepancies, plot holes, or just have questions, I ask that you email me at cjethingtonbooks@gmail.com and bring those to my attention.

Here's to many more adventures with you.

About the Author

C.j Ethington lives in Utah with her husband (lovingly referred to as her second-in-command despite the fact that he is often the first), their four children, and her beloved coffee maker. She may not have her super hero badge yet, but deep down, she believes that anything is possible with enough coffee in her system. C.j. has been dreaming up stories since she can remember and sharing them since she could talk. With an insatiable desire to learn, she considers herself a career student. In other words, if they have a course for it, she'll be the first to sign up. Though, her love affair will always be with creative writing. Don't worry; her husband understands. After all, they did meet in English class.

Cinnamon and Salt is the first book in the Sentinel series and C.j.'s first published novel. Visit her website at www.cjethington.com and make sure to like her author page on Facebook at www.facebook.com/cjethington for updates and contests.